INTRIGUE

Seek thrills. Solve crimes. Justice served.

K-9 Security
Nichole Severn

A Stalker's Prey
K.D. Richards

MILLS & BOON

K-9 SECURITY
© 2024 by Natascha Jaffa
Philippine Copyright 2024
Australian Copyright 2024
New Zealand Copyright 2024

First Published 2024
First Australian Paperback Edition 2024
ISBN 978 1 867 29960 8

A STALKER'S PREY
© 2024 by Kia Dennis
Philippine Copyright 2024
Australian Copyright 2024
New Zealand Copyright 2024

First Published 2024
First Australian Paperback Edition 2024
ISBN 978 1 867 29960 8

MIX
Paper | Supporting
responsible forestry
FSC® C001695

Published by
Harlequin Mills & Boon
An imprint of Harlequin Enterprises (Australia) Pty Limited
(ABN 47 001 180 918), a subsidiary of HarperCollins
Publishers Australia Pty Limited
(ABN 36 009 913 517)
Level 19, 201 Elizabeth Street
SYDNEY NSW 2000 AUSTRALIA

Cover art used by arrangement with Harlequin Books S.A.. All rights reserved.

Printed and bound in Australia by McPherson's Printing Group

K-9 Security

Nichole Severn

MILLS & BOON

Nichole Severn writes explosive romantic suspense with strong heroines, heroes who dare challenge them and a hell of a lot of guns. She resides with her very supportive and patient husband, as well as her demon spawn, in Utah. When she's not writing, she's constantly injuring herself running, rock climbing, practicing yoga and snowboarding. She loves hearing from readers through her website, www.nicholesevern.com, and on Facebook at nicholesevern.

Visit the Author Profile page
at millsandboon.com.au.

K-9 Security deals with topics that some readers may find difficult.

DEDICATION

To my husband: for managing to keep me from going insane during COVID-19 quarantine so I could write this book.

CAST OF CHARACTERS

Cash Meyers—He can spot a threat from a mile away, but he was too late to stop the violent attack on a small New Mexico town. Pulling the only survivor from the debris was supposed to be part of his job as the first line of offense against the *Sangre por Sangre* cartel. But he never expected Elena.

Elena Navarro—The cartel abducted her youngest brother in a massacre of underage recruitment, and she will do whatever it takes to get him back—but she can't do it alone. Relying on the private military contractor intent on keeping his distance, she'll risk it all—including her heart—to stop the cartel lieutenant who doesn't forgive and never forgets.

Bear—The former DEA drug K-9 is more than Cash's asset. She's all that's left of his family.

Jocelyn Carville—Socorro's logistics officer might knit cozy mittens and host movie nights to aid operatives' spirits, but she's possibly the most dangerous asset on the team.

Socorro Security—The Pentagon's war on drugs has pulled the private military contractors of Socorro Security into the fray to dismantle the *Sangre por Sangre* cartel...forcing its operatives to risk their lives and their hearts in the process.

Ivy Bardot—Founder of Socorro Security.

Chapter One

"It's going to be okay." Elena Navarro tried to keep her voice low. It was hard to make sure her brother had heard her over the screams penetrating the windows and doors.

Another burst of gunfire contracted every muscle she owned around Daniel's small frame. She clamped a hand over his mouth to muffle his sobs. They'd hidden beneath their parents' bed, but there was no sign that her mom and dad were ever coming back. "I've got you. I'm not going to let anything happen to you. Okay?"

Daniel nodded, the back of his head pressed against her chest.

Alpine Valley was supposed to be safe. With only two hundred and fifty people in town, the cartel that'd slowly started consuming New Mexico shouldn't have even glanced in their direction. They should've been left alone. Instead, *Sangre por Sangre* had come for blood and recruits.

And Daniel was the prime age to get their attention.

She had to get him out of here. Had to get him somewhere safe.

"Listen to me. If we stay here, they will take you. I need you to do exactly what I say, and we'll be okay." Elena kept her gaze on the closed bedroom door while backing out from underneath the bed, her hand never leaving her brother's side. Carpet burned against her oversensitive skin, but it was nothing compared to the realization that her parents were most likely dead. "Come on."

He didn't move.

"Daniel, come on. We've got to leave." They didn't have much time. The cartel soldiers would start searching homes to make sure they hadn't left anyone behind. By then, it'd be too late. "Let's go."

"Quiero mama." I want mama. He shook his head. "I don't want to leave."

She didn't have time for this. They didn't have time for this. Elena fisted her brother's shirt and dragged him out from beneath the bed. His protests filled the room, and she struggled to get his flailing punches and kicks under control. He didn't understand. He was too young to know what the cartel would do to him if they got their hands on him. *"Para.* We have to go."

Hiking Daniel onto her hip with one arm, she quieted his cries with her free hand. She hugged him to her, his bare feet nearly dragging against the floor. She wasn't tall in any sense of the word, and Daniel had shot up like a beanstalk over the past years. He was heavy and awkward, but she was all he had left. She'd do whatever it took to get him out of here.

A flashlight beam skimmed over the single window of her parents' bedroom. Elena launched herself against the wall to avoid being seen. The jerking movement dislodged Daniel's black-and-red unicorn dragon, and he cried out for it.

The beam centered on the window.

"Shhh. Shhh." Her breath stalled in her chest. Time distorted, seconds seemed like an eternity and she couldn't seem to keep track of what must have been only an instant. That beam refused to move on. The sound of gunfire had quieted. All she could hear was Daniel's soft cries, but no matter how hard she held on to him, it didn't comfort him.

Shouts pierced through the panes. "I can hear you in there."

The flashlight arced upward. A split second before the window shattered.

Daniel's scream filled her ears.

They didn't have any other choice. They had to run.

Elena hauled him against her chest and pumped her legs as hard as she could. Glass cut through her heel, but she couldn't stop.

"Dragon!" Her brother's sobs intensified as he locked his feet to the small of her back, trying to wiggle free.

"We've got to go!" She ran down the hallway and

headed for the front door. It burst open within feet of her reaching it. A dark outline solidified in the doorway. The soldier's flashlight blinded her, but she kept moving. The back door. She just had to get through the kitchen.

"Where do you think you're going?" Heavy footsteps registered from behind.

Her fingers dug into her brother's soft legs as she raced across old yellow decorative tile. They nearly collided with the sliding glass door. Elena clenched the handle to wrench it open.

It wouldn't move.

Panic infused her every nerve ending. The broomstick. Her parents had always laid a broomstick in the door's track to deter break-ins. The flashlight beam gleamed off the reflective glass behind her.

"Nowhere to go, *señorita*," a low voice said. "And what do we have here? Daniel, right? That must make you Elena. Such a pretty name. Your parents are just outside. Give me the boy, and I will take you to them. Easy."

Easy? No. Her instincts told her every word out of his mouth was a lie. Elena turned to face the shadowed soldier, the light mounted on his gun too bright. She pressed her shoulders into the glass door and crouched. Her thighs burned as she tried to support Daniel's weight. "It's going to be okay," she told him.

"That's right." The shadow moved closer. "You know you can't win. Give me the boy. He'll make a fine soldier."

"Over my dead body." She found the thick broomstick with the broken handle. She swung it into the soldier's shin with everything she had.

His scream punctured through the roaring burst of gunfire. Flashes of light gave her enough direction to grab for the door handle, and she and Daniel fled into the backyard. Echoing shouts and pops of bullets closed in. She hiked Daniel higher up her front, his sobs louder now. They couldn't take her car. The cartel would have already set up roadblocks. Their only choice was the desert. Alone. Without supplies. "We're going to make it. We're going to make it."

She wasn't sure if she'd meant that for Daniel or herself.

"You're going to pay for that!" The soldier who'd cornered them in the kitchen tossed the broomstick onto the back patio. His beam scanned the opposite end of the yard, buying her and Daniel mere seconds.

Elena pried a section of chain-link fence free from the neighbor's cinder block wall. The opening wasn't big enough for both of them. She maneuvered Daniel through. "Go. Run, and don't stop. Don't look back. I'm right behind you."

"Come with me, Lena. Come on. You can fit." Another sob escaped him. He tugged at her hand to drag her through after him.

She shoved at him through the fence while trying to make the opening large enough to fit her, but it wouldn't budge. "Daniel, go!"

The beam centered on her from the back door. Another burst of gunfire caused cinder block dust and chunks to rain down from above. She ducked to protect her head as though her hands could stop a bullet. "Run!"

Her brother ran.

Movement penetrated her peripheral vision. Followed by pain.

A strong hand fisted a chunk of her hair and thrust her face-first into the wall. Lightning struck behind her eyes. Her legs collapsed from beneath her, but the soldier wouldn't let her fall. He pulled her against him. "You've got more fight in you than I expected. I like that. After we find your brother, I'll come back for you."

"No." A wave of dizziness warped his features. She couldn't make out anything distinctive, but his voice... She'd never forget that voice. The ground rushed up to meet her. Rocks sliced into the back of her head and arms. The shadow was moving to climb the fence as she tried to press herself upright. Daniel. He was going after Daniel. "You can't have him."

Her head cleared enough that she shot to her feet. She jumped the soldier as he tossed his weapon over the fence to the other side. She locked her arms around his throat and held on for dear life. She didn't know how to fight. That didn't matter. She'd do anything to stop these men from getting hold of her brother.

"Get off." Those same strong hands that'd rammed her face into the wall grabbed for her T-shirt and ripped her from his back. Air lodged in her chest as she hit the ground. A fist rocketed into the side of her face, and her head snapped back. "When will you people learn? You're not strong enough to fight us." He grabbed her collar and hauled her upper body off the ground, ready to strike again. "We are everywhere. We are everything."

She couldn't stop the wracking cry escaping up her throat as she cradled one side of her face. She spread her hand into the rock-scaping her parents had put in a few years ago. Her fingers brushed the edge of a fist-sized rock. Securing it in her hand, Elena slammed it into the side of his head as hard as she could.

The soldier dropped on top of her. Tears flooded down her face as she tried to get herself under control. She shoved him off, relief and adrenaline fusing into a deadly combination. This wasn't over. The man who'd come after her and Daniel was just one of many. There would be more soon. She had to go. "Daniel."

Elena clawed out from beneath the man's weight and stumbled toward the fence. She managed to squeeze through, but not without the sharp fingers of steel leaving their mark across her neck and chest. Darkness waited on the other side. No sign of movement. No sign of her brother.

She tested the sting at one corner of her mouth with the back of her hand and started jogging. Dead, expansive land stretched out in front of her. Only peppered with Joshua trees, cacti and scrub brush, the desert made it hard to tell where the sky ended and the earth began. And Daniel was out here alone.

"Lena!" His cry forced ice through her veins. Not from ahead as she'd expected. From behind. "Help me! Lena! Let me go!"

Elena turned back to the house. "No. No, no, no—No!"

Brake lights illuminated the sidewalk in front of her parents' house enough for her to get a look at two men forcing her brother into the cargo area of a sleek, black SUV.

"Daniel!" She lunged for the fence she'd just climbed through. Her bare feet slipped in the panic to get back over as fast as possible. She was on the edge of getting to the other side when her body failed her. She fell beside the soldier she'd knocked unconscious. Pain exploded down her arm and into her ribs. It wouldn't stop her.

Daniel's screams died as the cargo lid closed him inside the car.

"No!" This wasn't real. She ran as fast as her body allowed, along the side of the house and toward the front. "Daniel!"

She reached the corner of the house as the car sped away.

The butt of a gun slammed into the side of her head.

And the world went black.

CASH MEYERS GAVE a high-pitched whistle, and his Rottweiler, Bear, launched at the gunman.

Her teeth sank deep into the bastard's arm as the woman the soldier had knocked unconscious hit the ground. A scream echoed through the night, but it was nothing compared to those he'd heard on the way in. Of pain, loss. Of fear. Fires burned out of control from at least three homes that were torched during the recruiting party. *Sangre por Sangre* had raided a small New Mexican town for new blood. And left nothing but devastation.

Bear brought down her target, and Cash called her off with a lower-pitched whistle. His weapon weighed heavy in his hand as he approached the gunman and took aim. "How many others?"

A low laugh was all the answer he received, but Bear's low growl put an end to that. "Too many for you, *mercenario*." Mercenary.

Cash had been called much worse, but the truth was he and the men and women of Socorro Security were the only ones stopping the cartel from gaining utter control of this area. So he'd take it as a compliment. "It's sweet you're concerned about me, but I've got Bear. Who has your back?"

Nervous energy contorted the soldier's expression in the gleam of flames and moonlight. The man's fingers splayed across the dark steel of his automatic rifle. An upgrade from the last time Cash had a run-in with the cartel. "You'll need more than a dog to protect you if you kill me."

"Oh, I'm not going to kill you." He rammed the butt of his weapon into the soldier's head and knocked him out cold. "You're just not going to be happy when you wake up."

"Steh," he told Bear in German. She huffed confirmation as Cash tossed the soldier's gun out of reach and turned his attention to the woman who'd run head-first into the weapon's stock. Her face came dangerously close to being impaled by one of the cacti, and he maneuvered her chin toward him. Scratches clawed across her neck while swelling and a split lip distorted sharp cheekbones and smooth skin. She'd fought. That much was clear. He set one hand on her shoulder and shook her. "Hey, can you hear me?"

No answer.

Hell, he should've hit the bastard who'd struck her harder. Or let Bear get her pound of flesh. Cash scanned the street. Sirens pierced through the roar of flames and cries. Not even Bear's low whimper compared to the dread pooled at the base of Cash's spine. He'd been too late. He hadn't seen this coming, and now the people in Alpine Valley had paid the price.

Fire and Rescue rolled up to the burning house across the street. One ambulance in tow. It wasn't enough to treat the people gathering for medical attention. Older couples holding their heads, a man calling a woman's name, a toddler screaming in his mother's arms.

Sangre por Sangre had ruined lives tonight.

Because of him.

"Daniel." The woman at his feet cracked her eyes open. Flames reflected in her dark pupils a split second before she slipped back into unconsciousness.

Cash holstered his weapon. She'd taken a nasty hit to the head and then some. She needed medical attention. Now. He slid his hands beneath her thin frame, only then noting that she'd run to the front yard in nothing but a T-shirt and lounge shorts, and hauled her into his chest. *"Aus."*

Bear followed close on his heels like the good companion she'd been trained to be for the Drug Enforcement Agency. With more cartels like *Sangre por Sangre* popping up between the states and butting up against the Mexican border, deploying K-9s like her had become standard protocol, but Bear had taken one too many concussions during her service for the agency. Always the first to respond. Always the last one to leave. She'd dedicated her life to saving lives, and in return, he'd saved her when she'd faced being put down. They had an understanding. A partnership. She was part of the team, and he wasn't ever going to leave her behind.

Cash jogged the way he'd come and wrenched the back door of his SUV open. Bear waited for her turn as he laid the woman in his arms across the seat,

then took position in the front. He hauled himself behind the steering wheel and flipped around as fast
as he dared. Alpine Valley didn't have its own hospital, and the small clinic meant to handle non-life-
threatening injuries would be overrun.

Her groan practically vibrated through him from
the back seat and deep into bone. "Son of a bitch...
lied."

"That seems uncalled for." Cash barely managed
to dodge a police cruiser tearing down the street with
its lights and sirens on high alert. His mind raced
to fill in the blanks that came with her words. She
wasn't conscious. Whatever she'd been through tonight had taken hold and wouldn't let go. It was a defense mechanism. One part of her brain was trying
to process the trauma, while the other tried to force
her into action. "I'm going to get you help. Okay?"

She didn't answer. Out cold.

Putting her in his sights with the rearview mirror,
he couldn't help but catch a glimpse of the devastation behind. It'd take all night for Fire and Rescue
to get the flames under control. Cash hit the first
number on his speed dial on the phone mounted to
the dash. The line only rang once.

"What the hell happened, Meyers?" Jocelyn Carville, Socorro's logistics officer, didn't give him the
chance to answer. "Because from where I'm at on the
top floor, it looks like an entire town has caught fire."

"You're not wrong." Cash floored the accelerator

with another check in the rearview mirror. His back seat companion hadn't moved. "I need additional fire and ambulance units in response from Canon and Ponderosa sent to Alpine Valley. What they have isn't enough. I counted at least three homes on fire and two dozen residents injured. I'm bringing another in."

"Wait. You're bringing who in?" Jocelyn's voice hitched a bit higher.

"Doesn't matter. Can you get me the rigs or not?" he asked.

"I can have them there within thirty minutes." He could practically hear the logistics officer jabbing her finger into the phone. "You owe me."

"I'll have a box of Junior Mints on your desk by morning." Ending the call, he glanced at Bear staring at him from her position in the front seat. "What? I couldn't just leave her there. The clinic is going to be overrun. We have a perfectly good suite at headquarters. The doc will know how to help." She didn't look too convinced. "Don't give me that look. You would've done the same thing. Protocols be damned."

She cut her attention out the passenger-side window. Her side of the conversation was over.

Cash carved through town. The blaze overtaking Alpine Valley had spread and gave off a glow seen for miles. Every cell in his body urged him to turn around—to do what he could to help—but he had to trust the police knew what they were doing. He turned the SUV onto a one-way dirt road that led up the mountain that overlooked the valley, pinched between two plateaus.

Socorro Security had become the Pentagon's latest instrument in undermining and disbanding *Sangre por Sangre*. Their operation was smaller than most defense companies, but the private military contractors assembled under its banner were the best the United States military had to offer. Forward observers, logistics, combat control, terrorism, homicide—they did it all, and they did it for people like the woman in his back seat. To protect them against the crushing waves of cartels killing and competing for control.

The corner of the massive compound stood out from the dirt-colored mountains surrounding it. Modern, with sleek corners, bulletproof floor-to-ceiling windows, a flat roof that housed their own chopper pad and a black design that had been carved into the side of the range. The one-million-square-foot headquarters housed seven operatives in their own rooms, a fleet of SUVs, a chef's kitchen, an oversize gym, an underground garage, a backup generator, an armory and the best security available on the market. This place had become home after his discharge from the Marine Corps. A place to land after not knowing what to do next—but it was the medical suite Cash needed now.

He dipped the head of the SUV down in the garage with a click of an overhead button and pulled up in front of the elevator doors. He hit the asphalt, Bear jumping free behind him, and rounded to the back seat.

Cash tried not to jar her head more than necessary, hugging her against him. She was still unresponsive, but her delirious name-calling earlier was a good sign she'd pull through. She wasn't talking anymore though, and a sense of urgency simmered in his gut. He wasn't a doctor. While he'd taken a few hits to the head throughout his service, he didn't know anything more than the instinct to get her to a real doctor. He nodded to the elevator door's keypad. *"Tür."*

Bear pressed her front paw to the scanner, and the doors parted.

Once they were inside, a wall of cool air closed in around them as the doors secured into place. His grip automatically tightened on the woman in his arms as the elevator car shot upward. The swelling had reached its peak, but even underneath the bruising and blood, he had a proper glimpse of arched eyebrows, thick eyelashes and a perfect Cupid's bow along her upper lip. He guessed her age somewhere between thirty-two and thirty-six. No hint of silver or gray in a black mane that must've reached her low back. Fit. Someone who took care of herself. Her breathing was even, deep, and accentuated her collarbone across her shoulders. She was beautiful to say the least, but that hadn't stopped the cartel from hurting her.

Bear cocked her head at him, as though sensing he'd taken his eyes off the target. Hell. He hadn't brought her back to headquarters for his own viewing party. She needed immediate help she wasn't going to get back in town.

The elevator pinged, and a world of black expanded before him. The floors, the ceilings, the walls, the art. Monochrome and practical. Cash picked up his pace. He shoved through the door at the end of the hall, swung the woman onto the bed in the middle of the room and got the attention of Socorro's only doctor, seated behind the desk at the far end.

"Hey, Doc." Pointing to Socorro's only visitor, he tried to contain the battle-ready tension in his voice. "I brought you something."

Chapter Two

Come with me, Lena. She couldn't get his voice out of her head. *Come on. You can fit.*

She had fit through the fence, but not fast enough. Her heart threatened to stop beating at the realization. They'd taken her brother, and she hadn't been strong enough to stop them. "Daniel."

"Take it easy." That voice. She didn't know that voice. It was rough and deep, and masculine in a way that rocketed her defenses into overdrive. "Doc said you've earned yourself a mild concussion. It's going to take a few minutes to adjust."

"Where…" Her mouth was caked with dryness and something like dirt. Cold worked through her as the overhead vent pumped out air, and Elena forced her eyes open. Pain arced through her head at the onslaught of lights. "I think I'm going to throw up."

"Wastebasket is on your right," the voice said.

A monitor's rhythm jumped as panic and nausea won out. The garbage can found its way into her hold, and she emptied her stomach with as much grace and decorum as possible. Which wasn't much. It felt good and embarrassing at the same time, but she didn't have the energy to care about either.

"You gotta go slow. Breathe. You've been through a lot, but I give you my word you're safe. The cartel can't find you here." Details bled into focus. A strong nose—broken one too many times—filled a rugged face with a hint of bristle. Dark hair accented even darker eyes, and dirt or ash smeared down his jaw. "Do you remember what happened?"

She didn't know him. And she didn't know this room. The fight instinct that'd failed to keep Daniel safe ripped through her. It centered on a scalpel on a bedside tray and urged her hand to close around the steel. She swung the blade between them and hiked herself higher up the hospital bed. One exit. Through him. She didn't like those odds, but she'd fight. She'd never stop fighting. "Who are you? Where am I?"

A low growl reverberated through the room. Coming from…a dog?

"Platz." One word. That was all it took for the Rottweiler to lick its lips and lie down at the man's command. Mountainous shoulders flexed and receded under a black T-shirt as he scratched behind the dog's ears. "Bear's a drug dog. Former DEA. She's spent years training to sniff out the cartel's dirty little secrets, ain't that right, girl?" His voice softened when he spoke to—what was it?—Bear. Here she was, con-

vinced the cartel had kidnapped her right along with Daniel, and the man beside her bed was baby talking his dog. "She'll follow my every command, but she does not like it when people threaten me."

The scalpel shook in her grip. Elena gauged the distance between her and the door. "I think you have that backward. I'm the one who woke up with no idea who you are, where I'm at or what you want from me."

"Cash," he said.

A ransom request? Confusion took what little strength she had left. The cartel didn't negotiate. Ever. Not with people like her. They took what—who— they wanted and left the scraps of people's lives without second thought. There was no way in hell she'd ever be able to come up with money for her brother. "I don't have any."

A corner of his mouth hitched higher. "It's my name. Cash Meyers. As to where you are, welcome to Socorro Security."

"I don't… I don't know what that is." It was then that she realized the clothes she'd fallen asleep in were gone. In their place was a set of sea-foam green scrubs.

"I found you unconscious at the foot of a cartel soldier. He hit you pretty hard." Cash—if that was his real name—tapped the side of his head to make his point. "I returned the favor, took his weapon and brought you here for medical attention. That understaffed and underfunded clinic you guys rely on wasn't going to give you the care you needed. Figured you're better alive than dead."

She scanned the room. It was crisp, clean and white apart from the casing around a floor-to-ceiling tinted window. The landscape on the other side stretched out around the building, and in the distance, two pillars of smoke funneled upward. Her home was on fire. This wasn't the same clinic she'd gone to in Alpine Valley two months ago. This was calm and clean and white. Not barely hanging on by a thread.

Socorro Security. Judging by the location set into the mountain, this place must've been the military contractor her father had rallied against. Something about aggravating the cartels. Starting a war with towns like theirs caught in the middle. "I shouldn't be here. Take me back. Now."

"It's not safe in Alpine Valley right now, and you're in no condition to go back out there." That hard edge to his voice lost its sharpness, the same as it had when he'd spoken to his dog. "You got a name, or should I make one up?"

Her name? That was his response? The soldier who'd taken Daniel knew her name. How was that possible? Her exhale drained her harder and faster than she thought possible. Elena stretched her feet toward the floor. "I have to go."

Cash stood, blocking her path. "I'm not sure that's

a good idea. Concussion symptoms can strike when you least expect. Take it from Bear."

Take advice from a dog? Yeah. She'd get right on that. She scrambled to collect her clothing from the end of her bed. Bandages she hadn't noticed until now pulled at the tough skin along the bottoms of her feet. She'd run from the house without shoes. It'd be a long and painful trek back to town, but she could do it. She'd get to the police. She'd find a way to fix this. "You don't understand. I can't stay here. My family… They were caught in the middle of the raid. I have to find them."

Her parents must've rushed out of the house to fend off the soldiers. There was no telling what'd happened to them between the fires and the gunshots. Part of her didn't want to know. The other already did know she was the only one left who could get Daniel back.

"Hey." Cash raised calloused palms in surrender. "I'm not asking you to sleep it off and forget about them. I'm saying you're no good to them with potential brain swelling and permanent damage."

She didn't have time for that. Her brother was out there. Alone. Terrified. Possibly hurt. Who else was going to fight to bring him home? Elena clenched her clothing to her chest. She couldn't fight him, just as she hadn't been able to fight off those men, but she'd try. "Please move."

Hesitation smoothed his features into an unreadable mask. "Tell me your name."

He wasn't serious. Of all the things to focus on, he wanted to know her name. But if it was going to get him to move without her having to use force, she'd give in. "Elena. Elena Navarro. Now will you move?"

"That's a start." Cash angled himself to the side to provide a straight shot to the exit. "I'll make you a deal, Elena Navarro. You tell me why *Sangre por Sangre* raided a town of less than three hundred people tonight, and I'll drive you back myself."

"What makes you think I know anything about their motives?" Whatever painkiller they'd given her was starting to wear off, leaving her nerves raw.

A deadliness in his gaze threatened to consume him, as though he was looking for a reason to go back to Alpine Valley and find every single one of those men who'd attacked them. Who'd attacked her. Which didn't make sense. He didn't know her. They were just two specks of dust caught in an unforgiving desert. "Because that soldier who clocked you with the butt of his rifle wasn't going to leave you in that yard. He was about to drag you to his vehicle, and I want to know why. The cartel isn't known for keeping hostages unless they're recruiting, and you're not young enough to cross their radar for trafficking. So what do they want from you?"

Daniel's scream for help echoed through her mind. The pressure in her chest was closing around her throat as memories of his sobs and the feel of his hold around her penetrated the disconnected barrier she'd gotten good at building.

"It's rude to tell someone you just met they're too old to be trafficked." The words escaped her control, and her breath hitched. She'd meant them as a joke, but the truth was right there, wasn't it? Tears burned as seconds distorted in agonizing minutes, but there was no going back. "My brother. He's eight. I think my parents tried to stop the cartel from finding him. I'm not sure what happened to them. I knew *Sangre por Sangre* was going to take him. I tried to get him out of the house, to protect him. We almost made it into the desert, but..." The rest didn't matter. Elena took a step into him. "I need to go back. I know a police officer in town. Deputy McCrae. He can help me—"

"No. He can't, Elena." Something along the lines of pain ticked in the small muscles along his jaw. "I'm sorry. About all of it. It takes a lot of courage to stand up to those men the way you did, but these aren't people committing misdemeanors or getting caught with pot. The cartel is made of soldiers. They aren't ruled by the same laws as you and I are, and they certainly wouldn't think twice about putting anyone down who got in their way. No police force in the country is enough to break through their defenses."

"And you are?" The small amount of hope she'd clung to dissipated. "My father rallied against a group of private military contractors setting up their headquarters so close to our town. He thought having a military presence here would only aggravate the cartels. That we would be caught in the middle of a war. Turns out he was right. So now it's my turn to ask a question, Cash—or whoever the hell you are. Where was Socorro Security when we needed you?"

Physical pain etched deep into his expression.

It created a chain reaction within her that started with wanting to take back her accusation and ended with smoothing those lines from his face. But she'd wasted enough time. And she didn't owe him anything. Elena hugged her clothes to her chest and raised her chin a fraction of an inch. "I'll take that ride now."

"You still haven't answered my question." It was his turn to take a step toward her. "You told me what happened to you and your family, but not why that soldier wanted you specifically."

Shame and guilt and grief combined into a toxic emotional storm. Her name on that soldier's lips grated against everything she was. There was no denying it. Everything that'd happened tonight hadn't been because Socorro Security had failed to do their jobs. It'd happened because of her. "Because his lieutenant ordered him to."

"You're going to need to fill in some blanks here, Elena." Every cell in his body wanted to head back to town and interrogate any soldier he could find, but rushing in without intel or a strategy would only come back on Socorro. Not to mention put Elena in more danger. "Why would a drug cartel lieutenant raid an entire town to get to you?"

"Would you believe me if I told you he's my ex?" Elena released her grip on her dirt-stained clothing and tossed it on the bed. "Of course, I didn't know who he really was until it was too late. I still don't. He used a fake name, told me a bunch of lies to cover up the fact he was working for the very people terrorizing us. Now I'm starting to think raiding Alpine Valley was a cover, and taking Daniel was… punishment."

Cash had had run-ins with the cartel before. Part of the job he'd signed up for, but he'd never wanted to hurt them more than he did right then. Intercepting drug runs, raiding compounds, seizing assets—none of it was good enough. He swallowed the welt of rage clawing up his throat. "Punishment for what?"

"For leaving him," she said. "I don't live with my parents because I don't have ambition or a job or because I don't know how to take care of myself. After we separated, I didn't have any other choice. I had a whole life before I met him. I was a different person before him."

"You were married." The thought shouldn't have bothered him. They weren't friends. Hell, they were barely acquaintances, but the fact rooted deep through muscle and aggravated his insides.

"For a whole three months. That's when I started

seeing the man he kept hidden while we dated. Little things, really. The battery on my phone kept over-heating. I took it apart and found some device in-stalled in the back. I think he'd been listening to my calls and following my movements." She picked at her thumbnail, as though trying to distance herself from the conversation, from having to relive what she'd been through. "After that, he moved us to Albuquer-que. Wouldn't let me call my parents or make lunch dates with friends. Another time, I thought someone was following me, so I ducked into a shop, and one of his buddies I'd met a few weeks before walked by. After a few weeks, the small things started add-ing up, but until then I never even realized what was happening."

"He was isolating you." Standard protocol in an abusive relationship. Dominant versus submissive. Weak versus strong. But Cash had no doubt in his mind—based on the defensive marks on her hands and face—that Elena Navarro didn't let anyone have a rule over her. Leaving a relationship such as hers took an unfathomable amount of determination and courage, and, hell, if that wasn't the most admirable thing he'd ever seen. "Did he hurt you?"

Her gaze went distant and sad beneath the swell-ing around her eye. Elena grabbed her opposite arm, the scrapes and bruising fully exposed to him. "I checked the mail. Something he'd told me not to do when we first got married. Inside there were bills addressed to a name I didn't recognize. Several. To the point I didn't think the mailman had made a mistake. When he left for work the next morning, I had my friend in the police department run the name. Deputy McCrae told me who I'd really married. I don't know how, but he found out."

Tension flooded through him.

"I escaped. I drove to Alpine Valley, and I never went back," she said. "I needed to start over and to be around the people I care about. Now those people are either dead or hurting, and he's not going to stop until I come back."

"Do you want to go back?" He didn't know why the question held as much weight as it did. There was nothing more despicable than a man who mistreated a woman or children, and she'd managed to escape of her own free will. Not all of them did. Cash knew right then and there he would do whatever he could to help her. Help her brother. Help her town.

"Not to him." Her expression broke under a scoff. "But if it comes down to my life or Daniel's, I'll do whatever it takes to protect my brother."

Cash whistled low to wake Bear, who'd apparently gotten tired of waiting around and collapsed on the stuffed bed the doc kept in the corner. He grabbed for his keys. "All right. Then we'll find him."

"What?" Those dark eyes that'd glimmered with fire and deliriousness held him hostage.

"I'm holding up my end of the deal. You told me

why the cartel wants you. I offered a ride back into town in return." He'd already made up his mind and was heading for the door. "We'll start with that."

"Just like that?" Suspicion bled into her voice. "You don't... You don't know me. You said it yourself. The cartel is brutal. They don't live by the same laws as we do. There are thousands of them and two of us. We'd be better off going to the police. Even if they can't help directly, they know people who can."

"Actually, it's more like thousands of them and seven of us. Not including Socorro's K-9s." Bear followed on his heels. The distrust radiating off Elena centered between his shoulder blades as he headed down the hall. He didn't blame her. Everything she'd been through and feeling the physical result of her choices guaranteed trust issues, but she wasn't at fault. The blame was on him. For not seeing the threat before it was too late. For not getting there fast enough. But he'd make this right. "I need to brief my team before we go. Until then you're welcome to crash in my room. Comes with a shower and a king-size bed, and the kitchen is just down the hall. Fully stocked."

"No." A strong hand latched onto his arm and managed to pull him to a stop. "You said you were taking me back into town. I don't want to sleep or shower or eat. There are people counting on me. I have to go back now."

"I know what you're feeling, Elena. I do. You feel

responsible for your family, for what happened to them. You feel like you're the only one who can fix it. But racing back into Alpine Valley is exactly what the cartel is expecting. They took your brother as leverage, to turn you into something pliable and obedient." He couldn't help but pick up on her fear, almost like a solid barrier between them. From their limited interactions, he figured Elena was the kind of woman to stand up to any challenge and stare it down until it broke in front of her, but this wasn't something she could take on herself. No matter how much she wanted it or how strong she thought she was. His arm burned where she splayed her fingers across his skin, and in that moment, it grounded him more than anything else ever had. "If you go back now, half-cocked, without backup or a plan, you'll be walking right into their hands. Is that what you want? Is that what you want for Daniel? Because I guarantee you, even if you do turn yourself over, they won't let him go. They'll keep using him to get you to cooperate, and you'll both be nothing but pawns used against each other."

Her mouth parted on a steady exhale, the force of which brushed the underside of his jaw. She slipped her hand from his arm, and an imagined tendril of cold raced to replace her touch. "No. I don't want that for him. Or me."

"Then let me do the job I was sent here to do." A force he didn't recognize bubbled up inside of him.

Something alive and instinctual. "And I'll give you my word—I will get your brother back."

Elena seemed to steady herself. The pulse at the base of her neck thudded hard against the thin skin there, but at a more even rate. "Why are you doing this? Why risk your life and the lives of your team for someone you just met?"

"Because cartels like *Sangre por Sangre* are like a virus. If they're left unchecked, the infection spreads and kills everything in its path." Especially those radicalized and funded well enough to do some major harm. "My room's just down the hall."

He didn't wait for her to follow. His instincts told him he'd made his point. She wouldn't try to leave on her own. But he could see her walking down this mountain and through the desert to get back home if she put her mind to it.

"You live here?" Her voice had lost some of its gusto. That was the exhaustion kicking in, maybe the concussion, too. She needed a heavy dose of rest. "It's so…"

"Sterile?" That was one way of putting it. Cash motioned her to the third door on the left of this hallway. He automatically angled in after her, noting the scratches across the back and side of her neck as she took in the room. It was weird. Her being in here. This was his space. Well, his and Bear's, and sometimes it ended up being more of the dog's, but it served its purposes. Gave him a place to decompress after an assignment, to recover with his hand in Bear's fur. In here, he wasn't a soldier. Cash was allowed to just…be. "Socorro has to be able to mobilize at the first sign of trouble. We're a security company. We go where we're told and follow orders to a T. No frills. No comforts. If needed, we'll leave this place and set up somewhere new. Although I'll admit I like the view."

Elena didn't answer, seemingly taking in every inch of the room.

From the floating nightstands, to the dark gray walls and wooden headboard of his bed. To the floor-to-ceiling window looking out across the barren land-scape. He'd never had any need for something more. Rather, he'd been told what he needed most of his life and accepted it at that.

She closed in on the window and set her hand against the glass as though she could reach out and touch the smoke plumes rising over what was left of Alpine Valley. "You can't fight the desert. All you can do is survive it."

Chapter Three

The smoke plumes had thinned throughout the night.

Fire and Rescue had gotten the blazes under control. Or let them burn themselves out.

Elena sat on the edge of the bed, willing the air to clear hour after hour. Helpless and angry and tired. A headache dulled the vision in her left eye. From staying up all night or the concussion, she didn't know. Maybe a combination of both. Didn't really matter.

She was stuck here until Cash and his team decided what to do with her. He hadn't said as much, but she'd known there wouldn't be any welcome party in her honor. Too much risk to let just anyone walk—or be dragged—through those heavy doors.

But Cash had brought her here.

Which didn't make sense. She could be lying about who she was. She could've made up her entire story, but he'd trusted her. He'd kept her from being abducted by the cartel for no reason other than she'd needed him, and brought her to the one place he considered safe.

But she didn't feel safe.

The cartel would know Cash's face now. They'd know what he'd done, that she was with him, and they'd find a way to get to her. Cash had to know that, too. "They're not going to stop."

The sun broke over the horizon in the east. The sky bled from purple to hints of blue and orange and worked to unravel the knot of anxiety inside. In vain. Cash hadn't come back for a few hours, but his Rottweiler had given up watching Elena with those dark eyes and finally gone to sleep in her cushioned bed.

She couldn't just sit here and do nothing.

Not while her parents were missing, possibly hurt. Not while Daniel was being held hostage. She'd done as Cash had asked. She'd waited until morning and given herself a chance to recover, but she didn't work for Socorro. She didn't have to follow orders.

Elena shoved to her feet. Cash was military. While the cartel only served their own agenda instead of a government's, they considered themselves soldiers. And soldiers liked to hide things. In the final weeks before she'd escaped her husband, she'd found thousands of dollars in cash, keys to apartments, identities she'd never seen before, and communications between him and other lieutenants throughout the organization. And weapons. So many weapons. She hadn't been able to use any of it, but it'd taught her a valuable lesson. Never take anyone at their face value.

Not even a handsome knight in Kevlar.

Bear lifted her head, a low huff of frustration clear.

Elena ran her hands over the back of the bed's headboard, then down into the frame. "If you're just going to rat me out, you might as well help me."

She dropped to her knees and searched beneath the bed. Her stomach growled at the sight of a package of Oreos stuffed up between its frame and the mattress. She unburied it with anticipation. Peanut butter. Her favorite. Wouldn't hurt to get something in her stomach before slipping back into the garage for one of the SUVs. She pulled the package free and sat back on her heels. The ecofriendly wrapping could be heard through the door and down the hall.

Bear shot to her feet in a scamper of anticipation, her back feet nearly sliding out from under her.

Elena hugged the package to her chest. It was almost empty. Probably no more than a couple of cookies left. "If you think I'm going to share with you, you've got another thing coming, Cujo."

The Rottweiler cocked her head to one side with the best plea Elena imagined a dog could give. And it was working.

"Fine. Just one." She peeled back the sticky tab on top of the package. She'd been right. Only two left. Although the frosting didn't look like the peanut butter she was expecting, and the cookies themselves were cracked down the middle. Glancing at Bear,

Elena let the dog take the cookie from her hand as she bit down into hers. "Breakfast of champions."

The bedroom door clicked on steel hinges.

Cash scanned the room a split second before settling that compelling gaze on her and Bear. A hitch at one corner of his mouth released the tension that seemed permanently set into his face. "I see you found the Oreos."

"I was hungry." She tried to ignore the slightly chemical taste swirled throughout the frosting. That wasn't right. These cookies must've expired. Her stomach was ready to revolt as she chewed, but she was so hungry she didn't want to spit it out. "How old are these? They don't taste like peanut butter anymore."

"Couple weeks." His heavy boots thudded over the floor before Cash took a seat on the end of the bed. The mattress dipped with his weight, and it was then that she realized just how…big he was compared to her. Not intimidating. Not forceful. Just mountainous. "I think that's Bear's allergy medicine you're tasting."

"What? No." Elena dropped what was left of the cookie back into the package. The chemical taste coated her tongue and slid down the back of her throat. "Excuse me?"

"Bear's allergic to sagebrush, and she loves Oreos." He was trying not to laugh. She could see it in the slight tick of his eye, and right then she wanted to shove the rest of the Oreo down his throat. "The only way I can get her to take her medicine is by disguising it in a cookie, and from the look of it, she's already got her dose for the day. Thanks for that."

Elena tossed the package across the room and climbed to her feet. She needed water. No. Wait. Alcohol. No. Bleach. She needed bleach to get the taste out of her mouth. It was the only thing that would help. "But you…you hid it under the bed like a late-night snack." Her stomach threatened to revolt. She was going to throw up in front of him. Again.

"Yeah. She'll eat the entire package if I put it somewhere she can get to it." Cash grabbed the remnants of her cookie just as Bear took a step to scoop it up. Tossing it in the garbage, he pulled open one of the cabinets she hadn't gotten around to searching and produced a bottled water. "Good news is, you're not going to have seasonal allergies today."

She twisted off the cap and drank as though she'd been stranded in the middle of the Sahara for three days. It helped. But Elena couldn't help but think the aftertaste would stick around. "And the bad news?"

"You might experience excessive panting and an upset stomach." Cash settled against the built-in desk, massive arms folded across his massive chest. The man would claim the attention of any woman with a pulse with that strong jaw and the promise of reckoning in his body language.

But that smirk was back in place, and she wanted nothing more than to wipe it off by dumping the rest of her water on him. But then what would she use to get rid of the taste of dog medication?

"Ha ha." Elena clutched her water tighter. "I hope you know what you've done. You've officially ruined my love for peanut butter Oreos. Of which I'll mention was an impossible task until now. My mother would be very proud of you."

Her mother. It hit her then, that they'd stepped away from the urgency of the situation and had started talking as though they'd simply met on a day that didn't include a town-wide slaughter of her friends and family. The lightness she'd gotten lost in the past few minutes—the banter and easiness—drained. Leaving her empty.

Cash seemed to realize it, too. The uptick of his mouth was gone.

"You said you had to brief your team on what happened last night." Her mouth dried then. So much for excessive salivating and panting. "So what's the plan? How do we get my brother back?"

"You don't." Two words. That was all he was going to give her? After everything she'd been through?

Her heart threatened to explode straight out of her chest. The fire that'd driven her to fight back against those soldiers simmered beneath her skin. Pain arced through her head. Specks of black shifted in her vision, but she wasn't going to let it stop her from going home. "Then what have you been doing these past few hours? You said you would help me. You said—"

"I gave you my word I and my team would bring him home, and I intend to do just that." He pushed away from the built-in desk as though the conversation was finished. Wrenching open a cabinet door, Cash hit a keypad with a six-digit code. A safe door popped, and he collected a weapon, ammunition and what she thought was a shoulder holster from inside. He discharged the magazine from his pistol and started loading rounds. "I didn't say you'd have any part in it."

Wait. Elena rounded into his peripheral vision, almost stepping on Bear. She got a low growl in response, but the dog's interruption in beauty sleep wasn't high on her priorities right then. "This is my brother. This is my family."

"And how do you expect to help them, Elena? We're trained for this. We're good at this. Each of us has a specialty we've spent years honing. The people in this building—the ones who have my back out there in the field—they're masters of war and are willing to risk their lives for the greater good." He slowed then as though sensing she'd finished his real implication in her head.

Which she had. She wasn't any of those things. She wasn't even close. She was just Elena. She worked remotely for a genealogical website that helped connect people to their ancestry through sending out DNA tests and handing off vials of people's spit. She didn't know the first thing about taking on a cartel, and she knew it. But worse, he knew it. "You're right. I don't know how to shoot a gun or track a target or whatever the hell it is you people do here. I can't protect anyone the way you can."

That simmer under her skin was spreading, growing hotter. To the point it was going to burn her alive unless she did something with it.

"But I was married to a cartel lieutenant. And during that time, I learned a few things about his organization. Things he'd never want to get out."

Cash had slipped back into the soldier again—no more jokes, full-on attention—and she had the feeling being at the center of this man's universe would be a very dangerous place to end up. "Keep talking."

"I saw passports with aliases. I memorized his schedule and the faces of who came around. I documented it all." She stood her ground. Throwing herself in the middle of a war between two opposing military units wouldn't guarantee an ounce of the freedom she'd come home for, but it might get her brother back. She had to try. "And I found keys hidden all over the house attached to little white tags with addresses on them. So whether you like it or not, if your job here is to disassemble *Sangre por Sangre* as you claim, you need me to do it."

Cash didn't move, didn't even seem to breathe, for a series of seconds. Then, life. "In that case, welcome to the team."

He was going to regret this.

But they were running out of time.

The longer *Sangre por Sangre* held Daniel hostage, the faster the boy would slip through Socorro's fingers. Cash had seen it done before. The cartel saw kids like Daniel—male and female—as expendable and replaceable as well as psychologically more malleable. Why put years into training a soldier to point and shoot when you could threaten the livelihood and loved ones of a child to get the job done? It was a systematic disassembly of a kid's psyche that relied on protection and guidance. Within a few days, a soldier was born. Not weeks. Not months. Not years.

They couldn't wait. They had to move now.

Awareness added pressure between his shoulder blades as he led Elena across the compound to the conference room, as though he could physically feel her. As though he'd been centered in the crosshairs during that final assignment alongside the DEA a year ago all over again.

Right before his world had imploded. Well, technically exploded.

He automatically reached down for Bear, to hold back the memory, but she'd slowed to walk beside Elena. Traitor. Cash angled to put the two in his sights as he hauled the conference room door open. "Straitjackets are on the right, meds on the left, keep your hands off my crayons."

A crack of a smile softened the tension in her face as she crossed the threshold, and Cash couldn't help but catch her fingers tangled in Bear's fur. Like she'd needed a bit of support, too. Didn't matter how much she tried to convince herself. She was out of her element.

"Ms. Navarro, I'm Ivy Bardot." The founder of Socorro Security—and his boss—rounded the conference table, extending one hand. The redhead with more fire in her eyes than her hair gripped the seam of her blazer. A thousand secrets simmered in the former FBI agent's angled jawline and tight smile lines. Her slim figure beneath her signature slacks and blazers alluded to more investigative skills than strength, but Cash had seen the woman take down more than her share of hostiles without so much as losing her breath. There was an intensity about Ivy that had him clenching every time she turned those emerald-green eyes on him. "Cash has briefed us on your situation. I want you to know Socorro is at your disposal. We will use every resource to retrieve your brother from the cartel."

Elena shook the founder's hand, panic setting in to her upper lip. Her gaze flickered to the rest of the team as though trying to take it all in. The people in this room were operatives, through and through, and unless she'd grown up military, her nerves were going to get the best of her. It made Cash want to close the distance between them, to supply some kind of shield between her and what was coming. "I appreciate that. I don't know what Cash has told you, but I can't... I can't pay you."

"The Pentagon pays us, Ms. Navarro." Ivy backed off, seemingly sensing Elena's tenuous condition. The woman kept her past to herself—as most of the team tended to do—but despite her secrecy, there were some things Socorro's founder couldn't hide. Her intuition, for one. It'd built this place. It'd saved lives. And it'd given him a second chance. "I'm not sure if you're aware, but I met your father a few months ago when the Pentagon announced Socorro would be setting up headquarters here in New Mexico. He ambushed me in the middle of the survey for this site. I was impressed. There aren't many people who surprise me anymore."

Ivy took her position at the head of the conference table and motioned Elena to take a seat down the side, near the door. "He was adamant that we needed to stay away, that our presence here would only make things worse between residents and the cartel. He wanted us to ignore what's happening. Something the men and women in this room aren't willing to do. And I don't think you are either."

Elena pressed her hands into the top of the table,

rocketing Cash's defensive instincts into overdrive. "Then why didn't you do anything last night? If you were sent here to protect us against the cartel, why were they allowed to attack us at all?"

Her fear, her grief, her anger—it all bled into the space between Elena and his team. It stabbed through him and twisted as efficiently as though he'd taken a blade to the gut, and he wanted nothing more in that moment than to take the pain away. But he couldn't. He couldn't take back his mistake.

"I am sorry for what happened on our watch, Ms. Navarro. Truly." Ivy indicated the woman on her right, across from Elena. "Jocelyn Carville—our logistics officer—has recruited Fire and Rescue from the surrounding towns to provide aid, and the DEA is already starting their own investigation into why this happened."

Jocelyn waved from the other side of the table. Her long braid framed her face and brought out the soft undertones of her skin. Of all the operatives contracted to this team, Jocelyn stood as a bright light against the onslaught of violence, darkness and loss any chance she got. Movie nights, hand-knitted gloves and sweaters around Christmas, brownie bake-offs. Cash had never met anyone like her in the military, yet somehow she belonged in this merry band of contractors.

"I've got our combat controller tracking the cartel's

retreat to pinpoint where they're headquartered, and my security operative is checking in with your police department as we speak. Granger here has proven himself as one of the best from the FBI's joint terrorism task force recruited to dismantle some of the country's most dangerous organizations over the past decade," Ivy said.

Granger Morais nodded from the opposite end of the table.

"We're truly doing everything we can to make this right." Socorro's founder had let her attention slide to Cash then back. Ivy knew. She knew it'd been his fault. That an entire town had been burned to the ground last night, that an eight-year-old boy was missing, that the company's contract would fall under review. Because of him. "Cartels like the one who raided Alpine Valley last night claim thousands of lives every year as a result of territory wars, drug addiction and violence. They're linked to political corruption, assassinations and kidnappings, but the *Sangre por Sangre* cartel has somehow clawed its way to the top. They've started killing off the competition and taking more control throughout the state. Socorro is the only thing standing in their way. We have the entire US government supporting us, Ms. Navarro, but we can't do our jobs unless we know what we're up against. You were there last night. You fought them. Is there anything we need to know about before we get ourselves into a war with the cartel?"

"Tell them, Elena." Cash hated putting her in this position, but it was the only way.

All eyes went to Elena. All of this—taking down the cartel, finding her brother, helping a town get back on their feet—it all came down to her. "I was married to one of the cartel's lieutenants. I didn't know who he really was at the time, but I knew he was hiding something. I saw financial statements and mortgage payments to addresses I didn't recognize. I memorized names of my husband's friends and family who came to visit. Though I got the feeling none of them were actually related. So I took photos and made notes of who came to the house and how often."

"For how long?" Granger took note. Always focused, always forceful. Cash didn't normally have a problem with it, but directed at Elena, he had half a mind to tell the terrorism agent to back the hell off.

Elena didn't seem to notice. "Three months."

"Where is this information now?" Ivy signaled for Jocelyn.

Elena's voice—maybe even her determination—wavered. "In my phone. Where I left it."

Hell. She hadn't been carrying one on her last night when he'd dragged her out of there. The cartel had struck without warning close to midnight. She'd most likely been asleep. "Before the raid last night," he said.

"Yes," she said.

They needed that information if they were going to start picking off the scales of the dragon and get Daniel back. But taking Elena back there—where her brother had been abducted, where she'd been about to be abducted—wasn't for the faint of heart. Soldiers trained to live under constant stress and triggers. To be ready to fight at a moment's notice.

"Most phones nowadays have cloud backups," Jocelyn said. "If I get you a laptop, can you access the information remotely?"

"Not this one." The challenge was there. Just waiting to strike. What little he knew of this woman since last night had made one thing clear: she wasn't going to sit on the sidelines while someone else got muddy. She blamed herself for what happened to her brother, and Elena Navarro wasn't going to let anyone else pull that kid out of this mess. But she couldn't do it alone. Not with what he knew about her past and the cartel itself.

"Then we go get it," Cash said. Bear's huff at his feet told him she was all in. She'd had enough downtime. She was rearing for the next assignment. Just like him. It was a trauma response—the need to constantly be on the go, engaged. A distraction from the things really going on in his head. At least, according to the psychiatrist the Corps had forced him to see before his discharge. But in this case, his mental war games just might save Elena's brother. "In and out. We stay under the radar, especially law enforcement. No one even has to know we're there."

"All right." Ivy pressed to her feet, every ounce the leader a bunch of military misfits had relied on when they needed her most. "Cash, you'll lead the recovery of the phone. Jocelyn, I want you with him. Survey the situation and report back once you're clear of the town's borders. Take your K-9 units and stay off the main roads. If there's anything off or the cartel makes a comeback, I want to know about it—"

"With all due respect, Ivy." Cash had never interrupted his boss before, never questioned an order. But this was important. "That's all fine and dandy, but you're leaving out a key part of this operation."

"What's that?" Ivy narrowed her gaze on him.

"The intel we need won't be in Elena's house, and we'll be wasting valuable time we don't have trying to find it on our own." He turned to the woman who'd taken an entire security company hostage with the promise of completing their mission. "There's no way you kept those records on your everyday phone, is there?"

Pure resolve etched into her expression. The slight stiffening of her shoulders was all the answer he needed.

"She hid it. Most likely close enough to town to get to it if she needed it but just out of reach so no one would accidentally come across it." Damn it. Looked as though they didn't have a choice. "Which means she's coming with us."

Chapter Four

There was no way he could've known that.

She'd kept the information she'd gathered about her ex and his organization secret from everyone. Including her family and closest friends. To keep them safe. To compartmentalize what she'd done. Yet Cash had barged into her life and stripped her of any kind of secrecy. As though he'd known her for years. Which was impossible.

Dirt kicked up alongside the SUV as they cut through back roads into Alpine Valley. The smoke was gone, but there was still a burnt smell. From what little she could see through the dust, she caught sight of holes where homes and buildings should've still stood. Nothing but charred ghosts left behind.

Her heart squeezed harder than ever before. She'd done this. She'd brought this evil into their town, into people's homes, into their lives. Alpine Valley had never had a nightlife or a reason for tourists to stay more than a day. Its abundant, nurturing hot springs filled with healing mineral waters had attracted thousands over the years, but it was the men and women she'd known since birth that kept this town alive. Archaeological findings discovered near the dam, the pueblos that were later created, the church dating back to the sixteenth century—these were pieces of her history. Of this town's history. Stories and sites she'd known all her life And the cartel was slowly laying waste to everything in its path. Could all of this have been avoided? Could she have stopped the raid before it'd even started?

The SUV slowed to a stop, and the dirt settled enough for her to see the back fence dividing the desert from the line of her neighbors' homes. Cash and Jocelyn—complete with their K-9 partners in the cargo area—scanned the area like the good soldiers they were supposed to be.

"We'll take a look around." Cash slid one hand behind the passenger headrest and twisted to set those deep brown eyes on her. "Once I give the signal, you can take us to the phone. In and out, remember? No one can know we're here."

She heard Cash's instructions, but they failed to latch on. Because all Elena had attention for was the smoking remains of her childhood home. Air crushed from her chest. "No."

She shouldered out of the vehicle and raced for the hole she'd pried in the back fence to get Daniel out.

The boots and clothing Jocelyn had lent her were a tad too big, holding her back.

"Elena, wait!" Jocelyn's voice pierced through the hard beat of her heart between her ears. A duo of dog barks and the slamming of car doors penetrated her senses, but she couldn't stop.

A rock tripped her up, and she pitched forward. The ground rushed to meet her faster than she expected. It hurt, but the tears were already prickling in her eyes. It was gone. Her home—everything—had been burned to the ground. "No."

Strong hands hauled her into a wall of muscle and turned her away from the scene. Cash buried his hand into the hair at the back of her neck as the sobs took control. "I've got you."

Her instincts had her pushing away to get free, but Cash's tight hold battled to ground her at the same time. It was a war she had no control over. She couldn't breathe, couldn't think. Elena fisted her hands in his vest, needing his support at that moment more than she'd needed anything in her life. The soldier, the one who'd tried to abduct her before Cash interfered, he must've done this. "Why?"

"They're sending you a message." Calluses scraped against the oversensitive skin along her arms as Cash added a couple inches between them. "One you wouldn't be able to ignore. Could your ex know you were gathering intel on the cartel? Did you tell anyone what you'd been doing?"

She finally summoned the ability to release her grip on his vest and wiped her face with the back of her hand. "No. No one knows. I didn't want..." Elena sucked in a lungful of oxygen to regain her balance and risked a glance behind her. The emotional pressure she'd suffered reared its ugly head, and she broke. Right there in front of the man who'd saved her from a fate worse than her nightmares. "I didn't want this to happen."

Too late. Because the tighter she'd held on to that small ounce of power over her ex, the quicker she'd lost it. Until she had nothing left.

"This wasn't your fault, Elena. No matter what that voice in your head is telling you, you are not responsible for this." Cash seemed to hold her tighter then, willing his words to sink in through his touch. It was no use. She knew the truth.

But his willingness to put Socorro's mission on hold long enough to try to comfort her mattered. Seconds distorted into long stretches of breaths as she stared up at him. The early morning sun highlighted the difference between the structure of the bones above his eyes, one slightly lower than the other. She hadn't noticed that before. Hadn't allowed herself to slow down to notice. She wasn't naive. She understood exactly why Cash and Jocelyn and their partners were here. They wanted something she had. She was a pawn, a means to an end. In exchange for her help, they'd help her. A simple arrangement. But it was easy to imagine the past twelve hours hadn't happened when Cash Meyers looked at her as though he was willing to forget his assignment for her. Because there hadn't been a single moment her ex had made the effort once they'd gotten married.

And she should've seen the monster behind the mask long before she'd escaped.

Elena pried her grip from Cash's vest, only then realizing her fingers had gone numb, and took a step back. There'd been moments like this between her and her ex. Where he'd cared. Where he'd comforted her. Where he'd made her feel important and loved with grand gestures. Jewelry, trips, clothing, cars. She'd been blind to who he really was, and she couldn't let herself make that mistake again. "I need to check the house."

She didn't wait for an answer. She wasn't going to let Cash stop her this time. No number of words were going to fix this. The scrapes along her neck tingled as Elena maneuvered through the hole in the fence. She saved herself the injury this time, not in a hurry. As much as she needed to know what was inside, her stomach soured at the idea of finding her parents in the ashes.

Glass and rock crunched under her feet as she approached the mess of smoking wood. She shouldn't have been able to see the street from the backyard. Smoke burned at the back of her throat. The kitchen was almost unrecognizable other than the appliances.

Wood grain cabinets were now scorched with black streaks. The dining table where they'd spent every night as a family for dinner had collapsed. Yellow patterned linoleum had practically melted to the subfloor underneath. There was a diesel smell laced into the smoke.

But no signs of bodies. Then again, she wasn't entirely sure what burned remains were supposed to look like.

"Accelerant. Most likely gasoline." How Cash had fit through that hole in the back fence, she didn't know, but he was there. Helping her search. "Fits the cartel's MO."

She hadn't asked, but once again, he seemed to know exactly what was on her mind. Elena pulled up short of what used to be the living room. "I don't… I don't know what to look for."

"Do you want me to tell you specifics or trust I know what I'm doing?" he asked.

Trust. She didn't have any reason to trust him, and it didn't come as easy for her now as it used to, but she believed him. She couldn't say the words. Instead, she sidestepped to give him access to the living room. "Be my guest."

Bear shoved her nose into the debris and carved a trail down what was left of the hallway on her own. Toward the bedrooms.

Elena was sure her parents had left the house when the gunfire had started, but she'd been so committed to getting Daniel out of the house, she wouldn't have noticed if they'd come back.

"They're not in here," Cash said.

"How do you know?" In truth, she didn't want to know, but despite what little she'd learned about the Socorro operative, she couldn't discount the fact he might lie to keep her on task. Recovering her phone. "Doesn't gasoline make fire burn hotter?"

"It does. Up to twenty-five-hundred degrees, but even then, it's not hot enough to get rid of a body entirely." He marched through the room that'd housed so many memories over the years. Christmases with the tree by the window. Movie nights on the floor and a bowl of popcorn. Her *abuela*'s home-cooked meals around the too-big coffee table. "Human remains assume a distorted position referred to as the 'pugilistic attitude' when the muscles contract due to heat, making them easy to spot. There's nothing in this room other than furniture."

Bear returned, continuing her search through the rubble with something in her mouth. A stuffed animal. Elena couldn't be sure, but she could almost see the tail of a dragon between the dog's teeth. Daniel's dragon.

"Then they made it out." A spark of hope doused the surge that'd held her hostage all night. Her parents might've survived. "Maybe they fled to one of the neighbors' houses or the police. They need to know what happened to Daniel."

She headed for the front of the house where Jocelyn and her German shepherd—Maverick—surveyed the street.

But was blocked by the very man who'd saved her life last night. She backed up, remembering the scorch of his skin against hers. Hotter than the timbers around her. "What are you doing?"

"They can't know you're here, Elena. No one can know. It's too dangerous." Pure determination settled into the fine lines around his eyes, and in that moment, he wasn't the rescuer who'd teased her for eating dog allergy medicine. He was a security operative. A soldier. "We came back here to collect the intel you've put together on the cartel. Nothing more. And the longer we're here, the higher chances someone reports your movements."

Wait. "You can't be saying what I think you're saying." Her nerves were getting the best of her. It made sense her ex would know where she'd run—and maybe she'd been foolish to come back to Alpine Valley in the first place—but to allude that the cartel had been tracking her through the very neighbors and friends she'd known her whole life? No. "You think there are people in this town who are some kind of spies for *Sangre por Sangre*? That they're keeping tabs on me? They're not, and you're wrong."

He had to be. Because if he wasn't… She couldn't think about that. She couldn't imagine any of these people being okay with what the cartel had done.

Elena shoved past him and through the opening where her front door had once stood. It was a fifteen-minute walk to where she'd hidden the phone. And the sooner she had it, the sooner Daniel could come home.

Cash's words barely reached her as she added distance between them. "I hope that's true."

IT WAS ALWAYS the ones you least expected.

Cash had learned that lesson the hard way. Right as an entire DEA raid had blown up in his and Bear's faces.

Smoke clung to his gear as he left what remained of Elena's house behind. Jocelyn's attention drilled through him. She wanted to say something—most likely encourage him to be more human and not a robot, as she liked to say—but thankfully decided against it as they kept up with Elena.

Part of him wanted her to be right. To believe that this small town had just gotten caught off guard by the cartel. Not that they had anything to do with targeting Elena's brother and home. But Cash hadn't trusted that part of himself for a long time. He couldn't.

Bear brushed against his pant leg as though the same thoughts were running through her head.

He scanned the street. Three more houses had been burned to the ground, but the sound of sirens had died. No faces in front yards. No vehicles driving by. The town had come to a standstill. Residents had locked themselves behind closed doors and had no intention of leaving.

"Have you seen anything like this?" Jocelyn's hand hovered over the sidearm at her hip. The dark gray trousers and white button-down shirt did nothing to hide her weapon, and it only added to what Cash knew about her. Everything out in the open. Ask the logistics officer a question and she answered. No issue. It was one of the things he liked about her best. What made them a good team. "This place is a ghost town."

"Once." He'd trusted the wrong person and nearly ended up in the ground because of it. His gaze slid to Elena a few feet ahead. They moved into backyards as they worked their way down the street. Despite being surrounded by miles of desert, Alpine Valley provided life to an entire natural preserve. Trees over a hundred feet tall crowded in around them, branches clawing at his shoulder holster, neck and vest. It was amazing, really. An oasis in the middle of scorched earth. "Fire and Rescue must've caught the flames before they jumped to the trees."

"Lucky." Jocelyn clicked her tongue to call Maverick back to her side. The German shepherd did as he was told, then jogged ahead with Bear. The woman scanned the surrounding trees. No matter what threat came their way, Cash trusted Jocelyn would have his back. That was one of the things that set Socorro apart from the military. In the marines, he was expected to serve until his countdown to discharge ran out. With Socorro, every single one of them made the choice to stay. Out of loyalty to the team. "What do you think about her?" Jocelyn nodded to Elena up ahead.

His mind instantly went to the moment Elena had fit against his chest. He hadn't planned on pulling her into his arms, but watching her hit the dirt and try to claw her way toward her house had broken something inside of him. It'd been instinct—a connection between them he didn't quite understand and wasn't sure he wanted to. In less than thirteen hours, she'd taken hold of something inside of him. Raised a protective tendency he'd solely reserved for those he trusted. As much as he wanted to believe she hadn't known what she was getting into when she'd married a *Sangre por Sangre* lieutenant, there was something about her that triggered his defenses. And reminded him of the masks people wore. "She's in over her head."

Jocelyn didn't respond to that, which he took as confirmation of his theory. She was here on orders. Simple as that. And she didn't intend to fail.

"It's just up here." Muscle flexed through the back of Elena's borrowed jeans, and Cash's gut tightened. Jocelyn could've at least given her something unflattering to wear on their trek through the desert.

Temperatures spiked as trees thinned. Sagebrush, muted dirt and exposed terrain replaced lush foliage and shade. They caught a dirt trail hiking higher into Alpine Valley's historic site. Sweat built around his collar as he took in the outline of the mission ahead. The oldest mission in the entire United States had served as Elena's secret keeper. But like the town itself, there was no one in sight. Perfect location for an ambush. "Jocelyn, take Maverick around the backside. I don't want any surprises."

"You got it." Jocelyn's low whistle drew her shepherd to her side. Both jogged along the tree line, out of sight within a few minutes.

Cash positioned his earpiece. "You read me?"

Elena watched him, squinting due to the sun, as though memorizing his every move. The hair on the back of his neck stood on end the longer they remained out in the open, but the trees were their best chance at cover if this went sideways. Better to cover all their bases.

"Loud and clear," Jocelyn said in his ear.

"Good." He scanned unfamiliar terrain, taking in the ridges surrounding the mission. It was basic warfare. Attack from high ground, gain the upper hand. Like the cartel, the only help from above he trusted was the kind that came with a sniper rifle. "Watch your back."

"What? You worried about me or something?" The connection quieted, giving Cash enough room to focus on the task at hand.

"Where we headed?" he asked.

"Inside." Elena didn't make a move to walk up the incline. "I know why you're here, Cash. I know how important that intel is to you and Socorro. I hardly believe you'll risk your life for someone you just met, but I need to know you won't back out on your word to bring my brother home."

She was persistent. He'd give her that much. And careful. Hell, the truth was he couldn't blame her for either after everything she'd been through. To learn the one person you trusted the most wasn't at all what they'd advertised. He'd been there. He'd lived through the betrayal, the heartache, the anger. And it'd taken him over a year to come to terms with the consequences. There'd only been one bright light that'd come out of it. His dog. "What makes you think I wouldn't risk my life for someone I just met?"

Seemed she didn't have an answer for that one.

Cash started up the incline. The sun beat down on him, but it was nothing compared to the heat generated every time he found himself this close to Elena. It didn't make sense. He'd helped dozens of Socorro clients over the years. Some in more complicated situations than hers. He'd never felt this…connected to any of them. She was different. He didn't know how yet, but the guilt suffocating him from the inside urged him to find out why.

They reached the entrance together. The early sixteenth-century mission pueblo was associated with both Native American and Spanish colonial history and had played an integral part in the heritage of the country as a whole. This was sacred ground in many respects, but organizations like *Sangre por Sangre* would only see it as a way to punish the people who dared to rise up against them.

Cash's survival instincts rocketed as the stone walls rose on either side of them. He'd studied the area when he'd taken the contract from Socorro until the very elevation changes had been etched into his brain. But he'd never come here. Too many corners with a possibility of an ambush. Too much unknown. Bear could only sense so much with permanent brain damage. Even on her worse days, she excelled by leaps and bounds ahead of him, but someday that wouldn't be enough.

Elena brushed her fingertips against the stone walls as she walked. Her lips moved without making sound, as though she were counting the bricks beneath her touch. She stopped suddenly and dropped into a crouch. "I need your knife."

"How do you know I'm carrying a knife?" He pulled his military blade from the inside of his right ankle and handed it off, grip-first. Any number of scenarios in which she turned that knife on him and made a run for it crossed his mind. He'd gone and put himself in a position he'd sworn never to again. He'd gotten personally involved in seeing this through.

"Soldiers always come prepared." Scabbed skin brushed against the tops of his fingers and sent an electric bolt of awareness down his spine. It was unlike anything he'd experienced, yet he couldn't say the same for Elena. She wedged the tip of his knife into the space between two stones and tried to pry one free. As though the reaction between them had never happened. Maybe it hadn't. "Army?"

"Marine Corps. Twenty years." The wind kicked up, cascading dust around her in a translucent veil of glitter. It enriched the color of her eyes and stood out in specks in her hair. Like she'd been touched by something otherworldly.

"And you thought two decades wasn't near long enough to take orders from people who aren't in the mess with you?" Elena handed him the knife and gripped both sides of the stone she'd worked free. Tugging it lose, she set it beside her and crouched to get a better look inside.

He didn't have any reason to answer her question. In fact, he didn't owe her anything, but Cash couldn't fight his need to explain. "I was discharged after a joint assignment between the DEA and the Corps went sideways. I'd been tracking a cartel coming up out of Colombia. Thought I knew everything I needed to know."

Elena pulled a stained dishrag from the hole she'd made in the wall, staring up at him. "What happened?"

"Didn't so much as get a foot in the compound before we were made." His grip went to the butt of his sidearm. "Bullets started flying, and at the time, I just kept asking myself where the hell I went wrong. It wasn't until the smoke cleared, I figured it out." A scoff escaped his control, meant to break the tension, but there was no detachment that could make it better. "Turned out I'd trusted the wrong person. A K-9 agent with the DEA. He'd given us everything we needed to raid. Layout of the compound, how many cartel soldiers would be there, how to find the drugs, but I found out later he'd been taking cartel money for years. We'd been fed bad intel from the start."

Her throat convulsed on a strong swallow. "You knew him?"

"Yeah. I knew him. Bear, too. They were partners since she was a pup, but there was an explosion during the raid. The cartel had known we were coming and constructed IEDs to slow us down. Bear put herself in the line of fire to save her handler, but he didn't make it. She was discharged due to too much head trauma after that." A heaviness he hadn't allowed to take over distracted him from the task at hand.

"That's how you and Bear were partnered?" she asked.

"Seemed fitting. She was already comfortable with me, and I wasn't going to let her be put down." There was more to it than that, but they'd wasted enough time. "Is that the phone?"

Elena dropped her attention to the rag in her hand. "Yeah. I charged it the last time I was here a couple weeks ago. It should have enough power left to get what you…" Unwrapping the package, she revealed a slim, shiny, silver flip phone predating anything that could connect to the internet. Brand new from the look of it. Her panicked gaze shot to his. "I don't understand."

"What's the problem?" he asked.

"This isn't my phone." She shot to her feet. "Someone else has been here."

Chapter Five

Nobody should've known where she'd hidden that phone.

She hadn't told anyone. Not her parents. Not even Deputy McCrae. Without that information, what chances did they have of getting Daniel back?

Acid collected at the back of her throat. Cash had instantly contacted Jocelyn and gone on alert to search the mission, but there'd been nothing to find. Thousands of people visited the pueblos every year. Tourists, Mexican and Native American elders, architecture enthusiasts. This place had felt safe. Just enough out of reach to keep her eight-year-old brother from going through her things but close enough to get to the phone if she needed to run again.

Cash's words lanced through her. *The longer we're here, the higher chances someone reports your movements.* Could someone have followed her out here? Had her ex placed spies throughout town to keep tabs on her every move? Who she talked to, where she went and what she ate for dinner?

She turned the phone meant to look like hers over in her hand. Cash had already gone through it. The contacts list was empty. No sent or received messages. No call log. It was as though someone had tried to replicate her device, bought one, then come back here to make the switch. The only thing they had going for them was the SIM card. Maybe someone in Socorro could trace it back to a credit card purchase. Security companies could do that, right?

But more important, what did this mean for her brother? She hadn't followed through. Socorro and its operatives weren't going to get the intel she promised in return for bringing Daniel home.

The gusts coming through the SUV's windows whipped her hair around her face. A whimper pierced through the endless loop of thoughts tearing her apart bit by bit just before Bear's wet nose prodded the side of her neck from the cargo area. "What happens now?"

Neither Cash nor Jocelyn had said a word since they'd rushed her back to the vehicle, and she wasn't sure they would now. Bone threatened to break through the back of Cash's hand from his grip on the steering wheel. "Now we regroup. Try to come at this another way."

He didn't have to finish that thought. It'd already wedged between her ribs. Every second they wasted trying to pin down *Sangre por Sangre* lowered the chances of them recovering Daniel. This was her fault. She'd been responsible for the information she'd gathered living with her ex for those three months. She should've been more careful. She should've gone out there sooner.

"I remember one of the addresses I saved in the phone." It wasn't much, but it was a start. If they found a connection between the cartel and one location, they might be able to build from there. "Twenty acres of undeveloped property. I remember it because it was one of the addresses I was able to get photos of online. There was nothing out there, from what I could tell, but it seemed odd the cartel would just let it sit."

"Cartels like *Sangre por Sangre* own thousands of acres of undeveloped land." Jocelyn angled her chin over her shoulder, though not enough to get a direct look at Elena. "It makes moving their product— drugs, women and alcohol—easier across the state. Sometimes they're just used for logistics' sake."

It made sense, and of all the operatives Socorro employed, she supposed Jocelyn would be the one whose literal job it was to confirm that theory. But Elena's gut said something different. That the mortgage statements and environmental surveys she'd found for that specific piece of land represented more than a simple route the cartel used to avoid law enforcement. She didn't know why, but it felt important. She ran through the address over and over until it'd be impossible to forget.

All too soon, the SUV dipped into the compound's underground parking garage. Her vision struggled to adjust to the lack of input for a few moments, casting her into a world of darkness. She hadn't actually been conscious for this part when Cash had brought her here, and a thread of anxiety clawed up her throat.

Bear whined from the back seat, her cold nose grazing along Elena's neck, as though seeking comfort. Cash reached overhead, and the interior of the SUV lit up. That simple action not only seemed to calm the dog but took a weight off Elena's chest.

They pulled over in front of a shiny elevator. Jocelyn was the first to exit, before rounding to the back of the vehicle to get Maverick as Elena and Cash hit the asphalt. "I'll check in with Ivy, let her know what we found. Or didn't, rather. I'll keep you up-to-date."

"Thanks, Joce." Cash clicked his tongue, and Bear jumped down from the cargo area. It was sweet. Their relationship. Earlier he hadn't said as much, but she'd guessed Cash and Bear's handler had been close. It must've been hard. Not only to lose that friend but also to realize he'd been responsible for the operation's failure. To uncover that betrayal.

Jocelyn unlocked a door off to the right of the elevator using her keycard and disappeared inside, leaving Cash and Elena alone in the cavernous garage.

Elena didn't really know what would happen next. The intel she'd promised Socorro was missing, her brother was still out there, she wasn't sure if her

parents had survived the night and a cartel lieutenant had raided her hometown to find her. Her phone
was supposed to fix everything. Now she had nothing. She stared at the replacement. Who'd known
about what she'd done? Her ex? One of the men he
employed?

"You look like you're about to drop dead." Cash
pushed the button for the elevator. The doors parted
almost immediately, and he stepped inside. "Let's
get you something to eat."

"Yeah." She followed him inside. Because she really didn't have any other choice, did she? She had
nothing to go back to. Her ex—and the cartel—had
made sure of that. The only thing left to do was find
Daniel. The doors slid closed behind her, and she
made note of the floor Cash selected. Three.

The phone's plastic protested from the tightness
of her grip, catching Bear's attention, and she pocketed it into her borrowed jacket. "Is your dog scared
of the dark?"

"Weird, right? I always thought dogs had better
vision than we did, but there's something about the
dark she doesn't handle well. I have to keep a night-
light on, or she'll whine all night." He scratched behind one of Bear's ears. The dog's jaw loosened as
she closed her eyes. Cash slipped the SUV's keys
in the right pocket of his cargo pants. "I've asked
the vet we keep in-house for the K-9 unit. She has
a theory that Bear might've gone temporarily blind

from her last concussion. Anytime she can't see, it freaks her out."

Elena knew the feeling. The elevator pinged, letting them out on the same floor she recognized from before. Though this time the tall, dark and scary man beside her wasn't so scary. Cash directed her through the maze of sleek black walls, floors and ceilings until they reached his room. Left. Two rights. Fourth room from the end.

Motioning her inside, Cash stood sentry at the door as she crossed the threshold.

Her movements were subtle and quick. Just as she'd learned living with her ex. She closed the distance between them, nothing more than mere inches keeping her from touching him as she raised her gaze to his. "Thank you, Cash. For everything. If it wasn't for you, Daniel wouldn't have a chance. How am I supposed to repay something like that?"

He studied her from head to toe.

"You've still got a bit of ash and dirt on you. Bathroom's there. Fully stocked. Feel free to shower." His voice was husky, and she couldn't help but feel it rumble through her. "I'll have Jocelyn send over another change of clothes while I grab us something to eat other than a couple old Oreos disguising Bear's allergy medicine."

The aftertaste made a hard comeback at the reminder, and Elena grabbed her stomach to keep it from revolting all over again. She took a step back to find the nearest garbage can. "A toothbrush would also be good."

"You got it, Elle." The hitch at the corner of his mouth that'd twisted her insides earlier exploded into a full-blown smile she hadn't been prepared for. It stole the air from her chest and left her doubting every thought she'd had during the drive back to Socorro. Cash closed the door behind him.

Elle. No one had called her that before. Her family had always called her Lena. The warmth he'd given off evaporated. *Come with me, Lena.* Ice infused her veins despite the sun beaming through the windows. Elena pulled the phone from her pocket and flipped the cover open. The screen lit up. Ten percent battery life. She'd already determined the device had never been used before being shoved inside the mission wall. No reason for anyone to be looking for it then, right?

Pulling up the messaging screen, she entered the only phone number she'd bothered memorizing since she'd returned to Alpine Valley. Hesitation cut through her. If someone had been watching her movements on her ex's orders, reaching out could put her parents in more danger. But not knowing if they were safe was eating at her from the inside. She typed a quick message. Need to meet. You know the place. Tonight.

She sent the message. Cash would be back soon. She had to go now. Elena palmed the SUV's remote key she'd taken from his cargo pants and lunged for the door. Left at the end of the hall. Another left. Then a right. In less than a minute, she faced off with the elevator and hit the call button. Nervous energy had her scanning the floor for signs of Cash, Bear or any of his team. The elevator pinged, and she slipped inside.

She was in the clear. The fist around her heart released. There was no way the cartel was using twenty acres of land for nothing more than a drug route. The chances of finding Daniel there were slim, but she had to try. Her pulse thudded hard at the base of her throat as she locked on to the reflection in the silver doors. The bruises had darkened since last she'd noticed them. One bleeding up her cheek, the other across her opposite temple, but the swelling had at least gone down. She didn't look like she'd gotten into a fight with the end of a rifle.

The overhead lights flickered. Her heart rate skyrocketed out of control at the thought of getting stuck in the dark. The LED light above the door framed out a *G* for garage, and Elena stepped forward in anticipation of getting out of the car as fast as possible.

The doors parted.

The same wall of muscle that'd held her up at the sight of her childhood home burned to the ground blocked her path. Cash. "You know, I'm starting to think you don't like me."

COLOR HAD DRAINED from her face. Like she'd seen a ghost.

Cash only allowed himself a split second of concern before he stretched his hand out. "You're good, but you're not that good."

"You knew." Elena seemed to pull herself back from whatever terror had taken over. Even faced with an obstacle, she wasn't going to let herself crack. Admiration kept a tight hold on his consciousness, but sooner or later, the wall she'd built to keep herself under control was going to fall. He just hoped it didn't get her killed in the process. "Why let me get this far?"

"I wasn't sure of your motivation. Whether you wanted to run or if there was something you were running toward." Her body language didn't come across as nervous. More determined. That challenging gaze flickered behind him, to the fleet of vehicles parked within reach. Elena was gauging her chances of success against him. Wondering if she could outrun him. She couldn't. But, no. She wasn't trying to escape her problems. It wasn't in her genetic makeup. "You're going to that parcel of land your ex tried to hide from you."

A shuddering breath told him everything he needed. "I need to know what's out there. I need to know if that's where my brother is, and I'm not going to stop. You can lock me in your room or order Bear to guard me, but I won't stop trying to leave. I'm not going to sit here while you waste time coming up with an entire mission. Daniel doesn't have days. He needs me now."

Cash had made his decision the moment she'd stepped free from the elevator. Hell, he'd made it long before. Before her promise of inside intel on *Sangre por Sangre* fell through. Back when he'd taken down the bastard who'd intended to abduct her last night. There was nothing he wouldn't do for this woman. Because there was nothing she wouldn't do for those who needed her help, and that deserved respect. He headed for his SUV. "You navigate. I'll drive."

"What?" she asked.

"You got the coordinates, right? You know where we're going." He didn't bother turning around and wrenched the driver's-side door open. "You think there's more to that land than logistics. Let's see what the cartel is hiding."

Because there was no way in hell he was going to let her take on an entire cartel alone.

Elena didn't move to the passenger side of the vehicle, her hand still gripped around the SUV's remote. "What about Bear? I thought you two were inseparable."

"She's already in the back." Cash hauled himself behind the steering wheel and secured himself inside. Waiting. He centered his Rottweiler's face in the rearview mirror. "Up for another assignment?"

Bear licked the tip of her nose and along one side of her mouth in response. No complaints.

He started the engine with a push of a button as Elena climbed into the passenger seat.

"Shouldn't we wait for backup or something?" She slid her palms down the length of her thighs. She'd been prepared to fight him and lose. Not partner with him on a potential dead end. "Does your team know you're doing this?"

"No." Cash shoved the SUV into Drive and launched them from the underground parking garage. Sun cut through the windshield, making the landscape monochromatic and bright. "Best-case scenario, you're right. We find the cartel. If we're spotted and have to engage, I can ping the team for backup. The chopper cuts that down to ten."

"And the worst case?" The weight of each word told him she already knew the answer. "What then?"

"Worst case, you're wrong." He checked the side mirror to focus on something other than the effect her voice had on him. Soothing and compelling. Emotional. Strong. The combination pulled him into a false sense of security and refused to let go. "There's nothing out there. You get whatever this is out of your system, and we come up with a new plan to find your brother."

"Do you trust them? The people you work with?" Elena clutched the SUV's remote tighter, as though it were a lifeline through the violence and deception she'd already survived.

The question was simple enough, but the meaning… That was something else entirely. "You want to know whether or not Socorro will keep their word without you delivering on yours."

"I've been through it a thousand times in my head. No one knew I had that information about my husband's business dealings. And the fact whoever took it knew where I'd hidden it and replaced it with the same model of phone makes me think you were right. That the cartel has been watching me," she said. "I wouldn't blame your boss for believing I'd lied about it to begin with."

She wasn't talking about Ivy. She was talking about him. Cash checked the mirrors to ensure they hadn't been followed. A habit he couldn't afford to quit in his line of work. "You said husband that time. Not ex."

She didn't answer right away, seemingly trying to gauge how much to tell him.

Soldiers who climbed the ranks inside organizations like *Sangre por Sangre* were few and far between. Most had been brought in from right off the street as youths, most likely victims of their own recruitment tactics. They were encouraged to prove themselves at all costs and trained to compete with one another. For food, sleeping arrangements, the clothes on their backs, assignments. To make it as high as a lieutenant, a recruit would have to survive years of mental, physical and emotional abuse, not to mention learn to deliver it out to his subordinates when called for. Including those closest to him.

"You're still married." She'd told him as much, hadn't she? When she'd initially explained she'd run with nothing but a phone the lieutenant didn't know about and the clothes on her back. But the idea she was legally bound to another man set him on edge. Even if she was the one who'd wanted out of the relationship.

Though someone had known about what she'd done. The question was how.

"Hard to get a divorce when one party refuses to sign the papers." Elena directed her attention out the window, hugging herself around the middle as though to keep it together a little bit longer. "Not to mention beats the man who served him the papers to a pulp."

"Your friend the deputy? " he asked.

He barely caught her nod as they carved through a dirt road cutting across the county. There was nothing out here but weeds, dirt and death, yet Cash found himself not wanting to be anywhere else right then.

"He's with the Alpine Valley police department," she said. "Deputy McCrae. He was the one who got me out. He drove all the way to Albuquerque to help me escape, but he barely survived going back. Spent three weeks in an intensive care unit after surgery to relieve a blood clot in his brain. Came out with a shaved head, a four-inch scar and six broken ribs for his trouble. I would do anything to go back and not ask him to deliver those papers, but at the time, it'd felt like the only thing that would finally put an end to this."

But the world didn't work like that. Not with abusers.

"Brock McCrae." His study of Alpine Valley and their limited resources set the name at the front of his mind. The deputy had only been with the department two years. Good record. No reports of abuse of authority or excessive force as far as Cash could remember. Then again, a little town like that didn't usually see anything more serious than misdemeanors, and most of them came from bored teenagers planning to get out as soon as they graduated high school.

Elena turned that guarded gaze to him. "How did you know that?"

"It's my job to know all the players on the board." Big or small. But it hadn't been enough to stop the cartel from raiding and slaughtering a small town in search of their intended target. Elena. The sun arced into the western half of the sky, cutting through the windshield and diminishing his view. "What's so special about this land? Of all the documents you found with all the addresses, why this one?"

She pinched her hands between her knees. "I'm

not sure. I just know what my gut is telling me. It was important. When my…husband learned I'd checked the mail that day—it was the one and only time I saw a mortgage statement pertaining to that location—he was angry. Angrier than I'd ever seen him before."

It was easy enough to fill in the rest of the blanks, and the eighteen-year-old who'd enlisted straight into the Marine Corps after the largest terrorist attack had hit the country went on the defense. "He punished you for it."

"He locked me in our wine cellar for three days." Her voice detached slightly. Not in any big way, but in the smallest change in pitch. A memory she was better off believing had happened to someone else. "No food. No water or way to go to the bathroom. There was no electricity. No light. I clawed at that door, begging him to let me out, but he never came."

Elena brushed her thumb over her middle fingernail, and Cash only then realized it was missing. The base had started growing back some but stood out more than the others. "I can see why Bear might be scared of the dark. I am, too. I have to sleep with a night-light. Ridiculous, right? A grown woman paralyzed by a childish fear like that."

Cash had held himself in check since the moment she'd woken on that examination table in the doc's office. But he couldn't anymore. He reached over the center console and wrapped her hand with the missing fingernail in his. "It's not ridiculous, Elena, and you sure as hell don't let anyone tell you it is. They don't know. Nobody knows what you went through or what you've survived, including me. What I do know? You deserve good things in your life, and I'm going to damn sure be one of them as long as we're partnered together. Whether that means bringing Daniel home or taking down the son of a bitch who hurt you, I will not let you down. Ever. You understand?"

"I understand." A glimmer of tears reflected the afternoon sun as Cash released his hold. She swiped at her face with the back of her hand and sat forward. "Thank you."

Barbed wire fencing took shape through the windshield, cutting across their path, and Cash pulled the SUV off the side of the one-way dirt road. Bear *ruff*ed from the cargo area. Apparently not too pleased with his driving. As usual.

"This is it." Elena leaned forward in her seat. "We're here."

Chapter Six

They didn't have a plan.

She scouted the length of the barbed wire fence through the windshield. There was no gate from what she could tell. At least not for a few acres in each direction. The only reason to use a fence was to keep intruders out. Or someone in.

Elena shoved free of the SUV. Midday sun warmed her skin and instantly beaded sweat at the back of her neck. Shading her eyes, she tried to gauge the distance between them and the opposite border of land. She'd been wrong before. "This is more than twenty acres."

Cash rounded the hood of the vehicle, taking position beside her. "You sure these are the coordinates?"

"Yes, but that was months ago." She hated to think of what this new information meant. More acreage meant having to take more time to search. Time she wasn't sure Daniel had. "Is it possible the cartel has bought up more land?"

"Only one way to find out." He maneuvered to the

back of the SUV and hauled the cargo area door over-head. Bear jumped free, seemingly scanning their surroundings for herself, and a bit of relief eased through Elena. From what Cash had told her, Bear trained for things like this. She could sense danger before they stepped into it. Like their personal radar. Cash extracted a large set of bolt cutters from the cargo area and tossed them on the ground. He released the magazine from his sidearm and checked the bullets inside, then slammed it back into place. In seconds, he'd locked the vehicle and presented her with the bolt cutters. "You know what this means, don't you? We're about to trespass on cartel land. Your ex's land. Once we cross that line, there's no going back. No more running."

He was giving her a choice. Either confront her ex to save her brother or go back and put the past behind her as she'd intended. But it wasn't really a choice at all. Not for her. Elena accepted the bolt cutters, surprised at the weight. "I understand."

"Let's do this." He followed her to the fence, his massive body shading her from the sun.

Elena centered the bolt cutters against one link and clamped down. The metal broke as easily as uncooked angel-hair pasta. Daniel's favorite snack whenever she caught him in the pantry. She repeated the process until an uneven section of fence separated from the main frame—too loud in the silence of the desert.

"Ladies first." Cash held the section of fence back as she crawled through with the bolt cutters, then followed far more gracefully than she'd ever managed. "We stick to the fence. Scout the perimeter. If anything happens, we can get out fast. This is surveillance only, Elena. We see something, we call for backup. We do not engage. Agreed?"

Her heart threatened to override logic. "What if we find him?"

"The odds of your brother's survival are better if the entirety of Socorro has our back." He was waiting for her to agree to his terms. Wondering if he could count on her in a sticky situation. Because the last time he'd trusted the wrong person during an assignment, he'd lost someone important to him and gained Bear in the process.

She wasn't a soldier. She didn't have a weapon other than an oversize pair of bolt cutters, not to mention none of his training. He was the expert here, and deep down, she understood his number one priority would be getting her out alive if faced with danger. "Okay."

"Watch where you're stepping. Scorpions and snakes are faster than you think." Cash took the first step, leading them along the fence. He kept pace as easily as if they were on a stroll along a cemented sidewalk instead of navigating loose rock, weeds and potential threats from wildlife. Not to mention armed gunmen who'd given up their morals a long time ago.

Bear jogged alongside her master, snout to the ground, with Elena taking up the rear of their little search party. The fence rattled with a gust of wind and stripped her nerves raw. Her mouth watered at the sudden intensity of the sun overhead. It was searing the skin of her scalp where her hair parted down the middle.

She shouldn't be out here.

Twenty-four hours ago, she'd been living an entirely different life. Recovering from her marriage at home, with her family, secure in knowing she could unravel her ex at a moment's notice if provoked.

Now her parents were missing, her brother had been taken and the information she'd risked her life for had been stolen. There was nothing left. Nothing but a Rottweiler and her grumpy, sarcastic handler in the middle of a desert determined to swallow her whole. And, somehow, they'd become her only comfort. "Who was he? Bear's first handler. You said you knew him. Were you friends?"

"His name was Wade." Cash refused take his eye off the path up ahead. It was easy to imagine him dressed in his combat uniform. Solely focused on the task at hand. That kind of intensity had transferred into his new life. One ripped apart by betrayal and loss. Just like hers. "He was my brother."

Her step hitched, but Cash didn't seem to notice. "Your brother. As in—"

"Same parents." His voice shifted down. Most likely unnoticeable to anyone else, but in the time since he'd saved her life, she'd become acutely aware of each and every change in his demeanor. "I'm older by eleven months. We enlisted around the same time. Right after September 11. I remember that day so clearly. He'd just graduated high school. I was still trying to figure out my life—what I wanted to do. We were sitting in front of the television, watching the whole thing play out, and we just looked at each other. We knew right then and there what we were meant to do. Next day, I went down to the Marine Corps recruitment office. Within five years, I ended up one of the top weapons experts and strategists. Wade went into the army for intelligence."

"That's how he ended up with the DEA?" Elena hadn't missed the part where the Meyers brothers had instantly responded to an explosive need for help when the country needed them most. It was what Cash had done last night. Charging into an unknown situation for the sake of a stranger. It was admirable, ethical and, in her opinion, one of the greatest sacrifices someone could make for another. And he'd made it for her. "Gathering information against the cartels?"

"Was damn good at it, too. He wasn't like other

analysts. Didn't like sitting behind a desk, punching in data for eight hours a day. He wanted to be in the field, investigating the tips he got himself before sending them up the ladder. Made a hell of a case vetting all the intel himself. Managed to convince the higher-ups to keep him and Bear in the field. Within a few weeks, the DEA had actionable intelligence to tear apart the Colombian cartel. Watch your step." Cash pointed out a scorpion the size of her fist, hidden by its near translucency against the desert floor. "At least on paper."

"But he started taking money from the very people he was supposed to be fighting." She craned her head back over her shoulder, searching the flat, dead landscape for something—anything—to confirm they were in the right place. That she hadn't made another mistake.

"I don't know where it went wrong." A heaviness she'd come to hate tainted his words. "Wade wasn't a gambler. Didn't have financial issues as far as I could tell. Wasn't in over his head on his house or in debt. He didn't need their money. Best I can guess, they threatened someone close to him."

"You." It made sense. While *Sangre por Sangre* didn't hail from Colombia, their tactics overlapped in more than a few areas. Personal relationships would always be an easy target, and from what she'd learned of Cash, she bet Wade Meyers would do whatever it took to protect the people he cared about. Her heart hurt at the idea. Because in much the same way, they were in similar positions. Him with his brother. Her with Daniel.

"Yeah." Cash left it at that.

They walked several hundred more feet along the perimeter in silence. She wasn't sure how much distance they'd covered, but the backs of her thighs had started protesting the uneven terrain.

"Platz," he said.

It took her brain too long to process Cash's sudden command. Faster than she thought possible, his body encapsulated hers. He tugged her to sit against him, her back to his front, behind a large brittlebush. Bear dove for another section in the bush, then sat absolutely still. Cash practically melted into the leaves, enough for them to prod at her overheated skin as yellow flowers closed in around her vision. Her breath puffed too hard out of her chest as she listened. "What is it?"

"Shh." He unholstered his weapon. His arm was still gripped around her waist. Solid and warm.

The sound of footsteps crunched from a few feet away. Goose bumps rippled down her exposed arms as a shadow crawled in front of them from the opposite side of the bush. Elena reached for the bolt cutters she'd dropped, but Cash laid his hand over hers.

Static breached through the protective layer of

brush, and the shadow's arm shifted upward toward the head. *"No hay nada aquí."* There's nothing out here. *"Me dirijo de vuelta."* I'm headed back.

Her chest threatened to explode from holding her breath, but Cash's hold remained on her. Grounded, strong. It shouldn't have meant anything in that moment—especially given the danger they were in— but his touch was the only thing keeping her from spiraling.

The shadow eased away from them, but even then, Cash waited a few seconds before releasing her. "Slowly."

She tipped her balance forward and crawled on all fours into the open. No sign of the man, but a scuff of boot prints encircled the opposite side of the bush. They were in the clear. For now. "Just so you're aware, I don't take German commands."

"If I hadn't told Bear to get down, she'd have given us away." The dog crawled free of her hiding spot as though she understood Cash's every word. He holstered his weapon. "I wasn't worried about you."

"Oh." His words shouldn't have wounded her at all, but she couldn't help but twist his meaning into something along the lines of not caring for her at all. It was silly, really. After what he'd done for her, she knew better. But the effects of her marriage had yet to wear off. "Why do you think he was out here? We haven't seen anything since we left the car."

Cash nodded northeast, directing her attention to

the half-built structure at the bottom of a man-made valley she hadn't seen until right then. "I think he's guarding that."

ELENA HAD BEEN RIGHT.

Which meant his and Socorro's attempts to track and gauge *Sangre por Sangre*'s movements and assets had failed.

The compound was bigger than anything he'd seen. Constructed from massive resources no amount of inside intel had tipped them off to. Dug deep into the earth, half of the structure peeked out between mountains of dirt shoved to the side. Haulers and excavators worked in slow motion as Cash added up the number of armed men patrolling the perimeter of the site.

Cash had jogged back to the SUV for his gear. Lowering the binoculars, he handed them off to Elena, who was flat on her stomach beside him. He'd always worked alone during his missions. Analyze the threat. Report to Ivy. It was kind of nice to have someone who didn't bark back. Though that feeling didn't stay long. "I count thirty-five armed, six excavator drivers and at least thirteen others."

"You think they all work for the cartel?" She pressed the binoculars against her eyes.

"Organizations like *Sangre por Sangre* don't let outsiders in. Either they're in the ranks, or fated to die once they finish the job," he said.

"I can't believe nobody knew this was out here. The building has to be at least double the size of Socorro headquarters. This kind of project has to come with environmental reports and permits." She lowered the binoculars as though trying to take it all in with her own eyes. "You and your team really had no idea what they've been building?"

"No." A mistake he seemed destined to repeat at every juncture. Cartels operated out in the open. They took credit for attacks and assassinations. A project like this didn't fall into normal operating procedure. What the hell was going on here? "My guess—this place doesn't exist on paper. Wouldn't be surprised if the cartel paid off the right people or threatened or murdered whoever they needed to to keep it under the radar."

"What is it for?" she asked. "Why go through all the trouble?"

"A headquarters. See those piles of dirt?" Cash moved along the barely-there ridge providing cover for their positions. Bear had been on enough of these scouting missions to keep her head low and stay put. But Elena… She wasn't trained for this. She didn't understand the rules of warfare. She was just a victim caught in the cross fire. "They're going to bury the building once construction is complete. Satellite imagery over this area would just register the dirt. The building will give off heat, but combined with the desert, there won't be anything to differentiate the different sources. Within a year, the weeds will be back, and this place will be completely hidden in plain sight. *Sangre por Sangre* has always been left to operate under the banner of their lieutenants across the state. This will give them a place to create a stronghold."

"Unless we stop them." Elena handed back the binoculars. "Look. The backside of the building is already finished. There aren't any guards patrolling over there. We could probably circle around and drop down."

"Assuming there's a way to get inside from there." He'd known this was coming. The moment they'd crossed the site, she would've already come up with a way to get inside. "Elena, we had an agreement. Surveillance only."

"My brother could be in there." Desperation and a hint of anger solidified her expression. "Doesn't your entire organization exist for the sole purpose of dismantling the cartel? What better way than to catch them off guard? To hit them on their own turf?"

There was no reasoning with her. She'd already made up her mind.

"I'm not saying we leave and forget this place exists." The numbers weren't adding up. They were outmanned, outgunned and working blind. "We need a layout of the building, confirmation your brother is here and support—preferably more than thirteen bullets and a dog scared of the dark. We have no idea what we're walking into down there."

Bear craned her head toward them.

"Don't pretend you aren't." He hadn't meant to be so harsh, but this situation was coming dangerously close to the DEA operation that'd gone to hell and taken his brother. The intel they'd been relying on had turned out to be nothing but wishful thinking. He couldn't go through that again.

"He's here. I know he is, and I've waited long enough." She backed away from the ridge overlooking the construction site and shoved to stand. "You can wait for your team, but I'm not letting Daniel suffer one more second wondering if someone is coming for him."

Dirt kicked up at her heels as she raced along the barbed fence.

Bear's whine reflected the war tearing through Cash. He couldn't let Elena go in there without backup. Let alone unarmed.

"Does she think bolt cutters are a weapon?" Bear didn't have an answer for him. Cash dragged himself away from the ridge, keeping low as he followed in Elena's footsteps. Her frame shrank the faster she ran. He whistled low to call for Bear and slowed long enough to trigger the emergency signal on her collar. No matter where they were, the team would respond to the call. "Damn it."

He just hoped it was in time.

Battle-ready tension infiltrated the muscles along his neck and shoulders as Elena slid down the incline behind the compound. Dust funneled overhead, practically signaling anyone within a mile radius of her presence, but the soldiers and workers in the basin somehow hadn't noticed. Cash picked up the pace. Rock and dirt penetrated through his gear down the slope. The earth wall threatened to swallow him and Bear whole as his view of the site cut off. Solid ground caught them at the bottom and dragged Elena's attention from a set of double doors at the back of the structure.

He crossed the dry, cracked distance between them. Every cell in his body wanted the reassurance of her touch again—to make sure she was okay—but they were living on borrowed time as it was.

"What are you doing? Go back. Wait for your team." Surprise softened the curve of her mouth and dropped her hands away from a keycard panel installed beside the entrance.

"Couldn't let you have all the fun, now, could I?" He nodded to the panel. Top-of-the-line security. No access in or out without a corresponding keycard. But, being employed by one of the brand's installers, he'd come across this model before. And the bypass built into the system. "Watch out."

Cash entered a six-digit code. The panel LEDs lit up green and released the dead bolts securing both doors.

"How did you do that?" she asked.

"Socorro is one of two companies certified to install this brand of security system, but it turns out the override code is the same." He unholstered his weapon, setting Bear at full alert. "We have no idea what's waiting on the other side of these doors. Stay behind me. Use me as a shield if you have to. Bear will protect you if someone gets close enough, but there's no way for her to stop a bullet."

He crouched beside Bear and removed her emergency collar. "Anything happens to me, get out and put as much distance between you and this place as you can. The team can find you with this."

Elena pocketed Bear's collar and gripped both handles of the bolt cutters in front of her, nodding. "I'm ready."

She wasn't. Very few people who hadn't seen war could be ready for a situation like this, and letting her walk right into the enemy's hands was out of the question.

Cash wrenched open the nearest door and took aim. One foot in front of the other, he scanned the long hallway from left to right. No movement. No ambush waiting for them to cross the threshold. Cement walls tunneled ahead of them. The compound itself was still under construction, but overhead fluorescent lights had been installed in equal distance, lighting their way. "They're already up and running."

"How is that possible? Half of the building is a gaping hole." Elena's arm brushed against his shoulder.

He didn't know, but if the compound already had power, it stood to reason that *Sangre por Sangre* was further ahead on the project than he'd initially estimated. Like the Death Star. Cash moved along the wall, Bear taking up the rear, Elena sandwiched between them. *"Pass auf."*

His canine partner huffed confirmation, her nails clicking against the cement tomb they'd infiltrated. She'd guard Elena with her life if necessary.

But the place was a ghost town. No cameras in sight. No guards or offices in this section of hallway. None of this made sense. Why install lights and a security system if there was nothing here to protect?

His instincts provided the answer, and Cash pulled up short. "We need to get out of here."

"What? No." Elena refused to budge. "We have to find—"

Bear growled low in her chest, the sound echoing off the walls closing in around them.

He took aim at empty space along the corridor, but something was down there. Something that rivaled his human senses.

The power cut out. Bear whimpered from the tail end of their search party. Her fear of the dark would override any command he gave, and without her to protect Elena, he was operating blind. They had to get out of here. This whole plan had been a setup from the beginning. Just like before.

"Damn." Cash grabbed for his flashlight. He hit the power button. "Back up. Head for the door."

Elena's hand fisted around the shoulder of his Kevlar vest. Her gasp reached his ears as a single face emerged in the beam.

"Please. Don't rush out on my account," the man said. "I've been waiting a long time for my wife to come home."

The lights flickered to life, revealing the circle of armed men surrounding them from every angle. Including their exit. How was that possible? How could he have been so blind? He'd walked them right into an ambush.

"I'm not your wife." Elena's confidence embedded deep in his chest. Almost enough to convince him they might have a chance here. "You can't be married to someone who only exists on paper."

Physical tension pinched the man's mouth into a thin line. Like the guy had just eaten a bunch of sour grapes. Elena had hit her mark. "Take them."

The circle surrounding them tightened.

"Touch her, and you'll lose your hand." Cash gripped his weapon tighter as though the simple action would ensure their escape, but the truth was they were nothing against a small army. They weren't getting out of this without a few scars.

Bear's yip had him turning to amputate whoever'd put a hand on her.

Pain exploded at the back of his head. Lightning blinded him for a fraction of a second. Then darkness.

Elena's scream followed him into unconsciousness. "Cash!"

Chapter Seven

The rope was too tight.

Elena dragged her chin away from her chest. The fibers around her wrists scratched at oversensitive skin. A dull thud pounded at the back of her head, but all she could think about was the binding contorting her arms behind her back. Which didn't make sense. She should be far more concerned with a head injury than any damage done to her wrists. Was that a sign of a head injury? She didn't know.

She forced her eyes open, fighting the drug of unconsciousness. Her heart pumped blood too fast as she took in the darkness. There were no shapes to make out. No noise to distinguish through the pulse behind her ears. Her throat convulsed to fill the silence, but she was paralyzed against the inky blackness closing in. A weak sound escaped instead. Grating. Pathetic.

He was punishing her again.

How long this time? Four days? More? She didn't

know this room. It wasn't part of her own home this time. She couldn't see the door or make out a way to escape. But, knowing her husband, there would be no way to escape. There hadn't been the last time.

Pulling at the rope, she struggled to contain the tears burning in her eyes. No. No, no, no. This couldn't be happening. Her ankles had been secured. This wasn't punishment. This was domination. She hadn't obeyed, and he was going to make her pay.

It took everything she had to take her next breath, only one name forming in the sobbing inhale. "Cash?"

Movement provoked her senses from a few feet away.

A spark of hope zinged through her, and for the first time since she'd opened her eyes, her shoulders relaxed away from her ears. He was here. He'd get them out of this. She had to believe that. Because he was her only option.

"Did you really think you could just walk away from me, Elena?" he asked. "That I wouldn't find you?"

Dread pooled in the pit of her stomach. Not Cash. That voice had woken her in the middle of the night for months, even after she'd left it behind. Elena pressed her back into the chair he'd secured her to. She still couldn't see him, and her hands immediately worked to free herself and put as much distance between them as possible.

Warm light reached for the ceiling and spread

throughout the room at the pull of a string. It was a desk lamp, illuminating every cinder block wall and a single entrance. And beside it, her husband. He was looking tired. Too thin. Stressed? Though still handsome. His dark hair, peppered with silver at his temples, didn't come close to showing his age as much as the exhaustion around his eyes. His once terra-cotta skin tone had paled slightly. Not enough sun. A troll guarding his mountain of treasure. The white suit paired with a black button-down shirt had starred in many of her nightmares since escaping. He was everything she remembered and everything she wanted to forget.

"Where is my brother?" Fear threatened to bleed into her voice, but she wouldn't give him the satisfaction. She wasn't that woman anymore. The one he'd targeted, seduced, lied to and betrayed. She wasn't his plaything that he got to bring out whenever he got bored. "Where's Cash?"

Her husband slid off the edge of the desk, smoothing invisible wrinkles from his suit. In truth, she'd never seen the slightest flaw in his appearance, even in sleep. It would only take away from his presumed power. "Come now. We don't need to talk about that. You must've missed me. I certainly missed you."

Spreading his arms in front of him, the man she'd known as Metias Leyva—the one who'd asked her to take his last name—waited there as though she would stand up and walk right to him. As though he hadn't had his men knock her unconscious and tie her to a chair in the dark.

She wasn't sure how long she'd been out. How much time she'd wasted. How much time Daniel had left. "You can't miss someone you didn't know."

"That again? We've talked about this, *mi amor*." His laugh broke over the room. Like she'd recounted a joke she'd heard rather than the dysfunction of the life they'd tried to build together. He dragged a chair matching hers from beneath the desk with the lamp, and it was then she realized this room didn't have any windows. He'd trapped her in what seemed to be an office. Underground. Metias took his seat across from her, his knees brushing against hers. He'd done it on purpose. To remind her he was the one who had control. That she was at his mercy. As she always would be. "Do you remember what I told you the last time you were in a room like this?"

The memories were there on the cusp of her mind. At the ready to unravel her from the inside, but Elena wasn't going to break. Not here. And not for him. "Hard to forget the first time your husband locks you in a dark room for three days without food or water."

Eyes the color of dark chocolate—compelling and deep and fluid—centered on her and triggered her defenses. He set his palms on the top of her thighs and leaned in. A hint of his aftershave, the one she used to love, worked into her system. His hands were warm. Deceiving in so many ways. "I told you my work requires an extra layer of security. My associates wouldn't hesitate to take you from me if I made a mistake. Neither would the government of this country. Lying to you—it was the only way I knew how to protect you."

She'd heard this speech before. In that cellar after she'd lost her voice from screaming and her insides were trying to eat themselves. At the time, she would've agreed to anything he said to get the relief she'd desperately craved. She would've done anything. But time and distance and freedom had changed her. "Your work. You mean abducting children and turning them into soldiers, killing innocent people, destroying their homes and pushing them out of their towns. Running drugs and women and guns? That work? The work you chose over our marriage time and again. You didn't lie to me to protect me, Metias. You lied because you were scared I would see you for who you really are. A monster."

He moved so fast, she didn't have time to brace herself first.

The strike twisted her head over her left shoulder and stung across her face. Her eyes watered from the impact, but there wasn't a single bone in her body that regretted what she'd said. He stood and pulled the chair back where he'd taken it from. Turning back, Metias tugged a handkerchief from his pocket and wiped his hand clean. Couldn't leave any evidence connecting him to his atrocities. That wouldn't bode well for his work or the people he worked for, now, would it? "What happened to Alpine Valley was your fault, *mi amor*. I gave you everything. A home, clothing, food on our table. I pulled you from poverty in that nothing town and introduced you to a better life. This is how you repay me? By stealing information about my business and running away?"

He knew what she'd taken. How? For how long? She'd been so careful. Blood beaded at the corner of her mouth. She moved to swipe it away, but the rope had somehow grown tighter around her wrists. His wedding ring, the same ring she'd slipped onto his hand that day in the church surrounded by her family and friends, had busted her lip. The people he'd isolated her away from, that'd given up on trying to keep in touch. She wouldn't lick it away. She'd make him see it. See the kind of man he'd become. "That's the problem, Metias. A marriage isn't a debt to be repaid. It's a partnership—a relationship that requires give and take. But the only relationship you'll ever be able to count on in the future is the one with your hand."

That crooked smirk he intentionally used to make her feel less than human graced her with its presence, and her confidence waned. Scrubbing a hand through the beard scruff showing more salt than pepper these days, Metias shoved his opposite hand into his pants' pocket. His knuckles fought against the fabric there, as though he were wrapping his fingers around something. He rounded behind her, out of sight, and she found herself hating the idea of not being able to see him rather than confronting him head-on as she'd prepared for all these months. "You asked me before where your brother was. Strong *chico*, that one. A fighter. I knew it the moment I met him. Could see it in his eyes. You and he share that trait. You both endure physical punishment well."

What? What did that mean? Elena struggled to catch her breath. "What have you done? Where is Daniel?"

Metias penetrated her peripheral vision, a phone in his hand. A low whoosh registered. A message? "But that means you also share the same weakness. So here's what I'm going to do, Elena."

The door across the room swung inward. A man—familiar even through the dim lighting of the desk lamp—filled the doorway with mountainous muscle and an obvious pride, as though he'd just won killer of the year three years in a row. It was him. The one she'd suspected had been assigned to follow her through Albuquerque any day she dared leave the house alone. She hadn't been able to get proof before. Not with her husband's knack for hiding any real pieces of their life from her. Now she knew.

"I'm only going to give you one more chance."

Metias moved to wipe the blood from her mouth
with his thumb, and wasn't that the perfect example
of the man she'd once trusted to love her, to care
about her? Never one to lower himself for the ben-
efit of others. He locked on to her chin as she jerked
away from his touch, pinching her mouth in his grip.
"Apologize for what you've done. Forget about the
man you dragged into this mess you've made and
come home. Be my wife. Not behind me as before,
but at my side. Where you belong."

Cash. Her heart threatened to suction inside out.
He'd taken a brutal hit to the head with the butt of
the soldier's gun, and her face ached in remembrance
of where Metias's gunman had done the same to her.
She'd watched him drop so hard, she feared he might
never wake up. And Bear… The Rottweiler had tried
to protect them by going after Metias. And failed. It
was up to Elena to save them now. Because Metias
was right in a way. She'd gotten them into this mess.
"And if I refuse?"

She already knew the answer. It'd lodged in her
chest the moment Daniel had been taken from her.

Her husband leveraged both hands on the chair
arms, boxing her within his broad frame. "Then
you'll lose Daniel forever. And I'll finish burning
Alpine Valley and everyone in it to the ground."

THE TWELFTH HIT must've cracked a rib.

Cash's body swung backward from the momentum. He could barely see out of his left eye from the swelling. The cartel didn't condone trespassing. He'd be lucky if that broken rib didn't puncture his lung before the night was over.

"Who do you work for?" The soldier who'd turned him into a life-size piñata wasn't going to wait for an answer. He hadn't yet. The thirteenth strike cut a jagged ridge over Cash's eyebrow. *"Policia?"*

Stinging pain enveloped his face. He dropped his head back between his strung-up hands in an attempt to numb the pain, but the relief never came. It wouldn't. Not until he had eyes on Elena and Bear. But the chances of getting out of the makeshift cell they'd hoisted him into weren't in his favor. Not without his gear or weapons. The building itself was new, but a hint of human decomposition stained the air of what looked to be a gym pieced together with mismatched machines, barbells and dumbbells. Sweat, and blood and horror. He wasn't the cartel's first visitor to this area, and he certainly wouldn't be the last.

"No, man. He's not police. He came for the boss's woman." The fourteenth hit struck harder than the previous ones. Blood bloomed from a laceration inside his mouth as another soldier took his turn. He backed up, letting Cash swing freely. As though he were the one completely in control. "Big mistake, *vato*. Boss already laid his claim. There ain't nothing you can do now. When he's done with her, she won't even remember your name."

Elena. He'd given his word her ex wouldn't lay
another hand on her, and he'd failed. Her and Daniel. This place was a massive maze. Meant to con-
fuse and disorient anyone who wasn't supposed to
be here. Law enforcement, military, hostages. It'd
take days to search without a guide or a map. Lucky
for him, he had his pick. Cash muttered something
under his breath.

"What was that?" A soldier who'd gotten a few
good punches in stepped forward, but they'd been
scattered. No focus. Just intensity. "You begging for
your life already? Damn, I lose the bet."

His mouth moved, but Cash didn't let sound leave.

The soldier came closer. Close enough to make
contact.

Cash dropped his head back again. Then snapped
it forward. His forehead slammed into the soldier's,
and the recruit dropped hard with a hand to his nose.
Trying to keep the blood in. Wouldn't work.

The laughs died in an instant. Surprise and confusion rippled through the cell.

Anger radiated off the kid. Couldn't be any more
than twenty. But Elena's husband had left the soldier
with a hostage, which meant the *vato* puckering his
shoulders up by his ears had earned the lieutenant's
trust over years of service. A child soldier. And while
Cash hadn't seen a photo of Daniel, it was all too
easy to imagine Elena's brother becoming the one
thing she feared most.

Five hostiles. Presumably all armed. Little to no combat experience, but dangerous as a pack all the same. Like wolves. One alpha. The rest were followers but each was capable of defending themselves or taking down their prey alone.

The kid pulled a knife, blood dripping into his mouth and down his shirt. Harsh fluorescent lighting bounced off the blade. "You think you're funny, *cabrón*? Let me wipe that smile off your face, but before I do, I'll take that dog of yours and turn her inside out."

They wouldn't touch Bear.

Mostly because she'd eat any man alive before she let them close.

"Then let's get this over with." The words left his throat as more growl than English.

The recruit stabbed at him.

Cash twisted enough to avoid the soldier's lunge. The blade cut through his T-shirt at his low back, but the kid hadn't calculated his own momentum and met the cement face-first. Cash wrenched his upper body around as another attacker raced forward. He locked his legs around the soldier's neck and squeezed.

Two more moved in, a third staying on the peripheral.

He jerked his legs as hard as possible and choked out the fighter under his grip to take on the next two. Only he wasn't fast enough. One slammed into his gut. Air crushed from his lungs. The impact left him guessing which way was up as his binds broke free of the hook hanging down from the ceiling. His spine wrapped around the soldier he'd knocked out like a damn piece of Play-Doh, but Cash didn't have time to pull himself back together. He wrenched free of the ropes and hauled himself to his feet.

The fourth attacker came from behind. He locked Cash's arms to his side as the one with the knife got his bearings. A swipe of that blade cut through the front of his shirt and scored across his chest. Cash launched his elbow back into the bastard's face behind him. Then he kicked the knee out of the guy in front. A scream filled the small cell and echoed down the corridor.

The soldier at his back—roughly Cash's size—war cried a split second before the son of a bitch practically picked Cash up and hauled him back. They hit the floor together. Before he had a chance to catch his breath, two more attackers were dragging him across the floor by the legs. Cash reached for the closest thing resembling a weapon as he could get: a freestanding dumbbell.

He swung it with everything he had into one man's kneecap. The sickening crunch of shattering bone filled his ears, and he knew then the soldier would never walk right again. Without any use, the cartel would put him down. His attacker dropped to both knees, and Cash ripped the metal across the soldier's face. Another caught him around the middle from out of nowhere. He brought the dumbbell down as hard as he could.

A weight bench slammed into him from behind. He launched forward, saved from eating the floor by the weight in his hand. Cash caught himself against the wall and chucked the dumbbell at the abductor getting ready to throw the bench at his head. The soldier took the weight to the gut and dropped the bench on himself. Cash rotated his shoulder. "I've gotta get in better shape."

A fist rocketed into his face from out of nowhere. He spun into the fifth soldier who'd decided to get in the game and launched his knuckles into the man's jaw. It was a brawl with no end. He knocked one down and another got up, and he was quickly running out of adrenaline.

Strong hands shoved him backward, and he tripped over an unconscious body. His elbow slammed against the cement as he rolled his legs up and over his shoulders to keep him moving. Out of breath, he raised both hands in preparation of what came next. Only one soldier remained. The one who'd locked his arms back while letting the others see if a bunch of candy would break out of him if they hit hard enough.

Cash had misjudged the soldier's size. They weren't equal. If anything, the man had at least fifty pounds of hard muscle on him. No shot caller. Not one to make decisions. His job was meant to keep others in line. "Let me guess. They call you Tiny."

A broken-toothed smile soaked in blood flashed wide. Groans filtered through the hard pound of Cash's pulse behind his ears. Tiny came in for a right hook. Cash ducked and struck the soft tissue of the bastard's organs. Didn't make a damn bit of difference. A thick hand wrapped around Cash's throat and bent him over a stack of barbell weights at his back. Cash dug his grip into the soldier's forearm, then his elbow. Black dots floated across his vision. He had a minute. Maybe seconds.

He hauled his bloodied fist into the soldier's eye, but Tiny recovered too quickly.

His attacker locked his gaze on him. Then thrust his forehead directly into Cash's face.

The world threatened to rip straight out from under him. The black dots took over, his lungs empty. He'd taken on an entire army in hopes of getting Elena and Bear out of here. Instead, they'd be the ones looking down on his body.

Tiny threaded an arm between Cash's legs and hauled him overhead. Gravity took hold, and in a classic wrestling maneuver, the soldier deposited him onto the floor. The collision finished the job the others had started on his ribs.

He had nothing left. Nothing left to fight. Nothing for Elena or her brother.

Pain exploded across his scalp as Tiny fisted a

chunk of his hair. Bone threatened to break under another strike to the face. Once. Twice. His head snapped back into the metal foot of the weight rack, and the world exploded into color. White, yellow and that drugging black he'd followed down the rabbit hole once before. In that pale rainbow, a face materialized. One he felt he'd known his entire life, yet had just encountered less than two days ago. He wanted nothing more than that face to be real. To feel how soft her skin was, to get lost in her warmth, to have those dark brown eyes look at him with something other than fear. To have her believe he was the good guy. That his brother's betrayal didn't run in his veins. Two days. That was all it'd taken for her to remind him of his purpose.

An outline shifted above him, and Cash's hand seemed to move of its own accord in survival mode. He clutched one of the stack weights and brought it forward. A scream nearly punctured his eardrums as Tiny's hand folded as easily as a dish towel against the steel. No. He wasn't giving up. There was something deep down that wouldn't let him—a drive to make this right. He'd given Elena his word that he'd bring her brother home, and that was exactly what he was going to do. Whether he was dead or alive for their reunion.

Cash struggled to his feet. Blood dripped from his mouth, adding to the stains already taking over the cement. The four other soldiers were down for the count, and they wouldn't be getting back up. He grabbed Tiny by the hair and pried the man's head back on his shoulders. "You're going to tell me where you're keeping my dog. Then you and I are going on a field trip."

Chapter Eight

She could feel him staring at her. The man Metias had left behind to watch her.

I have a matter that needs attending to. I'll give you some time to think about my offer. Her husband had kissed her forehead then, as though merely telling her he'd be late for dinner, and closed the door behind him. The unspoken warning in his tone filtered through her head on a loop. He'd given her time, but patience had never been one of his virtues.

She could either run back to him—submissive, apologetic and weak—or lose her brother forever.

And Cash… Where was Cash? Where was Bear? Were they still alive? Part of her had lit up at the possibility that the matter Metias needed to attend to involved the private military contractor and his Rottweiler giving the cartel hell. Cash would fight. In the limited amount of time they'd known each other, she knew that much. An internal mission drove him to overcome any situation—especially any that involved his K-9 companion—but what that meant for Elena, she didn't know. Would their deal still matter to him here? On the surface, she wasn't in physical danger. Metias wouldn't outright kill her for escaping their marriage. But if she refused to return to his side, would that give him reason to add her to the list of dead at his hands?

Her body ached. The ropes around her wrists had cut through skin and were rubbing her raw from the tension. Every move Elena made, every sound, was being catalogued by the brute guarding the door, but she couldn't stay here.

Because she'd already made her decision.

She'd made it the night she'd run from that house. Metias hadn't expected that of her. He'd been counting on her being too weak from starvation and dehydration and fear. That was why he'd agreed to let her have a few minutes of privacy to wash away the blood, sweat and tears from three days in that cellar. He hadn't counted on her climbing through the window, contacting someone for help or avoiding the perimeter patrol of men he'd set to keep the unwanted out.

She wasn't going back.

But that left Daniel at the mercy of a man who didn't have a compassionate bone in his body. A man who would want to keep his leverage as close as possible.

Elena scanned the bunker office for the dozenth

time. Metias had left the lamp on. He'd given her that much, at least. Books, a desk, the chair. None of it would help her out of these ropes. But something like a pen or a letter opener would do. She just had to give herself the opportunity to search. A fresh water bottle, complete with beaded condensation running the length of the plastic, stared back at her from the desk. Her husband would've placed it there on purpose. To break her, to remind her that her life was once again in his hands.

She'd surrendered her power for the chance of a family and a new life outside of Alpine Valley. She'd betrayed herself, but knowing Daniel's life depended on her, knowing Cash and Bear would do whatever it took to see this through, it was time for her to take it all back. To stop hiding. Stop playing the role of victim. To take a stand against the virus infecting the town and people she cared about.

Sizing up the massive boulder-sized man ahead of her, she cleared her throat. There wasn't any scenario in which she'd be able to overcome him physically, but she didn't have to. All she had to do was outsmart him. She'd done it with Metias. She could do it with a guard. Elena nodded toward the bottled water sweating against the desk. "Could I have some water?"

He didn't answer. Didn't even seem to comprehend her question for a series of moments. Maybe considering the repercussions if he gave in to her request, then those of not giving in. Would Metias want him to give her water or not?

She licked her lips, drawing his attention to her mouth. Her voice softened at the slightest provocation. "I'm really thirsty. I won't tell him, if that's what you're worried about. I just… I can't think when my throat is so dry, and he wants an answer soon."

He gruffed and hiked his shoulders a bit higher, which exaggerated the tendons fighting for release along his neck. He wasn't like the others she'd met when Metias threw his parties and forced her to mingle with his friends. Most, if not all of them, came from the same handwoven rug as she did—umber skin, dark hair, even darker eyes. Sweat built along his skin that suggested they shared some kind of ancestry, but the guard's eyes pinched at the edges slightly. More Asian than Mexican. Out of place in *Sangre por Sangre.* Trying to fit in.

He didn't respond. For the stretch of what felt like two full minutes, her plea died between them, but then…he was reaching for the water bottle. Small ticks around his jaw testified of the internal battle waging inside his head. He still wasn't sure he was making the right choice, but Elena couldn't think about what would happen to him after she escaped. Not right then.

Survival. She was good at that.

The guard closed the distance between them and unscrewed the lid. Offering it to her, he set the screw threads against her lower lip and tipped the bottle up-ward. Liquid drenched the front of her clothing and settled between her thighs.

As she'd intended. She pulled back. "I can't… I can't drink this without my hands. I need the ropes off."

The battle contorted into outright war across his expression. This was the moment that would decide her life. He knew the risks. She saw it in his face. If he let her free, his boss would punish him. If he let her become delirious from dehydration, his boss would punish him. There was no right answer. Every choice ended with a consequence, but he needed to decide which one.

"Please," she said. "You know what he's going to do to me. To my brother."

She wasn't asking him for water. He must've seen it in her face, heard it in her voice. He stared at her, trying to devise a motive or weighing the possibility of getting out of this alive from her expression, but she didn't have anything left to give. He had no rea-son to follow through. In fact, he had every reason to walk right back to his position at the door, but he didn't. The guard rounded behind her.

In a frenzy of doubt and uncertainty, Elena closed her eyes. The sound of a blade skimming against leather—something she'd grown all too familiar with in her marriage—pricked at her nerves. Right before the ropes fell from around her wrists. Blood rushed back into her hands.

"I'll stall them as much as I can. Tell Ivy something for me." He kept his voice so low, she wasn't sure if she'd heard him right. "Tell her Echo got off his leash."

"What?" What the hell was happening? She'd asked him to release her hands. Now he was helping her? She felt the need to turn around, but every second she tried getting answers was a lost opportunity to escape. "You know Ivy?"

"You don't have much time." He shoved to his feet behind her, a serrated blade inches from her face. The guard pulled back his shoulders and watched the door as though preparing for an oncoming fight. "Metias keeps the new recruits on the second floor on the south side of the building. Your brother should be there. But I need you to do something first. You have to stab me."

"You're out of your mind." Elena got to her feet.

"If Metias comes back and it doesn't look like I tried to keep you here, he will kill me, and years of undercover work will be for nothing." He took a step into her, handing her the blade handle-first. "Just imagine I'm your husband. Should make it easier. And make sure to take the knife with you. You're going to need it."

"Ex-husband." Elena sucked in a deep breath. She'd never stabbed someone before, and her gut soured at the idea. Trying to get her balance, she shifted her weight between both feet. The knife felt too heavy in her hand. She was going to have to do this. Trust him. "Any preferences on location?"

"Right here. Not too deep." He tapped just below his right pectoral. "My liver will grow back someday."

"Just promise me you're not going to die." Was she actually considering this?

"We're all dying, Elena. It's just a matter of when and what we do with the time we have left," he said.

That was too philosophical in a moment where a stranger she'd believed to be a cartel member was asking her to stab him. "Who are you?"

"You're out of time." He notched his chin higher. "Metias will be back any minute. Stab me, then get to your brother. Now."

Elena pressed the tip of the blade into the spot he'd indicated and glanced up to gauge his reaction. "Thank you."

She pushed the blade through T-shirt and flesh.

His groan would stay with her for the rest of her life, but even worse, the sound his body made as she withdrew the weapon. Blood coated the once flawless steel. She'd thought the knife was heavy before. Only now it would weigh on her from this moment forward. "I'm so sorry."

He dropped to the floor, doubling over, and she backed away. "Tell...Ivy what I said. Go!"

Elena lunged for the door, clothing clinging to her from the water drenching her down to bone. She ripped it open without looking back and pumped her legs as fast as possible. Bunker-like lights flickered as she raced along the corridor. *Second floor. Second floor.* How did she get to the second floor?

Low voices echoed down the hall, and she pressed herself against one wall. Out of breath, she tried to keep her heart rate under control, but it was no use. She'd just stabbed a man at his request. *Echo got off his leash. Echo got off his leash.*

The voices had drifted farther away now. She took a single step toward an upcoming corner, blade pressed against her chest in defense, and rounded into a perpendicular corridor.

Confronting the man who'd sworn to have her in sickness…and in death.

SHE HAD TO be here.

Cash blinked to keep himself conscious, but he was losing the battle faster than he expected. He couldn't recall the turns he'd already taken or how long ago Tiny had finally collapsed. There were too many hallways, and he was on his own, but he wouldn't stop. Not until he put Bear and Elena in his sights.

His shoulder made contact with the nearest wall. He took a second to clear his head, but the only image his brain could come up with was of Elena. Of her passed out in the back of his SUV, then the horror on her face as he told her she'd mistaken Bear's allergy meds for an Oreo. Of her smile and the way it'd tunneled past his guard as he'd invited her into his personal space. A space he hadn't let anyone else—not even his team—step foot in.

Hell, she'd taken on a fight no one had ever won. Just imagining the trouble she was giving her ex and the soldiers in this very building was enough to make him shove away from the wall and keep going. Elena Navarro was everything he'd tried avoiding over the past year and the one person who could drive him to keep going. She challenged him in ways that messed with his head but strengthened his moral code. The kind of woman who protected those she cared about, who stood alone against an army determined to tear her to pieces for the chance to do the right thing. Who carried everyone around her with her strength. Because that was how she quietly survived. That was how she kept moving forward. And he needed a healthy dose of that strength now.

Pain arced through his back as he pushed along the corridor. His right leg dragged behind him. He was getting close. He could feel it, and with two more turns through the maze, he froze.

Barking.

Incessant. Distant. Undeniably familiar. Bear.

"I'm coming, little lady. Keep it up." Cash picked up the pace. For as much pressure squeezed the oxygen from his lungs at the thought of putting off finding Elena, he wasn't going anywhere without his dog. Bear had been there. Suffered at his side after the explosion that got her kicked out of the DEA. Even

temporarily blind and through the painful nights following her injury, she'd refused to leave his side. Because she'd known. She'd known his loss. She'd felt
it herself when they'd recovered Wade's body miles
from the raid site where he'd died. The Colombian
cartel had done a good job of making his brother unrecognizable, but he and Bear had known the moment
they'd seen him. The whine of a K-9 that'd lost her
handler would stay with him for the rest of his life.
He wouldn't put her through that again. He wasn't
walking away.

An alarm sounded overhead.

Piercing agony ripped through his head in a swirl
of red lights and sirens.

Covering his ears, he made out heavy footfalls
coming down the corridor. Cash took a sharp right
turn to get out of their path, his back against the wall.
A group of armed men sprinted in two straight lines
down the hall, hustling as though the building were
about to collapse.

Someone could've found the mess he'd left behind
and raised the alarm, or... "Elena."

He was searching on borrowed time. They had to
get out of here. Cash couldn't hear Bear's warnings
over the sound of the alarm, but she was close. He
kept low and moved fast past a handful of doors, instincts on high alert for another swarm of soldiers.
Then he heard it. A single bark. Pulling up short,

he backed up, pressing his ear to the last door in the hall. There it was again. "Got you."

He didn't know what waited for him on the other side of the door. Didn't care. Ripping the door open, Cash rushed the armed gunman pointing a weapon at his dog as the soldier turned to confront the intruder. He cocked his elbow back and rocketed his fist into the guy's face.

The soldier dropped harder than a bag of cement, and Cash collected the man's automatic rifle as a reward. Bear cocked her head from behind a chain-link kennel, as though she'd been waiting for him all this time. "Don't give me that look. I got here as soon as I could."

He unlocked the hatch keeping her inside and crouched. Threading his fingers into her soft coat, he checked her over for injuries. Relief washed over him as he set his forehead against hers. "Good to see you, too."

Teeth bared, she stared down the soldier who'd threatened her with coal-black eyes. "Don't mind him. He's not getting up for a while. Think you can find Elena?"

With a lick of one side of her mouth, Bear hustled out the door and into the hallway. After a split second of consideration, she charged right at full speed.

He struggled to keep up with her, biting the inside of his mouth between his molars to take his brain's attention off the pain. The alert had been going for several minutes. The entire building was about to go under lockdown. No one in or out. Bear took a sharp left up ahead, out of sight. Tucking the rifle against his chest, Cash put any adrenaline still lingering in his veins into catching up.

He slowed at the corner, cutting his gaze the length of the corridor. Bear was there. Circling some kind of puddle on the floor. Heel-toeing it against the far wall, he cleared the hall. "What you got, girl? What is it?"

Bear lay down beside the stain. One of her cues to indicate human remains.

Blood. An entire foot-span seeped into the concrete. Fresh. No crusting around the edges where there was less volume. "Where is she?"

Bear's whine bled through the resounding peal of the alarm. His gut filled in the answer to his own question, but he wanted to outright reject it. No. Whoever'd lost this much blood would be well on their way to bleeding out, but it wasn't Elena. He hadn't failed her. He hadn't walked her straight to her death. She was alive. He had to believe that. Because if she wasn't… If she wasn't, then what the hell good was he?

Drops spattered out from the puddle left behind, and Cash couldn't help but follow. *"Such."* Track.

They moved as a team, Bear at his side. Shadows darkened in corners with each flash of the emergency lighting. He hiked the butt of the rifle into his shoulder and followed the trail. Elena would be at the end. There was no other option. Not for him.

The slam of something heavy ricocheted through him. Cash spun, finger on the trigger, in time to catch a barrier wall lowering down, cutting off his escape from behind. The building had gone into lockdown. Windows, doors, the garage. They wouldn't be able to get through any of it. *"Geh rein!"* Go!

Bear launched forward as a steel door started dropping four feet ahead of them. She cleared the door in record time, but his leg had gone numb. Limping didn't do a damn bit of good. The door would secure in five seconds or less. He had to move. Now. Sliding the rifle underneath, Cash lunged. His shoulder took the brunt of the impact as he rolled. The steel lock pin caught on his shirt, tearing through the thin fabric, but he'd made it.

Just in time to watch the third door seal them inside the corridor. Hell. They'd been cut off. The alarm cut out. The lights returned to normal. The threat had been neutralized. Cash listened for movement on either side of the steel barriers. There was no way through these doors without heavy machinery. No way to get to Elena.

Bear's barking echoed off the walls, then quieted as the crackle of a PA system filled the resulting silence. Cash collected the rifle he'd taken off the unconscious soldier back in the kennel and checked the rounds left in the magazine. Full load.

"You've made quite a mess, Mr. Meyers." The voice. He'd heard it before. In the dark. It was smooth, the kind that could just as easily start a war as it could declare world peace. Elena's ex. The cartel lieutenant responsible for the destruction of an entire town and the kidnapping of an eight-year-old boy. "Yes, I know who you are. Just as I know you triggered an SOS signal to the rest of your team. Unfortunately for you, they never received it. I did find something you lost though."

A struggle sounded over the intercom. Heavy breathing. "Cash, go! Get out while you still can!" Her voice muffled as though someone had shoved a gag in her mouth.

Elena. The muscles down his spine hardened one by one. It didn't matter that he couldn't see through one eye or that his leg might never recover. He'd shoot as many cartel soldiers as it took to get to her. "You son of a bitch. I warned you what would happen if you touched her. I'm going to find you, and when I do, you're going to wish you'd listened."

A bright laugh cackled through the system. "You know what, Mr. Meyers, I like you. Come." The door to his right retracted back into the ceiling from whence it'd come. "Let us do this man-to-man as in the old days. Two men fighting to win the fair maiden's heart."

The blood spatter trailed along the corridor. What would he find at the end? Not a fair fight. That much was clear. Cash positioned the rifle's stock into his shoulder and took aim, Bear on high alert. Another door retracted, leading him through the maze in turn. Until the last revealed the group of soldiers waiting on the other side.

The lieutenant—a man close to his midforties—took position in the middle, his white suit stark against the backdrop of cement and fluorescent light. With Elena restrained over his left shoulder. "Ah, yes. The man who took down five soldiers with nothing but a dumbbell and his own strength. I'm glad to see the dog survived. I'm an animal lover myself."

Cash tracked the bloodstains into the mass of men pointing guns back at him and locked his gaze on Elena. Red stained the cuff of one of her shirt sleeves, and his heart double-timed it into his throat. "You good, Elle?"

She dropped that bloody cuff away from her midsection, exposing the tip of what looked like a serrated blade in her palm. Tucked beneath her clothing. Not her blood. "Yeah. I'm good."

Chapter Nine

He'd come for her.

She wasn't sure why that was such a surprise other than the fact that no one other than her parents had dared cross Metias. They'd tried to get to her, spotting the signs she'd married a monster from a mile away, but her husband had isolated her well. It was only after she'd come to terms with her failing marriage that she realized she had to be the one to take that first step. That she needed to be brave.

And she'd do it again. Not just for herself this time. For Cash.

The tip of the blade pricked her palm. Surrounded by Metias's men, she wasn't sure how they were going to get themselves out of this, but she trusted the man who'd saved her from a cartel abduction once before. Elena rotated her forearm toward her body to conceal the weapon. It was still stained with the guard's blood. Now it would save her and Cash's lives.

"Here's what's going to happen, Mr. Meyers. You

and your dog have done enough damage, so I'm going to give you the chance to walk away." Only Metias didn't negotiate. It was a lie. There was no way her ex would let Cash or Bear survive after what they'd done.

"Just like that?" Interest sparked in Cash's voice, but an underlying suspicion narrowed his gaze. He was too intelligent to believe a word out of a warlord's mouth. "And Elena? Her brother? What happens to them?"

"They'll stay here. Of course." Metias glanced back over his shoulder to the men behind him, a scoff escaping that perfect mouth. "Where they belong."

"In that case." Cash cut his attention to her, and in that moment, she knew. She knew what he was about to do, and he was relying on her to do her part. It was the only way they were going to get out of here alive. "No deal."

In her next breath, she gathered every ounce of courage she could hold on to. "Metias." She waited for her ex to turn toward her. "This is for locking me in that cellar."

Elena let the blade drop from inside her shirt sleeve and grabbed the handle before the knife hit the cement. She stabbed the blade into the side of his thigh. His scream pierced her eardrums as she lunged to escape the ring of his security detail.

One caught her around the waist. A bullet threw his head back, and the soldier hit the floor. Bear growled from somewhere behind her. She wasn't sure, but she couldn't slow down enough to try to keep track of her and her handler. The second floor. This was her only chance to find Daniel.

A rain of gunfire ricocheted off the wall to her left. Cut off by a deep grunt and a bellowing howl. Covering her head as though her hands could stop bullets, she wrenched free of the circle of remaining guards. Oxygen caught in her chest as a strong hand threaded between her rib cage and arm.

"I've got you." Cash had to feel her shaking. It'd be impossible to miss, but they were still in the middle of a *Sangre por Sangre* complex with no way out but up. "Don't stop. Keep moving."

The shaking was getting worse. She tried to take a full breath but was on the brink of losing any control she'd somehow held on to.

"After them!" Metias's voice barreled through her and kick-started something in her brain. If she stopped to get herself together, she and Cash would die.

The outline of a soldier materialized ahead.

Cash didn't hesitate. He raised the automatic rifle slung around his chest and fired. The threat didn't stand a chance against the hail of gunfire and collapsed. Bear's claws scratched along the cement as loud as a typewriter. "Are you hurt?"

"No. It's… It's not my blood." The feel of the blade penetrating the flesh and organ of that guard was still fresh. Elena wiped her hands down the front of her jeans to drown the memory, but it was no use. She'd stabbed a man. Not including her ex-husband. And now she was carrying his blood with her. "Second floor... We have to get t-to the second floor." She caught herself against the wall as they reached the end of the maze. Stairs vibrated under their ascent. "Daniel's there."

Cash took aim up the boxy windup of steel stairs as though he'd done it a thousand times before. Anyone looking down would instantly see them, but he kept moving up, focused and routined. Hesitating at the first landing, he leaned to one side to get a better view before charging up to the next platform. A low growl seemed to enunciate his every step.

A spatter of bullets exploded from above.

Bear knocked into her shin, and Elena made contact with the wall. Out of the way. Cash twisted around, exposing the swelling and blood marring his handsome face. She'd seen it before but had underestimated the damage. He wouldn't be able to see out of his left eye, yet as he squeezed the rifle's trigger, every round found its mark. He latched onto her wrist and pulled her after him, and the raw skin there burned at his touch.

Her ears were ringing. Her hands were shaking. They stepped over the two soldiers who'd tried to kill them. One grabbed for her ankle, but Bear ensured his release with a snap of teeth and warning.

"This is it." Cash hugged the gun to his chest,

barrel pointed down as he surveilled what waited for them on the other side of the heavy door with nothing but a rectangle of two-paned glass. "How do you know Daniel's here?"

"One of the guards. He told me this is where Metias keeps the new recruits. He was…trying to help me." But could she trust he'd given her good information? Was she supposed to believe he wasn't really *Sangre por Sangre* but an impostor? A plant to mine the cartel for intel? *Tell Ivy Echo got off his leash.* Her gut said yes, but it'd lied to her in the past. About Metias. About her ability to keep her family safe. About her choice to collect information about the cartel. She'd been wrong. About everything. "He let me go. He was helping me."

She was rambling now. Trying to justify her reasons for wanting to stay when every other thought in her brain was telling her they needed to get the hell out of here, that Cash needed a doctor or an entire emergency medical team. But she couldn't go. Not without Daniel.

Cash centered himself in her vision, and it took everything she had left to keep him there. The tremors raced up her arms. Made her cold. She wanted to reach out for him, needed that contact to keep her standing. He angled the gun down and behind his back on its lanyard and gripped both of her arms as though sensing exactly what was happening. "Easy.

Breathe. Look at me. We're not leaving here until we search the floor. Okay? So let's find him."

She nodded. It was easier to breathe with his hands on her right then. The invisible connection they'd both somehow entered into over the past two days steadied her more than ever before, and she had no doubt in her mind she was only alive because of a stranger and his dog. "Okay."

Cash shifted the rifle back into his hands, and they went through the door. It was quiet. Darker than the basement without overhead lights. A set of rare windows in a compound meant to be buried allowed a wash of sunlight through the open room but it didn't carry far with a layer of tint. Fifty or more empty cots—disheveled and slept-in—peppered the entirety of the floor.

"I don't... I don't understand." Elena pressed her hand into one cot. The once-white sheet was cold. An indent in the center of the pillow told her someone had been there. The information the guard had given her wasn't wrong. But whoever'd slept there had been gone awhile. Same with the rest. "Where are the recruits? Where are the guards?"

She moved through the sterile room, searching each cot for something—anything—to confirm Daniel had been there or where he might've gone. The soldiers they'd encountered had all been men. Not boys. Metias had them moved. He'd known exactly why she'd come, and he'd done what he could to make sure she'd fail. To punish her. His offer to let Daniel go had been a lie. Even if she'd agreed to come back to him, he never would've let her see her brother again.

Frustration and a toxic dose of grief pressurized behind her sternum. She'd survived three days in a cellar, a cartel raid and house fire, an abduction and getting shot at. But this… This would be what broke her. Anger pushed tears into her eyes. "He's not here."

Cash scanned the room. A low rumble of voices infiltrated the silence. He headed for the nearest window. "We have to go."

It wasn't supposed to be like this. Bear nudged at her legs from behind, urging her to follow Cash, and Elena's body complied, but her mind? It was someplace else altogether. On the black, red and gold dragon-unicorn she'd gotten for her brother for Valentine's Day last year. The one he'd dropped during their escape from the house. She should've gone back for it as he'd asked. She should've given him something to hold on to when he'd gotten scared and wondered if anyone was looking for him.

She failed to process Cash's commands. He turned to her, shouting something she couldn't hear over the ringing in her head. The window shattered under the strength of his bullets, and a burst of descending sun beamed into her face. She brought her hand up to block the onslaught. Everything seemed to play out in slow motion. Cash hauling one leg over the windowsill. Bear hopping up on her hind legs.

Even the door slamming open behind them.

A flood of soldiers swarmed inside, though they were still too far away and slowed down by the layout of cots to reach them. What was the point? Without her brother, why bother escaping at all? The answer solidified in front of her as Cash took her hand and tugged her after him into the sunlight.

Because without her, Daniel didn't have a chance at all.

HE ALMOST HADN'T made it.

"You're lucky to be alive." The doc beamed a flashlight straight into his eyes, and a whole new kind of pain ignited through his head. "Tell me what happened."

"I started swinging. A few guys might've gotten in the way." He'd blacked out on the way back to headquarters. If it hadn't been for Elena taking the wheel, *Sangre por Sangre* would've been on them. It wouldn't take long before the cartel struck back. That was how it worked out here in the desert. An eye for an eye. Blood for blood. And from what he'd gauged from that lieutenant, this had become more than a territory war. This was personal.

"Right. I'm betting they look a lot worse." The dark blue scrubs and dark cardigan only added to Dr. Nafessa Piel's allure. Black hair framed a slim face and accentuated sepia, reddish-brown skin. In truth, Cash didn't know a whole lot about her.

As Socorro's one and only doctor on call, she took doctor-patient confidentiality to a whole new level. She didn't let anything slip. "Headache? Nausea? Vomiting? Dizziness? Any fogginess?"

"Is it bad if I say all of the above?" He'd known there was a possibility of a concussion considering the beating he'd taken before returning the favor to the group of soldiers in the gym. And the way his brain was rattling around in his head like it had after the explosion from his brother's DEA raid was a pretty good sign that something wasn't right. "The woman I brought in. Elena. Where is she?"

The flashlight was gone now. In its place, the doc pressed a cold stethoscope to his back and pulled his shoulder back. "I cleared her while Jones and Granger were pulling you out of the car. No serious injuries. Breathe in for me."

Seeing as how Elena had cleared her physical and Dr. Piel held the future of his assignments in her thin hands, he did as he was told.

"I don't hear any fluid in your lungs, but you're going to have to take it easy on that rib. As for the leg, nothing broken as far as I can tell. The X-rays should be back in a couple of days to confirm it, but you're most likely looking at a dislocated knee joint. Once the swelling goes down, I'll be able to reset it." She moved around the room, discarding her latex gloves in the trash and grabbing up her tablet and stylus to take notes. "Until then, get some rest, take an ice bath, elevate that knee and keep a compression sleeve around it. Should be good as new for you to mess up within a couple weeks."

He shifted his weight onto his good leg as he dropped off the exam table. "Don't know what I'd do without you, Doc."

"Probably die." She didn't even bother looking up from her notes as she said it. "All of you operatives think you're invincible. I just hope I'm there when you realize you're not."

True enough. The men and women of Socorro had seen their share of pain and violence and scars. It was what made them the elite—the right choice in fighting an enemy who didn't play by the rules. Each member of the team knew the stakes and the devastation that could follow if they didn't take risks. And sometimes that included believing they were invincible from time to time.

His leg bummed out on him halfway to his room. The brace Doc Piel had strapped around his knee helped with stability, but his endurance had gone to hell. She'd insisted on putting Bear in the kennel for the night instead of his room to give him a chance at some solid sleep, but the memories were right there at the front of his mind. They weren't going to give him the chance. Every mistake he'd made. Every hit he'd taken. Every drop of blood he'd lost.

"Damn. What house dropped on you today? Jones just told me he had to drag you out of the garage."

Jocelyn slowed her approach, every thought splayed across her face as usual. Right now her expression was broadcasting concern. Like a mom who'd just found out her kid had gotten into a fight at school. "Your face is a mess."

"Good to see you, too, Joce," he said.

She gripped his head between both hands and prodded at the butterfly stitch at the corner of his eye. "You should've called me. I'd have been there to back you up."

"I did." He didn't like this. The boundaries she insisted on breaking in an effort to bring the team closer together. The movie nights, the birthday parties, the dinners together at the table. None of it made up for what they'd each lost. Pretending it would only made things worse. They weren't a family. Hell, they weren't even friends most of the time. They were a highly-skilled operations unit. Yeah, they trusted one another. They had each other's backs when the time came, but this personal stuff? He didn't want any part of it. Didn't need it.

Except when the going had gotten tough back in that compound, there'd only been one person on his mind. Elena. It would've taken a massive amount of courage to confront her ex like that, let alone stab the man. He thought back to what the doc had said. Elena hadn't suffered any serious injuries, but the blood on her sleeve had been fresh. Cash maneuvered past

Jocelyn, leg be damned. "Cartel must've killed the signal. Nothing was getting through."

"Don't wait so long next time," she said. "And eat some vegetables. Not that garbage you call a cookie."

Because there would be a next time. The entire team was on alert. Waiting for the cartel to regroup and strike. It was only a matter of time, but tonight… He didn't have to worry about tonight. Cash hobbled down the hall and shoved into his room. She was there, sitting at the edge of his bed as though waiting for him all this time.

She pushed to her feet as he closed the door behind him. Not a word.

"Hey." He didn't know what else to say. Honestly, there wasn't anything he could say. They'd barely survived the search for her brother and come back empty-handed. She'd risked her life and her mental health, knowing what waited for her on the inside of that building, to bring her brother home. And she'd failed. A rock-bottom pit he was all too used to staring up from. "You hungry?"

Elena crossed the distance between them. She slammed into his chest, securing her arms around him so tight he felt as though she'd crack another of his ribs. Only Cash didn't care. She angled her ear over his heart, and a sense of calm he'd only felt when Bear climbed into his bed at night took over. "I'm sorry."

"Don't." He threaded one hand into the hair along

her nape, urging her to look up at him. She locked near-black eyes on him, so intense he could've sworn he saw himself in the reflection of her irises. Deep purple and blue bruises bloomed along one cheek, and a wave of rage crested at the sight. "What happened back there wasn't your fault. None of it. You understand me? I knew what I was getting myself into when I agreed to help you find him, and there was nothing you could've done differently."

She pressed one hand against his chest. "How bad is it?"

"I won't be running a marathon anytime soon, but seeing as how I wasn't interested in killing myself for a medal to hang on my wall before, I think I'll survive." He released his hold in her hair, loving the way it felt between his fingers. How it caught on the calluses, then slid free. It was slightly damp. She'd showered, and it was then he realized she'd changed. His oversize shirt and sweatpants did nothing to hide the woman underneath, and Cash couldn't help but appreciate her style.

Her smile cracked despite the tension moving in on the corners of her mouth. She slipped her hand from his chest, taking a bit of warmth with her. "You always know just what to say. Has your team learned anything more since we escaped the compound?"

He knew what she was asking, but he didn't have any answers for her. "Satellite images recorded a blizzard of activity in the minutes after we broke into the compound. From the look of it, six soldiers were moving a group of people out of the building into a truck on the other side."

She seemed to steel herself for the conclusion. "Daniel?"

"That's what it looks like," he said. "Metias must've ordered the evacuation after he ambushed us in the corridor. Since then construction has been halted, and the fleet of vehicles we suspected on site was deployed."

"Looking for us." It wasn't a question. They both knew what was coming. All they could do was prepare for what happened next.

He nodded. "They followed the SUV's tire tracks up until about a mile out. Guess they were hoping we'd have car trouble. Catch us out in the open. Would have, too, if it weren't for you behind the wheel."

"You make it sound like I wasn't the one who almost got you killed." Elena hugged herself then, goose bumps traveling up her arms. She was holding herself together as though expecting to shatter into a million pieces right there in the middle of the floor. The adrenaline, the fear—it drained fast and left the body in shock if you weren't prepared for it. "Thank you. For coming for me. I wasn't sure…"

Cash countered the space she'd added between them. "If I'd hold up my end of the deal. I would've done the same in your position. Trusting someone with your life like that. It feels…wrong sometimes. We tell ourselves we're strong enough, that we are all we need, when it comes right down to it. But in the end, we really don't want to be alone."

"No. We don't." A softness transformed her expression as she looked up at him, and Elena took that last step separating them. "Cash, I know Ivy arranged a room for me to stay in tonight, but…could I please stay here? With you? Because I really don't want to be alone."

He didn't have to think his answer through. "Yeah. You can take the bed. I'll sleep on the couch. That's usually where Bear passes out, but she's in the kennel tonight. Though I've gotta warn you—I might wake up smelling like dog in the morning."

"No." She skimmed her fingers down his forearm and interlaced her fingers with his. She tugged him forward despite the differences in their sizes. "Not on the couch."

Chapter Ten

The swelling had gone down in his face.

Elena pressed her head into the pillow as sunrise broke over the mountains from the east. It cast across the bridge of his nose and highlighted the damage done less than twelve hours ago.

He was still asleep. All dark bruises, lacerations and intensity, even unconscious. Cash had done as she asked. He'd stayed with her. Held her. For the first time in the past three days, she'd let herself unravel, and he'd been there to hold her together.

But she could still feel a thin coat of blood on her hands. The guard's. Metias's. She'd scrubbed her skin raw during her shower last night, but it wouldn't come off. She wasn't sure it ever would. Holding a man's life in her hands had all at once been powerful and terrifying. Metias had deserved what she'd done, but she couldn't help but wonder what became of the operative who'd helped her escape.

Silence secured her in a vulnerable blanket of unease. She'd been running on fumes for so long, it felt wrong to stay here in bed, memorizing Cash's face. Every angle, the cleft in his chin, the scar cutting through his eyebrow. All of it puzzled together to create a work of art. And she appreciated art. She wanted to remember this moment. The one encapsulating two people who'd been through hell and survived. Together.

"You're supposed to be asleep." His voice seemed to stick to the edges of his throat.

"I've never been a great sleeper." Elena buried deeper under the comforter they shared. Despite living with a Rottweiler, Cash had managed to keep the bed hair- and odor-free. Instead, there was a hint of the bodywash she'd found in the shower last night. Something clean and masculine. Something specific to the man beside her. She breathed it in a bit deeper.

He twisted with a grimace of pain in his expression to read the alarm clock on the nightstand over her shoulder, bringing him closer. "How long have you been up?"

"Long enough to notice your tattoo." She hadn't believed what she'd seen at first. This ex-military operator had gotten a tattoo on his hip of a muffin with bulging biceps, a tattooed anchor on one arm and a banner wrapping the entire piece of artwork. "Stud muffin."

His laughter punctured through the room and wedged under her rib cage to break apart the vise around her lungs. Cash scrubbed a hand down his face. He smiled then, stretching the split in his lip, but he didn't show any signs of noticing. "Right. I could tell you I don't remember getting it or that my marine buddies played a prank on me, but the truth is, my brother's is much worse."

"You and your brother got tattoos together?" She could imagine it. A younger version of the soldier in front of her and a DEA analyst making an undeniable pact to go through a unique kind of pain together. Judging by the lift of his mouth, it was a memory Cash obviously cherished. Even after everything that'd happened between them, he would still have that. He still remembered the good times. Could she say the same if she lost Daniel?

"Day we enlisted." He shook his head, flexing the muscles and tendons along his bare shoulders. While they hadn't done more than hold each other through the night, the temptation to test that strength for herself was there. Just beneath the surface. "Crazy, I know, but it made sense at the time."

"No. I think it's sweet." She tugged the comforter down, exposing the tattoo, and traced a line around the muffin's top. "The two of you taking on the world together with matching hip tattoos."

"Wade's is a pink doughnut with sprinkles," he said.

Secondhand embarrassment pooled in her stomach. "Oh, no."

He hiked himself onto his elbow, as though nothing outside of this room mattered. And it felt good. While she'd initially feared what being the center of this man's attention would result in, she found there wasn't anywhere else she'd rather be right then. "It says 'I'm a-dough-rable' in cursive."

"That's terrible." She wanted to cringe and laugh at the same time. "But I would've loved to have seen it." The words were already out of her mouth before she realized her mistake. "Cash, I'm sorry. I didn't mean—"

"Don't worry about it. What's done is done. Wade made his choice, and he paid for it. Nothing anyone can do about it now." The smile was gone then. "That tattoo was the only way to identify his body. Cartel dumped him in the middle of the desert."

"You went back for him." Of course he had. Because that was the kind of man Cash Meyers was. The kind that trusted little but once he did, he went the added mile. Who suffered betrayal and loss and heartache but ensured justice for those he cared for. Who kept his word to a woman who'd nearly gotten him killed. He was rational and ethical and kind, and once he started a mission, he finished it. No matter the cost. He didn't hold grudges. He fought for the weak and put others first. He was the opposite of her ex in every way, shape and form, and her heart beat harder at the thought of being one of the people he fought for.

Elena shifted closer, framing her hand along his jaw. Her thumb found the butterfly bandage at the far side of his left eye and smoothed the edges. His exhale brushed along her neck as he set dark eyes on her. He could feel it, too. That need to get close, to rely on someone other than himself. Metias had stolen that and her ability to forge relationships from her, but he couldn't touch this. Not if she didn't let him.

She kept her gaze locked on him as she pressed her mouth to his.

It was probably the most inappropriate thing to do to a man who'd just told her how he'd been able to identify his brother's body, but Cash seemed to accept this for what it was. Pure need. Fire licked up her insides the moment he penetrated the seam of her lips. His hand found the sensitive spot at her lower back and hauled her into his body. He was strong, stronger than any man she'd ever known, and she needed that strength. He held on to her as though he might break if he let go. Like she mattered.

This was insanity. People weren't supposed to meet like this. In the middle of a war between a brutal cartel and the small towns they were trying to take over. Maybe if she'd had a normal life—one without Metias, without the threat of losing her brother, without not knowing if her parents were all right—they could've met someplace else. He'd still brood, and she'd like that about him. They'd flirt, and she'd laugh at his sarcasm. They'd go on a date and make plans to do it again.

Instead, they were here. In a dorm-like room with an empty dog bed shoved against the wall and the sun coming up over the mountain. Each seeking something only found in the other, and Elena poured everything into finding what she needed. Protection, safety. Control. Somehow since the night of the raid, Cash had pulled her free of sinking into an endless well of loss she wasn't sure she would ever escape. Loss of the life she'd imagined, of her family, of any semblance of the woman she thought she knew.

Now there was something bright to hold on to. She and Cash knew grief and betrayal. They knew loneliness. What if they could create something new? What if they could forget the violence and bloodshed outside of these walls and just be? What she wouldn't give to be able to do that for him, to help him escape his pain as he'd done for her.

His heartbeat raged against her hand as he urged her calf around his thigh, inching them closer in every regard. This wasn't a biological reaction to danger that drove her. This was something more. Something real. And it was everything.

She'd hidden away from this, left the ability to trust and feel behind in Albuquerque. She'd had to. To survive. To protect herself. Afraid it would slither back into her heart and finish her off for good. But Cash had barreled through her every intention to keep him at a distance, and she ached at the thought of what she'd missed by shutting everyone out. At what could've happened if she'd just said yes to Deputy McCrae for dinner or if she'd been able to live with a husband who kept secrets. Deep down though, she knew. It was Cash. No one else would do. Because none of them were him.

The tick of something quick and heavy grew louder, pulling Elena from the drugging kiss.

Cash ducked his chin. "Oh, no. Prepare yourself."

"For what?" Her question went unanswered.

Until Bear bounded through the dog door, tongue flying, eyes alive. She launched her entire frame up onto the bed and padded between Elena and Cash in tight circles. The dog's tail hit Elena in the side of the face with enough force to knock her back onto her pillow. Playful growls vibrated through Bear.

"I know, girl. I know. I missed you, too." Cash propped himself up in bed, the comforter sliding down to reveal a perfectly outlined set of ab muscles that Elena had been so close to testing for herself. He scratched at Bear's neck and ruffled her coat. "You couldn't just give me a few more minutes though?"

It was endearing and cute, the way Cash and Bear loved each other, and the view of them reunited stuck in her throat. What she'd felt before had seemed real in the moment, but her heart hurt now. Watching

them, seeing how happy they made each other...
She didn't fit. Just as she hadn't fit in her marriage.
She was a nobody to them. An assignment. She'd
shoved her way into their lives because she wanted
her brother back. Helping her was a job, and one kiss
wasn't going to change that. And she'd been a fool
to believe it could mean more. She tried to breathe
around the ache inside but couldn't seem to fill her
lungs. "Excuse me."

"Everything okay?" he asked.

"Fine." Elena didn't let herself slow down as she
swung her feet to the floor and rounded the bed toward the bathroom. She closed the bathroom door
behind her and secured the lock. Twisting the shower
handle to the hottest position, she swiped at the tears
and unpocketed the phone she'd kept hidden from
Cash.

Her darkest shame rose as she read through the
message inbox.

Happily-ever-after didn't exist. At least not for her.

ELENA DIDN'T TASTE anything like dog allergy medicine.

There'd been mint from the toothpaste in the bathroom and a sweetness to counter it he couldn't describe. She'd been soft and hard all at the same time,
hesitant and demanding, stripped of that emotional
armor she wore yet raw for him.

Mere seconds with her had alleviated hours of
pain, frustration and doubt of this assignment, and

he wanted nothing more than to escape back into that cocoon they'd built around themselves the past few hours. Because inside it—with her—he'd felt like himself for the first time in over a year. Not the whatever-it-takes contractor he'd become, but the man who'd jumped at the opportunity to work alongside his brother and the DEA. The one who'd known where his path would take him since the day he'd enlisted in the military and was up for the challenge of making the world a little bit safer.

He'd lost sight of that side of him after his brother's death. Something inside of him had gone cold. Empty. He'd felt it, like a void continuously shifting and growing in his chest. It didn't matter how many assignments he and Bear had taken on or what the job was. Nothing had come close to healing that hollowness.

Until last night. As he'd held Elena. Inhaled the sharpness of her shampoo and conditioner, slid his hands along her skin. He'd enjoyed his fair share of women throughout the years. Some he'd met through Wade, others in a nearby bar. Always temporary. Yeah, he thought he'd been in love as a kid with his high school girlfriend before they'd figured out they were on separate trajectories, but last night… Something had changed.

Something inside him had trusted her enough to tell her about Wade when he hadn't mentioned him to another living soul other than the DEA higher-ups and his commanding officer after their operation blew up in his face. Elena wasn't like the others. She didn't conform to what she thought he might want to hear or try to be someone who hadn't been through some terrible stuff. She was honest. She was good. And she made him want to leave the past in the past. To move forward. To take the good when it came.

But Elena hadn't said a word since they'd left Socorro headquarters. Didn't even seem to notice him as she studied the open landscape through the windshield.

They'd agreed to warn Alpine Valley of the potential for another raid from the cartel. Her friend, the deputy, had come back clean. No outlandish debt other than the mortgage on his small home. No payments into his accounts other than from the city. Not even a speeding ticket. Cartels like *Sangre por Sangre* liked to use small-town police forces to keep an eye out. Departments were plugged in to their communities, trusted in most cases and able to gather intel under the banner of public safety. Deputy McCrae's background check didn't highlight any of the telltale signs Cash had uncovered when he'd looked into his brother's activities leading up to his death. They would trust him. For now.

The SUV's shocks absorbed the change from desert dirt to asphalt as he drove them into the town limits. The smoke had cleared, though that only exposed the damage done. The small church that'd held the weight of its ancient bell off to their right—barely able to contain fifty people during mass—had collapsed in on its scalded and blackened frame. The art gallery had somehow managed to survive, though the sign on the front door had been turned to indicate they were closed. Three men of varying ages boarded the windows of the BBQ restaurant but turned to stare down their vehicle as Cash and Elena drove through. "Guess I should've brought something a little less flashy."

"They're scared." Her solemn expression reflected back from the passenger-side window. "They're wondering what comes next. How they'll rebuild. If it'll happen again. If they'll find their loved ones. They didn't have any warning."

His gut soured. The night of the raid had played back through his head so many times over the course of three days. She was right. The people of this town hadn't gotten any warning because he hadn't given them any. It'd been his responsibility to track the cartel's movements, to raise the alarm for places like this one, but he'd been too late. There was no excuse or reason he could give her for allowing the men, women and children digging through the rubble of their homes to lose what they had.

Because if he did, she'd see the truth: that he was no better than his brother who'd sentenced dozens of agents and marines to their deaths the day of the DEA raid.

Or maybe she already had.

Maybe that was why she'd added the distance between them since waking in bed together this morning.

"The station is just up ahead." She pointed through the windshield to indicate a collection of single-level buildings grouped together at the end of a cul-de-sac made up of businesses.

Wood logs placed evenly throughout a makeshift lot indicated parking spots, while a low fence divided the asphalt straight down the middle. The main building stretched the length of three trailers with red wood bannisters leading visitors and police to two separate doors. One end for court proceedings, the other for the police department. Two vehicles— a truck and a police cruiser—had backed in for an easy exit on the right end of the structure, and Cash did the same.

He shouldered out of the vehicle, scanning a small park across the road with Cat Mesa towering protectively over the village. Then he turned at the sound of the building's glass front door squeaking outward on its hinges.

The officer dressed in a black police uniform with a gold shield over his heart jogged down the stairs. A thick brown beard and mustache hid most of the man's features, but not enough for Cash to make out the concern splattered across the officer's expression. The nameplate pinned opposite his shield read *B. McCrae* in black lettering. This was the cop Elena trusted. "Elena, holy hell. When I didn't hear from you, I'd assumed the worst. Are you all right?"

McCrae didn't wait for an answer and wrapped her in a strong hug, practically lifting her off her feet. A ping of defensiveness tendriled through Cash as he caught the cop tucking his nose into Elena's hair to take a full breath. She'd said McCrae and she had been friends for years, since high school, but Cash's gut said the cop was obviously interested in something more.

She pushed herself free from McCrae's arms and took a step back. A flush of pink spread through her cheeks as she glanced toward Cash. "I'm alive, thanks to Cash and his team, but it hasn't been easy. I'll tell you everything, but I need to know my parents are okay first. Have you seen them?"

"You haven't heard?" McCrae bounced his attention between Elena and Cash, then took her hands in his. "I responded to your message. I've been trying to get a hold of you for two days to give you the news."

"Message?" Cash took position at Elena's side. They'd been careful about keeping her activity off the radar. Never staying in one place too long when they left headquarters, no phone calls, no outside communication at all. His gut tightened. The phone. The one they'd recovered from the ruins. Oh, hell.

He'd checked it for spyware, contacts and messages, but the logs had been empty. In an age where people didn't bother to memorize phone numbers with them a touch away, he hadn't considered she'd risk her life by making contact to someone in town. What had he done? "What message?"

She didn't take her eyes off McCrae. "Where are my parents?"

McCrae pulled his shoulders back, accentuating a broad chest that got attention more than a couple times a week in the gym. "They're at Lovelace Westside Hospital. Your dad... He took the brunt of what the cartel did. I don't have all the details, but I know he had to go into surgery to stop some internal bleeding. The chief is with them now. He's watching over them in case the cartel decides to finish what they started. But, Elena, I've gathered statements from everyone in town. They all say the same thing. The raid started at your house."

Elena's knees gave without warning, but Cash was right there. He caught her against his chest a split second before she turned into him. He held her as he did last night—keeping her in one piece, not missing the way McCrae seemed to gauge Cash for himself.

Bear's whine matched the turmoil cutting through him. Her ex-husband and his cartel had systematically torn Elena's life apart. Not just with abducting her brother but going after her aging parents in the same blow. Metias was isolating her all over again, taking away everything she loved, everything she had to fight for.

Psychological warfare at its worst, but the son of a bitch wouldn't win. Because she wasn't alone this time. And Cash would spend the rest of his life and every resource he had protecting her if that was what she required. "We're going to take them down, Elena. Every last one of them. They're going to pay for what they've done."

She added a couple inches of distance between them. "How? Their guard is up now. They're looking for us as we speak. Socorro might have the resources, but based on what we saw in that compound, we're outnumbered five times over, and I'm sure that number is higher since we escaped. And Metias won't stop. He knows I was collecting information on the cartel, and he will kill every last one of you, my parents and my brother to get it back. What you're asking... It's impossible."

Cash swiped his busted knuckles along her cheek, catching a stray tear cascading down the bruised side of her face. "Except you're not alone in this anymore. Besides, I do my best work when the odds are stacked against me."

"You really think we can stop Metias from hurting more people?" she asked.

"I told you the day I met you—I've got your back," he said. "If anything had changed, I would've let you know."

He brushed his thumb over her smile as she leaned into his palm.

McCrae raised his hand—as though they were in the middle of a classroom working out an unsolvable math problem—hesitant and awkward. "I might have a way."

Chapter Eleven

Brock McCrae led them to a small, out-of-the-way desk once Cash had agreed to surrender his weapon into a locker at the front of the station. Made sense. The only guns police wanted within arm's reach were their own in case a situation broke out. But the way Cash kept glancing to the locker and crossing and uncrossing his arms said he obviously didn't like it.

"Have you heard of Sensorvault?" Brock fingered the scroll wheel of his computer mouse, and his ancient, dust-covered monitor responded a few seconds later.

Elena glanced from her friend to Cash, then back. "Is that one of the little wizard boy books Daniel has been reading the past couple of years?" He'd been asking her for weeks to read them to him at night before bed so they could have a full-blown movie marathon together. She'd always found an excuse to put it off. Now she wanted nothing more than to get that chance again. To read him just a few pages of one of his books. To tuck him in to bed. Hell, even to step on one of his LEGOs would be welcome at this point. But they'd lost everything. His toys, those books, their home.

Her stomach was still twisted at the image of Metias's men manhandling her sixty-four-year-old father. What kind of person could give that order? And why had she fallen in love with him in the first place? Elena turned her gaze toward Cash. And was she making the same mistake now?

"Not exactly." Brock's laugh shook through his office in the corner of the police department. Department was an overstatement. In Alpine Valley, the police station consisted of two double-wide trailers welded together to create some semblance of unity between the court side and the police side. Two desks, one of them belonging to the police chief and vacant at the moment, assisted the handful of officers committed to serving and protecting their small town. Dark wood paneling had been installed halfway up the wall—a half-hearted attempt to jazz the place up. Above that, gray paint peeled at the meeting place between the walls and the drop-down tile ceiling. The lights in here were something from eighties-style kitchens, but two large door-sized windows let in enough light to ensure visitors wouldn't suffer from seasonal affective disorder come winter. It was a wonder Brock and his fellow officers could do their jobs with the lack of resources on hand, but the community believed in them all the same. "Though it does tell a great story."

Bear nudged at the deputy's desk with her snout, slicking wetness all along the faux wood. There must've been some kind of food inside. Elena had known Brock to stash sweets as long as she'd known him.

"Sensorvault is a database put together by the largest internet host in existence. It collects GPS data from every phone at any given time and location and stores that information in the database only accessible by law enforcement." The words fell from Cash's mouth as though she'd simply asked him what the weather was outside. This kind of stuff was what he'd been trained for, serving in the marines and employed under a security company. This was what he was good at, and the way he maintained his focus doused the doubts circling her brain. "Geofence warrants are almost impossible to get though. You think we have a shot?"

She didn't let Brock answer. This sounded like an answer they could've used yesterday. "Wait. Are you saying we could look up anyone who was in the vicinity of where I hid the information I got on the cartel and identify who took it through their phone? Why wasn't this something you brought up earlier?"

"Socorro isn't law enforcement, and the internet host follows strict rules about who has access to their database. They are only compelled to reveal their data through a court order, and in this case, I'm not sure we have a strong enough reason to file one." Cash angled himself away from the small grouping they'd made around Brock's desk. Bear followed on his heels, always the constant companion. "Even if we did, we don't know when the phone was switched out. Hundreds of people have been up and around in those pueblos and ruins in the past few weeks alone. The host assigns the devices it tracks anonymous ID numbers. There's no way to tell who's in possession of the phone right this second without unfettered access to the database itself."

Elena had to stop herself from letting the headache at the back of her skull take over. This was why she'd wanted to go to the police the night of the raid. They could've started the process days ago instead of being forced to confront Metias head-on.

"True, but Sensorvault would narrow down the suspect list." Brock continued to scroll through what looked like a list of calls the department had responded to over the past few days. The words blurred the longer Elena tried to catch them, but he soon slowed to a stop for what he was looking for.

"You said you had a plan," she said.

"Judge Hodge was just pulled over for a DUI last week." Brock turned to them with nothing but pride on his face. "All we've got to do is get him to sign the warrant request. Election is coming up this winter. It'll work."

"Blackmail? That's your solution?" Cash scrubbed a hand down his face. A scoff rushed past his mouth as he turned from them. "What makes you think your judge is the kind of man to give in to blackmail? What's to stop him from stripping you of that badge and having you and us arrested for attempted extortion and coercion?"

Elena read through the dispatch log on McCrae's screen. *Initiated-Motor Vehicle Stop. Arrest(s) made. Driving under the influence. Deputy Brock McCrae.* The time and date stamps for arrival and clearance were all there, spanning about thirty minutes, but the log didn't identify the driver or a license plate. Still, without the information she'd collected and stored on that phone, they had no chance of tearing apart Metias's organization. They had to try.

Brock didn't seem to have an answer of his own, but Elena didn't need one. She'd already made her decision. "This is how we bring down the cartel."

"You can't be serious," Cash said.

His disapproval struck harder than she expected. Over the course of the past few days, she'd relied on him to make the right choice. Depended on his moral compass and his idealism. They were what made Cash…Cash, and they made up a big part of why she trusted him. A man so determined to prove his integrity was the extreme opposite of the one who'd isolated her from everyone she loved and what she wanted.

But Daniel was in more danger than ever since their escape last night. And following the rules hadn't gotten them anywhere close to getting him back. He had to see that. "The cartel won't stop, Cash. You don't know what it's like, living in fear all the time in a town like this. Knowing that you're not the one who gets to decide your future and just praying day in and day out that you won't be their next target. They'll keep spreading, like a plague. They'll keep corrupting everything they touch. The people here were lucky. They might not be so lucky the next time. And the information I collected could put a stop to it. We can bury Metias and kill the snake. We just need to find that phone."

"So we follow their rules, is that it?" Cash pointed a strong finger at the floor, stepping into her. "We level the playing field by becoming the exact thing we're fighting? Is this really what you want to become?"

Something tightened in her chest, but it didn't dissuade her from the option in front of them. Not when the stakes were so high. This wasn't about her or Metias or what'd happened over the past few days. This was about an eight-year-old boy who only wanted to come home to his family. "Wouldn't you if you were given the chance to save Wade?"

A hardness he'd never turned on her solidified his expression in place at the mention of his brother.

It was her turn to take a step toward him. Dragging his hand from his side, she framed it between hers. The skin along the back of his knuckles was broken and bruised, and in that moment, she saw through to the man underneath the scars and the defensiveness and sense of mission. "Brock, can you please give us a moment?"

The deputy took a loud, cleansing breath of his own, shaking his head. He shoved to his feet and locked access to his computer with a few taps of his keyboard. "Uh, yeah. Take as long as you need. I'm going to check in with the chief at the hospital."

She waited until the glass front door closed, secluding her and Cash from the rest of the world. Her thumb traced the raised edges of dead skin around his wounds. "You're not him, Cash. Your brother. What he did... There was no excuse for the damage he caused, for the trust he betrayed." Elena dropped her hold on his hand, notching her chin higher to meet his gaze. "And that's not you."

The small muscles along his jaw ticked with his racing pulse. "We were cut from the same cloth. Wade and me. We liked the same movies, talked the same way. Even dated a couple of the same girls at some point. We both knew what we had to do the moment we saw that second plane crash into the World Trade Center tower. We spent nearly every second of our lives together up until we enlisted. We didn't have the kind of relationship most siblings did. There weren't fights over who got to take the car that night or yelling about tearing a hole through a shirt of his I'd borrowed. After Dad died, we stepped up— together—to take care of Mom. Because it was the right thing to do. He was my younger brother, but I was the one who looked up to him."

Cash shifted his weight between his feet. "What if what corrupted him is in me? What if it's just waiting to claw itself out?" He had to take a breath then, his massive shoulders stiff and weighed down. "If I give in, even for something as easy as this, what's to stop me from following in his shoes? If I take that step, that's it, Elena. There's no going back, and who knows what I'll do. Or who I'll hurt."

She swallowed the constriction threatening to choke her from the inside. Taking on the pressure and the weight of his admission as her own. She had a choice. Protect Cash from himself or go after the information she'd collected to protect her brother from the cartel. Elena pressed her hand over his heart. "Okay. Then we won't go through the judge. What if we call the phone instead?"

Confusion rippled across that handsome face. "You want to call your phone to see if someone picks up?"

"No blackmail. No coloring outside the lines." She ripped a piece of paper from Brock's notepad and scratched out the number, then handed it to Cash. It was a long shot, but there was still a chance she could fix this. "One call."

"And if it doesn't work?" He picked up the phone on Brock's desk and dialed the number on an ancient LAN line that should've been put out to pasture years ago. "What then?"

She didn't have an answer.

Because a cell phone had started ringing from one of the chief's desk drawers.

"YOU'RE SURE?" Cash handled the phone with a sandwich bag from Deputy McCrae's lunch to avoid compromising any prints on the device they'd recovered in the chief's desk.

"It's my phone." Elena nodded. "The dented corner on the bottom came from me dropping it on my driveway the night I ran from Albuquerque. Brock was there."

"It's the same phone," McCrae said. "I just don't understand why the chief would have it in his desk. Unless he took it off someone during a search or an arrest."

"Or he has it because the cartel ordered him to recover it." Occam's razor and all that garbage. The simplest answer was usually the correct answer, and it wouldn't be the first time Cash had known law enforcement to get in bed with the very people they were publicly committed to taking down.

"No. No way. The chief isn't working for those bastards. Not in a million years." McCrae grabbed for the phone, then pulled back as Cash dodged the attempt. Frustrated was an understatement. The deputy was taking Cash's suggestion personally. "You don't know him like I do. That man bleeds blue through and through. He patrols on his off-hours. He helps anyone he can, even if it's just to rake Mrs. Baker's leaves out of her front yard. Hell, he's not even from here. He's a transplant from somewhere back east, but he's spent the past five years serving this town. Without him, it would've been overrun a long time ago."

"I have no doubt your chief does his job well, but we can't discount the possibility he's working for *Sangre por Sangre* on the side." Cash bagged the device. "Cartel informers are good at what they do. They're recruited because they can stay under the radar, get access civilians can't, and they're very good liars. It's hard to spot one unless you know what you're looking for."

"Let's say you're right. Okay? The chief—a man I've known and respected for half a decade and has a complete knowledge of the latest tech and forensics in investigative cases—is working for *Sangre por Sangre*." McCrae pointed to the phone. "Don't you think he'd be smart enough to get rid of this thing before someone caught on? Lock it up, at least?"

Elena rolled her bottom lip between her teeth and bit down, claiming Cash's attention in an instant. Given the choice between blackmailing a judge to get her brother back and going about this whole mess the long way, she'd shown her true colors. Coura-geous in the face of losing everything she'd fought for. Honorable. A hero in her own right. And damn, if that didn't make him love her more.

Love.

That single thought paralyzed him down to a cellular level. Hell, where had that come from? He wasn't in any position to feel anything for anyone but a Rottweiler. He'd loved someone once, and that kind of vulnerability had torn him to shreds with Wade's betrayal. He couldn't go through that again. Because emotions and feelings overrode any order, any assignment, any situation. If he couldn't do his job, people died. Cartels grew. And towns like Alpine Valley disappeared off the map.

But Elena had met him on the battlefield. She'd taken up position at his side and held her head high as the enemy had centered her and her family in the crosshairs. She'd gotten them out of the cartel's and her ex's stranglehold by risking her life for others. She'd backed his decision not to lower their tactics in line with the very people she hated most, and, yeah, he loved her for that. For all of that.

But everything between them had been built on a lie. And the part of him that missed having a part-ner that wasn't a K-9 who was scared of the dark—someone to joke with, to ease the weight of the world, to love—knew he and Elena would never work until he came clean about the night of the raid.

"The chief wouldn't have been able to get to the information on that phone without my passcode," she said. "Could be the only reason he hasn't handed it over. It wouldn't do him any good to give it up without knowing what was on it."

"She's right. Any good informant working for people like Metias knows leverage is their best bet of getting what they want out of the deal." Cash forced his head back in the game. They'd recovered the phone. They had to chance to cut off the head of the snake, but finding the device in the chief's desk exposed a variable they hadn't planned for. That the snake was actually a hydra. Cut off one head, two or more grow in its place. "If the chief couldn't access the intel Elena stored, he would've wanted to bide his time long enough to get the passcode before meeting with his handler."

"The chief helped me unload my things from the car that night I moved back." She raised that enigmatic gaze to Cash, and it was as though they were right back in his bed. With nothing but the two of them. "Metias must've tipped him off about what I'd done. I kept the phone on me instead of in my bags because I was terrified the cartel was coming for me. I hid it in the ruins the next day. The chief must've followed me to be able to make the switch."

"Or he could've been doing what the chief does and simply did you a favor by helping out." McCrae shoved his hand through a full head of hair. "This…

This is ridiculous. The chief doesn't have a handler, he isn't handing over information to the very people we're trying to protect this town from and he isn't some spy. The man barely says a word to the officers in this department. Our best bet is to hand the phone over to the DEA and their crime lab and let them deal with anything that comes of the information on it."

The deputy had a point. They'd involved Alpine Valley police by coming here instead of bringing the intel straight to the DEA. But the moment McCrae handed off the phone into evidence, they'd lose their leverage to bring Daniel home. "That could take weeks. Socorro is far more equipped to see this through."

"I can't just hand over a piece of evidence to a bunch of mercenaries in the hopes you'll keep us in the loop, Meyers." McCrae tried to hold back a laugh. The pressure was getting to him. He wasn't in any position to make these kinds of decisions. Could be one of the reasons the man hadn't seen a promotion in all the time he'd served Alpine Valley. "Do you have any idea what would happen to me? To my career?"

They were going in circles. Losing what precious little time Daniel Navarro had left. The boy had already been in the cartel's hands for three straight days. Long enough to make him forget the life he'd had before his abduction with the right psychological tactics.

"Then we eliminate the chief as a suspect right

now." Elena relieved Cash of the phone and flipped it open through the bag. The screen lit up, and she pressed a series of numbers through the plastic to gain access. Always one to take action rather than wait for a plan. It countered every instinct that'd been ingrained into him through his training, but following her lead had gotten them further than working out all the details ahead of time. "I took hundreds of photos of documents and names in the weeks I was married to Metias. If the chief's name or face isn't in any of them, we'll know who we can trust. It'll take some time, but it's better to know what we're getting into than to look over our shoulders for the rest of our lives."

She scanned through the photos, and with each passing second, the deputy seemed to get more agitated. They weren't breaking any laws. The phone belonged to Elena, but an official DEA investigation had been opened with the cartel's raid on the town. The chief could return any second, and McCrae would find himself in hot water for sharing intel outside of the department.

Cash couldn't explain it—the feeling they were missing something. Bear stared at him. She hadn't indicated anything suspicious, though she'd taken up sitting beside the deputy's desk corner. Like she was waiting for Cash's permission to proceed. She'd only done that one time before. Waited instead of charging full tilt at a threat. It'd been inside the warehouse where the DEA and Marine Corps had set up their staging area before her final assignment.

Her paws kneaded the carpet, just as they had in the hours before their entire world had changed. He didn't have reason to order her to search the trailer, but her behavior wasn't lining up. Though she hadn't worked in drug or explosive detection for over a year, Bear would never forget.

Something was off in this trailer.

Cash could feel it. He scanned along the filing cabinets lined up along one wall. If *Sangre por Sangre* had infiltrated the Alpine Valley police department, it stood to reason they'd want to keep an eye on developments from within. Surveillance, recording devices, wiretaps on the LAN lines. Socorro had utilized and worked with all of them. It'd be easy enough to spot.

"Here's something." Elena's face brightened with the potential of a lead. She glanced from McCrae to Cash, drawing them in with her excitement. "It's a list of handwritten names I found in Metias's desk. I originally thought it was a rundown of his aliases, but they're so different from each other. It makes more sense that they're other people he's keeping tabs on. Maybe informants?"

Cash couldn't get a good look at the list on an inch-and-a-half-by-one-inch pixelated screen, but she seemed to be able to make out the names well enough.

The deputy took a step toward his desk.

Bear's ears lifted away from her face slightly as she tracked McCrae's move from her position.

And it was then Cash knew.

Confusion cocked Elena's head back slightly. "The chief's name isn't on here. I've been through everything. No mention of him anywhere." Elena lowered the phone to her side. "But there is one name I recognize." She turned toward the deputy. "Yours."

A nervous laugh burst from McCrae's chest, and Cash reached for his weapon. Damn it. The deputy had made him surrender it at the door with a promise to give it back once they left the station. "That's insane, Elena. We've known each other since we were kids. You've eaten dinner with my family. You know I'd never work for people like the cartel. Come on. I'm the one who came to get you when you wanted to escape your marriage. This is all some sick game your ex is playing with you. You have to believe me."

Cash took a step forward, positioning himself closer to the deputy. "Elena, how did you reach McCrae when you needed out of Albuquerque?"

"I had to buy a phone Metias didn't know about. I messaged him." Elena's gaze widened. "With this phone."

"Well, I was really hoping to avoid this, but what are you going to do?" McCrae's innocence bled from his face as he withdrew his sidearm and took aim. At Elena. Bear's defenses instantly went on alert with a series of barks and warnings at the deputy. "You were right. An informant has to have some kind of leverage to get what he wants out of a deal with a cartel like *Sangre por Sangre*. So I'll be taking that phone now."

Chapter Twelve

"You son of a bitch. You knew. You knew what the cartel was going to do, and you let it happen anyway." How could she have been so blind? Cash had tried to warn her, but she hadn't wanted to see it. Until it was too late. "You knew they were going to take Daniel. He's only eight years old!"

She lunged to get her hands on the friend she believed she'd known as well as herself, but Cash held her back. Brock loaded a round into his weapon, and her heart shot into her throat. Would he really shoot her? After all the years she'd trusted him?

"Now, Elena. Don't be trying to blame all this pain and suffering on me," the deputy said. "If you'd just been a good girl like you were supposed to and kept your nose out of cartel business, Metias wouldn't have had any reason to send his men to look for you and this phone. Lucky for me, I'm observant. I didn't recognize the number you messaged me from that night in Albuquerque. Took some doing, but I was able to match it to a cash purchase on a day you were seen in town. But it was the way you held on to it as though it were a lifeline after I picked you up outside of the city. I put two and two together. You were hiding something."

Elena squeezed the phone in her hand harder. The plastic protested under her grip, and she wanted nothing more in that moment than to destroy it so the weasel had nothing to offer *Sangre por Sangre*. Only then she'd have nothing to use as her own leverage to get Daniel back. Was this how Cash had felt when he'd learned what his brother had done? So much anger that had nowhere to go? Building until she feared she'd explode from the pressure?

"So you started informing on Elena to her ex." Cash angled himself in front of her, but it wouldn't be enough. Bullets were known to go through bodies even as massive as his, and she wasn't sure he could take any more after what the cartel had already done to him.

"Well, subterfuge certainly doesn't come quite as easily to me as it does to you, Elena. I kept an eye on you, trying to figure out what it was you were up to. Call it an inner sense of curiosity. Days went by, then a week. I gave you as many chances as I could, but when you still didn't tell me what was going on, I followed you up to those ruins." Brock cut his attention from Elena to Cash. Trying to mentally work out who he'd shoot first. Her chest tightened at the thought of any of those choices. But sooner or later, he would make a choice. "Found your phone hidden in the wall. You were smart to password protect it, but that left me in a predicament. Because I didn't have anything I could give Metias in exchange for what I wanted most. You could've trusted me, Elena. We could've been a team. You, me, we could've started the life together we'd always talked about. I just needed you to trust me. Now we're going to have to do this the hard way."

"Talked about?" Her stomach turned at the thought. She'd known. For years. The signs had been there since before she'd gotten married and let herself be swept away. Brock had asked her on dates in high school, but she'd wanted out of Alpine Valley, and he'd set his heart on becoming a police officer. They'd been friends. Movie nights, high school dances, hikes together. He'd listened to all the unimportant things she thought she wanted out of her life, like moving away, traveling the world, making something more of herself than a small-town New Mexico girl. There'd been countless nights the two of them had just stared at the stars from the hood of his dad's car wondering what the universe held for them. She'd celebrated his acceptance into the police force. Once Metias had entered the picture, he'd asked her to not go through with her engagement. But the only other option had been staying in a town she was desperate to leave, with a man she'd never see as anything more than a friend.

Only now that friend wanted something more.

"I do trust you." Elena took a step toward Brock, toward the gun barrel slightly shaking in his hand. She hadn't been able to convince Cash of her interest the time she'd lifted the keys for his SUV from his pocket, but he was a trained military contractor. Brock… Brock was a nobody from Alpine Valley who hadn't even graduated at the middle of his class from the police academy.

"Elena." Cash's warning sliced through her. There was so much power in that single whisper of her name. She'd read once a name was the sweetest word someone could ever speak to a person, and they were right. Her name falling from his mouth drilled through the pain and anguish and balled into a tight knot of hope. With that one warning, he was promising to fight for her, to protect her, to have her back and follow through with recovering Daniel from the cartel. But it was so much more than that. It was a map of their future together. One where the things they'd been through didn't hurt anymore. Where she didn't have to bear the weight of pain and injustice alone. It promised healing and Oreos that weren't laced with Bear's allergy medication. He was promising a partnership born of love, and she wanted that. With him.

"It's okay. He's not going to hurt me. Because I know what he's planning to negotiate with the cartel for." Elena raised her hands in surrender, pinching the phone between her thumb and palm. "Me."

"That's one of the reasons I've always liked you,

Elena. You accept people for who they really are."
Brock motioned toward her with the gun. "Now,
here's what's going to happen. You're going to hand
me that phone, then you and me are walking out of
here. We'll use what you gathered to take down *Sangre por Sangre* and get your brother back. Together.
Like it should've been from the beginning. I tried to
warn you about Metias, but you wouldn't listen. But
you're listening now, aren't you?"

"Over my dead body." Cash moved to intercept,
but Brock seemed to breathe new life into his gun
hold. The weapon raised a fraction of an inch and
centered on Cash. Bear exposed her teeth, a terrifying
growl vibrating through her hundred-pound frame.
She didn't like when people threatened her handler.

"That's far enough." Brock redirected his aim, and
it took everything inside of Elena not to step between
Bear and the gun. "One more step and the doggy
gets hurt. You wouldn't want that, would you, Meyers? From what I could find on you, the two of you
have been through quite enough already since your
brother died. I wouldn't want to break up the band."

"Brock, you don't have to do this. Okay? Nobody
has to get hurt." Elena took another step to claim the
deputy's attention. Because it was the only way to
ensure Cash and Bear got out of here. "You have me.
Let them go, and the phone is yours." Acid churned
in her gut. "I'll be yours. Just like you wanted. All
you have to do is let them leave."

"Elena, no." Cash's voice dipped into dangerous territory. "You're not going anywhere."

"You think I'm that foolish? I know you'd say anything to make sure you were the only one who suffered. Because that's who you are. That's what makes you so easy to manipulate, Elena." Brock's mouth thinned into a smile she'd never seen before. A combination of amusement and corruption that set her defenses on high alert.

"But would you still feel the same way if you learned Cash Meyers was the one who failed to warn Alpine Valley the cartel was making their move the night of the raid?" His low laugh infused Elena's nerves with dread. "Did you ever ask him what he did in the Marine Corps? What his job for that security company is? He's a forward observer, Elena. He's the one who tracks the cartel's movements to give towns like ours a chance of evacuating. Makes me wonder what he was doing the night *Sangre por Sangre* took Daniel from you. Where was his warning?"

What? No. That didn't... That didn't make sense. Cash would've told her. Elena turned to put him in her sights, waiting for him to explain. To give her the answer she found herself so desperately needing in that moment. "Cash?"

His guard was back in place. The one that'd taken her days to work through. He held her gaze long enough to convince her of the truth. Brock wasn't lying. Not this time.

That cutting sense of betrayal she'd felt realizing her lifelong friend had given her up to the cartel was nothing compared to the twist of an invisible blade through her heart, handled by the man in front of her. The one she'd let hold her through the night, who'd saved her life and put a fantasy of real partnership and a future in her head. The one who'd convinced her she didn't have to be this broken remnant of a marriage she never should've gotten into in the first place. Heat assaulted her then. Shame, hot and undeniable, worked beneath her skin and eviscerated everything she thought she'd known about him. Her ex had made her feel small and worthless. Weak. Cash had given her the chance and the guts to be strong.

But it'd all been a lie from the beginning.

Her heart crumpled right there in her chest. Beaten black and blue to the point she wasn't sure it could ever be revitalized. "It's true, isn't it?"

Cash finally broke his vow of silence. "Elena, I'm—"

"I'm sorry. We are simply out of time for heartfelt apologies." Brock struck without warning. He fisted Elena's hair and dragged her back into his chest. She reached up to pry his hands free, but the harder she fought, the more force he used.

Violence spread through Cash's eyes, and she swore every muscle in his body flexed under the pressure. "You're going to want to get your hands off her. Now."

Bear lunged without a command. She clamped onto Brock's arm. His scream triggered a high-pitched ringing in her ears a split second before the gun went off.

The bullet threw Cash back.

He hit the floor.

Blood bloomed across his T-shirt in an instant.

"No!" Elena tried to reach him, but the deputy only held on tighter. "Cash!"

"Get off of me!" Brock's foot connected with Bear's ribs, and Elena's would-be protector belted an injured whine as the Rottweiler rolled across the floor. Unmoving.

Elena threw back her elbow as she'd seen Cash do in the middle of a fight, connecting with bone and cartilage, but the deputy recovered faster than she expected. She hadn't hit him hard enough to break his nose.

Brock sucked in air between his teeth as he surveyed the bloody damage done to his forearm. "That's enough of that. Looks like our ride is here." He shoved her toward the trailer's front door, a glimpse of a large SUV taking shape through the glass. "And, believe me, we don't want to keep him waiting."

OH, HELL. DYING HURT.

He hadn't liked it the first time an assignment had blown up in his face, and he certainly didn't enjoy it now. Cash managed to roll off his bullet-ridden shoulder. Blood soaked into the already-stained industrial carpet underneath him. The shot had gone straight through. Sitting up, he clamped a hand over the wound. Son of a bitch.

Deputy McCrae had been the informant.

Not the chief as they'd been led to believe.

The pieces of the puzzle were starting to make sense. He'd just put them together too late. But there was still time. For Elena. For her brother. A dark outline of hair and muscle whined from across the trailer, and dread took over. "Bear."

Cash crawled on one hand and both knees toward her. She flinched at his approach. "Shhh. It's me. It's okay."

The lean muscles behind her legs and down her back relaxed, but only slightly. He ran his good hand along the length of her side. He'd blacked out from the impact of the bullet. "What happened, huh? What'd he do to you?"

Bear set her head back against the floor, blinking those big dark eyes he trusted with his life. She'd tried to protect Elena. That much was clear. Following an order he'd given days ago. A line of blood stained the hair around her mouth. She'd taken a bite out of McCrae. The bastard had been lucky she hadn't torn him to pieces. Another whine broke through the pound of his heartbeat behind his ears.

"I'm sorry." He wasn't sure who he'd meant the apology for. For Bear, in pain and unable to move from possible broken ribs to match his own, or Elena.

The hurt in her expression had seared itself into his brain. It'd been the last thing he'd seen before the bullet had ripped through him and was the only image in his head now. He'd done nothing but ask her to trust him these past few days, and he'd broken that trust. He'd betrayed her as easily as his brother had corrupted their joint DEA mission.

Corrupted.

That was what he was. The fear there was something waiting inside of him, something dark and evil and defective, had kept him on the edge to prove he wasn't anything like his brother. To take on more assignments, to push himself harder than the rest of the team. Thousands in donations, hundreds of hours of community service, countless volunteer opportunities whenever he got the chance—it'd all been for nothing. None of it had erased that hollowness that'd taken over Wade's conscience. And now, he was just like his little brother.

A fraud.

The night of the raid. It was still so clear in his mind. He'd had no other leads in recovering Wade's body for over a year. Over and over again until the days blended together and hope had disintegrated, he and Bear had hit the dirt the moment the sun crested the plateaus. They'd searched through blistering heat, sunless mornings and dozens of grids laid out over the course of hundreds of square miles. Then Socorro's source within the cartel had passed along coordinates and sworn his intel was good. And it had been.

The remains had been picked over to the point the buzzards hadn't even bothered circling anymore. Unrecognizable. While the elements took their pound of flesh, the body's clothing had protected some of the dehydrated skin beneath a pair of cargo pants and the man's shoes. Teeth had been removed. The sun had dried up any blood left in the body. Not even Doc Piel would've been able to do anything to rehydrate the body's fingertips to get prints. But Cash had known the moment he'd seen the tattoo. The broken outline of a doughnut reading *A-dough-rable*.

There was supposed to be a sense of relief, of closure, from finally completing his personal mission, but it'd never come. He'd wanted something more as he'd stared at his brother's remains. But bodies couldn't talk. They couldn't apologize or explain or argue. He'd waited. He'd waited for Wade to stand up, to brush himself off and crack that ridiculous grin of his, but all Cash had gotten was a dead man. Until hatred and grief and pain had exploded to the point he found himself screaming into the night. Bear had simply lain down next to Wade as he raged. It wasn't until an hour later—maybe more—that he'd caught sight of the fires. By then it'd been too late.

The cartel had taken his brother's identity as a final nail in his coffin, but Wade's corrupted legacy would live on regardless. His actions would continue to ripple out. Affecting the families of the men and women who'd died in that explosion, strengthening the cartel's reputation, helping organizations like *Sangre por Sangre* spread like the disease they were by weakening law enforcement one mission at a time. All stemming from one choice. One man. The person Cash had trusted most in the world.

And now his choice to keep the truth from Elena about that night would follow the same track. It'd separated her family and lost them a vital piece of their lives. It'd paved the way for Metias and *Sangre por Sangre* to find Elena. And it'd undermined Socorro's ability to protect the people and the towns systematically becoming targets of the cartel.

Recovering Wade's body was supposed to fix everything. But it hadn't. It'd only made things worse and distracted him from what should've been his only priority: Elena.

But he wouldn't let her pay for his mistakes.

She deserved better. Better than Metias. Better than McCrae. And better than him.

Cash set his thumb beneath one of Bear's ears—her favorite spot to be scratched—then followed the ridge of her collar to the emergency SOS signal embedded in the leather. He collapsed beside her. "I'm going to get you out of here. Okay? Just as soon as I remember what it feels like to use this arm."

She directed that dark gaze to his, then let her eyes slip closed as he threaded one hand beneath her neck and the other under her hip. Tucking his knees beneath him, Cash braced for the pain that came with hauling her into his chest. Blood seeped from his wound, faster than before. The quicker his pulse picked up, the harder his heart pumped out blood through the injury, but he wouldn't stop.

Because this wasn't finished.

McCrae might've gotten what he wanted with the intel Elena had stolen, but it wouldn't be enough for the cartel. Nothing could ever be enough, and they would never stop. Not until there wasn't anything left to control.

Cash stumbled forward, his injured leg barely taking his and Bear's weights combined. One knee gave out, and he dropped at the corner of McCrae's desk. His elbow slammed onto the cheap faux wood. Nerves screamed in protest at the pressure, but it was there Cash noted a sprinkle of white powder dusting the edge of the desk.

Bear had sat in this exact spot. She hadn't been waiting for an order. She'd tried signaling Cash to the presence of drugs, and he'd missed it. It made sense now. He'd run a background check on the deputy for the same signs he'd noted in Wade's financials and phone records, but paperwork didn't always reflect drug use.

Cartels these days were careful. They didn't need corners. The drug game had turned into a boutique-style delivery service, usually under the cover of some other business. Pizza, flowers, internet orders—sometimes more than one. Text a number, place an order, pay with a credit card or checking account. McCrae would've been subject to background checks throughout his career. He'd known exactly how to hide his dirty little habit. From his friends, family, his chief. And now he had Elena.

Movement registered at the station's front door.

"Lucy, I'm home." Jocelyn Carville cleared the room in a fraction of a second and crossed the distance between them. Her hand instantly went to the butt of her weapon. Maverick raced through the room, circling Cash with an added bounce to his step. "Damn it. I swear one of these days I'm going to roll up to find you dead. Tell me what happened."

"The deputy happened." Cash managed to get to his feet with her taking some of Bear's weight. "Son of a bitch has been informing on Elena since she came back to Alpine Valley. He took her and gave me a bullet as an early birthday present. My guess is he's headed straight back to the cartel. Background check was clear, but check this out." He nodded at the thin powder coating the desk.

She whistled low, gaining Maverick's attention. The German shepherd sniffed along the desk then sneezed with a violent shake of his head before pawing at the carpet. "Well, it's not drywall dust. You think he's a frequent consumer?"

"Enough to cloud his judgment when it comes to

getting in bed with *Sangre por Sangre*." He should've seen it. McCrae's determination to blackmail a judge for a geofence warrant, his offer to take the phone into evidence. Both had been to buy himself as much time as possible. He'd been the one to switch out the device for a replica and plant it in the chief's desk. "Joce, I need you to take Bear."

Understanding hit as they carried the Rottweiler to Jocelyn's waiting SUV. He could see it in the way the logistics officer lowered her gaze to the bullet hole in his shoulder, then came straight back to his face. "You can't be serious. You're injured. Running after her in this condition isn't going to work out for either of you."

"I can't leave her to fight them alone. You know that." Cash groaned low and deep, mirroring Bear's moan, as they got her into the cargo area of Jocelyn's vehicle. Maverick hopped in and lay down beside his K-9 teammate. Protective and concerned. Cash added pressure to his wound in hopes of controlling the bleeding. In vain.

"You're out of your mind if you think I'm going to let you fight them alone in this condition," she said. "Elena's at least in one piece."

"I've got a field kit in the car." Pain stabbed down his arm. He wasn't sure how much a field kit would help, but it was better than bleeding out in the middle of a cul-de-sac. "You can stay to help patch me up, but I'm not asking. I'm telling. I'm going after Elena. So

I need you to get Bear back to the vet. I can't do this if I'm worried about her. Understand?"

Jocelyn cut her attention to Maverick and back. She'd make the same choice if it came right down to it. They all would. She grabbed her field kit from behind Bear and rolled it out. "Fine. But if you die, I'm going to tell everyone you watch rom-coms when you think no one is awake."

"You're not supposed to know about that," he said. "I was careful."

"Oh, but I do." She twisted off the lid to the bottle of alcohol and dumped a good amount onto a piece of gauze, waiting for him to make the next move. "And I have proof. So you better come back alive."

Chapter Thirteen

Someone would find Cash before it was too late.

He wasn't dead. He wasn't, but no matter how many times she'd begged the men in the SUV to go back, she'd been ignored.

Deputy McCrae's knee rubbed against hers from his position beside her. Not Brock. The man sitting next to her wasn't her friend. He wasn't her confidant or the one she'd relied on to get her out of Albuquerque and her marriage. She didn't know him anymore. He'd taken her trust and twisted it into something ugly and left Cash with a bullet in the process.

Her lip throbbed in rhythm with her racing heart rate. She'd tried to claw her way out the back of the SUV, to escape as distance shrank down the police station through the back window, but McCrae had been prepared for her to fight. And not opposed to hurting her to get what he wanted. Bastard.

"Cheer up, Elena. The dog is still alive." McCrae knocked his knee into hers as though they were simply joking about that cheesy horror movie they'd watched together last Halloween. "I'm not a total monster."

She had a few recent experiences to refute him, but there was no point. Squeezing herself against the window, she tried to drown the nausea churning in her gut. Every touch, every look, every word out of his mouth made her sick. Alpine Valley faded as the trees thinned along the borders of town. Coming home had been her only option after she'd left Albuquerque. She hadn't appreciated it. Not really. The protective cliffs, the shade the trees had provided all her life, the sheer beauty of an oasis dead center in one of the hottest deserts in existence. "It's not the dog I'm worried about."

Though Bear had taken a solid kick to the ribs. The Rottweiler hadn't moved an inch as McCrae dragged Elena out of the trailer. The idea of Cash losing his partner hurt despite the fact he'd been partly responsible for the pain and anguish she and her family had been through. What had McCrae called him? A forward observer. The man in charge of seeing the threat coming from a mile away, of ensuring towns like Alpine Valley had warning before the strike. Like an air raid siren for tornadoes. Though something had kept Cash from warning them the night of the raid. Maybe if he had, she might've been able to get Daniel to safety. Maybe they could've escaped the violence and the loss and betrayal.

Tears pricked at her eyes.

"Oh, come now. You can't honestly tell me you're worried about that Socorro thug. I did you a favor," McCrae said. "If you think about it, he's the reason the cartel got their hands on Daniel in the first place. You should be thanking me. Mercenaries like him are nothing but *Sangre por Sangre* soldiers on an imaginary leash. You don't want that in your life."

"And what about corrupt cops?" she asked. "How are they any different?"

His laugh was all the warning she had before McCrae gripped the back of her neck and thrust her face into the back of the front passenger seat. Lightning struck behind her eyes from the momentum, but her nose was largely saved by the leather. It took a few seconds for her vision to clear, but Elena caught the driver's gaze on her from the rearview mirror. She'd met him before. Not in the compound. In Albuquerque. One of the men her husband had brought around the house before she'd run. She couldn't read his expression, but she knew one thing for certain: he wouldn't help her.

"Don't worry, Elena." McCrae unpocketed the phone he'd taken from her. "I'm going to take good care of you. You'll see."

Gravity took hold of her insides as the SUV angled down into the compound construction site. Dirt kicked along and pinged off of the SUV's doors though the engineers and excavators had halted work on the actual structure. Dread forced acid into her throat. Cash had risked his life to get her out of this building. Now she might never see the outside of it again.

Her heart threatened to pound straight out of her chest at the thought. Of not seeing him again. He'd lied to her about the night of the raid. From the very beginning, he'd witnessed what had happened to homes and families displaced because he'd failed to do his job. But though she wanted to hate him as much as she hated her ex or Deputy McCrae, he wasn't like them. No matter what McCrae said. Cash wasn't just some soldier with an imaginary leash. He was a protector. One of the very best.

Without him and Bear, she wouldn't have made it out of Alpine Valley that first night. Or survived Metias's psychological torture. Without Cash, she'd have never found a reason to laugh or let someone just hold her through the night. And while nothing physical had happened between them apart from that kiss, those hours in his arms had fortified her in a way she never thought possible. Had given her hope and a reason to keep fighting. Not for others. For herself.

Sunlight vanished as the driver pulled into the underground parking garage, and every cell in her body went on high alert. She couldn't see him through the dark tint of the windows, but he was there. Waiting for her. Metias. She could feel it. She rocked forward as the SUV was thrown into Park, and the air in her chest evaporated.

"Time to claim what's mine." McCrae reached across her lap and shoved the door open. On the other side, her husband stood to greet them.

Only there was no smile this time. No warm welcome or the familiar mask of deception he liked to hide behind. Metias stood proud with his arms at his sides, his expression as severe as the time he'd caught her going through the mail. And a pistol gripped in one hand. "You and I have much to discuss, *mi amor.*" He cocked his head to one side, looking past her. "I take it you've brought me what I asked for, Deputy."

"Got it right here." McCrae nudged her out the door, and Elena was forced to face the man she'd run from not once but twice. The deputy kept a tight lock on her arm, but she wasn't going to run this time. "Took some doing, but she says it's everything she collected."

"Bueno." Metias nodded and two soldiers materialized from the shadows. "Then you and I have concluded our business. Elena."

Her ex said her name like calling a dog to heel. It was nothing compared to the way Cash made her feel. Safe. Strong. Confident. Metias didn't care about her. She was a trophy in his eyes. Something to be won through the pain of others. And Cash... He'd put her first in every scenario they'd gone into together. Ensured she had a place to sleep, food to eat. Only asked to touch her with her permission instead of taking what he felt he was owed. Yeah, there'd been a moment—maybe a few—she'd questioned his motives, but the difference between the two men with actual power over her was clear.

One used domination. The other let her choose her path, and she loved him for it. She loved Cash, and there wasn't a damn thing McCrae or Metias could do about it. They'd taken everything from her, but they couldn't take that, and the second she figured out how to get the hell out of here, she'd find him.

"Now hold on there, honcho. I don't believe we have." McCrae moved the phone back into his uniform pocket. He tucked her into his side body. "I went through an awful lot to get this information for you. Had to shoot a man. That requires a lot of cleanup on my end. Our business isn't even close to concluded."

"You want to change the deal." Thin skin around Metias's eyes seemed more translucent as though a demon were about to stretch through and possess him from within. "I'll tell you what, Officer…"

"Deputy. McCrae." The deputy enunciated every syllable. His grip tightened around her arm, punishing and painful.

Elena didn't dare move. Didn't dare to take her next breath. She knew what it meant to disobey the man in front of them, and every instinct she owned screamed at her to get as far from the deputy as possible. She tried to wrench her arm free, but there was nowhere she could run.

"McCrae." Metias let the deputy's name roll off his tongue with constrained flair. "I admire your passion. You believe you deserve something for your hard work. I commend that. I've promoted men within my organization for showing such vigor." Her ex closed the distance between them slowly, gauging his prey. He motioned to her lip. "I take it you are the one who did this to Elena. She's stubborn, no?"

McCrae's chest puffed up as big as a bird's in mating season. A smile she'd always been disarmed by pinched the edges of his mouth. "Had to throw her into the back of the headrest to stop that mouth of hers."

Metias's laugh belted from his lungs, hard and brash. But when the laugh died, so did the humor on his face. Her ex raised his weapon and fired. Once. Twice.

The deputy's body jerked beside her, and soon his grip disappeared from her arm entirely. Blood splattered onto her shirt, neck and face just before he collapsed to the ground. McCrae stared up at her as his final breath leaked from the holes in his chest. Dead.

"I believe that concludes our business." Metias used the barrel of his weapon to signal one of the men waiting in the wings. *"Consigue el teléfono."* Get the phone. The soldier did as he was asked, pulling her phone from McCrae's jacket, and in a fraction of a second, her life—and that of her brother's—was entirely in her ex-husband's hands. One of which he was extending out to her right then. "Welcome to our new home, *mi esposa*."

"I'm not your wife, Metias," she said. "I don't care what the courts say."

"Let's hear what you have to say after you see the gift I brought for you." He snapped his fingers as men in power did, expecting for his needs to be instantly met. And they were. A second pair of men stepped free of the shadows cast by the underground garage's overhang.

With her brother between them.

Metias rounded behind her, his mouth too close to her ear. "I can forgive the fact you stole from me, Elena, but I will not tolerate you making a fool of me. This has gone on long enough. I gave you a choice the last time we were together. I'm still waiting for your answer. Come home to me, make this right and your brother goes free. Refuse—" her ex raised his weapon again, to the side of her head "—and you both die."

HIS LEG ZINGED with numbness as the compound came into view.

Cash kept low along the crater's rim, looking down into the construction site. The trek across the desert upped the chances of finishing him off, but signaling the cartel of his approach would only sign his death warrant sooner.

He dragged his backpack higher up his shoulder. Elena was down there. He felt it as if she were calling to him. The connection they'd built in a matter of days pulled him unlike anything he'd ever experienced. It wasn't physical or mental or emotional. It was all of those things combined into something otherworldly and terrifying. He'd loved and lost. But this... This was worth risking his life for. Worth risking everything for.

They'd survived despite having no layout of that compound, not knowing how many soldiers they were up against or what they were getting themselves into. Because they'd worked as a team. He'd always been the kind of operator who needed a plan, who'd worked out every detail so he could predict the oncoming threat. But if there was one thing he'd learned since taking this assignment, it was that nothing was impossible. Not as long as he and Elena were together.

Cash surveyed the site for movement, but if the cartel had regrouped at the half-finished compound, satellites picked anything up. No movement. No signs of life or an ambush. But experience warned him not to take enemy lines at face value.

He dug his heels into the dirt and descended the steep incline. Rock and dust infiltrated his gear and slowed him down at the bottom. Taking cover behind one of the excavators, Cash swung his backpack forward and pried the zipper open. *Sangre por Sangre* would've narrowed down his and Elena's entry point from their last visit to the compound. There were no guarantees the override code would work for the security system any longer. He needed another plan to get in.

One that brought the cartel out.

He handled the explosive and detonator carefully as he attached it beneath the excavator's operator's seat. Then moved on to the next and the next. His senses rocketed into overdrive as he tried to keep out of sight. His injured shoulder tingled from overuse. Jocelyn had done a fine job cleaning him up, but chances of infection and blood loss were still high. He had to keep moving.

For Elena. For her brother.

The guilt that'd eaten at him since the moment he'd hauled her into the back of his SUV the night of the raid reared its ugly head and wouldn't let go.

Wade hadn't deserved his obsession all these past months, and if Cash hadn't been out in the middle of the desert looking for his body, Elena and Daniel might not be in danger now. His brother had betrayed everything they'd stood for growing up and had forgotten their agreement to fight for justice and change the world for the better. What had gone wrong? When was the moment Wade made his choice to denounce everything they'd sacrificed for?

A low growl escaped his chest as he got eyes on the compound's underground parking garage. It didn't matter. His brother was dead. Cash wasn't ever getting an answer, but he couldn't help but imagine the countless scenarios in which Wade would've crossed that line. The same line Cash would cross to save the woman he loved if she required it of him.

Understanding hit there—in the shadow of the cartel's physical manifestation of resources and control. His brother was younger, but he'd always taken on the role of protecting Cash when they'd been kids. Like the time Cash had climbed into the skeleton of an abandoned barn to outrun a group of boys determined to beat him to a pulp. Hadn't done much good. They'd thrown rocks to try to bring him down. One had sliced through his eyebrow and left behind the scar he had today. Wade charged into that building and punched the leader square in the face. Knocked the kid out cold. The others hadn't even dared try to take Wade on after that.

A heaviness ached behind Cash's sternum. He hadn't thought about that day in a long time. Too angry. Too busy. Too…empty. His brother had fought by his side the day of that task force mission. Always had. And that was what hurt the most. Wade hadn't just betrayed his oath to serve and protect his country and the people at the mercy of the cartel. He'd betrayed Cash. Walked him straight into that ambush, knowing what waited for him on the other side.

The memories were still there, right on the cusp. He'd played them over and over in his head, and that same gut feeling of a setup took up residence as he approached the garage. He shook it off. Only difference between then and now? He knew what he was getting himself into this time. And what he would do to get Elena and her little brother out.

Blood seeped through the gauze and T-shirt protecting the wound in his shoulder, but the pain had receded in the past few minutes. He'd take full advantage.

Cement overhung the entrance with a barely-there security system blocking vehicles without a keycard from driving down into the belly of the beast. Still no sign of *Sangre por Sangre* soldiers. He made quick work of the remaining explosive charges in his bag, setting them around the perimeter. From the layout he'd catalogued during their first visit to the site, he mapped Metias's office on the far side of the complex. Cash surveyed the spacing between devices, then jogged clear of the building. The cartel had somehow blocked his emergency SOS signal two days ago. He wasn't going to make the assumption one would get through now. Unpocketing the radio he'd pried from the console of his SUV, he switched it to the channel he needed. "When in doubt, have a backup plan."

He hit the push-to-talk button.

The charges detonated simultaneously. Cement, dirt and glass ripped through the air like a series of volcanoes ridding themselves of debris. A wave of pressure from the blast raced across the desert floor and shoved Cash back. But he didn't have time to watch his work unravel. The entire garage had been swallowed by failing framing and cement. Boulder-sized chunks crumbled away from the main supports and exploded on impact. He dodged the first one. Then barely missed the second as he sprinted into the collapse. A wall of heat slammed into him as darkness overtook his vision.

The building's security system screeched high alert and triggered the sprinklers overhead. He navigated through the blast site and into a corridor still standing, then unholstered his weapon. Voices echoed down the hall to his position. No bodies in the debris. The blast had done its job in knocking out the cartel's main escape, but that still left him to deal with the panicked soldiers responding to the alarm.

Water pooled beneath his boots and streaked down his face as he moved. Twisting from one side to the other, he cleared each door branching off the main hallway. A loop of one memory—of him and Wade clearing a building a hundred miles from here—overlapped the onslaught of blaring noise and thundering response.

Two soldiers turned the corner up ahead, and Cash's finger automatically tightened on the trigger. They both took aim, but he was faster. Each bullet found its mark. The metallic *tink* of casings hitting the floor shoved him back into the present. The here and now. Where the only thing that mattered was getting to Elena.

His shoulder ached every second he fought gravity to keep his arms up and his hold tight around the gun. Sprinkler water infiltrated his vision as he cleared the next corner and moved on a trajectory to the back of the building. Bear would've done her share to make sure the path was clear, but he'd have to rely on his own instincts now.

The wall six inches from his face exploded in a rain of bullets.

The impact kicked up dust.

Cash pulled back to keep himself from taking another bullet. A series of clicks registered through the rhythmic silence of the alarm. He rushed the soldier whose gun had jammed ten feet away and cocked his elbow back to clock him dead between the eyes. The recruit crumpled as quickly as the structure's garage had, and Cash confiscated his weapon. "Stay down."

A seismic rumble seemed to ripple through the walls. Cash set his hand against the nearest column to keep his balance. He'd taken out the main supports under the garage. It was only a matter of time before the front half of the building collapsed in on itself. He just hoped he had enough time.

He set one foot in front of the other. The strap of the automatic rifle dug into his shoulder with every step. But it wouldn't slow him down. Another shift of the building had him picking up the pace. He was working blind, only able to rely on the fractured memories of his first visit to the compound with a concussion, but they would have to be enough.

He wasn't leaving without Elena or her brother.

He wouldn't fail her as he'd failed Wade.

He wouldn't allow their bodies to be left in the middle of the desert for him to find months from now.

Because the truth was, he should've been there for Wade. He'd known it since the moment he had recovered his brother's body in the middle of the New Mexican desert. He should've been more involved in his brother's life. Listened better. Taken the time to check in more often rather than losing himself in the next assignment. Maybe then Wade would've trusted him with whatever he'd gotten himself into. They could've put their heads together to get him out.

And Elena… Hell. He didn't know what would happen between them when this was over and danger wasn't waiting to ambush them at every turn. But he was willing to find out. Willing to put the obsession aside, cut back on the number of assignments he took on for Socorro, face the hurt and the pain for a chance to start anew. To do whatever it took to keep her in his life.

Her confidence in him, in the kind of man he was, was the only thing keeping his head above water. She'd dropped into his life at the precise moment he'd needed her the most, given him a chance to prove he could overcome that corruption he and Wade shared deep down. It wasn't the donations and service that defined his goodness. It was her. She'd exposed a piece of him he'd wanted to bury forever, and he'd do whatever it took to earn her trust back. To earn her love. She'd brought him out into the light, and Cash suddenly found himself afraid of the dark.

He checked the rounds left in the gun's magazine and carved through the building without stopping. "I'm coming, Elle. Just hold on a little while longer."

Chapter Fourteen

The building shook beneath her.

Elena clutched onto her brother just as she had the night of the raid, clamping a hand over his mouth to quiet his sobs. He'd assumed more scrapes and bruises since that last time she'd seen him, but he was alive. He was here. In her arms. They were going to make it out of this. "It's going to be okay. I've got you."

Words were all she had. Because unless she was sure one of these walls made up the exterior structure and magically created a hole in it, they weren't going anywhere. Still, her heart believed them. She threaded her fingers into his hair.

The alarms drowned out the sound of Metias's order, but the three men on guard around the room seemed to be able to discern his instructions. They each peeled away from their fearless leader and headed for the door, guns clutched against their chests.

Sprinklers hissed from overhead and drenched them within seconds. Something had happened. Maybe an explosion or a fire. An accident? Had Socorro gotten news of what'd happened to Cash and decided to carry out a raid of their own? Her mind raced with the possibilities. None of it mattered. It was the opportunity she'd been waiting for. A distraction the cartel wouldn't be able to ignore.

Metias wiped the thin veil of water from his face, baring his teeth like a wild animal warning an oncoming predator. "The two of you are coming with me. Let's go."

"No." She wasn't sure if her voice carried over the blare of the security system screaming for them to evacuate.

Pulling an oversize gleaming silver pistol from beneath his white suit jacket, Metias lunged for Daniel when neither of them moved at his insistence. He went to tear her brother out of her arms, but Elena stepped between them.

"Get away from him!" She moved Daniel behind her. She'd let him go to men like Metias once. She wouldn't let it happen again. Water soaked through her clothing and down into bone. It froze her from the outside in, but there was a raging heat already simmering beneath her skin. One she'd left dormant for far too long. "You don't get to touch him. Or me. Ever. Do you understand? We will never be what you want us to be. I'm not coming back, Metias. I'm not your wife anymore. I don't love you, and if you think I'll subject myself to you because you threaten me into submission, I'll fight. Every second of every day, I will try to get away from you. I don't care if you lock me in another cellar or the trunk of a car or whatever else the hell you have planned for me."

The fire overtook her then, countering the cold. Bolstering her strength and chasing back the doubt clawing for attention.

She clamped her jaw to control the tremors rolling through her. "I give you my word—I will make your life a living hell. You think you have enemies now? You have no idea what I will do to you if you lay another hand on Daniel or me."

Shock smoothed Metias's expression into something unreadable and foreign. It was only with a slight crack of his smile that she realized she'd gotten through to him.

She should've known by now that smile warned of pain.

He brought his pistol up. The metal slammed into the side of her face and knocked her off balance. Throbbing agony ripped across her temple and scalp as she fell.

"Lena!" Daniel tried to catch her in his tiny arms as she hit the floor. He dug his fingers into her arm, trying to tug her over his lap, but he wasn't strong enough.

Her vision went black for a series of breaths. The loss exaggerated Metias's footsteps as he crouched beside her. Water squished—too loud—in her ears. Warm liquid slithered into her hairline. Blood.

"If you think three days in a cellar without food and water is the worst I can do to you, *mi amor*, you are sadly mistaken." He pinched the edges of her mouth in a strong grip, pulling her upper body off the floor as her eyesight cleared. "I told you before. Nobody walks away from me. As for Daniel, well… There's no reason for you to fight me if you have nothing to live for." Metias raised the gun and took aim. At her brother.

"No!" Elena latched onto her ex's gun arm and shoved him back as hard as she could. The gun exploded mere inches from its target. Daniel's scream drilled through her a split second before Metias slammed his forehead against hers. A wave of pain and dizziness rattled her from the neck down, but she only tightened her hold on the bastard's arm. "Daniel, run!"

Everything blurred as Metias slammed her into the nearest wall. Her head snapped back and made contact with the cement. The gun fell from his grip and hit the floor with a thud, out of reach. A strong hand wrapped around her neck and squeezed. He had her pinned there, her vision growing dark against the red emergency lighting. The alarm warbled in her ears. She couldn't breathe, couldn't think. Pressure from the air locked in her chest built just below his hand, and she scratched at his face with everything she had to get free.

"Get away from my sister!" Movement from behind Metias's shoulder claimed her attention right before Daniel swung something heavy into the back of the man's head.

The hold around her throat released as momentum thrust Metias to one side.

Elena gasped for a full breath. Her legs gave out, and she slid down the wall, desperate for oxygen. A hard thud registered as an eight-year-old hand slid into hers and pulled. She rolled forward onto her knees, trying to get her feet under her, but her body refused to obey her commands.

Metias locked on to her ankle and dragged her back. She was caught between the two of them as the building warned for everyone to get out. Rocketing her free foot back, she slammed her heel into the bastard's face. He let go, and she crawled out of reach.

This was it. This was the moment she left it all behind.

Her mistakes, her failures, the pain of abuse and hunger for something more.

It didn't fit into her life anymore, just as Metias no longer fit. In its place a brightness spread through her where self-punishment had reigned and taken control. A space where possibility and hope flooded through her. One where maybe her and Cash's differences didn't matter. Where they spent mornings curled up in bed, cuddling Bear close as the sun rose over the plateau through the window of his bedroom. She'd pretend to be annoyed at his sarcasm but secretly love it at the same time. He'd send Bear to the kennel and kiss her as though he were starving for her touch. They'd be there for each other when the bad days took over and protect one another from whatever came next. Because that was what two people in love were supposed to do. No games. No manipulation or lies. Pure support and understanding and partnership. It was everything she'd wanted in her marriage and everything she'd been denied by a dominating force she hadn't been strong enough to fight. Until now.

She was going to get out of here. She was going to find him.

Elena tightened her hold on her brother's hand and shoved to her feet. She wanted that life more than anything. The door was right there. She just needed to get to the other side, and they'd be free. She scooped Daniel into her arms, his legs locking around her waist.

A second shot exploded throughout the room.

Elena froze short of the door. She ran her hands the length of Daniel's small rib cage, checking him for wounds, but there was no blood.

Then the pain hit. It stole the air from her lungs and suctioned every thought from her brain.

She'd been checking the wrong body.

In an instant, the life she'd laid out ahead of herself vanished. Her hold on Daniel slipped, and he clutched on so tight she thought the medical examiner who performed her autopsy might see the hand-shaped bruises. He was dragging her down. She dropped to her knees as the tears burned, mixing with the sprinkler water across her face.

"I thought I made myself clear, *mi esposa*." Metias's voice sounded too close yet far away at the same time. "You're not walking away from me again."

"Get up, Lena." Daniel was standing in front of her now. Terrified and desperate with a sob contorting his small face. He pulled on her shirt twice. Three times. Each exposing his lack of strength and helplessness. And her heart broke for him. His life hadn't been nearly long enough. "Come on!"

"Go." Elena shoved at him, tried to put some distance between them as the gut-wrenching throb in her lower back intensified. To give him a chance of survival. But he wouldn't budge. Sweat built along the back of her neck as the reality of their situation set in. She was going to lose him again. No one was coming to save them this time. But she'd fight until her last breath to give him a chance. "It's okay. I'll be fine." She nodded for the door. "I'll find you. Go. Now."

She pried his grip from her shirt. It was going to be okay. One way or another. He'd never have to worry about Metias or the cartel again. Her hand shook as Daniel pulled free. He charged for the door. Pressure increased between her shoulder blades as her ex crossed the room toward her.

"He's never going to make it, Elena. You know that." Deep pain rippled down her back as Metias secured his hand around the tendons in her neck, but it didn't have the power over her he thought it did. "When I'm finished with you, I'm going to find him. I'm going to end your entire family for what you've done."

"That's going to be hard to do." Elena swallowed the pain flaring up her back and down one leg from the bullet still lodged deep in her flesh. She gripped the hammer Daniel had dropped, a leftover tool from the construction on the building, beneath her. "When you're dead."

She rolled onto her side, bringing the iron mallet in contact with the side of Metias's head. Right where he'd struck her with his weapon. He fell back with a groan and landed on top of her outstretched legs. She watched as Daniel wrenched the door open to escape, relief bursting through her chest at the sight.

Only to see him come to a stop as he took in the mountain of muscle and hostility waiting for him on the other side.

CASH GRABBED FOR the boy and hauled Daniel behind him.

The explosion had started a fire on the other side of the building. The flames had reached the hallway and were closing in fast. They didn't have long to get free of the building.

Cash launched at the son of a bitch trying to

get his bearings behind Elena. "Get Daniel out of here! Go!"

He blindsided Metias the moment the cartel lieutenant tried to bring his weapon around.

They collided into the wall on the other side of the room. Cash brought his elbow down into Metias's face while a solid fist to his side knocked the oxygen from his chest. Elena tried to get to all fours in his peripheral vision, but she wasn't making progress. He caught a right hook in the face, twisting him around, but he stopped the second from landing. He pinned Metias against the wall by the throat. "What did you do to her?"

"What I promised." A bloody smile split the lieutenant's mouth at one corner. "You think I would let her walk away from me to be with somebody else? Elena is mine, Mr. Meyers. Till death do us part."

"Do you think this is some kind of duel, you son of a bitch? That whoever is still standing at the end wins the damsel's heart? You're so hard up for attention, you have to threaten, abduct and abuse a woman and her eight-year-old brother to make yourself feel like a man? Well, the world I fight for doesn't work that way. Elena isn't yours. And she isn't mine. She's whoever the hell she wants to be, and neither of us get to say what that is. You're nothing but a dominating and manipulative piece of garbage who gets off on the misery of others." Cash rammed his forehead into the man's face. "And you don't deserve her."

Metias recovered quickly. His backhand connected with the laceration in Cash's temple. The lieutenant followed it up with a two-strike boxer combination. Cash fell back into a table shoved against one wall. Swiping his nose with the back of his hand, he gauged Metias's next move. His ribs protested the twist of his torso and reminded him he was no spring chicken in this fight. He shoved away from the table and hauled his knee into the lieutenant's gut. The cartel leader doubled over, and Cash took advantage. Metias hit the wet carpet, eyes closed against the onslaught of pain and sprinkler water from overhead.

A juvenile scream pierced Cash's eardrums.

He turned to catch a lick of flame crossing the threshold into the room. The sprinklers weren't enough to douse the flames. Daniel had backed himself into the opposite corner, his hands over his ears as he tucked into a ball. Cash lunged for Elena, who lay motionless on the floor. A dark stain spread across her low back. Hell. She'd been shot. Single bullet. No exit wound from what he could tell. "Elle, can you hear me? Come on. Wake up."

No answer.

He had mere minutes to get them out of here. Cash searched for something—anything—to staunch the flow of blood, but the room had been emptied long before he'd found Elena and Daniel inside.

Movement registered in his peripheral vision a split second before a fist jabbed into his ribs. Cash's

roar drowned out that of the flames as they flickered through the doorway. Undeniable pain lashed
through him. His face hit the floor, fingers biting
into the carpet.

A rumble shifted through the room. The building
would collapse in on itself at any moment. He had to
end this. Now. It was the only way to get Elena and
Daniel out of here alive. Cash buried the agony ripping him apart from the inside and shoved upright.
The lieutenant came at him again, his arm cocked
back.

Metias's knuckles skimmed his ear as Cash dodged
the attack. The lieutenant clamped a hand over the
bullet wound in Cash's shoulder. The world—the fire,
the sprinkler water, the sobs coming from the kid in
the corner, even the cartel leader lunging for the gun
on the floor—it all sped up as though this were some
kind of out-of-body experience. His heart thundered
behind his ears as he grabbed Metias's white suit
jacket and launched his fist into the bastard's face.
Once. Twice. A third time. "You think because you
have a minuscule amount of power that you get to
hold on to it forever?"

The man's head snapped back on his neck as blood
exploded from his nose and mouth. It took everything Cash had to hold the lieutenant upright.

"Cash." That voice. He knew that voice. It'd become part of him the past few days. It'd replaced
the inner critic screaming at him that he should've

been better, that he should've done better for Wade, that it'd been his fault Alpine Valley had suffered as much as it had. That voice had opened him up to the idea of allowing love and life back in and moving on from the mistakes he'd made in the past.

His vision blurred as he struggled to put Elena in his sights. Whether from the concussion from a day ago or losing too much blood, he didn't know. Metias hung, beaten and weak, in his grip, but right then it didn't matter. Dismantling *Sangre por Sangre* for the sins of his brother didn't matter. Punishing Metias for what he'd done didn't matter.

Elena. Daniel. Getting them free of the violence and trauma they'd suffered at the hands of entitled jerks. That was all he could do. He hadn't been able to save his brother, but he'd be damned if he let the cartel take them. Cash released his hold on the lieutenant and let the bastard hit the floor under his own weight.

"Do it." Metias rolled his head back and forth against the sopping industrial carpet. Blood leaked down his face and stained that once-pristine white suit jacket. "Finish it. If you don't, the people I work for… They will."

The gun was right there. All he had to do was pick it up and seal the lieutenant's fate. Secure Elena's and Daniel's and Alpine Valley's futures. One pull of the trigger. That was all it would take. But Cash wasn't that man, despite his fears that something waited inside of

him to claw free as it had spawned from his brother.
He didn't get to decide who lived and who died, who
he helped and who he punished. And he didn't want
that responsibility.

Metias slipped into unconsciousness.

Smoke burned Cash's nostrils. He turned to find
tendrils of flames traveling across the ceiling. "The
fire will do it for me."

He left Metias there to save himself, extending both
hands out for the eight-year-old who'd seen enough
nightmares to last him a lifetime. Daniel hesitated,
his gaze cutting to his sister and back. "Hi, buddy. I'm
Cash. I'm a friend of your sister's. Let's get you back
home. Okay?"

The small, rounded face with the same-shaped
nose and brown eyes as Elena nodded, then Daniel opened his arms to let Cash pick him up. It took
more energy than it should have to lift the kid into
his chest, but he wasn't going to let something as
minor as a bullet wound and a couple broken ribs
stop him from keeping his promise.

"All right. Let's get your sister." Fire trailed up the
walls and soon engulfed the entire corner Daniel had
huddled against. Cash bit back the moan working up
his throat as he crouched to pull Elena into his side.
She was conscious—barely—and able to shuffle one
foot in front of the other, but it would take all of them
working together to escape.

Flames lashed out from the partially finished

walls along the hallway. Cinder blocks hissed as Cash dragged them inch by inch down the corridor. But it wasn't enough. He wasn't enough.

His leg had gone numb. Nothing but a tingling where feeling should be. Blood soaked through the gauze Jocelyn had used to patch the hole in his shoulder. Soon he'd have nothing left but the oxygen in his lungs, and the fire would take care of that in time. His body would shut down until all he was capable of was losing the woman he loved. "We're going to make it."

Every muscle in his body screamed for relief. One more step. Then another. The fire was stretching across the floor, cutting off their escape. Black smoke built along the ceiling, and before he had a chance to warn either Elena or Daniel, they were surrounded. Blind. With no way out.

Coughs seized each of their lungs and seared the back of his throat. He was losing his grip on Daniel despite the lock the kid had around his neck.

"Cash." Elena struggled to stay upright on her own, but Cash wouldn't let go. He couldn't lose her. "It's too late. We'll be trapped. Go. Get Daniel out of here."

"There's no way in hell I'm leaving you." He hauled her into his side. His ribs took the brunt of the impact, but he didn't care. "No matter what happens, we do it together. Got it? You and me and Daniel."

She fisted her hand in his T-shirt.

Cash forced himself to take another step forward. The building groaned as the fire spread. Daniel's cries ricocheted through him. A growl clawed its way up his throat as they moved as one, but the flames were getting too close. "We're going to make it."

There was no other option. The hollowness that'd gutted him over the past year had finally started shrinking. Healing. Because of Elena, and he needed more time. They needed more time.

The alarm cut out. Pops and whistles of the fire closed in from every direction. And in the distance... Barking.

Cash wouldn't let himself latch on to the sound. Because if he did, if he lost his focus for a fraction of a second, Elena and Daniel would pay the price. The barking came again. Closer. Louder. Impossible. "Bear?"

His Rottweiler dove through the flames and landed a few feet in front of him. She hiked onto her back legs in excitement. A wrap of white bandages encircled her midsection, a guiding flag as the smoke thickened. She barked louder than ever before.

"Over here!" a female voice called.

A burst of frigid white clouds fought back the flames enough for him to identify Jocelyn Carville and Jones Driscoll in the corridor. Followed by Scarlett Beam and Granger Morais. The logistics coordinator left the others to continue work on clearing a path while she swung a portable oxygen tank complete with a mask from her back to her front. She closed the distance between them and set the mask over Daniel's mouth and nose. "We're here, Cash. Tell me what you need."

Chapter Fifteen

She wasn't very good at dying. Despite Metias's efforts.

Dim lighting eased through her eyelids. The rhythmic ping of the machine monitoring her heart rate and other stats had been set on low, and there was still an ache in her lower back.

"Welcome back to the land of the living." The voice Elena had feared that first time she'd woken up in this room flooded through her.

Only this time she didn't want to run.

Not that she could with a fresh bullet wound in one of her oblique muscles. She'd been lucky. Another inch to the left, and her ex-husband would've paralyzed or killed her as he'd intended. Her heart hurt at the idea. They'd been happy once, hadn't they? How had it ended like this in such a short amount of time? The questions would always be there. One thing she knew for certain was that no matter what she'd done differently, their story would've ended the same.

Elena tried to sit up higher, but an added weight

prevented her from adjusting. A headful of tussled brown hair tickled the inside skin of her arm, its pint-size owner passed out and tucked into her side. Her legs had gone to sleep from her brother's position over the top of them, but she didn't care. He was alive. He was safe. He was home. Because of Cash.

She swiped the painkiller-induced drowsiness from her eyes, caught off guard by a yawn. She'd let Daniel sleep awhile longer. After everything he'd been through, she didn't see a reason to rush him back to normal. They'd need time, recovery. Together. "Not sure I want to stick around. Getting shot hurts."

The world had gone on living, but so much had changed.

Cash's low laugh filled the room with a warmth she'd missed. His upper body was stiff with the sling supporting his left arm and shoulder. He leaned forward in the chair, pulling a package from behind him with his uninjured hand. Gift wrapped with a bow. "You might change your mind after you see what Bear got for you. She felt bad about before. Thought she could make it up to you."

Setting it on her lap, he took a seat on the edge of the bed, those compelling dark eyes sliding to Daniel to ensure he hadn't jostled her brother awake. It was the little considerations like that—awareness of the people and their needs around him—that she loved the most.

There was that word again. Love. She thought

she'd been in love once before. She'd been willing to follow it through countless lies, secrecy and abusive behavior. Only to end up running from it altogether.

This…felt different. Whole. As though she'd been missing a piece of herself all her life, and no matter how many times she'd tried to fill that hole, the puzzle pieces didn't fit. Until now. Because the missing piece wasn't escaping Metias, wasn't bringing her brother home or falling for Cash. It was learning to trust again. Having the courage to stand up for others. And forgiving those who'd wished her dead, including Deputy McCrae and her ex. All of it countered the pain and betrayal she'd suffered at the hands of others and gave her the greatest gift she could imagine. Love for herself. And for the man who'd charged into her life with a gun in one hand and an offer of survival in the other.

"Bear is an excellent gift wrapper." Elena pulled at the jute string expertly tied around the package and let the fabric fall away. Bright blue packaging peeked out from inside. "You brought me Oreos." Her stomach lurched at the memory of the last time she'd taken a bite out of one of Cash's cookies. "I'm not going to throw up after I eat them, right?"

"Depends on how many you eat in one sitting, but no." He grabbed for the package's tab and pulled as slowly as possible to keep the noise down. Daniel stirred but refused to wake. She knew that a bomb could go off in this room and the eight-year-old wouldn't notice. But she appreciated Cash's effort all the same. "They're not laced with dog medication, if that's what you're getting at. It's a brand-new package."

"Thank you." She pried a single cookie from the sleeve and took a bite, watching him do the same. Double-stuffed. Even better. The sugar hit her system almost instantly, but her stomach wasn't quite convinced it was safe. Well worth any nausea. "For everything. Daniel and I wouldn't be here if it weren't for you."

"From what I saw when I walked in that room, Metias was the one in trouble. I could see it in your eyes. You weren't going to let him push you around anymore," he said. "I was just there for support."

She raised her hand then, tentative and slow, as though approaching a wild animal. Tracing his bottom lip, she avoided the cut matching hers. There were others. At his temple, across his knuckles, along his handsome face. Every one of them had been earned from his choice to protect and fight for her. "Support looks good on you."

Her gaze drifted to the bullet wound in his shoulder, to the gauze taped beneath his shirt, and remembered what had led to him getting shot in the first place. Deputy McCrae's words were there, right at the front of her mind, and wouldn't let up. But she didn't want to lose this feeling. She didn't want to go back to being unable to trust him or wondering if he was hiding something from her. She'd had an entire marriage made of lies. She couldn't do that again.

"Ask me. You have the right to know." He'd read her mind again. She didn't have any explanation for it other than the fact that when two people survived what they had together, when they fought side by side for one another, they were exposed and vulnerable to that person. Cash slid off the edge of the bed, and those mere inches of distance between them stabbed through her. "Ask me."

"Is it true? What McCrae said at the station? Were you the one who was supposed to warn us the cartel was coming?" Her voice didn't sound like her own, but rather a puppeteer using her.

"Yes." He stared down at her, all heat and sorrow and stillness. "I was a forward observer in the Marine Corps. It was my job to see the threat coming before it struck. I studied patterns of attacks and consulted my commanding officers on how to respond or which targets to strategize around."

"And you do the same job for Socorro." It wasn't a question. McCrae had made it clear when he'd laid the cartel's sins at Cash's feet at the station. Though at the time, she hadn't put much stock in his words while he was holding a gun to her head. A tear escaped down her face without her intention, and she wiped it away with the back of her hand. "So what happened the night of the raid? Why didn't you warn us before *Sangre por Sangre* attacked?"

"Wade happened," he said.

That name—so simple and yet so heavy—pressurized air in her chest. The monitor to the side of her bed responded with an uptick of her heart rate for all to hear. Cash wasn't the type of operator to let his personal issues interfere with his work. He was one of the most focused and determined men she'd ever met. So if a dead man's history had somehow interfered with Cash's job, there was only one explanation as to why. Her voice broke. "You found him."

"Yeah." Cash lowered his voice, as though not quite able to wrap his head around his own words. "I found him."

"When you said his tattoo was how you and Bear identified him, you meant that night of the raid. You've been looking for him all this time." Elena grabbed his uninjured hand in both of hers. The wound in her back hollered for her attention, and she had to right herself to get it to stop.

Concern deepened the lines between his brows, and Cash dropped to his knees. He took her hand in his, letting her squeeze out her pain. "Take it easy. I'm here."

Her fingers brushed through Daniel's hair as she breathed through the upset in her back. She didn't know what she would've done had her brother not come home. Elena memorized the shape of his face, how his nose turned up at the end, and it was easy to imagine him asleep right there in her lap as something more permanent.

She knew what she would've done.

She wouldn't have ever stopped. The cartel would've had to kill her before she accepted defeat. She would've done whatever it took to hold him again. She'd broken into a cartel compound. She'd partnered with military contractors. She'd faced her worst nightmare. All for the chance of accomplishing what Cash had. And blaming him for letting his heart lead him that night instead of his head didn't feel right. "I'm so sorry."

"No. I am." He skimmed a calloused thumb under her eye and caught a wayward tear before it fell. "I should've told you the truth from the beginning, but I was scared if I did, you'd see me as someone just like the people we were fighting. That you wouldn't want me. I've spent years surrounded by a team I trust, but I'd never felt so alone as I did when Wade died. Then you came along. You're the most incredible woman I've ever met. You're stronger than I am, more courageous. You'll fight until your last breath for the people you love, and I wanted to be one of those people, Elena. Because I love you."

"How could I not want someone as inspiring and humane and hopeful as you are?" Her smile tugged at the laceration in her bottom lip. "If I'm any of those things you just said, it's because you were the one to show me how first. You're everything I've been missing, Cash. I love you, too."

He lunged from his kneeled position on the floor and crushed his mouth to hers. The impact pushed her deeper into the bed, but Elena found herself wanting him even closer. Bullet wounds be damned. She dragged him over the edge of the bed, and the monitor off to the side spiked with an erratic beat.

"What are you guys doing?" a small voice asked.

She broke the kiss, letting her breath come back to her. Heat flooded her face and neck. Her brother had just witnessed her making out with a man in the middle of a hospital room.

"Hey, buddy. Remember me?" Cash offered one hand in greeting. "I'm Cash."

FIRE AND RESCUE never recovered Metias's body from the compound.

Midday sun beat down on the back of his neck as Cash straightened. He chugged a mouthful of water as he took in the dozens of helping hands working to rebuild Alpine Valley.

It wasn't hard to imagine the cartel lieutenant had run with his tail between his legs. No purchases on his debit or credit cards. No cell usage or hits on any of the aliases Elena had catalogued over the course of her marriage to the son of a bitch. Even the Albuquerque house had been emptied. From what Cash knew of *Sangre por Sangre* upper management, Metias was living on borrowed time. What he'd done in the cartel's name was bad for business. And they wouldn't let that slide.

The DEA had rounded up a handful of soldiers and seized multiple shipments of drugs. The kids Metias had abducted and started training were left to social services, which was in the process of identifying and hunting down their families. Though some had been with the cartel for so long, they weren't quite sure where they belonged.

That was where Elena came in.

She searched missing person reports, local interviews and witness statements, and she administered and collected DNA tests from those kids the cartel had abandoned after the fire. She was doing everything in her power to ensure each of them made it back home to their families, and she hadn't stopped since the moment Doc Piel had cleared her to leave the medical suite. The woman was unlike anything he'd encountered, even in war-torn cities and towns overseas. She cared truly and deeply about every kid she was helping, and he loved her for it.

A loud bark sounded from the ground, and he caught sight of Bear directly under his position. She was signaling the approaching SUV as though she'd sensed them from a mile away. Which was entirely possible considering who was rolling up on the construction site.

Cash holstered the hammer in his work belt and made his way toward the ladder braced against the framing he and a few other locals had put together over the past couple of days. Fixing what the cartel had destroyed was slow but rewarding. Clearing the debris, replacing broken windows, sanding down and painting singed siding, patching bullet holes in the stucco—it all served to ease the weight he'd carried these past couple weeks. But it was rebuilding the family home that'd served as a refuge for Elena that bridged the grief between who he'd been and who he wanted to be for her.

The SUV pulled to a stop along the curb just as Cash's boots touched down on solid earth. Jocelyn and Maverick rounded the head of the vehicle. She brought her hand up to block the sun from her eyes. "It's looking good considering there was nothing here but a pile of ashes a week ago."

"It's coming along." He wiped his sweaty hands on a towel hanging off his belt. "She hasn't seen it yet. I was kind of hoping it'd be a surprise, but it's getting harder to keep her away every day. It's only a matter of time before she finds me out." Cash tried to read the logistics operator's motive for coming into town. "You here to bring me lunch or what?"

Maverick bolted straight for Bear, and the two started chasing each other around the worksite. Her ribs were on the mend, and if Metias hadn't shot the man responsible for kicking Cash's dog in the side, Cash would've returned the favor the first chance he'd gotten.

News of Deputy McCrae's actions had spread like wildfire, and the people of this town were ticked off. With reason. State police were now investigating McCrae's reach and misconduct while also vetting every other officer in the department. Some hadn't passed with flying colors, but there were no signs the chief of police had anything to do with what'd gone down. That left Alpine Valley more shorthanded than they'd already been, but sometimes the smallest forces made the biggest impact.

"I brought you something else." There was a heaviness to Jocelyn's voice he didn't like. Someone who baked cookies and hosted Christmas parties shouldn't sound like she did. She pulled a set of photos from a file folder she'd tucked under her arm. "Looks like Elena won't have to file those divorce papers after all."

Hell. Cash shuffled through the photos, each one more detailed than the last. Remnants of a white suit stood out in one. "Metias?"

"We found him about two miles east of Albuquerque. Took some doing," Jocelyn said. "They tried to hide their work, but a hitchhiker had seen the smoke and went to investigate for herself."

It was a common punishment among cartel families. A warning. The tire strung around the victim's neck would have been filled with an accelerant—most likely gasoline. Untraceable and cheap. Once the fire had been extinguished, there would've been little trace of the body or those responsible. "DNA?"

"They're working on it. Teeth were busted. They worked him over at least a couple hours before they put him out of his misery, but the ME is hoping there's something salvageable from bone marrow for a comparison and ID." Jocelyn's voice softened. "You want me to tell her?"

"No. I'm heading to meet up with her in a few minutes." Cash handed back the photos. He wouldn't need them. "I'll tell her. Thanks anyway. You coming to the service?"

"I'll be there." Jocelyn took a couple steps back. "Just got to run these by the police chief first."

He whistled to get Bear's attention, and both Maverick and she responded by returning to their handler's sides. In less than a minute, Jocelyn was behind the wheel of her SUV, pulling away from the curb. Cash scratched behind Bear's ear as he watched them go. "Let's go see Mama."

The Rottweiler's tail double-timed it at the mention of Elena's new nickname all the way to the truck. Cash tossed in his work belt, calling his goodbye over the bed to the men and women continuing work on the house. Pulling a flannel shirt from the back seat, he picked off clots of dog hair and threaded his arms into both sides. Not exactly appropriate attire for a funeral, but he wasn't a suit kind of guy. Never had been.

He hauled himself into the driver's seat. His shoulder pinched at the motion, but the more he put it to work, the better it felt. That was the thing about taking a bullet. You either came back stronger or you let it put you out of the game for good. And he wasn't finished.

Trees blurred through the side windows as he wound his way through town. He'd been all over the world during three tours in the Corps, but nowhere felt like Alpine Valley did. Like home. Cash pulled onto a single lane stretch of asphalt that was fenced off with overgrown trees and over two acres of headstones. And right there at the gate was the reason he had no interest in ever leaving this place.

Bear huffed to be let out of the truck the moment she saw Elena, and Cash understood that more than most. Just being near that woman was special. They both felt it. "Yeah, yeah. I'm moving. Hold your horses, dog."

He shoved out of the truck, nearly getting run over by Bear's insistence to reach Elena first. A wide smile transformed the woman's face as the Rottweiler bounded straight for her. Bear was practically climbing up Elena by the time he reached her, and Cash dragged the dog back. "Hey, no jumping." Every cell in his body was pulled in by hers, and Cash leaned in to show her exactly how much he'd missed her most of the day. "Hi."

"Hi. You must be working hard over there at the site." She leaned into her crutch, staring up at him as though he were the most important person in the world. And, hell, if he didn't want to be that for her. Her support system, her protector, her hero. Because she deserved it all. "I haven't seen you all day. How's the rebuild coming along?"

"Great. Moving faster than we expected, but it's hard to slow down with so many helping hands." Cash took her crutch for her, letting her use him any way she needed. The armrest tended to chafe with how much she was on her feet collecting information on the kids from the compound. If it was up to him, he'd be there with her all day. But kids who'd been taken from their homes, from their families, didn't trust men like him. Soldiers. Strangers. They only trusted Elena, and he didn't blame them a bit. "Jocelyn visited the site a little while ago. Wanted to let you know they found Metias."

"Oh?" she asked. "What hole he did crawl inside?"

"He didn't, Elena." Cash kept his hand on her elbow in case the news hit harder than he expected. "They found him. With a tire around his neck."

"The cartel killed him." She didn't let her emotions betray her. It was a habit she'd had to learn during her marriage to Metias, but he hoped, with time, she'd realize she didn't ever have to hide from him.

"I'm sorry." He didn't really know if that was true after what they'd been through.

"Me, too. But it's over now, isn't it? We don't have to spend the rest of our lives looking over our shoulders. Wondering if he'll come back." Elena's hand on his arm was grounding and exciting all at the same time. A single touch was all he needed, and everything outside the bubble they built around themselves didn't seem so important. "Are you ready for this? We don't have to go in. We can send everyone home, go back to Socorro, stay in the room and forget the world exists."

"I'm good." And he meant it. From the ashes of grief, loss, fear and betrayal, something new had been born inside of him. Becoming a private military contractor had given him a sense of purpose after Wade's death, but it was this new life he and Elena were in the process of building for themselves that kept him going. "I've been waiting for this day for a long time."

They walked through the cemetery's gates as one and headed for the small gathering of people waiting beside the casket. They all looked up at him as they approached and cleared a path to give him and Elena a front-row seat. Seven in total, including Elena's parents. The headstone had already been installed.

Wade Meyers. Beloved son, brother and friend.

The bishop of the local church greeted the attendees and asked if there was anyone who'd like to say something about the deceased, but Cash only had attention for the way Bear sat at the head of the gleaming wood of the casket. Her eyes had started watering as though she knew exactly who was inside that box. The rest of the Socorro team had noticed, too. There would be no military funeral. No seven-gun salute or hammering of pins into the wood. All eyes were on her, and no eulogy would meet the hurt Bear felt from losing her best friend. And it was enough.

"Rest in peace, brother." Cash unpocketed the medal he'd been given the day he and Wade had enlisted in the military. His father's. It was his brother's turn to hang on to it now. He set it on top of the wood and watched as the casket was lowered into the ground. Within minutes, the service was over. Condolences and handshakes passed in a blur, and soon, he and Elena and Bear were the only ones left at the grave site.

"Tell me what you're thinking," she said.

"I'm thinking it's time to go home and appreciate the life I have left. With you, Bear and your family." Cash took her hand in his and planted a kiss on her mouth. She tasted just as he remembered. Of hope. Of love. And a little bit of Oreo frosting. "What do you say?"

"I'll go home with you on one condition—" Elena

flashed a wide smile up at him "—Bear spends tonight in the kennel."

Cash wrapped his arms around her midback and kissed her again. "I think that can be arranged."

* * * * *

Don't miss the stories in this mini series!

NEW MEXICO GUARD DOGS

MILLS & BOON

A Stalker's Prey
K.D. Richards

MILLS & BOON

K.D. Richards is a native of the Washington, DC, area, who now lives outside Toronto with her husband and two sons. You can find her at kdrichardsbooks.com.

CAST OF CHARACTERS

Bria (Brianna) Baker—Actress, whose most famous role is Princess Kalvana.

Xavier Nichols—West operative.

Dane Malloy—Director of movie.

Mika Reynolds—Bria's agent.

Bennie (Bernard) Steele—Member of the paparazzi.

Rob (Robert) Gindry—Bria's old friend and costar.

Chapter One

Brianna Baker took a deep breath of crispy, New York morning air and picked up her pace along the Central Park path. There was probably another twenty-five to thirty minutes before dawn broke through the dark skies overhead and Bria wanted to be back at her Upper West Side townhouse before then. The morning air was invigorating and the forty-six-degree temperature was motivating, but the best thing about getting her morning jog in before the sun came up was that there was little chance that anyone would recognize her.

The brief snatches of time where she could be alone, unrecognized and just breathe and be herself, were what had kept her sane since her acting career had taken off and propelled her into celebrity status.

She wasn't complaining, at least not out loud. Acting had been her dream for as long as she could remember. And the fact that people, millions of people, thought she was good enough to spend their hard-earned dollars going to see her movies was thrilling and humbling in equal measure. But that fame had a price. The loss of her privacy for one. And lately, a nearly debilitating insecurity. The third movie in which she starred as Princess Kaleva, warrior princess, sent to Earth from an alien planet to retrieve the five elemental stones needed to save her people from certain death, had broken box office records in the US and overseas. She was officially an international superstar.

She was proud of the Princess Kaleva movies. They were showing little girls everywhere, especially little brown girls, that they were strong, powerful and smart and that they could be anything they wanted to be. But what she really wanted was to be taken seriously as an actress. But ever since she'd taken on the Princess Kaleva role, her agent had found it difficult to convince the Hollywood honchos that she could do the more serious roles.

Which was why she'd lobbied hard for the part of wife and mother, Elizabeth Stewart, in *Loss of Days*, a film about a family in crisis as a result of a child's drug addiction, when it had come up. It was a bonus that the majority of the filming, although on a tight six-week schedule, was going to be done in New York. In her heart, the city was still her hometown, even after fifteen years in California. It had taken some convincing and several auditions, but she'd won the part. And now she was weeks away from finishing the film she felt in her bones would prove to all of Hollywood that she could play serious, dramatic roles and not just be a busty superhero.

Princess Kaleva had pushed her into the ranks of celebrity, but *Loss of Days* was going to earn her the respect as an actress that she really coveted.

She picked up her pace. Although the sun had started to peek over the trees, the portion of the trail she was on remained deserted. She'd been jogging the same loop around the park since she'd come back to New York a little over a month ago to shoot the film. It totaled just over two miles and she wanted to make it the whole way before the park was packed with people.

She pushed through an uphill stretch of the path, her lungs burning. When she got to the top, she stopped, taking a moment to catch her breath.

Footsteps ricocheted off the trees behind her.

Bria glanced over her shoulder.

A figure jogged up the hill in her direction. From the size and gait, she pegged the person as male, but the shadows and a baseball cap pulled down low on the man's head obscured his face.

A bolt of unease shot through her. She began jogging again. She hadn't told anyone on her team about her morning jogs. Mika Reynolds, her agent, would have told her in no uncertain terms she was a fool for venturing out so early, and Eliot Sykes, her public relations manager, would have admonished her for jogging alone. But one thing she hadn't completely adapted to in terms of her recent celebrity was the complete and total lack of privacy that seemed to come along with it. And she wasn't sure she wanted to.

Bria shot another glance over her shoulder. The man was moving quickly, at more of a run than a jog, and with purpose.

She turned and began to sprint, less concerned with pacing herself than she was with getting to a more public space.

He's out for his morning run. He's not chasing you.

She tried convincing herself but survival instincts, honed over thirty-five years of being a woman in the world, pushed her forward.

She could hear the crunch of leaves indicating that the man was still behind her.

A level of fear she hadn't felt for a long time flooded her body, pushing her forward. She was still a bit of a distance from the entrance to the trail and she hadn't seen anyone other than the man behind her.

Without thinking, she plunged into the trees. Between the noise she was making crashing through the brush and the sound of her heart drumming in her chest, she couldn't tell if the man was still behind her.

She was probably overreacting. The man was most likely just another jogger out for a run, wondering why the weird lady had jumped into the woods.

But a voice inside her head screamed that that wasn't it at all.

She raced through the shadows, branches scraping against her arms and snagging her leggings. Darkness still clung to the dense woods, making her hasty decision seem ever more perilous.

She ran until her lungs threatened to burst, then crouched behind the thick trunk of a tree. She forced herself to listen past her own breathing for sounds that someone else was close.

She didn't hear anything she wouldn't have expected to hear in a thicket, but it was little comfort. If she stayed here and someone really was after her, had she just made it easier for them by darting into the trees? She had even less of a chance now of running into other people.

She couldn't stay cowering behind here forever. She pushed to her feet and plowed forward.

It seemed like it took forever, but finally, she saw the glow of streetlights.

Bria burst through trees, falling onto a walking path in front of a middle-aged man in a suit and carrying a briefcase. He started, freezing for a moment with wide eyes. She could only imagine what she looked like to him.

After a second, he rushed forward, concern plastered over his face for the wild woman who had literally just fallen at his feet. Thankfully, he didn't seem to recognize her. The last thing she needed was to have photos of herself online, leaves clinging to her leggings and twigs sticking out of her hair.

Bria assured the man that she was okay and didn't need an ambulance or the police.

He started away slowly, shooting a glance over his shoulder at her.

She attempted to smile, reassuringly only, but her eyes darted back into the darkness of the trees she'd just burst out of. She couldn't be sure, but it seemed as if the shadows shifted, taking the shape of a head and shoulders.

A car horn honked in the distance, tearing her gaze away from the trees for a moment. When she turned back, there was nothing to see but a solid wall of darkness.

Chapter Two

"I want to hire West Investigations, specifically Xavier Nichols, to provide for my personal protection while I'm here in New York." Brianna Baker sat on the other side of the conference room table at West Security and Investigations headquarters, the hem of her perfectly tailored skirt riding up high enough to reveal a silky smooth, caramel-colored thigh, sufficient to make a man's thoughts wander but not high enough to be tasteless.

Ryan West kept his gaze firmly fixed on her face. Not only was he a happily married husband and father, Ms. Baker was a potential high-profile client.

A potential high-profile client who was apparently familiar with Xavier Nichols, one of West Security and Investigations' best personal-protection operatives. A situation which was, in a word, interesting.

"May I ask who referred you to Xavier?" Ryan asked, not bothering to hide the note of curiosity in his voice.

Ms. Baker hesitated. "Let's just say his reputation precedes him."

It was all he could do to keep himself from laughing in her pretty face at that. If anything Xavier's reputation should have her running for the hills. He was good at what he did, protecting high-priority targets, but he had the people skills of a surly porcupine and communicated mostly in grunts and glances dark enough to turn lesser men to ash.

There was more to multi-award-winning actress Brianna Baker's story, a lot more if Ryan was reading her correctly. And his was a business that required him to be able to read people correctly. "Unfortunately, Xavier has just been placed on a new assignment. But, as I'm sure you are aware, West Investigations is the best in the business. I'm confident that another protection specialist can meet your needs."

"I'm sorry, but that won't work for me." She uncrossed her legs and reached for her handbag. "If Mr. Nichols isn't available, I'll have to find another way to solve my problem."

"One moment, please, Ms. Baker." Ryan held up a hand stopping her before she headed for the door.

She flashed a smile. "Please, call me Bria."

"Bria," he said with a nod. "Xavier happens to be in the office today. Why don't I call him in here and you can explain why you want to hire West Security and Investigations, and Xavier, specifically, to both of us."

She nodded, relief coursing across the delicate features of her face. "Yes, I think that would be a great place to start. Thank you, Mr. West."

"Ryan, please." He reached into his suit pocket for his phone, noticing as he did that some of the tension that she had been holding in her shoulders had faded away.

Brianna Baker was scared. And whatever it was she was afraid of, she believed Xavier was the man who could help her.

BRIA'S ALREADY RACING heart began to thunder once Ryan West declared that Xavier was on his way into the conference room. She was an actress, an award-winning actress no less, but right now, she couldn't find it in her to act as if seeing Xavier for the first time in fifteen years wasn't threatening to completely undo her.

She channeled her character from *Loss of Days*, Elizabeth Stewart, the matriarch of a rich, high-powered family. Elizabeth was always in control. She never let anyone close enough to read her thoughts or pick up on her emotions.

Be Elizabeth.

Bria took in a deep breath and let it out slowly as they waited for Xavier. She realized that Ryan West was studying her. She got the feeling he didn't miss much. That, she was sure, was what made him so good at his job.

She hadn't come to West Security and Investigations just because Xavier worked there, but if she was being honest, she would have at least checked out any private security firm he'd been employed by. Luckily, West was actually one of the best in the country. That was great because she needed the best.

Her stalker had gotten past every security measure she and her people had implemented to date, and if he really had been chasing her on her jog through Central Park earlier that morning that meant he'd followed her across the country as well. She was terrified of what he would do next.

So terrified that she was doing something she'd never thought she'd do. Turning to the man whose heart she'd broken and begging for his help.

Well, maybe not begging, but certainly asking for his help, which required her to swallow a heaping dose of humble pie. But it was worth it if West Investigations found her stalker and stopped the campaign of harassment he'd been on for the past six months.

And if she and Xavier rekindled something in the meantime…

No. Absolutely not. She wasn't there to rekindle anything. Despite the doubt that had crossed Ryan West's face, Xavier's reputation as a personal security specialist, a fancy name for bodyguard, was sterling. She wasn't embarrassed to admit she'd kept tabs on him over the years. He wasn't the kind of guy who had a social media presence, at least not one that she'd been able to find, and she'd deny it to anyone who asked, but she'd tried on more than one occasion.

But she knew he'd gone into the military after she'd broken up with him, become a decorated soldier in the army, then stepped into the private sector working as private security at West Investigations. He'd provided New York-area event security for several actors and actresses she knew. It had been easy to wheedle information about him from there. Actors were notorious for gossiping. And the actresses she knew that he'd worked for previously were more than happy to dish on the tall, dark and handsome bodyguard, even if he was more than a little surly. The surliness only made him sexier.

To that she could attest firsthand.

The conference room door opened behind her and she felt her entire body tense.

Ryan West stood, but Bria remained seated. She wasn't sure she could stand if she'd tried. Her back was to the door, but she could feel Xavier behind her. It had been like that since the first moment they met. Like they were on a special frequency, just the two of them. Whenever they were in proximity of each other, the air pulsated.

Xavier had yet to speak.

"Xavier Nichols, I'd like you to meet Brianna Baker."

Bria turned the chair and stood, facing her first

love, hell, the only man she'd ever been in love with, for the first time in fifteen years.

Fear, excitement and desire raced through her.

He'd changed over the years. He'd always been tall and lean, but now he filled out the dark jeans and long-sleeved gray T-shirt he wore. His shoulders were broad, his arms more muscled. His hair was still cut short, but the touch of gray just beginning to crop up around his temples gave him a slightly distinguished air. But the eyes, they were the same. Dark brown, just like his skin, that looked at her as if they could see straight into her soul. Eyes she used to love getting lost in.

Eyes that were gazing back at her now with open surprise and something else she couldn't put a name to.

"Bria." The sound of her name in his dark baritone swept over her like a warm ocean breeze at sunset.

She closed her eyes for a moment, remembering the last time he'd said her name like that. They'd been wrapped around each other in a dump of a rental house they'd gotten with a couple of friends in Atlantic City.

"Brianna." He said her full name this time and she opened her eyes, plunged back into reality. "What... what are you doing here?"

"Xavier, I need your help."

Chapter Three

Xavier stared at the vision in front of him. It took a lot to surprise him. He was a Bronx native, an '80s child who'd bounced from relative to relative and had seen his fair share of messed-up crap while doing it. And then he'd enlisted in the army, which had resulted in a whole new visage of nightmarish events.

But walking into West's conference room and seeing Brianna Baker, in the flesh, not just on a movie poster or in a commercial for whatever new film she was in, shocked him to his core.

He couldn't count the number of times he'd imagined, dreamed of what it would be like to see Bria in real life again. He'd played the meeting in his head thousands of times over the years, but none of those fantasies had prepared him for the moment he found himself looking into her beautiful brown eyes.

"What are you doing here?" He repeated the question. His brain was struggling to do anything other than drink in the woman standing in front of him.

She was gorgeous, even more so than she'd been

when they were twenty. The barest hint of makeup accentuated her warm golden-brown complexion and high cheekbones. Long, beachy waves cascaded over her shoulders. And her figure, a perfect hourglass. High, firm breasts and shapely hips that he longed to pull tightly against his body. Legs that went on for days, ending in the sexiest strappy black heels he'd ever seen. His mind instantly went to a vision of her wearing those heels and nothing else before he shook it loose.

"I need your help." Bria bit her lip, cutting into his fantasy. "West Security and Investigations' help."

He tensed and took a step forward, reaching out for her before letting his hand drop back down to his side. Damn. After all these years, he still wanted to wrap himself around her and protect her from every bad thing in this world. But he didn't have that right. Not anymore. So he went the more professional route. "What's wrong?"

"I have a stalker."

"Why don't we all have a seat and you can give us the details," Ryan said.

Xavier cut his gaze toward Ryan, only then remembering that his boss was in the room.

Bria had always had that effect on him. There was no one but her when she was near.

Bria sat back down, crossing her long legs.

His brain cycled to a memory that had him kissing up the length of those legs.

"Xavier." Ryan's voice pulled him back to the present. Ryan watched him through narrowed eyes.

It would have probably been more appropriate to move to the opposite side of the table and sit next to Ryan, but he slid into the chair next to Bria instead.

Ryan picked up his pen and held it at the ready. Every operative had their own style, but Xavier knew that Ryan felt taking notes by hand was less distracting for their clients during initial interviews. "So Bria, please, tell us how West Security and Investigations can help you."

"As I said, I have a stalker, which given my profession, isn't surprising. However, the stalker's outreach has…intensified over the last week."

Xavier's chest tightened. "Intensified how?"

Fear flashed across Bria's face for a brief moment before it was gone, replaced by what looked to him like rehearsed calm. "He, I say *he* because most stalkers are male, but I don't actually know if it's a man or woman, sent me flowers at my house." She paused for a moment, almost as if she needed to fortify herself before speaking the next words. "I get flowers from fans sometimes, so that's not the issue. It's that the roses were black. And withered. Dead. And the card that was with it was not like the usual fan mail. It scared me." A tiny shudder moved through her body.

Again, he fought the urge to reach out and pull her against his body.

"We'll need to see the note."

She pulled the compact rectangle of a bag hanging from her shoulder onto her lap and extracted a small card.

YOU ARE MINE. AND I'LL BE COMING
TO TAKE WHAT'S MINE VERY SOON.

He handed the card across the conference room table to Ryan, looking up at Bria as he did.

She was trying to look calm, unruffled, but she'd never been able to keep anything from him. He could see the fear in her eyes and it ignited fury inside of him.

And terror. Because, even after fifteen years, if anything was to happen to her, he didn't think he could go on. His heart thudded in his chest.

"Do you have any idea who could be behind this?" he asked.

Bria shook her head. "No. Like I said, I get lots of questionable fan mail. The flowers were delivered to the set and a PA, a production assistant, signed for them and brought them to me. The PA didn't pay attention to the delivery person, and there was nothing with the flowers that indicated what florist they'd come from."

Ryan scribbled something on the notepad in front of him. "We're going to keep this note if you don't mind. Run a few tests on it. They'll probably turn up nothing useful, but you never know."

Bria nodded her assent.

"You said the flowers and this most recent note were a ramping up on the part of the stalker." Xavier rolled his chair a fraction of an inch closer to Bria. He might not be able to touch her, but he was damn sure going to stick close. "When did the stalker first get in touch with you?"

"It started with weird emails about six months ago, as far as we can tell."

"Who is *we*?" Xavier asked.

"I don't actually read my own fan mail, and it became too much after the first Princess Kaleva movie for my assistant to handle along with her other duties. Now I use a public relations firm. They read any fan mail I get and respond appropriately. Most threats are logged and never make it to my attention, but if the threat is deemed credible, I'm notified, as are the police and anyone else who may need to know."

"We'll need the name of the PR firm and whoever handles your fan mail there, as well as your assistant's name and contact information."

"That's not a problem. The PR firm is Eliot Sykes Public Relations. My assistant's name is Karen Gibbs. She stayed in Los Angeles because her mother is ill and she can't be away for six weeks, but I'll let her know she should cooperate and get you whatever you need."

"Thanks," Ryan said. "Now, can you tell us more about these emails?"

"They're anonymous, so it's hard to say for sure

that the emails and the flowers are from the same guy. The emails were weird at first but mostly harmless, so my PR team didn't even tell me about them initially."

"Weird how?" Xavier pressed.

A flash of something, hesitation maybe, went across Bria's face before disappearing just as fast. She pulled an envelope out of her purse and handed it to him.

He read each email before passing the printout across the conference table to Ryan. There were over a dozen of them. The first few were all some sort of variation on the same. "Your movies mean everything to me." "We belong together." "I'm your biggest fan." "No one loves you more than me." Pretty typical fan mail. But then the messages progressed to the more personal. Asking Bria out to dinner. To marry him. To have his child.

Hell no. The words screamed through his head. Even though he hadn't said them out loud he hadn't been able to beat back the growl that rumbled in his chest.

He focused on the emails again. Their tone grew even more possessive. "You are mine" and "We belong together" being the most popular themes, it seemed. Then the messages changed, but were somehow even creepier. "I'll keep your secret." "Don't worry. I'll never tell." "Your secret is safe with me, my love."

Not a threat, at least not implicitly, but they made his skin crawl just the same.

He looked up at Bria. "What secret?"

"I have no idea." Bria's gaze slipped away from him.

"This person clearly believes he knows something about you," Ryan said. "Can you think of anything he could be referring to?"

"You have to understand. This person might not even really be thinking about me as me. Lots of fans conflate the character an actor plays on screen with the actor themselves. This secret might be the secret of some character I played who knows how long ago."

Maybe, but Xavier didn't think that was it, and from the look on Ryan's face, he wasn't buying it either. There was something Bria wasn't telling them. But they could circle back to it later.

"The note with the flowers and the emails use slightly different language at times. The note doesn't mention your secret, whatever that may be, and it's an explicit expression of ownership and domination."

"I noticed that, but all the notes came from the same email address, so they must be from the same person. As for the flowers, it's too much for me to contemplate that there are two people out there stalking me at the same time."

It wasn't out of the realm of possibility, given the level of her fame, but there was no need to worry her with that thought at the moment.

"Have you spoken to the LAPD?" Ryan inquired.

Bria's face twisted into a frown. "Yes. They took a report but said there was nothing they could do. No laws have been broken and they didn't think the emails or notes were a direct threat. They suggested I hire private security if I was concerned."

Ryan's brows arched. "There are several excellent private security firms in Los Angeles. Why did you wait until you got to New York to seek private protection?"

A good question and one that Xavier should have thought of the moment she'd started explaining her problem. Bria should have had personal security the minute the tone of the emails had shifted.

He caught her glance in his direction before she focused all her attention back on Ryan.

"I was hesitant to take that step. I didn't want some creep forcing me to change how I live. Until this morning."

Xavier's heart rate ticked up as her voice trailed off. "What happened this morning?"

"I think someone chased me while I was on my morning run in Central Park."

"Why the hell were you running through Central Park when you have a stalker?" Xavier exploded.

Ryan cut him a hard look, but Bria spoke before Ryan could admonish him.

"Because it's how I clear my head," she shot at him angrily. "I won't be held a prisoner. You should know that up front. If West Investigations can't provide protection while letting me maintain my shooting schedule and some semblance of a normal life, I'll find a security firm that can."

Before he had a chance to tell her just that, Ryan held up both hands. "Hang on, both of you. Why don't you tell us about what happened in the park and we can go from there."

Bria explained that she liked to jog in the early morning to clear her head and because there were fewer people out to recognize her. She was out running on one of the paths in Central Park that morning when she'd felt a man coming up quickly behind her. She'd gotten scared enough of the man to cut through trees. She was pretty sure he'd followed her into the woods, but it had been too dark to see his face or any distinguishing features.

Xavier bit his tongue against the urge to admonish her for dodging through the trees. She'd increased her risk, darting into a secluded area. It was one thing to care more about her career than she did about him, but he couldn't believe she'd been so cavalier about her safety. Traipsing around New York alone and unprotected in the wee hours of the morning was just reckless.

"So you aren't absolutely sure you were being chased?" Ryan pressed.

Bria bit her bottom lip. "I'm not 100 percent positive but—"

Ryan held up a hand again. "I'm not doubting you. You did the right thing getting away from someone you thought could be a threat."

Bria's shoulders relaxed.

Unfortunately, every muscle in Xavier's body remained tense. "What about your agent and the producers of your movie? What's their take?"

Bria turned her gaze to him. "Be diligent. Watchful, but they aren't worried."

"But you are worried." Xavier stated the obvious.

"Look, I've been in this industry for over a decade. I've had my fair share of racist fan letters, creepy fan letters and even outright threatening fan letters. This feels different. And frankly, I'm more exposed here in New York, working on location instead of on a studio lot with tons of studio-provided security."

"So you would be paying out of pocket for your security?" Ryan asked.

Xavier shot a glare across the table at his boss. Money? That's what Ryan was thinking about? Who would foot the bill? Well, maybe that was his responsibility as the president of West Security and Investigations, but Xavier didn't care what it cost. Bria was going to have the full weight and protection of West Investigations protecting her 24/7 until they'd caught this sicko stalker, even if he had to pay for it himself. Something he wouldn't have had a hope in Hades of doing when he'd walked away from her fifteen years ago, but now it wouldn't be a problem.

He'd done well for himself working in private over-seas security after getting out of the army and currently with West Security and Investigations. Not only could he protect Bria now, he could provide for her in the way that he'd only dreamed of when they'd been a couple. The way she deserved.

Bria's back straightened. "Money isn't an issue. A simple Google search will return estimates of my net worth and I assure you even the highest number is an underestimate."

Ryan held up his hands. "I didn't mean to imply you couldn't pay our fee. I only wanted to get a sense of whether we'd be working within the parameters set by a studio or the producers of your movie."

Bria let out a long slow breath. "I'm sorry for jumping to conclusions. No. No, if West Investigations decides it can take me on as a client, you will be working directly for me." Bria cut a glance in Xavier's direction.

"Consider us hired. As of right now," Xavier growled.

Ryan frowned. "Ms. Baker has requested that you be in charge of her protective detail and I explained that you'd recently been assigned to another protective detail, so that might not be possible, but—"

"It's not only possible, it's done. I'll get Jack to take over my current assignments."

"Xavier." Ryan's voice came low and authoritative.

Xavier met his boss's gaze straight on. He respected Ryan West, and considered him and Ryan's brother Shawn among the few people he'd categorize as friends. But this was Bria. There was nothing he wouldn't do when it came to her safety. If he had to, he'd go it alone, quit his job, take on Bria's protection on his own. He still had a few contacts in the world of foreign private security and mercenaries. He'd pay them whatever it took to establish his own team, but frankly, he knew it wouldn't be the same as having West Investigations on Bria's side.

After what seemed like hours, Ryan gave a faint nod and Xavier started breathing again.

Good. West was the best chance they had of finding Bria's stalker and stopping him before Bria got hurt.

The mere thought of her being hurt had his gut twisting into little knots.

"Well, Ms. Baker, it looks like Xavier is available to head up your protection detail," Ryan said.

Bria exhaled audibly. "There is one other thing. The press hasn't picked up the fact that I've got a stalker. So far. I'd like to keep it that way for as long as possible."

"West Security and Investigations always protects its clients' confidentiality," Xavier responded.

A small smile of relief turned up the corners of her mouth.

An instant yearning to send that smile blooming wider speared him. He shoved it away. She'd made it more than clear fifteen years ago that nothing was more important to her than her career, including him, and he doubted that had changed. She'd come to him for his professional services and that was all.

He'd find the sicko stalking her and neutralize him and then they'd both go back to living their separate lives.

Just like she wanted.

Chapter Four

Ryan had his assistant go over the contract with Bria while he settled Xavier into his office.

"Okay, we don't have a lot of time, so give me the CliffsNotes version."

"We used to date when we were kids. She ended it. The end."

"She ended it."

"I'm over it."

Ryan's brows arched. "I can see that," he said sarcastically.

Xavier frowned. "I'll be fine. Bria's in trouble and I can help her in a professional capacity, so I will."

"And if your prior personal relationship gets in the way, you'll let me know, right?"

Xavier glared. "It won't."

"If it does…" Ryan pushed back.

Xavier nodded, then turned on his heel and went to find Bria. She'd just finished signing the documents that officially made her a client of West Investigations.

"I need to get to the set," she said when Xavier reentered the conference room.

"Your protection detail starts now. I'll take you." He led her from the room to the secure garage where West parked its small fleet of cars.

If he'd had his way, Xavier would have taken Bria to a safe house and squirreled her away until he came up with a comprehensive plan for her safety. Actually, he wouldn't have minded keeping her hidden until they caught the creep stalking her. But Bria had put the kibosh on any thoughts of a private refuge, temporary or otherwise, while her movie was shooting. So instead of heading for a safe house, he was driving her to the building where the movie was filming most of its interior scenes.

"Princess Kaleva made me a celebrity but *Loss of Days* is going to put me on the map as a serious actress," she explained on the drive to the set.

He made a right onto 42nd Street and drove past Bryant Park.

He shot a glance across the car, but Bria was focused on her phone and didn't seem to have noticed where they were.

They'd been all of nineteen years old when they met in this very park. He'd been heading home from his job as a stock hand at a grocery store in Midtown that no longer existed. Back then, he lived in a tiny studio apartment with a roommate, supplementing his income and picking up whatever side hustles he could to make ends meet. It was a hard life but he had never known anything else.

Cutting through the park, he'd seen Bria sitting on a bench, reading.

She was luminous. He stared at her for far longer than he should have before sliding onto the bench next to her.

She didn't spare him so much as a glance. He finally gathered his courage and asked her how she liked the book.

"It's a play. And I'm in it," she answered, with a smile that made his knees go weak.

"You're an actress."

"Well, I want to be. Someday," she'd responded boldly. "Right now I'm a student at the New York Acting Conservatory downtown." She looked at him expectantly.

He didn't have a clue about the New York Conservatory or any type of school, to be honest. Higher education had been so far out of reach for him he'd never given it a thought. "Sounds fancy."

"Well, it's not Juilliard, but it's a great school and I was lucky to be accepted." There was that brilliant smile again. "My name is Brianna, but you can call me Bria."

He took the hand she extended, and from that moment on, he was a goner. They'd sat on that bench talking, well, she talked and he listened, for another hour. And then he spent the last forty dollars he had to his name, buying her an early dinner at a local café.

They were together for a year. The best year of his life. Bria was kind and outgoing and he was gruff and spoke only when it was necessary, but somehow, they fit. What he felt for her, what they had together was deep, passionate. He'd never known anyone like her before. Never loved anyone like her before.

He'd realized early on that being with her made him want to be a better man. Her ambition had stoked his own, although he hadn't been sure what to do with it. Bria had opened his eyes to the difference between a job and a career that he loved. She made him think about things he'd never contemplated before. About right and wrong. About how to be a good person, a better person. About his future. He hadn't been sure about what he wanted to do for the rest of his life, but he knew he wanted Bria at his side and she deserved more than he'd ever be able to give her on a stock hand's salary.

Then one day, without warning, she'd ended it.

They'd met for lunch at a dingy café not far from her campus, which sold lackluster sandwiches at student-friendly prices. Bria was unusually quiet while they ate and the anxiety encircling her had knotted his stomach until he couldn't take it anymore.

"What is it? I can see something is bothering you," he'd said.

She dragged her gaze from her half-eaten sandwich to his face. "I think we should break up."

The words felt like a sucker punch to his jaw. "Why?"

"I got a part in a pilot. It films in LA. I have to be there right after graduation."

"That's great. But that's no reason to break up."

She reached across the table and grasped his hand. "Xavier, I love you. I do, but this pilot could be my big shot. I need to focus on my career. And your life is here in New York."

He squeezed her hand and pulled her forward so their foreheads met across the table. "If you love me, let's try to make this work. We can do the long-distance thing, and maybe once I've saved a little bit of money, I can move to the West Coast."

Bria closed her eyes. He watched a single tear drop trail down her cheek.

For a moment, he thought she'd agree. That he'd convinced her that their love was strong enough to overcome whatever hurdles life and her career might throw at them.

She stuttered out a breath and pulled away from him. "I'm sorry. I think this is for the best."

Emotions roiled through him, but his pride wouldn't let him beg. He'd stood, taken one last, long look at the woman he loved more than life itself, and walked out of the café.

Three weeks later, he heard that she'd moved to Los Angeles.

FINDING STREET PARKING was out of the question in Midtown, which forced him to park in a garage a block from the film site. He was vigilant in looking for potential threats as he led Bria to the vacant building that the production crew had rented to film the movie. The guard at the door took one look at Bria and waved them both through, much to Xavier's dismay. Lax security. They got a couple of curious glances as they navigated the labyrinth of the people and equipment, but no one questioned his presence.

Finally, Bria stopped in front of a door. "This is my private dressing room."

She reached for the knob and he quickly stepped in front of her.

"Let me go first." He opened the door, noting that it had not been locked. Not that the lock would be much deterrent anyway. A credit card and a good shove would overcome its resistance. The room was small. He could see at a glance there was no one inside.

Bria swept past him into the room.

"The security in this place sucks," he said, turning the flimsy latch. "I want to get you a better lock for this door and I want you to keep it secured. When you're inside and when you're not here."

She gave a brisk nod. "Okay." She turned back to her phone.

He got it. This was awkward. Things between them had not ended on a good note. But as long as she was willing to abide by his rules, they'd get along just fine.

Her dressing room was on a corner on the ground floor, a perk he assumed for the star of the movie. It had windows set high and running along two of the four walls. He tested the latches on the windows and determined they too were a joke. One good yank would be all it took for someone to force one open from the outside.

"The locks on these windows are no good either."

"I know. That's why you're here," Bria said, scrolling through her phone.

"I only saw a couple of security cameras, which isn't nearly enough for a space this large. And flimsy locks on the doors and windows."

Bria shot him an incredulous look. "We have security guards. I don't think it's that bad."

One of Xavier's brows arched. "You don't. I just walked right in, and despite no one knowing the first thing about who I am or what I'm doing here, I wasn't stopped."

Bria shot him a withering look. "You were with me."

His other brow went up. "And? Every single person in here should be wearing a badge identifying them as a member of the cast or crew. If they're here on an authorized visit, they should have a badge that says so. Security cameras should be recording 24/7, at the very least in the public spaces and at the entry and exit doors. I should call Ryan. Have him get our expert out here to work up a full security system." He grabbed his phone from his back pocket.

A laugh burst from Bria. "You're kidding, right? I mean, this building is almost a hundred years old. There's no way the owners are going to let you drill holes in the walls and run the kind of wires you'd need for something like that."

A low rumble tripped from his lips.

Bria smiled wryly. "I see your communication skills haven't improved over the years. Look." She set her phone next to her purse on the vanity and crossed to him.

She stopped close enough that he could smell whatever exotic fragrance she was wearing. Her scent had every cell in his body standing on alert.

"I don't want to tell you how to do your job, but you're not going to be able to approach this the way you usually do," she said, looking up at him with her gorgeous brown eyes.

He frowned. "If we did this how I want to, you'd be safely ensconced in the safe house while I tracked down this scumbag."

"And I've explained why that won't work for me." She threw her arms out to the side. "Don't you get it? This is it. This is my shot. No more wearing a skintight superhero uniform in movies that are more about my physical assets than my acting chops. This movie is great, and I'm damn great in it. Once the acting world sees that, I'll finally be taken seriously as an actress."

He closed the space between them and curled his hands around her shoulders. "Bria, there is no doubt in my mind that you are brilliant every time you step in front of a camera. You always have been. You have a gift. But it can't come at the cost of your safety."

His gaze was locked on hers. Heat crackled in the space between them. He wanted to kiss her so badly that it was a physical hurt. But he couldn't. Shouldn't. Getting involved now would cloud his judgment. He needed to be clearheaded, focused and—

All remaining thought fled when Bria went up on her toes and pressed her lips to his in a hot, rough kiss. A kiss that sent him hurtling through the past, and returning for a future with the woman in his arms.

Instinctively, he pulled her closer, deepening the kiss.

She made a little mewling sound that sent his manhood straining against the front of his slacks.

A knock sounded at the dressing room door.

Bria jerked back, her hand coming up to cover her kiss-swollen lips. She stared at him for a moment, desire still swimming in her eyes.

The knock came again. "Ms. Baker? Mr. Malloy would like to see everyone on set in five minutes."

Bria licked her lips and looked away. "Yes…o-okay. I'll be there in a moment." Footsteps faded away on the other side of the door. She turned back to him. "That can't happen again."

He was still breathing heavily and, he noted, she was as well. "Why not?" The question came out gruffer than he'd intended, but dammit, there was something still between them. He knew she felt it too. Why not explore it? See where it could lead.

"Because," she straightened to her full five-foot-eight height which was still a good six inches shorter than his six-two, "I'm here to work. I can't be sleeping with my bodyguard if I want people to take me seriously."

Her answer was frustrating in more ways than one, mostly because she was right. After all, he'd been thinking the same thing just moments earlier. But those moments in-between, when his lips were on hers and her body was pressed against his, had sent all rational thoughts fleeing. All rational thoughts but one.

"Why did you come to me?" He asked the question he'd wanted to ask from the moment he'd seen her sitting in the conference room. "Why did you come to West Investigations for your security?"

West was one of the best, sure, but there were other outfits that could have handled her stalker. Firms where he wasn't employed. But she'd sought him out specifically. If not because she still had feelings for him, then why?

"Because I trust you. Despite everything, you may

be the one person I trust most in this world. And I'm scared. You once told me you would never let anything happen to me. I'm hoping you really meant that."

He remembered that. They'd taken a day trip to Coney Island. He'd coaxed her onto the roller coaster, not realizing how afraid she'd be. She was shaking as the roller coaster car made its way up the inclined tracks.

"Don't worry," he'd said, wrapping his arms around her. "I'd never let anything happen to you. I promise."

Another, more insistent rap sounded on the door. "Ms. Baker? Please, to the set now!"

"Coming." She started past him.

He caught her arm. "I meant it then. I can back it up now. I won't let this stalker or anyone else hurt you."

Chapter Five

"Cut! That was great, Bria. Just great. I do want to try it one more time," Dane Malloy, the director of the film said.

Dane was a perfectionist. Usually that didn't bother Bria at all since she had more than a little perfectionist in her as well. But she was exhausted, physically and emotionally. Between her stalker, seeing Xavier again for the first time in years and doing the same scene now for nearly an hour, she just wanted to go home, slip into a warm bath and relax. But that was not to be.

They did the scene two more times before Dane was satisfied and let her go for the night. She walked back to her dressing room with Xavier so close on her heels that she could smell his spicy cologne. It sent a zip through her blood, cut through her exhaustion and almost, almost, had her catching a second wind.

She kicked off the four-inch heels she'd been wearing for the scene the moment she entered the trailer and reached around the back of her dress for the zipper.

After a minute of flailing, she finally gave up and turned to Xavier. "Could you help me, please?"

The smirk on his face was equal parts infuriating and sexy. "I was enjoying watching you, but yes, I will help you. Turn around."

She did as he said. There was nothing intrinsically sexual about what he was doing, but the moment his hands touched her body, she trembled with want. She recalled kissing him earlier and her heart raced.

His touch was featherlight and he lowered the zipper, slowly, much more slowly than was necessary.

She reveled in each simmering second.

After an electrifying, excruciating moment, Xavier's hands stopped moving. He stepped back.

Bria glanced over her shoulder. "Thank you."

Xavier's expression was unreadable. "You're welcome."

She headed for the small bathroom in the corner of the dressing room and quickly changed into her street clothes. After splashing water on her face, she looked at herself in the mirror. "Simmer down. He's here to protect you. Nothing more."

She looked at her reflection again. "Yeah, right."

There had definitely been something between them when they'd kissed. They'd never wanted for desire in their relationship. The overwhelming passion she felt for him was rivaled only by the passion she felt for acting. It's why she'd ultimately broken it off, because she couldn't see a way to sustain both, at least she hadn't thought she'd be able to do it when she was twenty years old.

The industry was hard and grueling. It took everything you had and then some to make it. And she'd wanted to make it. It wouldn't have been fair to Xavier to try to squeeze in a relationship with him between auditions and tapings. She'd done the right thing for both of them back then.

And now?

They were both successful adults. She could be choosy about her projects now. She could afford to take downtime between each film. Maybe they could make it work.

"Are you ready to go?" Xavier called through the bathroom door.

She shook the thought from her head and opened the door. "Ready to go." She slipped oversize sunglasses on even though it was far too dark for them already.

Xavier held her elbow gently and led her from her dressing room.

Between takes, she'd noticed him talking to Dane, several of the other actors, the set security, and one of the producers. She had no doubt they were discussing the lack of cameras and flimsy locks on the doors and windows.

She had no problem footing the bill for a few wireless cameras and latches but even celebrities had to budget. They'd have to discuss his plans later that evening.

The thought gave her pause. Her contract with West was for full-time security. But she wasn't comfortable with a stranger staying in her house. Xavier had been with her all day, but this was a job for him and he'd expect to have some time off. Another thing they needed to discuss.

It was late, but in New York, that just meant a change in uniform for the thousands of people still out and about. Instead of suits and conservative dresses with kitten heels, New Yorkers donned their going-out threads. Sparkly minidresses. Skinny jeans. Crop tops.

Bria kept her head down, hoping not to be recognized while Xavier deftly navigated them through the people.

They stopped at the corner of 42nd Street. It only took a moment for the walk light to begin flashing.

Bria stepped off the curb.

The roar of an engine cut through the normal roar of the city.

She froze. A dark sedan hurtled through the intersection, its grill pointed directly at her.

Almost as suddenly as the car appeared, her feet were off the ground and she was flying through the air. Because she still remembered every inch of his body, she instinctively knew that the brick wall that had slammed into her was Xavier.

He twisted himself so that when they landed he took most of the impact, hitting the pavement on his back and sliding for a fraction of an inch. Quickly, he locked his arms around her as he rolled them both to the far side of the street. Once again she found herself hurtling through the air, this time because Xavier had sprung to his feet, taking her with him and hauling her onto the sidewalk.

"Are you all right?" he asked, running his hands over her arms, his eyes roving over her body, looking for injuries.

Words escaped her and her mind struggled to catch up to everything that had happened.

Was she okay?

As if in answer, a sharp pain stabbed her in the side. Her knees buckled.

Xavier wrapped his arms around her waist, holding her up.

A young man darted up to them. "Oh, man, I saw the whole thing. That guy was crazy."

Xavier focused on the man. "Did you happen to get the license plate number?"

"No, man." The guy shook his head. "I'm sorry. It all happened so fast."

An older man hustled over. "Not so fast. That car was parked there for over an hour," he said with a smoker's rattle.

The younger man frowned at the older man, clearly

unhappy with being contradicted. "I don't know about that. I was just walking by."

Xavier's arm tightened around her. "Are you sure?" he asked the older man.

The man nodded. "I'm sure. I own this store." He jerked his head toward the bodega they were standing in front of. "I keep an eye on all the comings and goings around here."

"Did you get the license plate?" Xavier asked.

The man shrugged. "I don't keep that good an eye out. But I'll tell you one thing. That wasn't an accident."

Chapter Six

Xavier insisted on getting Bria off the public street, once he was sure she was unharmed.

"Maybe we should wait for the police," Bria said after they were back in his car and had pulled out of the garage.

"I'll take care of that when I know you're somewhere safe."

"You can take me to my house." Her hands still shook, but she was feeling somewhat steadier than she had in the moments immediately following the car's attempt to hit her and Xavier.

Xavier slanted her a look. "I need to take you somewhere safe."

"It is safe. No one knows I own a place in the city. I own it through a bunch of different LLCs. I even pay for a small suite at the Four Seasons when I'm in town to throw the tabloids off my scent. That's where the paparazzi think I'm staying while I do the movie."

Xavier still looked as if he was ready to argue.

"Please?"

He gave a grunt but said, "Where is this place?"

Bria gave him directions to her Upper West Side townhouse.

They drove in silence for several minutes before she could no longer hold back the questions. "The driver could have just been distracted, right? I mean, it might not have been intentional."

"That's possible," Xavier responded in a tone that made it clear he didn't believe the hit-and-run was an accident.

"But you don't think so."

He shot her a glance. "No, I don't. Even if the driver was distracted, there was time to swerve, but he didn't."

"But the stalker, he's been sending me notes, candies, flowers. Then chasing me this morning." Because she was sure now that she had been chased this morning. "And now to try to run me down. That's—" She paused, finding it difficult to get the next words out. "That's a serious escalation. Why would he want to do that now?"

Xavier shifted lanes, going around a slowing cab. "You've made several changes that could have induced the stalker to alter his methods. Leaving Los Angeles for New York, for instance. Hiring private security. The notes that you showed us from this guy are definitely creepy, but the most recent with the flowers was different. More aggressive than the others."

Bria shifted in the passenger seat so she was looking across the interior of the car at him. "More aggressive, how?"

"The 'you are mine' phrase was repeated, but the next line is even more aggressive. 'I'll be coming to take what's mine.' It sounds like there is some anger there. Anger, certainly possessiveness and a host of other things. The forensic psychologist that West Investigations uses may be able to help us there."

Her hands began to shake more violently.

Xavier must have noticed. He reached over and turned the heat on.

The blast of warm air was soothing and she was grateful for it.

Xavier eased the car to a stop at a red light.

"You know as well as anyone how much I've always wanted to be an actress. And yeah, I knew that there would be a downside to becoming a celebrity, but I'm honestly starting to wonder if it's worth it. I mean, how long am I going to have to look over my shoulder? Even if you find this guy, and there's no guarantee you will, there's always the potential that someone else will take his place."

A spark lit in his eyes. She'd always found his protectiveness sexy, and that hadn't changed. If anything she found it that much more seductive now. "And I'll always be there to protect you from whatever threat crops up. You have my word on that."

The light turned green and they began moving forward again.

Xavier navigated the busy evening traffic deftly, but it still took nearly a half hour to make it from the set to her townhouse on West 77th Street. She directed him to the garage at the end of the street. Like most New Yorkers, she didn't have her own car and therefore didn't need one.

He parked, then quickly led her to the townhouse.

Hers was the second unit from the corner, surrounded by a black ornate metal fence. Three stories with stairs that led to a large black door flanked by a series of narrow triple-paned windows on either side of the door. The front yard was small, but instead of paving over it as many of her neighbors had, she'd hired a gardener to maintain the small patch of grass and plant flowers in a miniscule flower bed. Although she owned a two-bedroom penthouse in Los Angeles, she considered the townhouse her true home.

"I'll want to take a look at your security system first thing," Xavier said while Bria worked the series of locks on the front door. She glanced at him, but his eyes were trained on the empty street, scanning it for the hint of a threat.

"Not a problem." Bria pushed the door open and led Xavier into the home's narrow foyer to a cacophony of beeps. She shut the front door behind them and engaged the locks before entering the six-digit code that neutralized the alarm and reengaged the security system. "It's a top-of-the-line system installed by Dustin Home Security Professionals. I spared no expense. I have a service that comes in to check on the house regularly. Since I'm away so much, it seemed prudent."

"Dustin systems are good. It's a brand that West Investigation recommends highly to our clients."

She kicked off her shoes and left her purse on the side table by the door. "Come on, let me show you around."

Xavier made a move to step in front of her. "Maybe I should clear the house first."

"Xavier," she said, unable to keep the exasperation out of her voice, "did you see what I had to go through to get in here? There's no one inside. Come on. You can clear the house as I show you around."

She'd purchased the house out of foreclosure six years ago with the check from the first Princess Kaleva movie. It had been a fixer-upper, but that was the only way she could afford a townhouse on the Upper West Side, even with a multimillion-dollar budget. She'd spent a year renovating, taking down walls wherever it was feasible and opening up the main floor as much as possible. Then she'd spent a small fortune on a designer who'd helped her give the space a clean, modern look while keeping a sense of hominess.

She led him into the living room, which flowed into the formal dining room before opening up to the eat-in kitchen and attached family room. Upstairs there were three bedrooms, one of which she used as a home office, and a bath in addition to the main bedroom and en suite bath. Back on the main floor she pointed to the door leading down to the basement.

"The basement is the only place I haven't gotten around to renovating yet. I want to put a full theater down there someday, but right now, it's unfinished. I keep the door locked."

Xavier tried the handle, but it didn't give.

"I told you. Locked." Bria headed toward the kitchen at the back of the house.

"It's a fairly open flow. You can almost see through the front windows from the kitchen here in the back," Xavier said. "The windows could be a problem. I want you to keep the curtains closed."

"They aren't typical windows. You can see out but you can't see in. I like my privacy."

"Still. Keep the curtains drawn at all times," Xavier said gruffly.

She blew out a sigh. "Sure. Want a glass of wine? I could use a glass of wine." She bent, reaching for the door to the wine cooler tucked under the island.

"I can't drink. I'm on the clock. Do you mind if I take a closer look upstairs and in the basement?"

"Sure, knock yourself out." She grabbed a bottle of white and straightened. "The key to the basement door is in the drawer in the side table in the foyer. I'm going to make mushroom risotto for dinner if that's okay with you."

Xavier's brow went up in surprise. "You cook?"

She laughed. "A lot has changed in the last fifteen years. I've learned. Eating out isn't as much fun with people asking for your autograph every few minutes."

"I can see how that would put a damper on dinner," he said, giving her a small smile of his own before heading upstairs.

Bria poured herself a large glass of wine, then got cooking. Risotto was fairly easy and quick to make, which was why she always kept the ingredients for it in both her homes. The food that was provided on movie sets could be hit or miss. They only had a few more weeks left of shooting and Dane seemed determined to make the most of them.

She could hear Xavier moving around, first in the basement, then on the second floor above her head while she prepared dinner.

It was surreal to have him in her house. Not that she'd never thought about it. A part of her had always hoped their paths might cross again one day. And that maybe their timing would be better. That some spark of what they'd felt for each other would still be there. At least she knew that part was true.

The spark was definitely still there, at least on her side, and she was pretty sure he felt it too. The circumstances were terrible, but she couldn't help hoping that maybe after they'd identified her stalker and neutralized him, they might find a way to start again.

Xavier came back downstairs just as she finished cooking the risotto.

"Perfect timing. I thought we could just eat at the island," Bria said, waving to the bar stools.

"That's fine, but before we do I want to give you this." He pulled a small device from his pocket. It looked like a key fob for a car but with a single button.

She frowned at the device. "What is that?"

"It's a panic button. I want you to keep it on you at all times. If for some reason we get separated, you can hit the button and it will send a signal to West's headquarters that can be followed."

She shot him a bemused look. "You're LoJacking me?"

"No." He tried to hide it, but she caught the slight upturn of his mouth. "It will only send a signal if you hit the button. If you push it by accident, you can hit it again twice, quickly, to turn off the signal. Totally in your control."

She took the device from him, her hand brushing along his. "I do like to be in control." The statement came out sultrier than she'd intended and she could see that Xavier had heard it that way as well.

His pupils were dilated and he looked at her with a fiery desire burning in his eyes.

She was on the verge of stepping forward and giving in to the kiss she wanted to press against his lips when he stepped back.

Disappointment flooded through her, but she pushed it away. "Let's eat."

She set the panic button on the counter and busied herself with piling risotto on two separate plates. She slid one in front of Xavier before placing the other in front of the empty stool and sitting down.

She hadn't realized how hungry she was until the earthy aroma of mushrooms and cheese hit her nostrils. She ate hungrily.

"This is good," Xavier said after a few bites.

"Don't sound so surprised," Bria teased back.

He smiled. "It's just that I don't remember you being that good of a cook."

She laughed. "Fair enough. Early on in my career, I did a straight-to-video movie where I played a chef. The movie was forgettable, as in so bad I hope anyone who saw it has already forgotten about it. But the production did hire a real chef to work with me so that I looked like I knew what I was doing. He taught me a few dishes and I found that I enjoyed cooking. It's relaxing."

"Seasoned with Love."

Bria felt her eyes widen with surprise. "You've seen it?"

"I've seen every movie you've been in," Xavier said quietly.

A surprising warmth flooded her at his words. "I doubt that. There were several early on that I wasn't even credited in."

"Every one," Xavier reiterated firmly, his eyes locked on her face.

She didn't know what to say to that. Did it mean something that he'd taken the time to watch all her work? Or was it just one old friend supporting another? And did it even matter?

Questions she wasn't sure she wanted to know the answers to. So instead of pursuing them, she changed the subject.

"Did you find everything you wanted? I mean, is my security up to your standards?"

"Your security system is pretty good. Better than pretty good actually, but there are a few upgrades I'd like to make."

"Whatever you think is best." Bria reached for her wineglass.

"I think it's best if you stay at one of West Investigations' safe houses."

She looked at him over the top of her glass. "Anything but that."

"Even if it compromises your safety?"

"I'm not just being obstinate," she said, setting her glass down on the countertop. "This is my home. It's one of the only places in the world right now where I can just be me. Bria. Not Princess Kaleva. Not Elizabeth Stewart or whatever other character I might be playing at the moment. It might be hard to understand—"

"I understand. I'm just…concerned."

He covered her hand with his.

A charge shot through her body. She wondered if he felt it too.

"Thank you for being concerned." Her voice was little more than a whisper.

Xavier pulled his hand back.

The loss of his touch felt as if she'd been thrown into a cold bath. She grabbed her empty plate and wineglass and carried them to the sink. "It's been a long day," she said, her back to him. "I'm going to head up to bed. Just leave the dishes. I'll take care of them in the morning."

She hurried toward the stairs without looking at him.

"Bria."

Xavier's voice stopped her before she got out of the kitchen.

She stopped without turning around. "Yes."

"I'm… Good night."

His words seemed weighted and she wondered if he was apologizing for more than just dodging a kiss. But that was a conversation she was in no shape for at the moment.

"Feel free to take whichever of the guest rooms suits you."

Bria hurried upstairs, shutting herself in her bedroom.

There was only one floor between them, but she wasn't sure the distance could ever be overcome.

Chapter Seven

Xavier was no cook, but he could do dishes with the best of them. He cleaned up the dishes from dinner and put away the leftover risotto. When he was done, he checked all the doors and windows in the house one more time. Bria's security was top-notch. He'd have expected nothing less from Dustin security systems, but he was taking no chances with her safety.

It was late, but he still put in a call to update Ryan on the situation with Bria. He'd spoken to one of the movie's producers and gotten the okay to have a security assessment done on the building as long as it didn't interfere with shooting. Ryan agreed to send someone to the set first thing the next morning to do the evaluation and change the locks on Bria's dressing room door and windows.

"How are the two of you getting along?" Ryan asked.

"We're fine. Just like I told you we would be."

Ryan's silence on the other end of the line spoke volumes.

"I need to get some shut-eye," Xavier finally said.

"Sure," Ryan responded. "Let me know when you need me to send relief. I know we argued for you to spend every moment with her."

"I'm not going to leave her until I know she's safe."

Ryan sighed. "I had a feeling you were going to say that."

They ended the call. He climbed the stairs to the second floor and paused outside Bria's bedroom. It was quiet and no light shone from under the door. She must have already gone to sleep.

He turned and crossed the hall, settling into the guest room directly across from Bria's room. He had an emergency go bag in the SUV, but he didn't want to leave Bria to get it. He slid the gun he'd had tucked into the waistband of his jeans under the pillow, shucked his boots and got into the bed, fully clothed.

An hour later he was still staring at the ceiling, wide-awake. The mattress was firmer than he liked, but that wasn't the reason he was finding it so hard to fall asleep. Every time he closed his eyes, he saw Bria step out into the street and the car bearing down on her. He could have lost her today. Lost her again, just hours after she'd walked back into his life.

He couldn't let that happen. He had to find the stalker and put him behind bars before he hurt Bria.

And then? Maybe he'd think about trying to convince Bria to give him a second chance. He'd been a fool at twenty, not to fight for her. Maybe they could have worked things out. But he'd let his pride get the best of him.

The irony of it was, some part of him had always believed they'd find their way back to each other. He'd tried telling himself that he was being a fool, pining for a movie star who had probably forgotten he existed, but the hope had never completely died out in his heart.

But now she'd come to him, needing his help.

A creak sounded in the hall.

His body went on high alert. He bolted upright on the bed and swung his feet to the floor. Grabbing his gun from under the pillow, he padded quickly to the door.

Pulling it open enough to peer through the crack, he found Bria standing in front of the door. He swung it open, taking in her purple-and-white-striped pajamas and the matching purple eye cover pushed to the top of her head.

"Bria? Are you all right?"

Lines burrowed into her forehead and worry shone in her eyes. "I just got a call from the night guard on the film set. Xavier, the stalker broke into my dressing room. He left another bouquet."

Xavier pulled the SUV to a stop in the alleyway at the rear entrance to the building. Logan DeLong, the head of set security and a former New York City police officer, was waiting for them. Logan was a white man in his midfifties, with thinning red hair and a beer gut. Logan was one of the movie crew that Xavier had spoken to while he'd waited for Bria to finish rehearsals earlier in the day. Logan had given him a feel for the number of staff usually on hand, the security measures, and generally, how the production operated on a day-to-day basis.

"I'm sorry for calling you so late, Ms. Baker, but I thought you'd want to know about the intrusion right away."

Bria reached out and squeezed the man's hand. "You did the right thing."

Xavier scanned the alley. "Let's take this discussion inside." He hustled the guard and Bria into the building. They made their way through a maze of hallways that formed the behind-the-scenes area until finally stopping in front of Bria's dressing room.

The door was open and the lights on. A bouquet of black roses sat at the center of the dressing table, an envelope with Bria's name spelled out in block letters sticking out of its center.

Bria wobbled when she saw the bouquet.

Xavier reached out a hand to steady her. "You okay? You don't have to be here for this."

She shook her arm free and pressed her hand against her forehead. "I'm fine."

Keeping one eye on Bria, Xavier turned to Logan.

"Take me step-by-step through how you found the flowers."

"Well, the cast had left for the night by eight, but a few of the crew hung around to finish some things. Everyone had cleared out by nine. I completed some paperwork and was doing a walk through the premises, like I always do, to make sure everything was locked up tight before the night guard comes on shift."

Xavier nodded.

"That's when I saw the light was on in Ms. Baker's dressing room," DeLong continued. "She doesn't usually leave them on, so I went to check it out. Then I saw the flowers. Most of the deliveries go through my office, but I would have remembered black roses. The whole thing seemed…off. That's why I called you, Ms. Baker."

"Did you touch anything in the room?" Xavier asked.

DeLong shook his head. "No, I didn't even go in."

"Okay. You two stay here." Xavier stepped into the dressing room. Grabbing a scarf that was lying on top of Bria's vanity, he took the envelope from the flowers and opened it.

There was a photo inside but no note this time. The photo was dark and grainy. Obviously, several years old, but it still clearly showed Bria and another man at what looked like a campsite or somewhere in the woods.

He brought the picture to Bria. "Do you recognize this photo?"

Bria's face went sheet white.

"Bria? Do you recognize it?"

"It's from a movie shoot," she whispered. "A long time ago."

"Who's the guy beside you?" Xavier pressed.

"He was my costar. Derek Longwell." She looked at him with an unfocused gaze.

"Do you think he could be the one stalking you?"

Xavier had kept the explanation for his presence vague when he'd spoken to the head of security earlier, but now DeLong's eyes went wide at the mention of a stalker. Xavier ignored him.

Bria looked as if she was barely breathing and he worried that she might pass out.

She shook her head, her gaze finally focusing in on him. "No, it can't be. Derek is dead."

Chapter Eight

Bria woke up to the smell of coffee and bacon the next morning. It took some effort to drag herself out of bed and into the bathroom, and the image she saw in the mirror reflected that. Dark circles rimmed her bloodshot eyes. The makeup people would have their work cut out for them today. She let the water in the shower heat to just shy of scalding, then let it pummel her awake. She dressed and headed downstairs, feeling only slightly more human than she had when she'd awakened.

Pausing at the doorway to the kitchen, she watched Xavier at the stove, dressed in the same tight black T-shirt and blue jeans he'd worn the day before.

Her stomach did a flip-flop. Why was a man in the kitchen always such a turn-on?

Xavier shifted to look at her, his eyes skimming over her from head to toe. He hadn't changed so much that she couldn't read the concern in his eyes. So the shower hadn't helped as much as she'd hoped to make her look human.

"Good morning." Xavier's voice's husky timbre shot through her.

"Good morning."

"Coffee is ready."

"Thank you." She ripped her gaze away and headed for the coffee maker. "You didn't have to cook breakfast. We could have ordered something in."

Xavier spared her an elusive grin. "I may not be able to handle risotto, but I can manage bacon and eggs."

Bria carried her coffee mug to the island and sat.

Xavier slid a plate in front of her, then grabbed a cup of coffee for himself and sat down next to her.

He gave her a few minutes to eat before speaking. "You're going to have to tell me about it."

She swallowed the eggs in her mouth. "Tell you about what?"

After leaving the set last night, she'd shut down Xavier's questions. The shock of finding the photo had thrown her back to a time she'd worked to put out of her mind. She needed time to process, which she'd spent most of the night doing, hence the bags under her eyes. But she'd known Xavier wouldn't be put off forever.

"The photo. I saw how you looked at it in your dressing room last night. You looked afraid."

"How could I be afraid of a photo?"

He looked at her in silence.

"I told you. It's an old photo of me and a former costar."

"What movie?"

"*Murder in Cabin Nine.* It was a cheesy B movie that never got finished."

"Because Derek Longwell died while you were filming it?"

Surprise shot through her.

"I googled his name last night after we got back. Not much about him other than that he mysteriously died on the set of *Murder in Cabin Nine.*"

"Yes, well." She swallowed again even though she hadn't taken a bite. "After Derek's death, the producers decided not to continue with the movie."

"How did he die?" Xavier pressed.

"I…I'm not sure. I think the official ruling was an accident. Derek drank a lot and I think they said he fell and hit his head." She couldn't bring herself to look him in the eye. After fifteen years apart would he still be able to tell when she was lying? But she didn't need to look at him to feel his eyes glued to hers.

"What aren't you telling me?"

The doorbell rang, forestalling her answer. Not that she knew how she was going to answer him. She couldn't tell him the truth. She hadn't spoken the truth to anyone ever and she certainly didn't want to tell Xavier. It would change the way he looked at her forever and she wasn't sure she could stand that.

"I'll get it." She rose.

He waved her back into her chair. "No. Let me.

We don't know who it is. You stay here." He stalked toward the front door of the house.

She bristled and followed him into the foyer.

He shot her a look that she ignored.

"It's my agent," she said, glancing out of the front window at the stoop.

Xavier opened the door.

Her agent, Mika Reynolds, jerked back looking stunned. "Who are you?"

Bria shouldered Xavier out of the way before he could answer. "Mika, come in." She turned to Xavier when he still didn't move. "Xavier."

It took another several seconds, but finally, he stepped aside.

Mika made no move to step into the house. "It's fine, Mika. This is Xavier. He's, well, he's my body-guard."

"A bodyguard?" Mika frowned. "Doesn't look like he's doing that great of a job. You haven't answered any of my calls?"

"Your calls?" Bria grabbed her cell phone from the back pocket of her jeans where she'd slipped it after getting dressed. She had half a dozen missed calls and even more texts from Mika and several of the produc-ers of the film. She'd never turned the phone's ringer back on after leaving the set. "I'm sorry there was an incident last night and I forgot to check my phone."

Mika didn't know the half of it. Bria hadn't even filled her in on the late-night flower delivery yet.

"Yes, I know. We need to form a plan about that actually..."

Movement behind Mika caught Bria's eye. A familiar form jogged up the walkway.

Bria felt Xavier tense beside her. "It's okay. I know him too," she said before turning back to the man making his way up the front steps. "Eliot! I thought you were in LA?"

Eliot Sykes swept her into his arms. "I grabbed a late flight out of LA to JFK."

"And I was already in town, taking meetings on behalf of another client," Mika said.

"You didn't have to come," Bria said, pulling free of Eliot's embrace. "Either of you. It was probably just a distracted driver."

"It wasn't a distracted driver," Xavier grumbled, "and can we take this discussion inside the house, please?"

Eliot kept one arm around Bria's shoulders as they stepped into the entry. "And you are?" Eliot asked after Xavier had secured the door.

"Her bodyguard," Mika answered from the love seat in the living room where she now sat.

"Bodyguard?" Eliot's arm tightened around her shoulder. "I thought you said you were okay."

"I am okay," Bria said, shrugging free of Eliot's grasp once again and putting some distance between them. "I told you both I was concerned about the notes I've been getting, and the flowers. There have been other incidents since I came to New York to start filming." She filled them in on the most recent notes, being chased on her jog in the park and the flower delivery last night, but left out the photo of her and Derek. As far as she was concerned, the fewer people who knew about that, the less explaining she'd have to do. Or avoid doing, as she currently was with Xavier. "I thought it was best to have personal security, so I went to West Security and Investigations. This is Xavier Nichols. Xavier, this is Mika Reynolds, my agent, and Eliot Sykes. He owns the firm that handles my media and public relations."

Bria walked to the love seat and sat down next to her agent. There wasn't enough space for Eliot to sit too, so he took a seat on the larger sofa in the room. Xavier placed himself at the far end of the living room, leaning against the wall.

Mika's face scrunched as if she'd smelled something foul. "The notes and flowers again. I told you it was nothing to worry about." Mika waved a hand in front of her face as if shooing away a gnat. "All the big stars have exuberant fans. It's almost a rite of passage."

Irritation bubbled in Bria's chest. Mika was one of the best agents in the business because she was laser focused on helping her clients build their careers, but sometimes her focus could be shortsighted. "It's a rite of passage that concerns me, then. We can't be sure whoever is sending them is harmless. My intuition is saying that whoever is doing this is serious, and even though the near hit-and-run could have just been a reckless driver..."

"I think hiring a bodyguard is the right way to go. Especially with this video making the rounds now," Eliot said.

"What video?" Xavier barked, pushing away from the wall and moving back to Bria's side.

Mika already had her phone in her hand. She tapped it twice, then turned the screen so that Bria and Xavier could see it. "Your bodyguard pushing you out of the way, rescuing you from the out-of-control vehicle. It's all over social media." She flicked a glance in Xavier's direction.

Bria watched herself freeze in the middle of the street, trapped in the glare of the white headlights bearing down on her. Her heart rate picked up, remembering the moment, even though there was no way she could be hurt by the vehicle while she was sitting on the sofa in her home. Then Xavier entered the frame, pushing her out of the way. The car roared past them and the recording froze on her and Xavier lying on the sidewalk, Xavier cradling her, staring down at her, his face a mask of concern.

"You can't buy this kind of exposure for the movie." Mika's excited voice cut through the memories.

Bria looked at the woman who'd been her agent for the last decade, who'd taken her on and helped make her into a star. It was as if she was looking at

Mika for the first time and she wasn't sure she liked what she was seeing. "We could have been killed."

Mika had the grace to look abashed. "Of course, I'm glad no one was hurt. That goes without saying."

Did it though? Bria couldn't help but feel like it was something that should be said.

"But it is undeniable that this will bring more attention to the film. And that's what we want."

Bria felt the frown she wore deepen.

"I think what Mika is trying to say in her characteristically tactless way is that we can use this incident to get some buzz for the movie." Eliot held his hands up as if to ward off an impending verbal attack. "I know how slimy it sounds, but this is the business. People are talking about your brush with death. We want them talking about *Loss of Days* and how brilliant you are in it and how it is going to make you an even bigger star."

"And maybe even garner some awards buzz." Mika did a little dance on the love seat next to Bria, her face glowing.

Bria glanced at Xavier, but his expression gave nothing away. She really wished she knew whether he was thinking that taking advantage of their near miss was an opportunity or opportunistic. "It sounds like a tasteless move to me."

Eliot slid to the end of the sofa closest to the love seat and reached across the sofa arm for Bria's hand. "It won't be. I promise. Don't I always take care of you? You're my best client and I'd never put you in an uncomfortable situation, but I do think a few strategically granted interviews right now, about the movie of course, wouldn't be a bad idea."

"About the movie? *Loss of Days* won't be out for another year at least. We haven't even finished filming."

"You should know better than that by now," Mika scolded. "It's never too early to start promoting a movie."

"How many interviews?" Bria asked.

"Three or four, tops," Eliot answered. "Just enough to make sure we're in control of the story. We want people to know you didn't suffer any injuries and that you were back at work the next day, ready to go on with this fantastic movie that everyone should see when it comes out."

"Okay," she said resignedly. "Two interviews. That's it, Eliot. I'm still filming, I don't have a lot of spare time."

Eliot beamed. "Great." He sprung from the sofa. "I'm going to get on that right now. It'll give you and Mika some time to discuss a few things."

Eliot strode from the room in the direction of the kitchen, already pulling his phone from his suit pocket.

The show must go on. Wasn't that what they said, she thought wearily. She only wished she wasn't a part of this madman's show.

Chapter Nine

Sykes was on the phone, his back turned when Xavier walked into Bria's kitchen. He studied the man for a moment. Sykes wore a fitted suit in a deep plum shade with a black silk shirt. A goatee dusted his chin and a Rolex watch encircled his wrist.

Finally sensing he wasn't alone, Sykes turned.

Xavier walked nonchalantly to the sink, took a glass from the shelf above it and filled it with water from the tap. He turned, sipping from the glass and watched Sykes.

Sykes's eyes narrowed when he realized that Xavier wasn't going to leave the room. "Excuse me, Ian. I'm going to need to phone you back." Sykes ended the call. "Can I help you with something?"

"You can. You can help by telling me about your relationship with Bria." Xavier leaned back against the counter, effecting a relaxed pose although his muscles were taut and he remained watchful.

"Bria is a client of my public relations firm. And a good friend. A very good friend." Sykes smirked.

Xavier knew Sykes was trying to get under his skin. Unfortunately, it was working. He itched to wipe the smirk off the man's face and tell him how his close friend Bria had pulled him into a smoldering kiss in her dressing room a day earlier or the ripples of desire that moved between them with every look. But letting Sykes get to him would give the man the upper hand.

"That so? Bria never mentioned you, but she always did tend to see the good in everyone. Even those who may not deserve it."

Sykes's eyes narrowed. "Always? So you aren't just some meatheaded bodyguard she hired yesterday?"

"Let's just say we go way back and are also very good friends."

He knew it was petty, but he couldn't help being pleased by Syke's scowl.

"I understand that your firm has taken over handling Bria's fan mail. I need to see everything you have."

"As long as Bria consents, you'll have it."

"How does it work? Does everything come to your firm directly?"

Sykes shrugged. "Most fan interactions occur online nowadays. Email and social media. The case manager assigned to Bria's account responds to the fans and flags the questionable stuff."

"What does the case manager do with the flagged communications?"

"Sometimes nothing. You'd be amazed how much negative stuff comes in. If it doesn't seem like a credible threat, well, we don't have the bandwidth to follow up on everything."

"And when you do get a credible threat?"

"We let the appropriate people know. Mika." Sykes's chin jutted toward the living room. "On-set security if she's working on a movie. And the police, if we deem that necessary."

"Not Bria?"

Sykes nodded. "We let her know too when there is a threatening message, although she has chosen to retain access to all her accounts and does still occasionally respond directly to fans." The expression on Sykes's face made it clear he didn't agree with that choice.

"And you notified the LA police department about the stalker's emails? The ones declaring that Bria was his?" Xavier continued his questioning.

Sykes shifted uncomfortably. "Not at first. I mean, there was no concrete threat. It wasn't the first time Bria got an email from a lovesick fan. No one thought the guy was a stalker. Not at first."

"When did you realize the notes were coming from more than just a lovesick fan?"

"When the black roses arrived at Bria's house. She freaked out and I can't say I blame her."

"And that's when the police were called?"

"Yes." Sykes flipped his phone front to back, back

to front nervously in his right hand. "Not that they did anything about it. In fairness, if they followed up on every threat to every Hollywood actor and actress, they wouldn't have time to do anything else."

Maybe. But he didn't care about every actor or actress. He only cared about one.

"Did anyone follow up on how the flowers got to Bria's house?"

Sykes's eyebrows squished together. "What do you mean?"

"Did anyone try tracking down the florist the flowers came from? Look into who delivered the roses?"

"I don't know." Sykes frowned. "I assumed the police would have done that."

"But no one followed up with the LAPD?"

Sykes shrugged again. "I guess not."

Xavier didn't try to hide his annoyance that there'd been so little follow-through initially, but it was something that he'd be sure to remedy, although the trail was probably stone-cold at this point.

"I really wish I could help you more," Sykes said.

"I bet you do," Xavier said without making an attempt to hide his derision.

Sykes frowned. "Look, I want to keep Bria safe as much as you do. Despite what you may think, I'm glad she hired you. Well, maybe not you but that she hired personal security. If there's anything I can do to catch the guy who is stalking her, I'll do it. But at the moment, I need to get back to work. So if you don't have any more questions…"

"I don't for now."

Sykes swept past him. Xavier followed Sykes back into the living room.

Bria looked from one man to the other. "Everything okay?"

"Fine," Sykes assured her.

"I set up the first interview with Ian Cole. I'll send you the details once I've worked them all out. Mika has your shooting schedule?"

"Yes." Bria nodded. "I have some time off coming up, so that would be the best time to do it."

"Great." Sykes smiled. "I'll let you know ASAP."

"Now, speaking of my schedule—" Bria rose from the love seat "—I need to get ready and head to the set. I'm lucky I don't have an early call time today, but I don't want to be late."

Mika and Eliot rose and headed for the door. Mika said a quick goodbye before pulling out her phone and heading for a black town car idling on the other side of the street.

Xavier bristled when Eliot stopped just outside the door and pulled Bria into another embrace. "I'm going to be in town for a few days staying at my place in Chelsea. Let's have dinner tonight." He shot a look over her shoulder at Xavier. "Alone."

"I don't know, Eliot. I'll have to see how filming goes."

Eliot's mouth turned up in a smile that didn't reach his eyes. "I'll call you later, then." He followed Mika to the town car.

Bria shut the door and turned back to Xavier.

"Nice friends you got there," he said before turning his back to her and heading for the kitchen.

"You don't even know them. They are an important part of my team. Mika is one of the best agents in the business and she's been a good friend to me. And Eliot has gone above and beyond, helping me handle everything with the stalker."

Xavier frowned. "You're right. I don't know them. But maybe you should consider this. Many stalkers know their victims personally. So maybe you should ask yourself how well you really know your team."

THE MOVIE DIRECTOR, Dane Malloy, called, "Action," and Xavier watched Bria become Elizabeth Stewart, matriarch of a not-so-upstanding political dynasty. She took control of the scene and demanded attention. Bria really was a damn good actress. Better than good. She'd been good fifteen years ago when she was a student, but now Xavier couldn't take his eyes off her. Admittedly, her acting chops weren't the sole reason for that. That kiss they'd shared had been brief but soul stirring. And he was determined to do it again. Soon.

"She's good." Ryan's familiar voice came from behind him.

Ryan held a tablet Xavier recognized as one they used when they were on-site conducting security reviews for clients.

"I didn't expect you to come out to do the assessment yourself."

Ryan shrugged. "I've never been on a movie set. Couldn't pass up the opportunity."

After Sykes and Mika Reynolds's unexpected visit this morning, he'd forgotten to let Logan De-Long know to expect someone from West Investigations would be coming by to do the security review. "How'd you get on set?" Xavier asked.

"Yeah, security around here is crap. I just told them I was with you and showed my West Investigations employee ID and they let me right through."

Xavier glared at the backs of the security guards, fifty yards or so away, who were supposed to be keeping the set secure. Frustration rumbled in his chest. He'd have to have another chat with Logan DeLong. And maybe get Bria to ask her bulldog of an agent to make a fuss to the producers of the film. After all, if anything was to happen on set, the lax security would be a huge potential liability for them.

He made a mental note, then turned back to Ryan. "Find any fingerprints on the vase of flowers?"

"Nothing," Ryan said. "Guy must have worn gloves. I did get the video from one of the few security cameras. Of course, I'd have twice as many around the set as they do, but at least they do have a couple of cameras. One caught our guy." Ryan pulled out his phone, and moments later, video began playing on screen.

A figure, clearly a man from the shape and size, walked into the frame carrying the vase of flowers he and Bria had found in her dressing room last night. The man kept his head down, and the baseball cap he wore obscured any hope of making out distinguishing features. But the vase of flowers in his hands was clear, as was the fact that he wore gloves. He was in and out of the frame in less than five seconds.

"None of the guards remember letting a delivery guy on set, but…" Ryan let the sentence trail off.

Xavier didn't need him to finish the thought. His tour of the movie set had revealed a number of weak points. Like the fact that there were multiple doors in and out of the building. The official entrance and exit that all cast, crew and visitors were supposed to use were manned. The other doors couldn't be opened from the outside but anyone inside could leave through them. Which meant they could accidentally or intentionally let a stranger on set without going through security, such that it was.

Ryan tapped the phone's screen, and less than a second later, Xavier's phone beeped with an incoming message. "I sent it to you. The techs at West are working on cleaning it up to see if we can get anything more from it, but they aren't hopeful. I've got someone following up with local flower shops here and in Los Angeles, where the first bouquet was delivered, but that's looking for a needle in a haystack."

Xavier wasn't surprised about that. He'd filled Ryan in on the lack of follow-up after the arrival of the first bouquet while Bria got ready to drive over to the set that morning. Neither of them held out much hope this would be a fruitful line of inquiry, but it was legwork that had to be done.

"We'll look anyway." Xavier turned his gaze back to Bria.

Bria chatted with her costar while the crew reset the scene.

"Anything on Derek Longwell?" Xavier asked without taking his eyes off Bria.

"Not a lot. I emailed you what we've got. He was a small-time actor living in LA. Only had a handful of credits when he died on the set of a movie filming in the San Bernardino National Forest a little over ten years ago."

"*Murder in Cabin Nine.* Bria was his costar," Xavier said. "What's the official word on how Longwell died?"

"Cracked skull. He had a blood alcohol level of .17."

"So, sloppy drunk."

"Exactly," Ryan confirmed. "We know he was out with some of the cast members at a local bar. No one remembers him leaving, but everyone agreed Derek was drinking heavily that night. The police theorize that Longwell fell along the path heading back to the hotel and hit his head. He wasn't found until the next morning when he didn't show up to the set."

Xavier turned the information over in his head. "So why would Bria's stalker leave a photo of Bria and Longwell with the flowers?"

Ryan jutted his chin in Bria's direction. "Have you asked Bria?"

"She said she didn't know."

"You don't believe her?"

"She's not telling me something, but if I push her too hard, she might dig in even more. She's got a stubborn streak," he said, thinking about Bria's refusal to go to a safe house.

One of Ryan's brows rose. "You may have to. The stalker left that photo for a reason, which means we need to know everything there is to know about Bria's relationship with Derek Longwell."

The idea that there was a relationship between Bria and Derek Longwell, or anyone else, made him want to punch someone. Maybe several someones. Of course, it was unrealistic to expect that Bria had remained celibate for the last fifteen years. He certainly hadn't. But that didn't mean he wanted to know the specifics of her relationships.

"So, you and Brianna Baker. I knew you were a man who kept his own council, but that's a pretty big secret to keep."

Xavier slid a side long look at his friend. "Wouldn't

you keep it to yourself if the best thing that ever happened to you dumped you like a hot potato?"

Ryan nodded sagely. "I probably wouldn't be screaming it from the rafters. I see your point." Ryan was quiet for a beat. "So, the best thing that ever happened to you?"

Xavier grumbled. He considered Ryan a friend, a good one, but that didn't mean he wanted to share his feelings with him. Especially when he wasn't sure about those feelings himself.

Ryan chuckled then sobered. "Look, man, I get it. The right woman can make us go a bit nuts, but Bria, she may be in some real trouble here. Her stalker is getting bolder. Sneaking onto the movie set, even after the shooting had wrapped for the day, was a big risk. Are you sure you can keep your head in the game?"

Xavier turned to look at Ryan head on. "Would you trust anyone other than yourself with Nadia's safety if the situation was reversed?" he asked, referring to Ryan's wife.

Ryan didn't hesitate this time. "No." He sighed. "Just let me know if you need anything. I'm headed back to the office to work on the cost estimate for the upgraded security suggestions." He dropped a set of keys in Xavier's hand. "I took care of the locks on Bria's dressing room door and windows and installed a wireless camera outside the door."

"Thanks, man."

Ryan patted him on the shoulder, then headed for the exit.

Another hour passed before the director finally called for a break for lunch.

A production assistant handed Bria her robe. She wrapped it around herself as she made her way to him.

"Was that Ryan I saw you talking to?"

Xavier fell into step beside her and they headed for her dressing room. "Yes. He did the security assessment, changed your locks and gawked at a real-life movie being filmed."

Bria smiled. "Tell him to let me know when he has some time and I'll give him a proper tour."

They arrived at her dressing room, but Bria hesitated. He read the anxiety in her eyes.

"Hey." He pointed to the camera Ryan had hooked up on the opposite wall from the dressing room door. "No one has been in or out since we left."

Bria took a deep breath and unlocked the door with the key he passed to her.

Inside, she fell onto the sofa. "I hate this. Being scared all the time. Looking over my shoulder."

"I know. I'm sorry you're going through this, but I promise you, we will find this guy."

His words hadn't cleaned any of the concern from her eyes.

"You can't be sure of that. Certainly not sure that you'll catch him before he does something else. Something worse."

His gut clenched because, even though he meant every word, she was right. He couldn't be sure they'd catch the stalker before he lashed out again.

He let out a deep, steadying breath, then sat beside her.

"You're right. I can't promise you this guy won't send another email or more flowers or attempt another hit-and-run. But I can promise you that I will not let anything happen to you. I will stand between you and any danger. I give you my word on that."

He wasn't sure who initiated it, maybe they both had. But in an instant, he was lowering his head to meet her raised lips. The moment their lips met, an electrical charge flowed through him.

Her lips parted beneath his and he took it as a sign and deepened the kiss. Her hands slid around his neck and he pulled her closer.

He'd known he'd wanted her the moment he'd seen her in Ryan's office, but the kiss just made it crystal clear how deeply he felt for her. He was throbbing with his need to be closer to her. And from the way she was kissing him back, she felt the same.

A ding sounded from the counter where Bria had left her phone while she was on set. She broke off the kiss, rising from the sofa and covering her swollen lips with a hand before turning her back on him.

"That was a mistake. Totally unprofessional of me."

"It might have been unprofessional of both of us, but I don't think for a second it was a mistake. Bria,

I think we should talk about what happened between us—" He broke off when her body tensed. "What? What is it?"

He stood and closed the short distance between them.

Bria turned to face him, her face full of fear. She held her phone out to him. "He...he sent me a text. It's you."

Xavier took the phone from Bria's hand. On the screen was a photo of Xavier with his arm around Bria, hustling her from the movie set into his SUV. A red circle with a slash through it had been superimposed over his face. The text underneath the photo read:

GET RID OF HIM. OR I WILL.

Xavier took a screenshot of the text, then sent it to his own phone. Then he pressed the call button on Bria's screen.

Alarm flashed over Bria's face. "You're calling him? You can't call him."

Xavier led her back to the sofa. "Don't worry. I've got this."

The phone rang, but no one picked up. It was a long shot. Just like tracing the number was a long shot. More than likely the stalker was using a burner phone. But that wouldn't stop him from trying.

He ended the call and started another. "We might be able to trace this."

Ryan wouldn't have made it back to West's head-quarters yet, so Xavier tried Shawn, Ryan's younger brother and co-owner of West Security and Investigations.

Shawn picked up on the second ring, and after a brief explanation, set out to trace the number that had just sent the text to Bria's phone.

"Shawn is on it," he said, punching off the call, "but it could take a while. Are you finished with filming for the day?"

Bria shook her head. "No, I've got another scene to shoot."

Damn. He'd hoped to be able to take her home, but he knew she wouldn't leave the cast and crew in the lurch.

"Xavier, I'm scared." Fear pulsed off her.

He reached out and pulled her into his arms. He dropped a kiss on the top of her head. "I know, but we're going to find this guy and stop him. I promise you that."

Chapter Ten

For the next three hours, Xavier prowled the edges of the set, never taking his eyes off Bria and the people around her. He'd always known how talented she was, but now he was getting a glimpse at just how much of a dedicated professional she was as well. The text message had clearly upset her, but she pulled herself together and headed back to the movie set when the production assistant called for her. She acted the scene over and over, never missing a line.

Over the course of the next several hours, she filmed scene after scene without letting on how shaken she was. Of course, he could see it. In the nervous glances around the set between takes and in the way her eyes sought him out the moment the director called cut. He made sure to stick as close to her as he could, both so that he could keep an eye on her at all times and to give her the sense of security that she seemed to need at the moment.

The notes and flowers were terrorizing for Bria, but until now, the stalker hadn't exhibited a direct desire to physically harm her or anyone else. But the text message with his photo, along with the attempted hit-and-run, couldn't be taken as anything other than a direct threat against them. An escalation in the stalker's MO. He wasn't scared for himself, he was scared for Bria. Because there was no way he was leaving Bria's side, which meant the stalker might escalate even further. And there was no way to guess what he might do next.

While Bria worked, Shawn called to fill him in on the attempt to trace the text message. The techs at West had done their best to locate a name or location for the call, but not surprisingly, the message had come from a burner phone. The device was currently off or disabled, so unless the stalker used it again, they were at a dead end with regards to tracing the text back to the sender.

The director finally called a wrap on the day's shooting just after eight that night. It took Bria another half hour to get out of her wardrobe and makeup, then they drove back to her townhouse on the Upper West Side.

West had secured several parking spaces in the garage across from Bria's townhouse and gotten permission, via a hefty fee, to install cameras so that the spaces could be monitored from the West offices at all times. It was the best they could do for the moment, since Bria continued to refuse to go to a safe house.

Xavier scanned the street as he hustled Bria toward her townhouse, wishing she'd agreed to stay somewhere that at least had an attached garage. They made it to the sidewalk in front of Bria's home when he noticed movement several yards ahead of them. A man huddled behind one of the lampposts that lined the sidewalk. The man's head popped out from behind the post, and the light from the yellow bulb overhead glinted off something in the man's hand.

Xavier propelled Bria through the gate surrounding her property. "Go inside and lock the door. Don't open it for anyone."

He didn't wait to see if she followed his direction before he took off down the sidewalk.

The man looked around the post again, his eyes going wide. He turned, darted between two cars parked at the curb and then dashed across the street.

Xavier caught him by the collar as he made it onto the opposite sidewalk and slammed him face forward against the side of a parked SUV.

"Who are you?" Xavier barked.

"What the hell!" the man stammered, trying to wrench himself out of Xavier's grasp.

Holding him in place with one hand, Xavier patted him down, ripping the man's wallet from his back pocket.

His California driver's license gave his name as Bernard Steele and listed an address in Los Angeles.

"Let me go! I'm going to call the cops," Bernard wailed.

"What are you doing here skulking on this street?"

"Hey, man. It's a free country!"

Xavier gave the man a shake. "Do you feel free right now?" he growled into the man's ear.

The click of fast-moving footsteps had both men turning their heads.

Bria appeared around the side of the SUV Xavier held Steele against.

"I told you to go inside and lock the door," Xavier barked, frustration lining his voice. "Stay back."

"Bria, get this jerk off of me," Steele stuttered.

Xavier pressed the man against the car a little harder.

"Xavier, he's not here to hurt me. Bernie is a photographer. Part of the paparazzi, to be exact."

Xavier hesitated before taking a step back and allowing Bernie to turn to face him.

"Paparazzi?" No one was supposed to know that Bria owned a home on this block. He was sure they hadn't been followed from the set when he'd driven her here, so how did the photographer know where to wait for Bria?

"Your man is crazy!" Steele glared at Bria. "He broke my camera."

Xavier scanned the asphalt. A black digital camera lay on its side next to the SUV's tire.

"I'm going to sue the hell out of you, Brianna Baker."

Xavier bent, picking up the camera. The screen was black and had a spiderweb of cracks running through it now.

Bria stepped closer and Xavier angled his body so that he was between her and Steele.

She frowned at him before turning her attention back to the photographer. "Let's just everyone calm down. My bodyguard may have overreacted a bit, but you were lurking, and there was no way to know you weren't actually a threat. How about I buy you a new camera and we can forget about this whole misunderstanding."

"Misunderstanding," Steele sputtered. "He assaulted me. I'm calling the cops."

Bria fisted a hand on her hip. "And how many times have you pushed and bumped and prodded me, trying to get that million-dollar picture? Maybe I should start calling the cops. As a matter of fact, I'm pretty sure New York has laws against stalking. Surely hiding in the trees outside someone's home in order to get a photo of them qualifies."

"I wasn't hiding in the trees or stalking you," Steele said unconvincingly.

Bria tilted her head and gave a saccharine smile. "Oh no? Well, that's how I'm going to tell the story. And we all know how convincingly I can tell a story, don't we, Bernie?"

Steele swore under his breath. "A new camera tomorrow."

"Tomorrow," Bria agreed.

"Fine," Steele acquiesced, taking a small step forward and finding Xavier blocking his getaway.

"Do you mind," Bernie spat, gesturing for Xavier to step back.

Xavier didn't move.

"Xavier," Bria said, exasperated.

"I have some questions for this guy, first." Now that he was more or less certain that Steele wasn't a real threat to Bria, he shifted so that he was at her back and she was less exposed to anyone else who might come along. He'd have liked to take his interrogation of the photographer inside, but having this man in Bria's house wasn't happening.

"What questions?" Steele crossed his arms over his chest.

"How did you know to wait for Bria on this street?"

Steele scoffed. "I'm not telling you that."

Xavier took a menacing step forward and was gratified to see fear leap into Steele's eyes.

"Xavier." Bria rested a hand on his bicep and a tantalizing heat flushed through his body despite the circumstances. "Bernie, I could still call the cops."

Steele let out a pained sigh. "Look, I can't go burning my sources. They'll stop talking to me if I do."

"Give me a break," Bria laughed. "You're not exactly Bob Woodward breaking Watergate. You sneak up on celebrities to catch them in an awkward photo."

"Way to minimize my life's work." Steele sniffed. "Really makes me want to help you guys."

"Steele!" Xavier bellowed. "You're testing my patience here." He leaned closer, crowding into the man's personal space.

Steele held his hands up in a surrender pose. "Okay, whatever, it's not even worth it. I got an anonymous tip. A call from a burner phone, saying Bria had a place on this block. I've been scoping it out for a few hours now. I was almost ready to give up when I saw you guys heading for the house."

Xavier held his hand out. "Let me see your phone."

Steele must have realized it wasn't a request.

He took his cell from his jacket pocket and slapped it into Xavier's hand. "The call came in earlier today. Around noon."

Xavier scrolled through the list until he got to the blocked number. There wasn't a lot of information to be had other than the time the call had come in and the length of the message, but he noted that the number was the same as the one that had accompanied the photo and threat against him to Bria earlier in the day. So their guy knew where Bria lived. Not good. He had to talk her into staying at a safe house whether she liked it or not. In the meantime, Steele might be their best lead when it came to finding the stalker.

"Was the caller a man or a woman?" Xavier asked Steele.

Steele shook his head. "Couldn't tell. It sounded like they were using one of those digital voice-changing apps or something."

Another dead end. Xavier fought against frustration. "Do you usually believe tips from random, anonymous callers?"

"Man, I get tips from all kinds of people. You wouldn't believe it. This one seemed like it might be credible. I knew Bria was filming in the city and she is from New York, so it seemed plausible she had a secret love shack somewhere in town." Bernie smirked.

Xavier itched to smack the smirk off the man's face, but that was likely to end the cooperation he was currently getting. "Notice anything unusual about the call? Background noise? A car horn? Anything?"

"Nah, man. It was a short call. The person gave me an address for Bria and said she was staying there while she was filming. Then they hung up."

A gust of wind blew down the street and Bria shivered next to him. He needed to wrap this up and get her inside where it was not only warm but safer than standing out in the open.

"Have you been taking photos on the movie set?"

"Not on set, because I haven't found a way in. Yet," Steele said, obviously put out about that fact. Given the pathetic nature of the building's security,

Xavier could only surmise that Bernie was lazy or bad at his job. "But I have gotten some good shots from hanging just outside the perimeter."

"Have you noticed anyone suspicious lurking around or asking about Bria?"

Steele grinned. "Man, there's always someone asking about Brianna. She's Princess Kaleva. Hollywood's It Girl of the moment."

The man was working on Xavier's last nerve, but he gathered what was left of his patience and tried again. "Anyone who struck you as a little too much of a fan? Maybe a little bit obsessed."

Steele cocked his head, thinking about the question. "Not really."

"No or not really?" Xavier growled.

Steele held his hands out in surrender pose. "No, okay, I mean there are just the usual lookie-loos, fans and whatever, you know."

Xavier held his frustration in check. Taking a step forward, he made sure to crowd into Steele's personal space again. "It's in your best interest to keep Bria's address to yourself. And I'm only going to tell you this once. If I catch you hanging around here again, you won't have to worry about calling the cops, understand?"

Steele tried for an unaffected stare, but Xavier was good at reading people. The man was scared. Good.

After a moment, Steele looked at Bria. "I better get that camera tomorrow."

"I said you would and you will," Bria shot back. "I'll have it sent to your office first thing."

Xavier handed over the broken camera but not before taking out the memory card.

"Hey!" Steele exclaimed.

"I'll hold on to this to help keep you honest," Xavier said. There wasn't much he could do if Steele had already backed up the photos and videos he'd taken of Bria to the cloud, but at least he'd have the originals. Maybe he'd caught something that could help them find the stalker, even if he didn't realize it.

"That wasn't part of the deal," Steele grumbled.

"It is now," Xavier barked back.

Bria gave Steele a what-can-you-do shrug and a movie star smile. "You'll have your new camera tomorrow, Bernie. The best model on the market." Bria held up three fingers in the Girl Scout salute. "I promise."

Steele took his broken camera and shot another glare at Xavier before stepping away.

"Bernie," Xavier called out, stopping the paparazzo before he got far. "Remember what I said, Steele. If I see you on this street again, I won't be nearly as friendly."

Chapter Eleven

Once they'd gotten inside and were safe behind a locked door and the alarm system, Xavier read her the riot act for not following his earlier instructions. Or what amounted to the riot act for him, which meant bluntly telling her how stupid it was not to have thought about her safety first. Then he'd started pressing again to take her to a safe house. She was too exhausted to argue with him, so she didn't. Instead, she shot off an email to her assistant about purchasing a camera for Bernie and grabbed a wine cooler and the leftover risotto from the fridge and took it to her room to eat alone and in peace.

The texted threat against Xavier had rattled her to her core. Xavier had always made her feel safe. He was the epitome of the strong, protective type, but the threat against him reminded her that he could be hurt just like anyone else. Tonight it had only been Bernie lurking in the shadows, but what if some night soon it was someone far more dangerous? She couldn't handle it if Xavier was hurt because of her.

Tomorrow she was going to tell Ryan West she wanted a different bodyguard. Or better yet, she'd fire West Investigations altogether. Ryan was right, there were other security firms just as good as West Investigations. Security firms that didn't employ the man whom she had feelings for. Feelings she knew had grown deeper in the years they'd been apart.

And then she wouldn't have to tell Xavier what she'd done during the *Murder in Cabin Nine* filming and watch as he realized the kind of person she was. She knew the photo of her and Derek was the stalker's way of telling her he knew her secret. But how? She'd never told anyone. It was her deepest, darkest secret. Did the stalker intend to expose her? Or was it a prelude to blackmail? She spent hours in her bedroom, her mind shifting between concern for Xavier's safety and fear that her terrible secret was on the verge of being publicly exposed.

She wasn't sure when she fell asleep. It felt as if she'd only been dozing for a moment when a loud noise jolted Bria awake. Her bedside clock read 3:58 a.m. She sat up in bed and the sound came again. A thud against the front door.

She climbed out of bed and went to the window, careful to stay to the side, even though she knew she couldn't be seen from outside. She peeked out.

She caught sight of the tail end of a black sedan before it sped out of sight. An Uber dropping someone off, maybe? But she didn't see anyone making their way to any of the neighboring houses. She scanned the street until her gaze fell on what looked to be a bundle of clothes lying in front of the black iron gate surrounding her front lawn.

Her heart hitched at the sudden realization that what she was looking at wasn't a bundle of clothes at all. It was a person and they appeared to be hurt.

A knock sounded at her bedroom door and she pulled it open to find Xavier standing on the other side. He wore his pajama bottoms and a wrinkled white T-shirt. In his hand was a menacing-looking black gun.

"Are you okay?" he asked, his gaze panning past her to scan the room.

"Yes. But I think there's someone outside who needs help." She waved him to the window and they both looked out together.

Xavier cursed. "Stay here. Lock the door and don't open it to anyone but me."

He glided down the stairs. She turned back into the room and grabbed her robe from the foot of her bed, shrugging into it before following him down the stairs.

He had the front door open and was making his way down the steps carefully, toward the person lying on the sidewalk in front of her home.

Xavier knelt next to the body of a man, feeling for a pulse.

She hurried to his side, then mentally kicked herself when she realized her phone was still in the house charging on her bedside table. A moment later, shock gripped her as she focused in on the face of the man lying in front of her, realization setting in.

Bernie Steele.

They'd just spoken to him only hours ago and now he was... She wouldn't let herself think what her eyes were telling her.

"I'll go back in and call an ambulance," she said, making a move to turn back to the house.

"Ask for the police." Xavier pulled his hand away from Bernie's neck and looked up at her from his crouched position. "He doesn't need an ambulance. He's dead."

Chapter Twelve

The street outside Bria's home swarmed with police and emergency services vehicles. The first officer to arrive on scene had separated him from Bria and now they were each being questioned by detectives separately. Thankfully, they'd deferred to Bria's celebrity, and the implied threat of a host of lawyers keeping them from their two best witnesses, and consented to doing their questioning in Bria's house. Bria was in the living room being questioned and he sat at the kitchen counter with Detective Oliver Roslak. Roslak had a mop of brown hair and wore a wrinkled black suit over an equally wrinkled blue shirt. Despite his slightly disheveled appearance, his gaze was sharp and intelligent.

"Okay, walk me through it again, if you don't mind," Detective Roslak said, casually looking down at his notebook.

"No."

Roslak looked up, startled by his matter-of-fact refusal.

He had already walked Roslak through everything that had happened from the time he and Bria returned to her house until the moment the first officers arrived. Roslak had tried to act nonchalant, but he knew enough about police work to realize that he'd be a suspect, at least for a while, given the encounter he'd had with Bernie right before his death. Bria and the security system in the townhouse would provide him an alibi of sorts, but he was a security specialist. He knew there wasn't a system in existence that couldn't be manipulated, and given his past and maybe current relationship with Bria, he wasn't sure how inclined the detectives would be to believe her.

Nope. He'd told his story and he wasn't going to give the man the opportunity to twist his words.

Roslak forced a smile, but his eyes were narrowed to slits. The combined effect made him look like a lizard. "This is just routine questioning. I just need to make sure I got the details right."

"I'm sure you do, Detective. But I'm not going to sit here and go through rounds and rounds of questioning. I told you what transpired tonight. We'll make the home's security information available to you and your medical examiner will tell you that Bernie was dead before his body hit the sidewalk. That should be enough to clear Miss Baker and myself."

"You think?" Roslak growled.

Xavier just smiled.

"Mr. Nichols, this is a serious matter. Now, I'm sure you don't want it to get out that you're not co-operating with a homicide investigation."

He folded his hands on his lap. "I'm sure I don't care. I've told you what I know."

Roslak slammed his notebook closed. "Okay, I'll tell you what I know. By your own admission, you and the victim got into a heated argument last night in which you put your hands on him. That's assault. I could arrest you for that right now."

Xavier held his wrists out. "Do it. You and I both know the charges won't stick, and after I've been charged, you won't be able to talk to me without counsel present. No lawyer worth their salt will let their client talk to the cops after a charge has been laid against them. And trust me, my lawyer will be worth his salt."

Brandon West, Ryan and Shawn's older brother, was a top-notch attorney, as was Shawn's wife, Addy. Both lawyers were used to swooping in and getting West Investigations' employees out of stickier jams that the one Roslak was proposing. They'd both probably read him the riot act for talking to Roslak without one of them present now, but he had nothing to hide, despite Roslak's unabashed suspicion.

Roslak swore. "Let me pose a hypothetical for you, then. You don't have to talk since you're so shy," he said with a derisive snort. "You and the victim got into it earlier in the evening. You're enraged because he's been following you. You rough him up a little bit and tell him to get lost, but he doesn't do that. You find him poking around later that night. Maybe he's even peeping in the windows, catching a glimpse of you and the woman playing slap and tickle."

Xavier clenched his fists and reminded himself that Roslak was trying to get a rise out of him. An arrest for assault when the propertied victim couldn't press charges would be thrown out in a heartbeat. But an arrest for assaulting a police detective would be much harder to make disappear.

"Or maybe he's just peeping on her," Roslak added, after taking a beat to see if his goading was working. "I hear nudie pics of the right celebrity can bring in real money."

"I wouldn't know," Xavier shot back. "You clearly hang out with a lower-brow crowd than I do."

Roslak scowled and continued. "You lash out at the victim. Stab him, and realizing that now you have to do something with the body, make up this ridiculous story about finding him on the front stoop."

"On the sidewalk in front of the house. And the only thing ridiculous here is your story. Bria allowed you to search the house. You didn't find a knife. There's no blood anywhere in or around the house, including out on the sidewalk where the body was found, which confirms that the murder happened elsewhere. Your hypothetical doesn't match up with the facts, Detective."

Roslak huffed but didn't say anything more.

"So, are we through here?" Xavier stood.

"For the moment." Roslak rose. "Stay available, Mr. Nichols."

"Always, Detective Roslak."

BERNIE WAS DEAD. From the snatch of conversation she'd overheard between the paramedics, who had arrived shortly after she'd called, he was dead before he landed on the sidewalk in front of her townhouse. He'd been stabbed in the chest, then transported to her front door.

A shudder snaked through her.

"Take me over the events of the evening one more time." Detective Ivy Morris held her pen poised over the small notebook in her hands. She crossed her thin brown legs at the ankle. Her boxy suit was ill fitting but didn't hide the curvy figure beneath.

Bria massaged her temples. "Do I have to? I already told you everything I know, which isn't much."

Detective Morris smiled sympathetically. "I know it's been a long night. Just one more time so I know I have everything straight in my head."

Bria sighed heavily and leaned against the arm of the sofa she was sitting on. Morris's partner was taking Xavier's statement in the kitchen. Bria glanced toward the back of the house, but she wasn't able to make out Xavier or the detective.

"Something, a sound, woke me up just before four this morning. I didn't know exactly what it was, but it happened again and it sounded like it was coming from outside."

"Did you have any idea what the noise was?" Detective Morris asked.

Bria shook her head. "No. It just sounded like a thud. Maybe like someone falling, but I can't be sure."

"It appears that someone threw two rocks at your front door. We found them on the porch and there's a bit of damage to the door."

Bria pressed her palms together. She hadn't noticed any rocks, but she took the woman at her word. So someone wanted to make sure that she and Xavier were the ones to find Bernie's body and not some passerby. And Bria was sure that someone was her stalker.

"Can you tell me what happened next?" Detective Morris prodded.

"I got out of the bed and peered through the window. I saw something that looked like a pile of clothes on the sidewalk in front of my house." She continued retelling the events of the night.

Detective Morris scratched out notes and nodded for her to go on.

"There was a knock on the bedroom door and Xavier asked if I was okay. I took him to the window to show him what was outside. He told me to stay inside, but I followed him out of the front door." She took a steadying breath for what came next. "I didn't realize it was Bernie at first, but I could see that it was a person, a man. I'd left my phone in the house, so I started to turn back to go call for an ambulance when I realized I knew the person in front of me."

"And by Bernie you are referring to Bernard Steele?" Morris scribbled notes.

Bria nodded. "Yes."

"And you knew him, how?"

"He's a paparazzo. He's followed me for years now, taking my picture."

"You live in Los Angeles, correct?" Detective Morris looked at her with more than a hint of suspicion. "He followed you all the way across the country for a picture?"

"Celebrity photographs are big business, Detective. The paparazzi will follow an actor or actress all over the world for the chance to get a million-dollar photo."

The woman looked at her with open skepticism. "Million dollar?"

"It's a figure of speech, but the right shot can sell for anywhere from one thousand to ten thousand dollars. Or more, if the photo is an exclusive."

Morris let out a low whistle. "That's a lot for a picture."

"Exactly. Bernie has made taking my photo a significant part of his business model."

"So you knew him well?" Morris was back to scribbling in her notebook.

"Knew him? Not really. We weren't friends. He wasn't the worst of the paparazzi though."

"I understand there was an argument between Mr. Nichols and the victim earlier in the evening." Morris kept her tone light, but Bria got the hint.

"I wouldn't describe it as an argument. Xavier was escorting me home when he spotted someone he believed might be a threat. He approached and we discovered it was Bernie. Xavier asked him some questions and then advised him not to loiter on the street in front of my home."

Detective Morris's brow went up. "That's not how one of your neighbors described it. They heard the victim yelling about a camera, that he'd been assaulted and threatening to call the police."

Bria shrugged. "Bernie dropped his camera. He was upset, and not unexpectedly given his line of work, he tends…tended—" she corrected herself "—toward the dramatic. I offered to buy him a new camera and he calmed down." Bria guessed she'd have to cancel that order now.

"That's a very different story than the one your neighbor told us."

She shrugged. "I don't know what my neighbor told you, but I was standing right there. That's what happened." Or close enough. There was no way she was going to give Detective Morris grounds to suspect Xavier any more than she already did. Her version of events was close enough since there was no way that Xavier had anything to do with Bernie's murder. She'd told her about the text message threatening Xavier, and about the other emails, notes and flowers she'd received from her stalker. Detective Morris had listened but didn't appear to be putting much stock into the idea that her stalker had progressed to murder, much to Bria's chagrin. It was obvious who could have killed Bernie, but Morris was far more interested in the confrontation between Xavier and Bernie than she was in hearing about the stalker.

"Okay, so after the...discussion between Mr. Nichols and Mr. Steele, what happened?"

"Nothing. Bernie drove off and Xavier and I went into my house."

She eyed her warily. "And then..."

"It was late and I was exhausted. I went up to bed."

"By yourself?"

Her face heated further. "Xavier is staying in the guest room if that's what you're asking."

Detective Morris gave an apologetic smile. "I'm not trying to pry into your personal life. I'm just trying to ascertain whether the two of you were together for the whole evening."

"I went upstairs to my room and he went up to his a few minutes after me."

"And about what time did you go to sleep?"

"I'm not sure exactly. I went to my room around nine fifteen, but I didn't go to sleep right away."

"So you can't vouch for Mr. Nichols's whereabouts after you went to bed at 9:15 p.m. Is that correct?"

Bria's back straightened. "Xavier didn't kill Bernie."

Detective Morris pressed her lips together tightly. "Ms. Baker, after 9:15 p.m., you can't say exactly where Mr. Nichols was, correct?"

Bria ignored the question for a second time. "Xavier didn't do this. He doesn't have a motive, but more importantly, if he'd left the house the alarm would have sounded."

"He's been staying here, but he doesn't know the alarm code?" Morris shot back.

"He does, of course," Bria gritted out. "But when the alarm is deactivated, even with the code, it beeps. It would have woken me, I'm sure of it."

Detective Morris didn't look convinced. She wrote something in her notebook. "Is there anything else you can tell me?"

"Would you listen if I did?" Bria said.

The detective closed her notebook. "Ms. Baker, I'm just trying to do my job here. A man has been killed and I intend to find out who did it."

Footsteps approached from the hall. Xavier and Roslak appeared.

"I've finished taking Mr. Nichols's statement," Roslak said.

Detective Morris rose. "And I've just finished up with Ms. Baker." Roslak looked from Bria to Xavier.

"Neither of you have any plans to leave town in the near future, do you?"

"I'm shooting a movie here for the next month," Bria responded. "And I'm pretty hard to lose track of. Just open any tabloid and there I am."

"I've no plans to leave town at the moment," Xavier answered far less sarcastically.

"Good. Good. Well, then we will be in touch."

Bria walked the detectives to the foyer. With the door open, she could see the ambulance and most of the police cruisers had left while she'd been giving her statement. The street was almost back to normal except for the unmarked sedan double-parked a few feet from her home. Still, she couldn't help but see Bernie's lifeless body lying on the pavement.

She closed the door quickly and turned, pulling up short when she found Xavier waiting only inches away.

"We need to talk," he said.

Bria stifled a groan. "Xavier, I'm really not up for it."

She moved to go past him, but he stepped in front of her.

"Too bad. It's no longer safe for you to stay here. Bernie knew you owned this place and apparently so did whoever killed him. And I'm sure that in a matter of hours, so will the entirety of the New York paparazzi, if they don't already."

This time she didn't try to stifle the groan that escaped from her lips.

He placed his hands on her shoulders. "More importantly, it's time for you to tell me everything."

"What are you talking about?"

"This secret of yours that the stalker thinks he knows. And the photo of you and your former costar. What is going on, Bria? Do you know who's stalking you?"

Chapter Thirteen

"Of course not." Bria stalked past him into the kitchen.

"Then, what are you keeping from me?" Xavier followed her.

She programmed the coffee maker and contemplated how loaded his question was. A lot had happened in the fifteen years since she'd broken up with him, but she knew that wasn't what he was asking.

He wanted to know about the photo of her and Derek Longwell. Why the stalker had left it for her.

She couldn't be sure, but she had a good hunch. And if she was right, if her stalker knew her deepest, darkest secret, her career was over. And most likely her freedom as well. But she also knew that Xavier wouldn't give up. He'd keep asking until he wore her down or he'd go out and investigate himself. And that, she didn't want.

If he had to know her secret, she wanted to be the one to tell him. Even if it meant he'd never see her the same way again. She took her mug from the coffee dispenser and carried it to the island.

Xavier hopped onto the stool next to her.

Bria wrapped her hands around the mug, soaking in its warmth and taking a sip to fortify herself before she said the words that could change her life forever. "Derek Longwell was the star of a C-list indie film that I got cast in about three years after I'd moved to Los Angeles. The budget wasn't big, but we all had visions of the film becoming a breakout indie hit like *The Blair Witch Project* and other indie films around that time period." She gripped the sides of her coffee mug. "The entire cast and crew was young and mostly just happy to have a paying job on a real movie."

"What happened?"

Bria slowly let out a deep breath. "I killed Derek Longwell."

Xavier looked at her impassively. "Start at the beginning."

Bria's hands shook just going back to that night in her memory. "The film's shoot was scheduled to take a little over a month. We were about two weeks, maybe a little more into it and shooting was going well. The cast and crew would often hang out at a bar about a few blocks from the motel where we were staying. Most of us were at the bar one night, celebrating after having spent two days shooting a pivotal scene. There was lots of drinking. Some drugs, although I never partook in that. The rest of the cast and crew was still going strong around midnight, but I was ready to call it a night, so I headed out to walk back to the motel. It wasn't far."

The trembling in her hands became more pronounced. She'd never told anyone what had happened that night, for good reason, but somehow telling Xavier was harder than she'd ever imagined. It wasn't just that telling him her secret could be the end of the career, the life, she'd worked so hard to build. It mattered to her that he believed her, and the possibility that he might not, that he might turn against her, was more terrifying than any of the other possible consequences of her confession.

He reached out and took her hand, the simple gesture giving her enough hope to continue telling her story.

"I didn't make it out of the parking lot before Derek caught up to me. He said it wouldn't be right to let me walk home alone at night. There was a path through a wooded area that you had to use to get back to the motel, so I was more than happy to have company. He was drunk, a little unsteady on his feet, but I'd seen him in much worse conditions since we'd started filming. We were on the path when he suddenly grabbed me and kissed me. I pushed him away, tried to make light of it but also let him know that I wasn't interested. But he didn't care what I wanted. He grabbed me again, pulled me into the trees and his hands were all over me. I fought back, but he hit me."

His grip on her hand tightened, not to the point of hurting her, but she could tell by the hard set of his jaw and the fire in his eyes that he was teetering on the edge of rage.

"I fell and he was on top of me." The memory slammed into her. She took a steadying breath before continuing. "I knew he wasn't going to stop, and as hard as I was fighting him, he was much stronger than I was. I don't even remember picking up the rock, but it was in my hands and I smashed it against the side of Derek's head. He screamed and rolled off of me. I didn't wait around to see if he needed help, I just got up and ran back to my room at the motel."

"You didn't call the police? Report his assault?" His words were little more than a growl, but she knew the anger wasn't directed at her. She could hear the pain in them.

Bria shook her head, the terror of that night as real at that moment as it had been twelve years earlier. "I think I was in shock or something. Derek was the star—" she made air quotes "—of the movie. His stepfather had put up most of the money that was being used to produce the film. Even if the director and crew believed me, their jobs were dependent on Derek, not me. I was expendable."

"You have never been expendable," Xavier said fiercely.

"I spent the whole night huddled in my room, waiting for Derek to break down the door and try to finish what he'd started or for the police to come and arrest me for assaulting him."

"But neither happened."

She shook her head. "No. The next morning everyone returned to set. Everyone except Derek. It wasn't unusual for him to be late, so no one was worried at first. I just tried to act like everything was normal. Like nothing had happened. I hoped Derek would be embarrassed enough by his behavior that he'd just make up some story about the injury to his head and let it go." She shuddered out a breath. "Eventually, we got word that a couple on an early morning hike had found Derek's body. I was terrified and sure that I was going to jail."

"Did the police question you?" Xavier asked softly, and although she could still hear the fury in the words, he seemed to have wrested it under control.

She nodded. "They questioned all of us. Maybe I should have told them the truth, but I was still a nobody then. Derek's stepfather was some bigwig hedge fund or investment banker or something. He had connections. I didn't know what he'd do to protect his stepson, even in death."

"The truth is Derek Longwell was a creep who assaulted you and you defended yourself. The truth is his death was an accident brought on by his own actions."

How many people were in jail who had told the truth believing the system would work? "I told the cops that Derek had walked me back to my room and said he was going to go back to the bar. He was drunk, everyone at the bar could attest to that. I don't think the police in that town had the wherewithal to conduct a real investigation. A few days later, they officially ruled Derek's death an accident. It was March, but we were in a densely wooded area and the temperature at night was consistently in the thirties or lower. They concluded he was drunk, fell and hit his head. I think the official ruling was a combination of blood loss and hypothermia from the cold. I've carried the guilt with me ever since."

"You have nothing to feel guilty about."

She wished she could believe him. "I could have called for help. Sent someone to check on him."

"You said it yourself. You were in shock. You'd just been victimized yourself and you weren't sure that summoning help was going to do anything other than open you up to further trauma. Your actions are understandable."

Bria rose and stalked across the kitchen, putting her now-empty mug in the sink. "My actions might be the reason the stalker is terrorizing me now."

"I will find whoever is doing this."

Bria kept her back to Xavier, her hands gripping the countertop on either side of the sink. So many thoughts had swirled in her head since finding that photo with the flowers, but there was one she just couldn't seem to shake no matter how ludicrous it seemed.

She turned to face Xavier, still using her hands to brace herself against the countertop. "I've been thinking that maybe, I don't know how, but maybe Derek is the one doing this."

Xavier cocked an eyebrow. "Maybe he isn't really dead?"

"I'm not sure, but no one else was aware what happened that night."

"We aren't certain that anyone does know about Derek's assault on you."

Bria shot him an incredulous look. "What other possible message could the stalker mean to convey by that photo and all the references to 'my secret'? Hitting Derek and not owning up to the truth of that is by far the worst thing I've ever done. Maybe—" She paused, swallowing hard before forcing the next words out of her mouth. "Maybe I should go to the police and confess everything? Then the stalker wouldn't have anything to hold over me and he wouldn't have any reason to go after you."

Her resolve to fire West Investigations to keep Xavier out of harm's way had faltered with the light of day and finding Bernie's body. She wanted Xavier safe, but she wanted him at her side too.

Xavier rose and crossed the tile floor. He cupped her face in his hands. "I can take care of myself. Confessing to a crime you didn't commit isn't going to get this guy to stop. That's not how stalkers operate. We are going to figure this out. The photo, the stalking, everything, but you have to trust me. Can you do that?"

She let go of the countertop and wove her hands around his waist, keeping her eyes trained on his. "The answer to that is easy. I already trust you. I always have."

Chapter Fourteen

Xavier stalked into the West Investigations headquarters. His emotions were still in upheaval from
Bria's revelation. She'd been attacked and may have
killed a man.

And I wasn't there to protect her.

He knew it was a waste of time to blame himself
for something he had no control over, but he couldn't
seem to stop himself. Bria thought she'd taken a life
and he knew firsthand how that weighed on a person. He'd had no choice, that someone was likely
to die at your hand was a fact of life for a soldier
at war, but that didn't mean he felt the significance
of that act any less acutely. He often felt it was the
exact opposite.

He should have been there, but he was here now.
And he would move heaven and earth to protect her.

Bria wasn't on the shooting schedule for the next
two days and he needed to talk to Ryan about their
next steps in person. He'd enlisted another West In-

vestigations employee, Gideon Wright, to stay with Bria while he was at West headquarters.

Ryan was in his office. He waved Xavier into a chair in front of his desk and set the report he'd been reading aside.

"Xavier, I'm glad you're here. Seems you had one hell of a morning."

He'd called Ryan before the police arrived at Bria's house and had given him a quick heads-up on having found the paparazzo's body in front of Bria's townhouse. Now he gave a more fulsome description of the morning's events.

"I don't like this one bit," Ryan said. "This is a huge escalation if the stalker is our killer."

"It is, and we know that Bria's stalker is motivated. He followed her across the country."

"And we know that a changed situation can push a stalker to act out." Ryan jutted his chin in Xavier's direction. "You're a new element in Bria's life and he issued a threat to you with that text message. It's possible that he saw the photographer as a threat too."

"And it would be a whole lot easier to get to him than it would be to get to me."

"Exactly," Ryan agreed. "If this guy wants to show Bria just how serious he is about making her his, killing a man who is, for all intents and purposes, also stalking Bria is one way to do it."

Xavier drew in a breath. "There's more I need to tell you."

Ryan shot him a weary look but gestured for him to go on. Xavier recounted what Bria told him about the night Derek Longwell attacked her.

As Ryan listened, his expression reflected increasing concern. "So Bria's stalker could be connected somehow to this actor Derek Longwell's death."

"It's possible," Xavier conceded.

"You know this information makes West's association with Bria much more complicated. She confessed to killing a man."

Xavier felt his body tense. "It was self-defense."

"I'm not saying it wasn't, but it doesn't change the fact that a man is dead and Bria didn't tell the authorities the whole truth concerning the incident," Ryan shot back.

"We're not turning her in."

Ryan sighed. "I have to think about this firm."

"Fine. I quit." Xavier stood. "I'll handle Bria's security myself, and if you go to the authorities, I'll deny I told you anything."

"Just slow down." Ryan held up his hands. "I'm not going to the police." The unspoken *yet* hung in the air between them. "I suggest we look into Derek Longwell's life and death ourselves. See if we can't pinpoint our stalker and maybe drum up some evidence that might support Bria's claim of self-defense."

Xavier held his hands fisted at his sides. "I'm never going to agree to turn her in to the cops."

"I gathered that. But it might not be up to you. If

her stalker really does know about what she did to Longwell, he could reveal it at any time. It will be better for Bria if we're already prepared when and if that happens."

Xavier hesitated for a moment before giving a terse nod. Everything Ryan said made sense even if he didn't like it.

"I need to talk to Bria. Without you in the room," Ryan said.

"Why? I've already told you what she said."

Ryan gave him a hard look. "You are too close to this situation. You don't just want to protect Bria, you want to save her and that's clouding your ability to be objective."

"I can be objective," he growled.

Ryan snorted.

"Fine, I'm not objective. I'm breaking the cardinal rule of private protection. I have feelings for the woman I'm supposed to be protecting. But you ought to know better than anyone how that feels. How it can make you crazy but also sharpen your instincts because you have something to lose if you make the wrong decision."

It was well-known among those who worked for West Security and Investigations that Ryan's wife Nadia was a client when the two of them met and fell in love. Nadia's brother had gotten himself, and by extension her, into a heap of trouble with organized crime. Ryan had thrown every resource West had at protecting Nadia and helping her out of the jam her brother had created, despite warnings from his brother Shawn and several other people.

Ryan held his hands up in surrender. "Fine. I'm a hypocrite. I'd do… I did the same thing you're doing. But that's how I know it can go disastrously bad. I did end up in the hospital and Nadia was kidnapped."

"I remember you were fine and you saved Nadia's life. All I'm asking is the chance to do the same for the woman I…" Xavier caught himself before he said what he'd been thinking. What he'd been feeling since he'd walked into the conference room days earlier and seen Bria sitting there. Hell, if he was honest, it was what he'd felt since the moment he saw her sitting on that park bench in Bryant Park fifteen years earlier.

He loved her. He'd never stopped loving her despite her having given him the heave-ho fourteen years ago.

"The woman you what?" Ryan said, his mouth upturning ever so slightly.

He was sure Ryan knew what he'd been about to say, but he wasn't ready to profess his love for Bria to Ryan out loud. "The woman I've been charged with protecting."

Ryan shook his head. "You've got your head so far up your…" he mumbled, letting the thought trail off. "Look, I'll concede that, despite your emotional involvement, you are the best person to watch over

Bria. But I need you to trust me. I need to talk to Bria
if West Investigations is going to help her."

I need you to trust me. Hadn't he asked the same
of Bria only hours earlier? He did trust Ryan. He'd
trusted Ryan, Shawn, Gideon and all of the other operatives at West literally with his life on more than
one occasion, but somehow it was harder to trust
them with Bria's life.

*Because she means more to you than your life
does*, the voice inside his head intoned.

And that was the heart of it. He'd willingly give
his own life for Bria's, but of course, he couldn't expect the same of anyone else at West Investigations.
Still, despite his earlier threat to quit and protect her
alone, he knew that having Ryan and the West team
on his side was the best chance they had of figuring
out the connection between Derek Longwell's death
and Bria's stalker.

"Fine."

"Good." Ryan was all business. "Gideon's with her
now?"

Xavier nodded.

"I'll have him bring her into the office. While I
speak to her, you should pull everything you can find
on Derek Longwell and the *Murder in Cabin Nine*
movie."

"Bria said the film was shelved after Derek's death.
His stepfather was one of the major funders and ap-

parently after Derek was gone, he didn't see any reason to continue financing the venture."

"Still, at the very least we need to try to dig up a list of the cast and crew of the film. Occam's razor. The most obvious answer to the identity of our stalker is that he or she worked on *Murder in Cabin Nine* or was close to someone who worked on the movie. If nothing else, it's the logical place to start given the photograph that was left with the flowers in Bria's trailer."

"I'll get started on that." Xavier rose and headed for the door.

"Xavier." Ryan's voice stopped him before he left the office.

Xavier turned back to face his boss and friend.

"Be careful. You may be right that your feelings for Bria are an asset now, but they could just as easily turn into a liability. And that could be dangerous for you both."

"I DON'T APPRECIATE being interrogated, especially by people I'm paying to protect me," Bria said, marching into the conference room where Xavier had spread out all the information he and West's researchers had pulled so far on the people closest to Bria. Eliot Sykes. Mika Reynolds. Bria's assistant, Karen Gibbs, who they'd confirmed was still in Los Angeles. They'd also pulled background reports on her costars on *Loss of Days* and her last two films.

The possibilities were quickly becoming over-whelming. Bria literally came into contact with hundreds of people while she was filming a movie and those number swelled into the thousands once they took into account promoting the movies, fans, reporters and any other number of events and award ceremonies she attended in a given year. The stalker could be among these people or completely removed from them. Someone whose connection to Bria was entirely in his or her head, making them virtually impossible to find.

He was currently focusing on the cast and crew from *Murder in Cabin Nine* given the photograph and what Bria had told him, but he really had no way of knowing if he was looking in the right place. *Murder in Cabin Nine* had been a relatively low budget film with a small cast and crew by Hollywood standards, but there were still more than twenty names on the list, including the director and producers.

Xavier rubbed his temples and tried to keep his frustration from bubbling over. "It was necessary. We need to know everything you know."

Bria fell into a chair on the opposite side of the conference room table. "And you didn't believe that I'd told you everything. Is that why you sicced Ryan West on me?"

The vein in his neck jumped. "I didn't sic anyone on you. And I believe you. But Ryan is right. I'm emotionally involved. I'm sure he was better at pressing you, getting you to remember things you didn't even know that you've forgotten, than I would be."

"You didn't trust me to tell you the truth," she said, hurt shining in her eyes.

"I didn't trust me. I didn't trust my feelings for you would let me be as objective as I needed to be to question you properly."

Bria looked away.

Neither of them was happy about the current situation, but deep down, he knew that Ryan was right to have questioned her himself. Now they had to move on and focus on what needed to be done.

"I'd like you to take a look at this list." He pushed the paper indicating the names of the cast and crew of *Murder in Cabin Nine* across the table.

She studied the paper for a moment before looking back up at him. "These are all the people who worked on *Murder in Cabin Nine*."

"Yes. Right now we're working under the theory that the stalker is connected to that film."

Bria shook her head. "I can't imagine anyone I've worked with doing this."

"Someone is, and right now we don't have a lot to go on."

Bria looked at the list again. "Honestly, I can't even remember most of these people." She pointed to one of the names on the paper and smiled. "Rob, I remember though. He was a sweet kid. Everybody's friend."

"Robert Gindry?" Xavier pulled up the information West had compiled so far on Gindry. It wasn't a lot. Gindry wasn't in show business anymore. He'd gotten out of the industry more than ten years before and was now an insurance salesman. And a pretty successful one, based on his address, which Xavier noticed was not that far from Manhattan. "He's not acting anymore and he lives in Connecticut. Just outside of the city."

Bria shook her head. "No way. I know it's been more than ten years since I've spoken a word to him, but Rob was the kindest, sweetest soul you'll ever meet. Everyone loved him. He was everyone's friend. You'll never convince me he's my stalker."

Xavier frowned. That was just the kind of sentiment a lot of predators relied on. Instead, he pressed on. "Anyone else on the list you can tell me something about?"

"The name Morgan Ryder is kind of familiar, but I can't quite grasp why."

He searched for information on Ryder in the files they'd pulled already, but came up empty. "Morgan Ryder. The name is pretty androgynous. Was Ryder male or female?"

Bria shook her head. "I honestly can't remember. I can't pull up a face to go with the name, but there's something about it. It's probably nothing. Maybe he or she is still in the business and we've crossed paths since filming *Murder in Cabin Nine*. Or maybe the name is just reminding me of a character in some script I've read. It could be nothing."

Or it could be something. There was no point in pushing her now though if she couldn't remember. "If you remember what it is, let me know."

"Of course I will."

"There are only two people on this list, that we know of, who live within driving distance. Robert Gindry and Tate Harwood, the director of *Murder in Cabin Nine*."

Bria's brow rose in surprise. "Tate is on the East Coast? I wouldn't have thought he'd ever leave Los Angeles."

"He works for a production company headquartered here in Manhattan. The home address we have for him is in Brooklyn."

"I take it you think we should pay Rob and Tate visits."

"I should pay Gindry and Harwood visits. You should stay safely ensconced in a safe house until your stalker is locked behind bars."

Bria shook her head. "No way. If you go to talk to Rob and Tate, I go with you."

"Bria."

"I'm not some shrinking violet who's just going to cower behind the big strong man while he protects her. And you'll have a much easier time getting Rob and Tate to talk if I'm with you."

"I've never had difficulty getting anyone to talk to me," Xavier growled.

Bria smiled. "I'm sure brute force has its place, but I don't think this is it. Especially when it comes to getting Tate to meet with you. You can't do anything for him, so he's not going to be inclined to give you any of his time."

"And you think he'll talk to you?"

She laughed. "Oh, I know he will."

Chapter Fifteen

The research West Investigations had compiled on Tate Harwood was thorough. His cell phone number was listed among the contact information. It took a moment to convince Tate that the call wasn't a joke or crank call, but just as she'd predicted, once she'd convinced Tate she was who she said she was, he agreed to meet with her. They agreed to a time the next morning and Bria ended the call just as Ryan led Detectives Roslak and Morris into the conference room.

Their arrival seemed to suck all the air out of the room.

Bria glanced from Xavier to Ryan. The two men shared a look, conveying information only the two of them were privy to. What was clear, however, was the tension in both their bodies and the hardness in their expressions.

Detective Roslak stepped in front of Xavier. "We have a few more questions about the night you found Bernard Steele, Mr. Nichols."

"Why don't you and Detective Morris have a seat,

then?" Xavier gestured to the chairs surrounding the conference room table. "I'll be happy to answer whatever questions you have."

Morris's smile was feral. "Actually, we'd like you to answer them down at the station if you don't mind."

Xavier's expression remained unchanged. "And if I do mind?"

"Then we'll have to change this from a request to something more formal," Detective Roslak answered.

Bria took a step closer to Xavier. "Wait a minute—" Her voice came out high-pitched and laced with all the fear for Xavier she felt at that moment. "What the hell is going on here? Xavier didn't even know Bernie."

Ryan laid a hand on her shoulders. "Let's stay calm here. Xavier, you go with the detectives. I'll have Brandon meet you at the station."

Detective Morris glared at Ryan. "An attorney isn't necessary. As we said, we just have a few more questions for Mr. Nichols."

"Let's not be cute, Detective," Xavier growled. "You're not really giving me a choice. Answer your questions voluntarily or you'll arrest me, right?"

Both remained silent.

"I'd say an attorney is most definitely in order," Ryan said.

Bria grasped Xavier's hand and squeezed. "I'm going with you."

She wasn't exactly sure why the detectives wanted

to talk to Xavier, but it was clear from the expressions on his and Ryan's faces that they thought the situation was serious. Whatever was going on, she wanted Xavier to know that he had her support.

He returned her squeeze and gave her a thin smile. "There's no need. Brandon West is one of the best lawyers in the city and there will be nothing for you to do at the police station but wait. Stay here where Ryan can look out for you."

She opened her mouth to object. "Please. It will be easier on me if I know you're safe. And if I'm not back in time to take you, Ryan or someone else from West Investigations can accompany you to your interview this afternoon."

She'd forgotten about the interview. Eliot had sent her the details last night and she'd forwarded it along to Xavier. She was to meet the reporter, Ian Cole, that afternoon at the Ritz Carlton.

She didn't like leaving Xavier to deal with the police alone. Every fiber of her being urged her to stay with him and fight whatever misinformed theory had led the detectives to drag Xavier down to the station. But she trusted him, more and more with each passing day. If he said it was best that she stay here at the West Investigations offices, that's what she'd do.

"Okay," she said reluctantly.

She watched Xavier leave flanked by the two police detectives, more scared in that moment than she'd ever been before.

THE DETECTIVES HAD led Xavier into a small interrogation room when they arrived at the police station and left him there saying they'd be back in a moment. He'd been staring straight ahead, body relaxed, breathing even, for the past half hour. The light on the camera in the upper-left corner was dark, but he knew better than to think that the camera wasn't on and recording. The stark gray cinder block walls of the interrogation room were intended to remind people of the inside of a prison cell, a not-so-subtle intimidation tactic used by the cops in order to get criminals to loosen up. The long absence and drab surroundings no doubt worked to induce most people to talk. He wasn't most people.

The door to the interrogation room finally opened. Brandon West strode in, laying his briefcase on the table before opening it and taking out a leather portfolio. Brandon took the seat next to Xavier while Roslak and Morris slid into the chairs on the opposite side of the table.

"Detectives, does one of you want to tell me why you dragged my client down here to ask him questions you surely could have asked him in a less... coercive environment?" Brandon snapped at them.

"I wouldn't call this a coercive environment for a former decorated soldier such as your client. He's deployed to Iraq and Afghanistan, so I'm sure he's been in much more difficult situations," Detective Morris said in a measured tone.

"I'm sure he has, although I do find your likening this situation to literal war zones interesting." Brandon flashed a smile.

Morris's lips thinned.

Detective Roslak cleared his throat. "As we told your client, there was really no need for you to come to the station, counselor. We just have some routine questions we wanted to ask him."

Brandon leaned forward and pinned Roslak with a look. "You and I both know there is no such thing as routine questions, so let's cut the crap. You ask your questions and I'll decide if my client is going to answer them."

Xavier held back a smirk.

Brandon West may wear five-thousand-dollar suits and spend more on one haircut than Xavier spent all year on shape-ups, but he was a damned good lawyer. Especially, when it came to keeping his brothers and their friends and employees out of the line of police fire. There'd been some talk among the rank and file at West regarding whether they should continue to call on Brandon on the rare occasions they ran afoul of the cops, given that he'd started dating one himself. But it didn't appear that his feelings for Silver Hill detective Yara Thomas had dulled his sharp edges at all. If anything they seemed to have been sharpened to a deadly point.

Roslak and Morris glared back across the table for a long moment before Roslak turned his gaze on Xavier. "Could you go over what happened last night again for us? Starting with your arrival at Ms. Baker's townhome and the confrontation with Bernard Steele."

Brandon tapped one finger against the table, his signal not to answer. "As I understand it, Mr. Nichols has already given you a statement, Detective."

"He has," Roslak gritted out. "We just want to make sure we got everything down correctly."

Brandon's smile was cool. "Why don't you tell us what you're confused about and we'll see if we can help you understand things a little better."

Roslak scowled. "Mr. Nichols, you stated that you had an argument with Mr. Steele. We were able to get the video Mr. Steele took with his camera in front of Ms. Baker's townhome from his online storage, and it seems as if you and Mr. Steele had more than just an argument."

"Is there a question in there somewhere?" Brandon asked in a tone that hinted at boredom.

"Did you put your hands on Mr. Steele?" Detective Morris asked.

Brandon tapped the table once. "If you have the video as you say, you already know the answer to that question."

"I did, and I told you I did in my initial statement," Xavier answered the question, drawing a look of rebuke from Brandon. He appreciated Brandon being here, but it wasn't his style to hide behind a lawyer.

"Yes, well, your statement made it seem as if it was a little skirmish," Morris continued, "but the video shows that it was a bit more than that. You threw the victim against a car, not once but twice and broke his camera, did you not?"

Brandon tapped the table. "Again, a question answered by the video. I don't see why you've brought my client in, detectives."

"We're getting to that, counselor," Roslak growled.

"I pushed Steele against a nearby SUV when I thought he was a danger to the client I was hired to protect. He dropped his camera when I did so. I don't know if it was broken but it couldn't have been too bad if you have video from it."

"Ms. Baker offered to buy Mr. Steele a new camera, did she not?"

"She did," Xavier answered before Brandon could tap.

Brandon sent him another look.

"In fact, Ms. Baker offered the new camera as something of a bribe, correct? To keep Mr. Steele from calling the police and having you arrested for assault."

"He's not answering that question. You're asking my client to speculate on not one but two people's motivations."

"Not a problem." Roslak waved the question off as if it was nothing. "How about this one? Mr. Nichols, you and Ms. Baker aren't just employer and employee or bodyguard and protectee, are you? You've had a long-standing relationship with her, haven't you?"

"Long-standing, no. Bria and I knew each other when we were younger. It's part of the reason she felt comfortable hiring West Investigations when she realized she had a stalker. But before she contacted West Investigations two days ago, we hadn't spoken in fourteen years."

"But if you hadn't spoken to her in well over a decade, why would she seek you out?"

"That sounds like a question that should be directed at Ms. Baker," Brandon shot back.

This time it was Xavier who shot Brandon a hard glare. The last thing he wanted was for the detectives to get the idea that they should drag Bria down to the station and start questioning her.

"You've been staying at Ms. Baker's townhouse for the last few nights. Protecting her." Roslak smirked. "Is that correct?"

It took work to keep his expression neutral and not allow the detective to see his disdain. "That's correct."

"And Ms. Baker indicated in her statement that she told you the code to shut on and off her security system. Is that also correct?"

"It is."

Xavier watched a hint of concern flare in Brandon's eyes. "Get to the point, Detective."

"The point, counselor, is that I've been thinking

about this case long and hard." Roslak folded his hands behind his head and leaned back in his chair. "Ms. Baker thinks she has a stalker. She's filming in New York and seeks out an old flame. Someone she thinks might still have the hots for her. Someone who she could maybe manipulate with stories of old times and promises of new ones." Roslak let the insinuation hang in the air for a moment before plowing forward. "Mr. Steele traveled over three thousand miles to take pictures of Ms. Baker. That sounds pretty stalker-y to me. Maybe you, or Ms. Baker, thought he was your guy. Maybe you decided to take matters into your own hands. You use your firm's considerable resources to find the rental Mr. Steele is staying in and you eliminate Ms. Baker's stalker problem."

"Sounds like all you have is a whole bunch of speculation, Detective Roslak, and unless you have more than that, we're done here." Brandon stood.

Xavier followed his lead and stood as well.

"If you want to speak to my client again, call me first." Brandon nodded at each of the detectives, who remained seated. "Detectives." He gestured to Xavier to head for the interrogation room door.

They strode through the halls of the police station and out the front doors in silence.

Neither spoke until they were safely ensconced in Brandon's BMW and on the road back to West Investigations headquarters.

"So what do you think about all that back there?" Xavier finally asked.

Brandon shot a glance across the car. "They're grasping."

"That's good, right? Like you said, it means they don't really have anything."

"Maybe," Brandon said. "Our problem is that people who are grasping tend to be desperate, and desperate people will grab on to anything that looks like it could help them. And right now, it seems as if they're reaching for you."

Chapter Sixteen

Xavier had left with the police detectives more than three hours earlier and Bria spent most of that time pacing the conference room. Ryan had offered to have someone drive her home but she'd insisted on waiting for Xavier to return.

She'd wanted to call in the top New York criminal defense attorney, but Ryan had suggested she wait. His brother Brandon wasn't directly employed by West Security and Investigation, but he had plenty of experience dealing with the NYPD.

Waiting for Xavier to get back to West Investigations headquarters was like torture. They couldn't possibly think that Xavier had something to do with Bernie's death. She'd made it clear in her statement that Xavier had come to her room only moments after the sound outside had roused her from sleep. He couldn't possibly have gotten inside and upstairs that quickly. Not to mention she'd seen a car speeding away. Whoever killed Bernie had to have been in that car, and it wasn't Xavier.

She was on the verge of marching down to the police station and demanding they let Xavier go when he walked into the room.

She rushed toward him and into his arms without pausing to think. "Oh, thank goodness. I was starting to think they'd arrested you or something."

She felt some of the anxiety she'd been carrying since Xavier had left with the detectives seep out of her body as he wrapped his arms around her waist.

"Not quite," the man who'd walked into the room behind Xavier said.

Bria looked over Xavier's shoulder at the man with him. He looked enough like Ryan and Shawn West that she didn't need to guess that he was their older brother Brandon.

"Ryan said I had nothing to worry about since he was sending you to represent Xavier. I guess he was right."

Brandon West shot her a dazzling smile. All the West brothers were attractive enough to have solid careers in the entertainment industry, but she could immediately tell that Brandon West had that extra something, the "it" factor that was necessary to make star status. And he was a lawyer. There was probably some sort of irony in that, but she was too worried about Xavier at that moment to ponder it.

She turned to Xavier now. "Are you all right?"

"I'm fine." His arm was still around her waist. "It was just a few questions."

Bria studied Xavier's face. It had been fourteen years since they'd been truly close but she could still read him. It hadn't just been questions.

"This is where I take my leave of you," Brandon said, stretching a hand out to Xavier. "Call if you need me."

The two men shook and Brandon left them alone.

"What did they ask you?" Bria asked as soon as the conference room door closed.

"It was just some more routine questions about finding Bernie."

Bria pointed a finger at him. "No, don't do that. The cops don't show up at your job and take you to the station just to ask routine questions."

Xavier was silent for a moment, considering.

She crossed her arms and waited.

"They think I might have had something to do with Bernie's death."

"That's ridiculous!" The words exploded from her.

"Don't worry about it. It will be fine."

Bria began pacing again. "This is my fault. I dragged you into this, and now the police consider you a suspect in a murder."

"Hey." Xavier stepped in front of her, stopping her pacing. He took both her hands in his. "You are not at fault for any of this. The stalker or whoever killed Bernie is the only one at fault here. What we need to do is focus and find that person."

The feel of his hands in hers steadied her.

She nodded. "Okay."

Xavier let her hands fall to her side. "We're going to talk to Tate Harwood tomorrow morning. We still have a little time before you have to be at your interview with Ian Cole. What do you say we go try and speak with Robert Gindry now."

Bria agreed, and minutes later, they were on the road to Connecticut. They spoke very little, both of them lost in their own thoughts. So much had happened in such a short period of time, and no matter what Xavier said, she couldn't help feeling guilty about having pulled him into the mess that was currently her life.

Xavier pulled the car to a stop at the curb in front of a yellow brick colonial with black shutters. The lawn had been recently mowed, as evidenced by the neat vertical rows still visible in the grass, and the hedges on either side of the front door were trimmed to exactly the same height. The house was the picture of the quintessential American home.

"I'm stating, again, for the record, I don't like you being here," Xavier growled.

"And I'm stating, again, for the record, that I don't care. Now, are you ready?" Bria unlatched her seat belt and reached for the door handle.

"Wait. Let me come around first."

She rolled her eyes, but waited for Xavier to open the door for her. "Thank you."

Xavier closed the car door behind her and started

up the walkway. "If I say we're leaving, we're leaving, okay?"

"Fine, but I'm telling you, Rob is not my stalker. He was the nicest guy ever."

Xavier slanted her a look as she reached out to press the doorbell.

"People change," he said.

"You've never met Rob."

A moment later, the door opened and a girl of thirteen or fourteen stood in front of them. Her head was down, her gaze focused on the cell phone in her hand.

"Hi. I was hoping to speak to Rob Gindry. Is this his residence?" Bria asked.

"Yeah. May I ask who's—" The girl's head came up and she choked on the remainder of her sentence. She stared in shocked silence for a long moment before letting out an excited ear-piercing squeal. "Dad!"

Bria wasn't unaccustomed to this sort of greeting from some people when they realized who she was, but the girl's voice reached an octave that made her flinch all the same.

She felt Xavier tense next to her. She reached out and placed her hand on his arm. The teenager wasn't a threat to anything other than their eardrums.

A crash sounded from the second floor of the house and then footsteps thundered down the stairs. Rob came into view, a baseball bat clutched in his hand just as a brunette woman careened around the corner, a rolling pin in one hand and a cell phone in the other. Both parents were ready to fight to the death in defense of their offspring.

Xavier pulled her back several steps, positioning his body between Bria, Rob and the woman Bria assumed was Rob's wife.

He needn't have worried.

"It's Brianna Baker. Princess Kaleva, at our door." The girl jumped up and down, yanking on her mother's arm as she did. The woman looked confused, unsure of exactly what was going on. It didn't escape Bria's notice that she still held on to the rolling pin as if ready to smack someone in the head with it any second.

"Brianna Baker?" Rob let the baseball bat fall to his side, a wide grin blooming across his face. He turned to his family. "I told you I knew her!"

He leaned the bat against a wall, then stepped out of the house, sweeping Bria into a crushing hug. He pulled back after a long moment. "I can't believe you're standing on my porch. Come in. Come in."

Rob swept them into the house. "This is my wife, Alexandria." He motioned to the woman, who set the rolling pin on a side table and extended her hand.

"Nice to meet you," Alexandria said, her eyes still clouded with questions.

"And this is my daughter, Cleo, who I will be talking to about not screaming as if she's under attack unless she is actually under attack later today."

"OMG, Bria. I love you. Like, Princess Kaleva is such an empowering female character. All my friends love her. We've seen every one of the movies. I mean, I've seen all of your movies. Dad makes us watch them. He said he knew you from his acting days, but, like, I would have never imagined you'd show up at our house. I have to call Tiffany."

"No." Bria reached out and touched the teenager's hand, looking from her to her parents. "I am sorry to drop in on you like this, unannounced, but it would be better if no one knew I was here."

Cleo's face fell. "But my friends will never believe I met you if they don't see you for themselves."

Bria smiled at the girl. "How about I take as many selfies with you as you want, enough so that no one could ever doubt I was here, but you can't post them or show them to anyone until after I've left?"

Cleo considered it for a moment. "Deal."

Alexandria smiled and hooked an arm over her daughter's shoulder. "How about we go get refreshments for Brianna and...?"

"Oh, please excuse my poor manners. This is my friend, Xavier Nichols."

Rob, Xavier and Alexandria said their hellos. Cleo barely acknowledged his presence, her eyes were still full of stars and glued on Bria.

"Okay," Alexandria said, turning her daughter toward the back of the house. "Let's get those refreshments started."

Cleo reluctantly let her mother lead her away.

"Come, please, have a seat." Rob led them into a

sunny living room with two well-worn sofas facing each other.

Xavier followed them but didn't sit down. "Do you mind if I take a quick look around the house?"

Rob's brows went up to his receding hairline.

"Xavier is my friend, but he's also my bodyguard."

Rob's eyes swept over Xavier. "That makes sense." He shrugged. "Sure. Go ahead."

Xavier walked through the attached formal dining room and disappeared around a corner.

"Cleo isn't exaggerating, you know," Rob said sitting on the sofa across from Bria. "I do take the family to every one of your movies. I'm so happy you're doing so well."

"Thank you, Rob. And it looks like you're doing well too." Bria gestured, indicating the home around them.

Rob smiled, waving away the compliment. "I gave up on acting, which I'm sure you know. To be perfectly honest with you, I never had the talent to make a real go of it, and once I met Alexandria, I wanted to be able to build the life she deserved. We moved to Connecticut, where Alex is from, after we had Cleo. I sell insurance now."

"Well, your family and your home are beautiful. It looks like you made the right choice."

"I did. And look at you. You've definitely been making the right career choices. Princess Kaleva. Maybe I should have curtsied instead of hugging you."

Bria laughed. "No need for that."

"So, what brings you to see me? Don't get me wrong. I think you just earned me the father-of-the-century award, but I doubt you've sought me out just to raise my stature in my daughter's eyes."

Xavier returned to the living room. She waited until he sat to answer Rob's question.

"I don't know if you've seen the papers recently, but I'm having trouble with a stalker."

Rob leaned forward. "I hadn't seen that. I make sure to keep up with your movies, but I can't say that I read the gossip rags."

Bria smiled. "You're better off for avoiding them." Her smile fell away. "But this stalker, he's been sending me emails for a few months now and recently started sending flowers. With the last bouquet he sent a photo of me and Derek Longwell on the set of *Murder in Cabin Nine*."

Rob let out a slow breath. "Derek. I haven't thought about him in years. He was talented. His accident was such a shame."

"We're looking into whether the stalker's motivation might have something to do with the film or Derek Longwell's death," Xavier interjected. "We're hoping you can help us."

Rob leaned his elbows against his thighs. "I'll help in whatever way I can."

"Bria said you were close to Longwell back then. Was there anyone else who he was close to?"

"Derek wasn't the easiest person to be friends with," Rob said pointedly. "He had a huge ego. I mean, we were all struggling actors for the most part, but he came from money. Even though he wasn't a name, he'd never had to worry about how he was going to feed himself or make the rent. He was one of us, but the money also separated him from us, if you remember."

"I do," Bria said. "I remember we all stayed in that crappy motel close to the area where we filmed but Derek had a car so he stayed a couple towns over in a nicer hotel."

Rob pointed at her. "Exactly. He'd buy everyone's drinks for the night, but he wouldn't go back to the motel with us. One of us but not really one of us, you know."

"So how did you and Longwell become so close, then?" Xavier asked.

"I don't know if I'd say we became close. My wife says I've never met a person who wasn't a friend, and that's true to a point. I do find it easy to befriend people, but a lot of that is that I'm a good listener and I don't judge, at least not outwardly." Rob chuckled. "People like to tell me their problems. Derek was like that. Our friendship was based largely on his complaining to me about how horrible his stepfather and mother were."

"The stepfather who was bankrolling the movie he was in?"

Rob nodded. "Derek could be a lot of fun, but he was a spoiled brat. Constantly complaining about his parents, but he always took the money they gave him." Rob shrugged. "We were young."

Xavier cut a glance at Bria. They'd discussed how they were going to approach Derek's assault on her on the drive over. They needed to know if Rob could possibly be the stalker. If somehow he knew that Derek had planned to attack her or if he'd figured it out and this was his way of getting revenge for his friend. Bria hadn't bought into the possibility when Xavier floated it, and she was even surer that Rob had nothing to do with the stalking now. Still, she knew Xavier wouldn't be satisfied without asking Rob directly.

"Rob, I have to ask you something. It's about our time on the film." She'd agreed with Xavier that they wouldn't give specifics about Derek's assault. The last thing Xavier would want her to do was to give Rob the idea that she might have had something to do with Derek's death.

"Sure. Shoot," Rob said.

"Did you know that Derek tried to force himself on me?"

The stunned expression on Rob's face was more than enough to convince Bria that he'd had no idea.

Rob pushed to his feet. "No. Absolutely not. When?"

"I was able to fight him off and get away," Bria said, ignoring his question, "but it occurred to me recently that I might not have been the first woman he tried that with. Or the only woman he tried to assault on the set of the film. And as you said, people talked to you."

Rob paced a short line in front of his chair. "Bria, I promise you, if I'd known he'd attacked you, attacked anyone, I would have turned him in to the cops myself. Derek never said anything to me and neither did anyone else."

Bria believed him. They asked a few more questions but Rob didn't know anything that would help them.

She kept her promise and took several selfies with Rob's daughter and wife before saying goodbye to the family, apologizing for leaving without partaking of Alexandria's homemade scones, and promising to keep in touch with Rob.

"Rob was no help at all," she said, frustrated, when she and Xavier were back in the car.

"Hey, that's the nature of investigations. We just have to keep talking to people until we find someone who can help." Xavier reached across the console and pressed a kiss to her palm.

She tried to let his reasonableness soothe her, but as he pulled away from the curb, she couldn't help feeling things were going to get a lot worse.

Chapter Seventeen

A little over an hour after leaving Rob and his family, they were nearly at the Ritz. Xavier's phone rang. Ryan's name rolled across the in-dash screen. He accepted the call using the buttons on the SUV's steering wheel. "Bria and I just left Robert Gindry's place. I've got to get her to the hotel for her three o'clock interview, but I'd planned to call you while she did her thing and brief you on what we learned or, rather, didn't learn from him."

"I'm not calling about that." Ryan's voice came through the car's speakers. "The press has gotten wind that someone was killed at Bria's townhouse last night."

He glanced over at Bria. Her eyes were wide with shock.

He swore. "Bernie wasn't killed at Bria's house. He was killed somewhere else and his body was left in front of Bria's house."

"You wanna make that distinction for TMZ?"

Ryan shot back. "Bottom line is there's a horde of media in front of Bria's place right now."

Bria's phone rang. She snatched it from her purse and looked at the screen. "Mika. Probably calling to tell me exactly the same thing Ryan is saying right now." She declined the call.

Xavier swore again. "So the whole world knows where Bria lives now."

A breath whooshed out of Bria's lungs. He reached across the gearshift and took her hand, giving it what he hoped was a reassuring squeeze.

Bria's phone rang again. "Eliot. They are going to keep calling until I answer," she said before declining that call as well.

"It's not safe for her to go back to her place," Ryan said, stating the obvious.

"Copy that. We'll head into the office now. We can game plan our next steps when Bria and I get there."

"No." Bria shook her head. "I have to go to my interview."

Xavier glanced at her. "You can't still want to do that?"

"I didn't want to do the interview in the first place, but Eliot was right about the importance of controlling the narrative. It will be even more important now. And with the interview already set up, I can actually get a jump on framing the story."

A ball of frustration knotted in his chest. More Hollywood shenanigans.

Bria's phone rang again.

"It's Eliot. I'm going to take it and tell him the interview is still a go. If you can't drive me to the hotel, I'll call a car." Bria didn't make the statement as a threat but as a matter of fact.

He swore for a third time, but made the right turn at the next light that would take them to the Ritz-Carlton, where the interview was scheduled to take place.

"Thank you," she mouthed before punching the button on her phone to connect.

Xavier switched Ryan's call from the car's speakers to the Bluetooth headset in his ear. "You caught that?"

"Yeah." Ryan sighed. "You're on your way to the Ritz Carlton now?"

"Yes. We're about an hour away if traffic isn't too bad."

"Okay. I'm sending Gideon and Shawn to back you up. We know that the reporter who is meeting with Bria knows where she'll be. It seems unlikely that they'd have tipped off their colleagues to the location of the interview. They'd probably want to keep their exclusive to themselves, but I'm not taking any chances with Bria's safety."

"I agree. We checked out this reporter right?"

"Yeah. Bria's PR guy sent the name to us yesterday. He's clean."

"Be safe and keep your eyes open."

"Copy that." Xavier punched off the call with Ryan and a minute later Bria ended hers.

"Eliot has arranged for us to enter through the back of the hotel to avoid the other guests. He also spoke to the reporter interviewing me, who assured him that he hasn't shared the fact that he's doing the interview or the location with anyone other than his editor."

"Ryan's sending Shawn and Gideon to back me up. I'll tell them to meet us at the rear of the hotel."

He made the call.

They spent the rest of the ride in a flurry of text messages and phone calls. Mika and Eliot had already arrived and were waiting with a change of clothes for Bria in the suite where the interview would take place. The reporter hadn't arrived yet.

Shawn and Gideon were standing at the staff entrance of the hotel when Xavier pulled the SUV to a stop. Shawn opened the door for Bria while Gideon jogged around to the driver's side door as Xavier climbed from the car.

"I've got a secure spot to park. Then I'm going to scout the perimeter and set up a lookout point in the lobby," Gideon said.

"Good. We're in suite 1248. Stay on coms. I'm hoping this interview doesn't take too long." Xavier looked across the hood of the SUV. Shawn was leading Bria inside the hotel. His gut clenched as she disappeared behind staff entrance doors. He trusted Shawn, but he didn't want to let Bria out of his sight.

"Got it." Gideon climbed into the SUV and Xavier hustled toward the doors Shawn and Bria had disappeared through.

He caught up to them getting into the freight elevator. The elevator jerked them upward.

"Not exactly how I imagined an A-list movie star traveled," Shawn joked.

"You'd be surprised how many freight elevators I've been in," Bria shot back. "A lot of my glamorous lifestyle is nothing more than its own form of Hollywood magic."

"A bit of Hollywood magic a lot of people would love to experience."

Xavier was more concerned with reality than playing make-believe. "Did you check out the suite?" he said, focusing Shawn back on the task at hand.

"Yes. The suite and the eleventh, twelfth and thirteenth floors. No suspicious activity. Once we get Bria settled, I'll walk you through the paths of exit I've identified."

Xavier gave a terse nod. "Good."

"Guys, this is not a military mission. It's just an interview with an entertainment reporter. I've done a million of these things." She took his hand. "Everything will be fine. I'll be fine."

The elevator doors opened on the twelfth floor and Shawn took the lead, Xavier falling in behind

Bria so that she was sandwiched between the two of them. They made their way quickly to suite 1248.

Sykes and Mika rushed to Bria the moment she stepped inside.

"Don't you worry about a thing," Mika said, pulling Bria into the suite's living room. "Eliot and I are handling the vultures in front of your house as we speak."

Mika pulled Bria onto the sofa and she and Sykes fell down on either side of her.

"I've been on the phone for hours now, making sure that it's clear that you are the victim in this horrid situation," Sykes said.

Bria frowned. "I'm not sure that's accurate, given that Bernie is the one who was killed."

Something flashed over Sykes's face. Xavier didn't know him well enough to know whether it was anger or hurt, maybe both. But his features smoothed almost immediately. "Of course the dead man is the true victim of this crime. I just meant that I'm doing everything I can to make sure the press keeps the focus on that fact and acknowledges that you had absolutely nothing to do with this man's death."

Bria covered her agent's hand with her left hand and rested her right hand on Sykes's leg.

Xavier clenched his teeth against the jealousy that swelled in his chest.

"Thank you, both of you, for everything you've done for me. I know it's been a chaotic few days."

Sykes leaned over and pressed a kiss on Bria's cheek. "That's what we're here for. Anything you need, you just let me know."

"What I need right now is to get ready for this interview." Bria gave Sykes's leg a pat and rose.

Mika stood too, gesturing toward the closed doors of the suite's bedroom. "I got a couple of options from Alexander McQueen or, if you're feeling a bit riskier today, there's a Versace dress in the mix as well."

"I'm sure I'll find something that will work."

Bria disappeared into the bedroom to change.

Shawn ran Xavier through the exit scenarios he'd worked through in case they needed to get Bria out of the hotel quickly. Xavier would like to walk the planned escape routes himself, but there was no way he was leaving Bria's side.

The reporter showed as they were going through the plan.

Xavier left the greeting and setting up to Sykes and Mika, but that didn't stop him from studying the man who'd shown up.

Ian Cole was tall, blond and blue-eyed, and fit. He'd be no match for either he or Shawn if he did try something, but Ryan had said his background check had come up clean, so there was no reason to expect anything to go wrong.

Then, why was his gut churning?

Bria was right, she'd done tons of these interviews. The likelihood that the stalker would show up here

was slim. Between Xavier, Shawn, Gideon, hotel security and all the many, many cameras throughout
the hotel, attempting something here would be risky
to the point of foolishness.

Which didn't mean the stalker wouldn't try. It
might even make it more likely he would. Killing
Bernard Steele had been risky and foolish and he'd
done it anyway. It was clear the stalker was escalat-
ing and maybe even losing his grip on reality. Who
knows what that might lead him to try.

The doors to the bedroom in the suite opened and
Bria swept into the living room.

He had no idea whether she was wearing Alexander McQueen or whatever other designer outfit
her agent had bought for her, but he knew she was
breathtaking.

She'd chosen to wear a dark green jumpsuit with
gold heels and matching gold jewelry. She'd pinned
her long straight hair back and added large bouncy
curls to the ends. She stepped out of the bedroom, her
eyes sweeping over everyone in the room. Her gaze
lingered on him for a moment before she crossed the
room to greet the reporter.

His fingers ached with the need to touch her, but
he hung back.

Just as Bria said, she was a pro at this. She handled
the interview deftly, wrapping the reporter around
her finger, exhibiting genuine grief over Bernie
Steele's death and imploring whoever had a hand

in it to come forward and turn themselves over to the police. The interview ended and Bria saw Ian Cole to the door. It was clear from the sappy look on Ian's face that the man was more than a little smitten with Bria.

Get in line, pal, he thought. Then, on second thought, *No, don't get in line. Bria is mine.*

He heard the words in his head, how they were almost exactly the same ones that the stalker had used in his note, and shuddered.

He wouldn't put himself in the same category as her stalker, no way. But thinking about Bria as his, that was objectifying her, thinking of her as something that could belong to him. Bria was and always had been her own person. She belonged to no one but herself and he wouldn't have it any other way.

As if she knew he was thinking about her, Bria looked over at him and winked.

No, she couldn't belong to anyone, but that didn't mean they couldn't be a team. Lifelong partners.

It was something he wanted to think about more but not now. Now his priority had to be Bria's safety. She couldn't go back to her townhouse. While she'd been doing the interview, he and Shawn had discussed the best place for her to stay.

They'd come up with an answer, but Xavier wasn't sure Bria would like it.

Bria closed the door behind the reporter and turned back to the room.

"You did amazing," Eliot said, crossing the room and pulling Bria into a hug that sent Xavier's jaw hardening.

"You did a wonderful job, darling," Mika said. "You had that reporter eating out of your hand. I'm sure the article will be very sympathetic toward you and everything you've been going through. Good news, since I hear that things haven't been going as smoothly as we might have liked on set." Mika's brows arched.

Bria frowned at her agent. "No movie ever runs smoothly. Things are just fine."

"Good." Mika gave Bria's shoulder a pat.

Someone knocked on the room's door.

Bria was closest to it, but Xavier stepped forward quickly, gently stopping her from reaching for the latch. He motioned for her to move back and looked out of the peephole.

A bellhop dressed in the uniform of the hotel stood in the hall. He held a long white box with a red bow.

Xavier opened the door.

"Hello, sir. A package arrived for Ms. Reynolds." The bellhop thrust the box at Xavier and waited expectantly.

After a moment, Sykes stepped up next to Xavier and thrust a wad of bills into the bellhop's hand before shutting the door.

Xavier turned to Mika. "This is for you."

Mika looked at him with an expression of surprise.

"Me? I can't imagine who'd be sending me something here."

Xavier sent a pointed look in Shawn's direction. "Do you mind if I open it?"

Mika waved a hand. "Go right ahead."

Xavier placed the box on the round table in the corner of the living room. Shawn came to stand to his right with Bria, Sykes and Mika standing on the other side of the table.

The fleeting thought that the package might be an incendiary device floated through his head, but that seemed unlikely, given the hands that the box had probably passed through on its way to the room.

Still, he lifted the top slowly, expending a small breath of relief when nothing exploded.

Relief quickly turned to anger as he processed what he was seeing inside the box.

Half a dozen black roses and a photo of him leading Bria into her townhouse. His face had been scratched out with a bloodred marker, and the word "die" scrawled across the bottom of the photo.

Chapter Eighteen

Bria leaned against the passenger door exhausted, thankful that no one could see her through the heavily tinted windows. Shawn, Xavier and Gideon had questioned the bellhop and every other hotel staff member who had handled the flowers, but no one knew anything helpful. Or at least, they weren't willing to share the information if they did. The only thing anyone could tell them was that the flowers had been delivered by a man in dark clothing and a ball cap pulled low over his forehead and eyes. The hotel security feed had confirmed that, but the man had been careful to keep his head down. The camera hadn't captured an image of him that was clear enough to be recognized. He carried a clipboard and looked like every other delivery person in New York City, according to the concierge who'd signed for the box. They'd gleaned one ominous clue from the concierge, however. The man had expressly stated that the package was for Ms. Reynolds in suite 1248, which meant he knew that Mika had reserved the room.

She hadn't wanted to believe someone close to her could be her stalker when Xavier suggested it, but now? Mika had insisted that, aside from Ian Cole, only she, her assistant and Eliot knew which hotel and room the interview would be taking place in. Xavier was having Ryan confirm with Ian that he hadn't let the meeting place and time slip to someone, but she knew he hadn't. In her experience, reporters were compulsive about protecting information regarding an exclusive interview. No way would a reporter have risked the competition finding out about the meeting and crashing it.

Which made it all the more likely that somehow, someone she trusted was betraying her in a terrifyingly upsetting way.

Bria opened her eyes and glanced across the car at Xavier. Not for the first time since this whole ordeal began, she was thankful that she'd gone to him for help. Even after their breakup and the years that had passed, he was the one person in the world she knew she could count on, no matter what. And at the moment, he was the only person she trusted completely.

And that made her wonder about the choices she'd made in her life up until now. Sure, she had fame and fortune. She'd achieved her goal of becoming an actress, and not just one who could pay the bills but one who'd never have to worry about paying the bills again. An actress with influence in the industry. A role model for other little Black girls to look up to and know they could achieve their dreams too if they were willing to work hard for it.

But she was also isolated. Surrounded by studio executives, agents, PR people and fans but very much alone when she bore down to the root of it all. When she'd needed help the most, she'd had to reach back fifteen years to get it. What did that say about the life she'd chosen for herself?

She knew what it said about the man she'd left behind for that life. It said that he was caring and generous beyond what she likely deserved.

It said that she'd made a mistake leaving him all those years ago.

She shook the thought from her head. She wouldn't have the career she had if she had stayed.

But what about now?

She had the career. The influence. The money. Maybe now she could have the man too.

"What?" Xavier said, breaking into her reverie.

"What, what?"

"Why are you looking at me like that? If you're worried, don't be. I'm not going to let anything happen to you."

"I know that." She sighed. "Do you think that the police will be able to find the delivery guy?"

At Ryan West's insistence, Xavier had called the police and they'd filed a report after he and Shawn had questioned the hotel staff. With Bernie being killed and left in front of her house not long after the confrontation with Xavier, Ryan felt that it was in Xavier's best interest to have everything on the record. There were too many innocent men in prison for Bria to be sure he was right about that, but Xavier had agreed with his boss.

"No. I don't think they'll look too hard either. No crime was committed. But filing a report puts on the record that you are being stalked."

"Yippee."

Xavier made a left turn and took the ramp for the Holland Tunnel.

"Where are we going?"

He shot a glance at her before focusing back on the road in front of him. "Your place isn't safe. Too many people know about it now, and the press are probably still lurking if they aren't just camping out there."

"I agree." As much as she hated it, her beloved townhouse just wasn't safe for her at the moment. "But you didn't answer my question."

"I'm taking you to my place."

Her stomach did a flip-flop. She wanted to see Xavier's place. To see how he lived. But spending the night at his place felt…emotionally dangerous. On some level, she knew it wasn't all that different from him staying at hers, but at her townhouse, she was on her own home turf.

"I don't have a change of clothes."

"I can have a female operative at West Investigations pick up some things for you."

"That would be great. Thank you." She smiled, relieved that one thing was easily handled, since there was so much else in her life at the moment that couldn't be.

"I'll make the call now. While I'm at it I'll also order us something for dinner. Anything in my fridge is well past its best-by date. Is Chinese food good for you?"

"Perfect."

He made the calls.

"Are you sure it's safe? I mean, people have seen you and I together. The stalker or the press might think I'd be hiding out at your place and look up your address."

Xavier arched an eyebrow. "They could look, but they won't find it. I own it through a private company."

"Ah." She smiled. "I totally get that." She'd had to purchase her townhouse in a similarly circumspect manner.

"Trust me. I have a top-of-the-line security system, my neighbors mind their own business and I have a friend across the street who is former Special Forces. It's unlikely anyone would find you here, but if they somehow do, they're in for a surprise. You can relax."

Relax. She was starting to forget what that felt like. But if she was going to relax with anyone, it would be with Xavier.

Her body heated at the thought of just how relaxed he used to make her.

Forty-five minutes later, Xavier pulled into the driveway of a small bungalow in a New Jersey suburb and hit a button on his sun visor that sent the garage door opening. He pulled the car in, shut off the engine and closed the door before getting out and leading her into a mud room off the kitchen.

The open space living room/dining room/kitchen felt more like a loft than a single family home. The peaked ceiling was lined with dark wood beams and a stone fireplace climbed the far wall. A brown leather sectional sofa was positioned so it faced a flat screen television but also took advantage of a large bay window looking out on the backyard. A wood-topped table that matched the beams overhead anchored the dining space, and the kitchen looked as if it had been newly remodeled with light granite countertops and stainless steel appliances.

"Your home is gorgeous."

"Thanks," Xavier said, flipping on the lights in the living room. "It didn't look so gorgeous when I bought it five years ago. I did a lot of work to whip it into shape."

"Well, it definitely paid off. It's very warm and comfortable."

"I'm glad you think so." He smiled. "And you should. You know, make yourself comfortable. Here, let me show you to the guest room."

He pointed out his bedroom as he led her down a short hall off the main room. Xavier kept walking but she paused at his door. Just as with the main living area, his room was masculine but lived-in. A king-size mahogany bed sat against the longest wall in the room flanked by matching, round bedside tables. A five-drawer dresser completed the set. From the doorway she could see into the small en suite bathroom, which also looked as if it had been recently updated with white marble flooring and a glass-enclosed shower.

Her mind jumped to an image of falling into the bed with Xavier, the soft linens at her back, his lust-covered face looming over her. Desire ran through her core.

"You're welcome to sleep here if you prefer it to the guest room."

She jumped at the sound of Xavier's husky baritone in her ear.

Heat flooded her face. There was no hiding what she'd been thinking. "I was just taking a look."

"Look all you want."

She moved toward him, going onto her toes and pressing her lips against his, softly at first, but when he responded, she deepened the kiss. His hands roamed down her sides, to her hips to cup her butt. She didn't want him to stop. She was edging them into the bedroom when the doorbell rang.

Xavier managed to pull back.

"That's dinner."

Another delivery person with terrible timing. She

sighed internally. This was one time she wouldn't have minded having dessert before dinner.

She waited until Xavier had paid for the food and shut the door firmly before stepping out of the hallway. He didn't need to tell her that it was important that as few people as possible knew where she was staying.

He grabbed plates, silverware and cups while she took the food from the bags and peeked into the cartons to see what he'd gotten. She hadn't paid much attention while he was ordering the food, but she wasn't surprised to see that he remembered her favorite dishes. Peking duck. Scallion pancakes. Dumplings. It was all here. More food than they could probably eat in two nights.

The smell hit her, reminding her it had been several hours since her last meal. Her stomach growled in anticipation and they both spent the next several minutes eating in comfortable silence.

"Thank you for letting me stay in your home," Bria said once she'd had enough food to take the edge off her hunger. She reached for the bottle of red wine Xavier had opened and poured herself a half glass.

"You're welcome. You're always welcome here."

She studied his face but found nothing there except honesty. "You really mean that, don't you?"

"Of course I do."

"Even after how things ended between us?"

He let out a long breath. "That was a long time

ago. I admit, seeing you again brought some of those old feelings, that old resentment up again. But you did what was best for you at the time, and obviously, it paid off."

She traced the ridge of her wineglass with her index finger. "I don't regret choosing my career then. At the time, I couldn't have managed acting and having a relationship. It was never about you though. It was always about what I had the capacity to handle at one time back then."

And now she wanted both. The thought raced through her head. She wanted him and her career. But she knew it might be too late for that.

"I get it. In a very real way, your decision was the best thing for both of us. I wouldn't have gone into the military if you hadn't dumped me."

"Really? I've been meaning to ask you how you ended up enlisting. I don't remember you mentioning wanting to join the army."

As much as her breaking up with him had hurt, the one silver lining was that it had led to his enlisting in the army. He'd never be sorry about that. "Because I hadn't even considered it until the night you broke up with me."

Her mouth formed a shocked O.

"I somehow found myself in Bryant Park that night, after you gave me my walking papers. I don't even remember getting off the subway, but I was sitting in the park, well after midnight, when a police officer found me."

"The park closes at night."

"That's exactly what he said. But he also saw that something was wrong. To this day, I don't know why but I just unloaded everything on him. My dead-end job. My girl breaking up with me. Everything. And Officer Jarell Hurt, who'd only gotten out of the army a few years prior, suggested that if I was looking for something to take my mind off a broken heart and a new career path that the army could be for me. Turned out it was one of the best decisions I've ever made."

"Wow, that's some story."

"Jarell is a good man. He's retired now, but we still get together regularly for a beer or to watch the game on television."

"Does he know Brianna Baker is the girl who broke your heart?"

Xavier looked away. "I told him." He picked up his empty plate and carried it to the kitchen sink.

She grabbed her plate and followed him. She reached across him and set her plate on top of his in the sink. Turning so there were only inches between them, she looked up at him. "And now? Are you going to tell him I'm back in your life?"

His hands fell onto her shoulders. "Are you back in my life?"

Chapter Nineteen

Bria stood pressed against him, her heart pounding against his chest. The need to sweep her off the ground and carry her to his bedroom was nearly overwhelming. He'd had sexual partners other than her, but he'd only ever experienced a need so palpably strong with her. From the look in her eyes, she felt it too.

Somewhere in the back of his mind, he realized becoming intimate with Bria again could be a bad idea. It would most likely lead to him alone with a broken heart just as it had before. But drowning in her beautiful brown eyes, heartbreak seemed a small price to pay to have her in his bed once more. Then she drew even closer, pressing her pelvis against his already stiff length and all reason flew out the window.

"I want you, Xavier." The way she said his name made him long to hear her say it again, but this time, as he thrust himself inside of her. "Tell me you want me too."

It wasn't a profession of love, but it was enough for him right now. More than enough.

He held her tightly against him. "You can feel how much I want you." He rested his forehead against hers. "But there's no going back if we do this."

"There's been no going back from the moment I saw you again. At least not for me."

That was all he needed to hear. "It's always been you, Bri. Always." He dipped his head down and claimed her mouth. She tasted like heaven.

Her hands traveled down his chest and across his hips until she gripped his backside. He grabbed the hem of her sweater and pulled it over her head, letting it fall to the kitchen floor. She wore a sheer, lacy black bra and when he dipped his hand under the material and cupped her breast, massaging her nipple with his thumb, she let her head fall back and moaned.

It was the most erotic and beautiful thing he'd ever seen.

"You are so damn gorgeous. Do you know that?"

She looked at him. "I missed this. I missed you."

Something inside of him melted at her words.

He swept her into his arms, taking her mouth in a hot, heavy kiss and carried her to his bedroom. He set her down in front of his bed. "I missed you too, sweetheart. So much more than I can say. But I plan to show you just how much."

He found her mouth again while her hands worked at the button of his jeans. Moments later, their clothes were littered across his bedroom floor and he finally had her where he wanted her. In his bed.

He took his time, his hands exploring. He brought his mouth to one breast and then the other, lavishing her nipples with the adoration they deserved. She was all curves and softness, a contrast to his hard edges, but somehow, they fit. At that moment, he would give anything to know that she would be in his bed every night for the rest of his life. But if all they had was tonight, he was determined to make it memorable.

He kissed his way down her body and then back up again until he worked his way to the sensitive flesh on the inside of her thigh. He felt her shudder in anticipation and his already painfully tight groin pulsed with need.

"Xavier, please. I need you now." Her face was flushed with desire.

He was determined that she should have her pleasure before he took his, so he focused on her luscious body.

He slid his hands beneath her bottom and tilted her up, bringing his mouth to her core. She was more than ready for him and it didn't take long for her to find her release. Her muscles clenched and her body vibrated as she tipped over the edge, screaming his name.

BRIA WAS STILL coming down from the climax Xavier had sent shooting through her body when he reached over to the nightstand and took out a condom. Watching him sheath himself renewed the never-ending desire she seemed to have for him. She hadn't been exaggerating when she'd told him she'd wanted him from the moment she'd seen him again. If she was being totally honest, she'd never stopped wanting him.

Now here he was, crawling up her body, seating himself at her opening. And she craved nothing more than to feel him inside of her, tipping her over the edge with desire again, and again, and again.

She reached out for him, guiding him to where she wanted him, opening her legs to accommodate his size. Her gaze was locked on his face, not wanting to miss his expression the moment he entered her for the first time in far too long.

He gave a guttural moan as he thrust himself inside of her. She opened wider, taking him in fully, adjusting for his girth and length. He felt amazing. So much better than she could have ever imagined.

And then he began to move inside of her, and all thought fled. All she could do was feel. And it felt so damned good.

Far too soon, she felt her body tensing again.

Xavier smiled down at her as a second orgasm rocketed through her body. And then his smile faded as he thrust into her harder, faster, deeper, barreling toward his own release.

She thrust her hips in time with him, wanting to give him as much pleasure as he'd given her, riding a third wave building inside of her.

Their bodies exploded in time with each other. She felt him pulsing inside of her even as the walls of her core clenched around him.

Xavier rolled onto his side, breathing hard and pulling her in close to him. Her heart raced along with his and she pressed a kiss to his chest. She lay in his arms, wanting to share with him what she was feeling at that moment. Wanting to say those three little words she should have said fifteen years ago.

But she didn't. Because those three little words weren't all that mattered.

They'd both built lives for themselves far away from each other, and at some point, they'd have to return to those lives. But maybe they could figure out a way. Other people did it. Why couldn't they?

But she didn't have to think about that now.

She wrapped her arms around Xavier and held him tightly. For now she could pretend that this, the two of them right here, would never end.

Chapter Twenty

Bria was still asleep in his arms when Xavier woke. Part of him wished he could stay where he was, holding her. He knew waking up next to her was temporary, but he couldn't help wishing that it wasn't.

Instead of dreaming dreams that couldn't be, he got out of the bed, taking care not to wake Bria, and headed for the bathroom. Showered and dressed, he reentered the bedroom, only to find the bed empty.

He found Bria in the kitchen, sipping freshly brewed coffee from one of his favorite mugs. She was barefoot and wearing the shirt he'd shed in a hurry before taking her to bed the evening before.

"I hope you don't mind," she said, a hint of hesitation in her tone. "I made coffee."

He crossed the kitchen and bent to place a kiss on her lips. "I don't mind at all."

He poured a mug for himself. "Tess, one of my co-workers, is going to bring you some clothes to wear. She should be here soon. Hopefully, the press mob has moved on and we can get back into your place sometime today."

"To stay? Or just for me to pick up a few things?"

"I think it's best if you stay here for the time being. Even if the press has backed off, your address is out in the public now. I want West to do a full security sweep and assessment. Your security was good, but you'll probably have to level up now."

Bria rubbed her temple with the hand that wasn't holding her mug. "Whatever you need to do."

He shot off a quick text to Ryan asking him to take care of the sweep.

Bria sat her mug on the counter. "I missed a call from Tate Harwood last night."

The slight smile on her lips told him she was thinking about what they'd been doing when the call must have come in. The memory put a matching grin on his face.

"Is that so?"

She swatted at him and he dodged out of the way.

"Tate says he's available to see us anytime today."

He couldn't keep the surprise off his face. "Really? It was that easy."

Bria's smile grew wider. "I told you he'd be falling all over himself to take the meeting. It probably helped that I hinted at maybe having a project I was interested in talking to him about."

"Okay, and how is he going to react when he finds out there is no project?"

Bria shrugged. "He won't be happy, but he'll get over it."

The doorbell rang.

"That's Tess."

Bria headed for the hallway leading to the bedrooms. "I'll call Tate back and set up a meeting for this morning. I have to be on set by two today." She disappeared down the hall.

He went to the front door, and after checking that it was in fact Tess standing on his porch, he let her in.

Tess's gaze moved around his home in a practiced, efficient scan. "Nice. We should have a company happy hour or two here."

He arched an eyebrow. "I don't think so."

Tess laughed and handed him the shopping bags she held in her hands. "Not a lot open this early in the morning. Had to hit the big box store. Nowhere near as nice as the stuff that Bria is used to wearing, but it'll do until she can get her own things."

"Thanks. I know she appreciates it."

Tess cocked her head to one side. "Huh. So."

He didn't like the way she was looking at him. "Huh. So. What?"

"The two of you are hitting the sheets. Honestly, I saw it coming a mile away, but Ryan won't be happy."

Xavier turned his back to her. He'd never been the kind of man to kiss and tell and he wasn't going to start now. "You don't know what you're talking about."

Tess laughed. "Okay, but I'll give you some advice. If you want to have a chance that Ryan doesn't pick up on the fact that you're doing the midnight rumba with a client, you should tap into your growly side some more. You are far too chill, for you, to convince anyone you haven't recently gotten laid."

He turned back to Tess with a scowl on his face.

"There he is. That's what I'm talking about." She laughed again.

"Thanks for the clothes. Now, get out."

Tess left, still laughing.

He carried the bags into the bedroom, catching Bria still on the phone with Harwood.

Even though she didn't have the call on speakerphone, Xavier could clearly hear Harwood's excitement on the other side of the line. He agreed to meet with Bria in his office in an hour.

"The power of being an A-list celebrity," Bria said after ending the call.

"An A-list ego to match," he teased.

"Gotta have something to balance out the self-doubt."

"Just make sure you use the power for good and not evil."

"Always," Bria shot back with a sexy smile that made his insides melt.

He left her to shower and change while he again read through the background information they'd compiled on Harwood.

Bria reappeared in the living room forty-five minutes later in skinny jeans, a fancy off the shoulder shirt and black pumps. Her hair was up in a complicated twist and her makeup looked expertly applied. It was simple, classic, but she still looked like a million bucks.

"Wow, you look great."

She beamed. "Tate's online bio with Panthergate Productions lists him as a producer. But based on my experience, that could mean anything from he's a glorified coffee boy to he's the brains of the operations. In either case, he'll undoubtedly want to exploit our renewed relationship to up his clout within the company."

"Tough business," Xavier said, taking the oversize sweater she carried in her arms from her and holding it open so she could shrug into it.

He wrapped the material around her shoulders and she turned slightly, leaning back against him and looking up at him with a wink. "Thanks."

He pressed a kiss to her neck and she sank back farther.

"What do you say to going back to bed?"

He pressed a kiss to the other side of her neck.

"I don't think we have time for what you're thinking," Bria said teasingly.

"You know you're thinking about it too," he teased.

She giggled. "Maybe, but we still don't have time now. Later."

He sighed and stepped back, letting his hands fall from her shoulders.

Bria turned and faced him. "When we get to Tate's office, let me do the talking, okay? He's bound to be a little put out when he realizes the project I mentioned to him on the phone is looking into Derek's murder, but he won't want to jeopardize our renewed acquaintance."

Xavier quirked an eyebrow. "So I'm to act like nothing more than your obviously lethal, devastatingly handsome bodyguard?"

She grinned. "Whose ego is showing now?"

He grinned. "Is madam ready to go?"

Bria grabbed her handbag and slid it onto her wrist. "She is."

The Panthergate Productions offices were on the east side of Manhattan, but they weren't far. Traffic was merciful and they arrived only fifteen minutes late. The building offered valet parking, and Xavier slipped the valet a fifty to keep the car in front of the building although he was pretty sure the young man would have done it for nothing more than the smile Bria shot him as she'd gotten out of the SUV.

Xavier strode into the building at Bria's side. It was as if she was a magnet, compelling all of the heads in the lobby to turn toward her. An excited buzz hummed through the air.

He swept his gaze over the mostly suit-clad people, most likely employees of the production company coming or going to lunch or meetings. None of the faces held a threat. They mostly reflected excitement.

A heavyset, middle-aged man in a light brown suit hurried through the security gate toward them. Xavier recognized him as Tate Harwood. The face was the same as the photo he'd seen in the background check Ryan had pulled, even if the man was now thirty pounds heavier and ten years older. His hair was almost completely gray with only a few stray patches of dark brown pushing through. The crow's feet around his eyes were the bigger indicator of his age, which Xavier knew was fifty-two.

"Brianna Baker," Harwood boomed in a voice just a touch louder than it needed to be. "How are you? How long has it been? Too long, much too long."

It wasn't at all subtle, but a glance at the faces watching them revealed that it was working. The gazes of the people in the lobby moved between Brianna and Harwood, alight with curiosity about the man who somehow knew Brianna Baker personally.

"Tate." Brianna air-kissed Harwood on either cheek without actually touching him. "You are so right. It has been too long. When I learned you were back in New York and working at a production company, I just knew I had to reach out to you."

Harwood folded her arm around his and began to lead her toward the bank of elevators. "And I am so glad you did." He sent a glance over his shoulder, taking in Xavier, who had fallen into step behind them.

"Oh, I hope you don't mind. Xavier goes everywhere with me. Personal security. You know how it is." Bria tapped Harwood's arm lightly. "Such a pain, but I trust him implicitly."

"Of course," Harwood said, sparing Xavier one more look before focusing all his attention on Bria. "And this is my assistant, Mary Beth." Harwood gestured to the woman who was holding the elevator doors open and waving off anyone who tried to enter.

They stepped onto the elevator and the doors slid closed before the elevator car started its smooth climb upwards.

"I've had Mary Beth order in refreshments from Pâtisserie la Reine. I remembered how much you like dessert," Harwood said.

"Oh, that is so sweet of you. Of course, I have to watch what I eat so closely now, I'm not allowed to eat half of what I really want to." Bria laughed the tinkling laugh he recognized from her interviews.

"The price of fame." Harwood joined in laughing with her.

The elevator stopped at the twenty-third floor, and Harwood led them into a glass-walled conference room. He clearly wasn't going to let a drop of reflected importance go unnoticed.

Bria seemed to be taking it all in stride. She may have been used to living in a fishbowl, but Xavier wasn't. Even though Harwood had firmly closed the door after they'd entered the conference room, Xavier remained uncomfortable with the number of people strolling down the hall and gawking from the other side of the glass.

Harwood's assistant bought in coffee and the pastries. Bria accepted the coffee and demurred on the pastry.

No one offered him refreshments at all. He did as Bria asked and took up a position in a corner of the room, faced the glass wall and faded into the background.

After several minutes of small talk and catching up, Bria got down to why they were there.

"Tate, I'm sure you're wondering why I called you out of the blue today."

"Well, I am a little curious, yes."

"The truth is the project I'm working on involves *Murder in Cabin Nine* and Derek Longwell's untimely death."

Harwood flinched.

"I know it's a tragedy that those of us who knew Derek were all affected so deeply by. Especially those of us working on *Murder in Cabin Nine* with him. I mean, you know how the cast and crew on a film can become family. We were the people closest to him in his last days and moments."

"Yes, well, the industry lost a great up-and-coming talent in Derek," Harwood said unconvincingly.

Bria leaned forward across the table. "I've been thinking about starting a production company. You know how brutal this business is, especially to women, and a Black woman, well, I've got—what? Maybe five to seven more years left as a lead actress."

Harwood nodded. "Your talent and skill as a performer is timeless and boundless. But I can't argue with the fact that this business favors youth over talent."

"Exactly." Bria slapped a hand against the lacquered tabletop. "I want to plant my feet firmly in the industry soil. Producing my own content would do that."

Harwood cocked his head, a look of confusion coming over his face. "Are you thinking about reviving *Murder in Cabin Nine*?"

"Heavens no. The script was terrible. I'm thinking about telling Derek's story. The up-and-coming actor whose career and life were ended in a haze of mystery far too early. Audiences love what-could-have-been stories. I mean, we are still seeing massive audiences for biopics about Marilyn Monroe decades after her death."

"Derek was no Marilyn Monroe."

"No, of course, he never had a chance to achieve what she did, but ten years ago, he was probably the equivalent of Tom Holland or Harry Styles. He could have been, at least, and that's all that's needed to make a compelling story. What could have been?"

"Maybe." Harwood's eyes darted around the room. He smoothed his tie. "I'm not sure what I can do to help you," he said, his tone decidedly chillier than it had been moments earlier.

"As much potential as Derek had, I think you and I both know that he wasn't perfect, and if I want to do this biopic right, I have to tell a balanced story. The good and the bad."

"I…I still don't see where you're going…"

Bria sucked in a deep breath and then let it out slowly. "I never told anyone this at the time, but Derek attempted to force himself on me. I was able to fight off his attack."

Harwood's back straightened. "I didn't know anything about it. I hope you know that if I had I would have fired him immediately. Father producer or no father producer."

Bria waved a hand. "As I said, I never told anyone. Times were very different then. But that's why I'm sure that I wasn't the only woman Derek pulled that crap with. You worked with Derek several times on several different films. I figured you might know of other women who had similar experiences."

Harwood pulled at his tie again and didn't look Bria in the eye. "I did work with Derek on a number of films, but I wouldn't have tolerated such behavior if I'd known…"

"Of course, you would have." Bria cut him off sharply. "Derek was your bread and butter. But I have no plans to use the biopic to focus on what you did or didn't do years ago. At least, not at the moment."

Xavier smirked internally at Bria's interrogation technique.

Harwood swallowed hard, his Adam's apple bobbing. "What do you want to know?"

"Was there anyone you can remember who might have known that Derek attacked me? Anyone he was close to on set?"

Harwood scoffed. "You were there. Derek wasn't close to anyone. He didn't have friends. Thought he was too good for everyone."

"He could be full of himself," Bria agreed.

"That's a kind way of putting it. He was a class-A jerk." Harwood sighed. "Look, I'll admit I'd heard rumors about Derek's heavy-handedness with women, but I knew nothing about him attacking you. And as far as friends who might have known, I can't help you. Hell, Derek's own stepfather didn't like him. Talked about him like he was something he'd scraped off his shoe. That's probably where Derek learned it from. Do you remember how he treated that one guy who worked on the film with us?"

Xavier's ears perked up.

Bria's brow furrowed. "What guy?"

"Oh, you must remember him. He had a small part, only a couple of lines. What was his name? Now, him I did have to talk to Derek about, get him to back off a little at least. Nice guy but very awkward, kind of quiet. The kind of guy bullies love because he's not going to fight back."

Everyone eventually fought back, that was one thing that Xavier learned. Some people just had a greater tolerance, but they also tended to be the people most likely to explode when they finally reached their limit.

"What was his name?" Harwood looked at the ceiling, thinking. After a moment, he snapped his fingers and grinned. "Morgan Ryder. I'm surprised you don't remember him, Brianna. Now that you've stirred up all these memories from the movie set, the one thing I remember about Morgan in addition to how badly Derek treated him is how big a crush Morgan had on you."

Bria shot a glance across the room at Xavier. "I don't remember him."

Harwood shrugged. "He was that kind of guy. Forgettable, I mean. It's funny though. I ran into him a few years back when I was still living in Los Angeles. He'd completely changed. Slick suit. Two-hundred-dollar haircut. Nice ride. A real poor-guy-makes-it-big transformation."

"I guess that's good for him," Bria said.

"Sure. It's great. Like I said, nice guy. Totally deserves it. I almost didn't recognize him and he seemed surprised when I did. He'd even changed his name or I guess stopped using his stage name. Morgan Ryder." Harwood guffawed. "He's still in the business, kind of. Owns his own PR firm. Eliot Sykes Public Relations."

Chapter Twenty-One

Xavier threw the door to Ryan's office open, pausing long enough to allow Bria to enter first before he strode inside with purpose. "Eliot Sykes is the stalker."

"We don't know that for sure." Ryan sat behind his desk, working on his computer.

Shawn was also in the office, tapping away on a laptop on the sofa.

"I'm sure," Xavier growled.

He'd called Ryan on the drive from Tate Harwood's office and briefed him on his and Bria's meeting with Harwood. Ryan had apparently briefed Shawn.

"I'm working on tracking down this Morgan Ryder. So far, no luck. I've got Tansy working on it also. She's better at scouring the bowels of the internet."

Tansy Carlson was the best computer tech and researcher that West Investigations had. If anyone could dig up proof that Eliot Sykes and Morgan Ryder were one and the same person, it was Tansy.

"I've tried calling Eliot," Bria said. "He's not picking up his cell phone."

"And his office says he hasn't been in contact for the last two days."

Shawn's head snapped up. "Two days. That means he's been off the grid since the paparazzo was dumped outside of Bria's house."

"Oh my…" Bria pressed her hand against her stomach as if keeping the contents from coming up. "I hadn't even thought about what it means if Eliot really is my stalker. He must have killed Bernie." She sat down hard in one of Ryan's visitors' chairs.

Ryan looked across his desk at her with sympathy in his eyes. "We will find him. And until then, we will keep you safe from him."

Xavier felt every one of Ryan's words right down to his bones.

Tansy burst into the office. "I've got it." She had a wide grin across her face and held a printout above her head triumphantly.

"You found Sykes?" Xavier advanced on her.

Tansy took a step back, confusion coloring her face. "What? No, sorry. I meant I found the proof that Sykes and Ryder are the same person." She held out the printout.

Xavier took it. It was a copy of a very old web page that appeared to have been focused on discussing Hollywood celebrities. The sheet of paper was full of comments about Morgan Ryder. A small, grainy, indecipherable thumbnail photo was in the top left corner, but when he flipped to the second page he found Tansy had managed to blow the picture up and print it out. It was still grainy, but it was without a doubt Eliot Sykes, aka Morgan Ryder.

"I bookmarked the site so we could get back to it whenever we needed to," Tansy said.

Xavier passed the sheets of paper to Ryan. "This has to be enough to take to the cops."

Ryan scanned the papers. "It proves Sykes is Ryder, but it doesn't prove that Sykes is the stalker. We need more before the police will do anything."

Xavier hissed out a breath. He knew Ryan was right.

"He lied to me," Bria said. "If nothing else, by omission. He must have known we'd worked together on *Murder in Cabin Nine* and he said nothing for nearly two years. That's something."

"Fire him. In fact, I strongly suggest you do, but it's not illegal to lie to your employer."

"I'd hold off on firing him." Shawn rose and joined them at Ryan's desk. "We don't know if he knows we suspect him. We may be able to use that."

"He's not answering Bria's calls," Xavier pointed out.

Shawn's mouth twisted into a grimace. "I said 'may be able to use that.' It looks like Bernie's murder has pushed Sykes past the point of playing the good guy PR rep. He may be fully engulfed in his own decisions about being with Bria and has completely jettisoned his outward life."

"Oh…" Bria pressed a hand over her mouth.

Ryan shot Shawn a hard look.

"Sorry," Shawn mouthed back.

"I think I need to freshen up." Bria rose.

"I'll show you where the ladies' room is." Shawn hurried to extend his arm to Bria and she took it with a small smile of thanks.

When they were gone, Xavier turned back to Ryan. "We have to do something now."

Ryan stood, came around his desk and faced Xavier. "We are doing something. We're protecting Bria. We're searching for Eliot. We're staying diligent. That's all we can do at the moment."

"It's not enough," Xavier growled.

"I didn't say it was. It's what we have." Ryan hesitated. "Remember when I said that you were too close to Bria to be responsible for her security?"

Xavier didn't respond. There was no way he was going to desert Bria now.

"I know you're not going to leave her protection to anyone else," Ryan said, reading his mind. "I'm just reminding you that if you let your emotions do the thinking, you aren't going to be as effective as Bria needs you to be."

"I can separate my emotions from my job."

Ryan scoffed. "Right. Like you've been doing? Everyone can see what you feel for Bria. And I can tell it's affecting you."

He wanted to deny it, but he couldn't. He wasn't

thinking as clearly as he would be if he was protecting anyone other than Bria. All he could think about was what he'd do if she got hurt or worse. He'd survived fifteen years without her, in part because he believed they were both doing what they were supposed to be doing with their lives. If they couldn't do it together, well, at least they were happy-ish apart.

But the thought of a world without Bria in it... He was sure he couldn't make it through an hour in that world. So he'd give his life to make sure that was a world that never existed.

"I can't deny I have feelings for Bria. Always have, always will. But we had our chance and she chose her career over me. We can't change that and I doubt she wants to. She'll go back to Hollywood when this is all over and I'll still be here. So whatever is going on between us now, it can't last."

Ryan's gaze moved to the office door.

Xavier turned even though he already knew what he'd find.

Bria stood there, Shawn behind her. Her back was ramrod straight, hurt shining in her eyes. She'd clearly heard every word he'd just said.

Damn. He hadn't meant to hurt her, but he'd only said out loud what they both knew to be true. Hadn't he?

The moment of silence seemed to go on forever before Bria spoke. "There's been a change in the shooting schedule. They need me on the set."

Shawn cleared his throat, nodding at Xavier. "If you want to stay here and keep searching for Sykes, I can take her."

"No. I'll do it," Xavier said.

"Thank you." Bria's response was icy enough to skate on. She turned, sending Shawn scurrying to move out of her way.

"I'd have thought it was impossible to make this protection detail worse," Shawn said, keeping his voice low as Xavier passed by him, "but you always have been good at achieving the impossible."

Xavier growled before hurrying to catch up with Bria.

Chapter Twenty-Two

Whatever is going on between us now, it can't last.

Stupid. Stupid. Stupid. That's exactly what she was for entertaining the idea that somehow she and Xavier could find their way back to each other. For thinking that he'd even want to. He saw the night they'd spent in bed together as nothing more than fun rolls in the hay for old times' sake and she'd been envisioning white picket fences. It sounded like the kind of script she'd toss in the garbage bin after the first five pages.

At least now she knew how he felt. It was ironic when she thought about it. She'd pushed him away fifteen years ago to pursue her dreams, and now he was pushing her away. Karma really was something else.

Well, she hadn't been voted People's Choice Awards' best actress twice in a row for nothing. She pushed her shoulders back farther and kept her eyes trained on the streets of Manhattan. She might have been heartbroken on the inside, nearly falling apart with grief for the future she'd already begun spinning in her head, but she wasn't about to show it on the outside.

Xavier pulled into a space in the small parking lot next to the set.

"Bria, I'm sorry about what I said back at the office. I was just—"

She held up a hand, cutting him off. "No need to apologize. I totally understand." She opened the passenger door and stepped out.

Xavier got out and hurried to her side, a frown on his face. "You're supposed to wait until I come around the car."

"I'm sorry. I forgot. I'm running a little late though, so could we hurry?"

She moved past him toward her dressing room. She stopped at the door. The room was big as far as dressing rooms went, but way too small for her and Xavier and all the emotions she had swirling inside. If he came in with her, there was no way she wasn't going to erupt and she had too much pride to let him see her fall apart over him.

She turned to face him. "The scene we're shooting this afternoon is important. I need to concentrate and prepare. Would you mind waiting out here?"

A part of her felt like a heel for even asking. A diva too special to let the hired help inside her precious space. The other side of her screamed to get away from Xavier if only for a little while. The screams won out.

The frown on his face deepened. "Fine," he spat. "I'll need to check out the interior first though."

She stepped aside to let him pass into the dressing room.

He was back in less than a minute. "It's clean."

"Thank you."

She showered and headed over to wardrobe and makeup with Xavier's words still echoing in her head. The fact that he trailed behind her the whole time made the words that much louder in her mind. But she pushed them aside when she was called to set and did her job. She'd always had the ability to get outside herself and into the role she was playing. It was one of the reasons she was so good at what she did. She was happy to see that her personal drama with Xavier hadn't changed that.

She managed to complete the scene in only three takes and headed back to wardrobe to change. Once again, Xavier waited outside her dressing room as she gathered her things. She took her time. It was hard enough riding in the same car with Xavier after hearing what he thought of their relationship. Or lack thereof. Spending another night under the same roof… She didn't think her heart could stand it.

He'd offered to take her to a safe house when she initially hired West Investigations and that seemed like the best option now, given the changed circumstances. Maybe Shawn or one of the other operatives could stay with her. She knew Xavier would resist the suggestion, but she was the client. If she insisted, Ryan West would have no choice but to go along with her desires.

Now she just had to tell Xavier.

She steeled herself and stepped out of the dressing room.

Xavier fell in step beside her after she locked the door and headed for the parking lot.

"I think it would be best if Ryan assigned someone else to my protection detail."

"No."

"You don't get to decide. I'm the client."

"You aren't just a client and you know it. I'm sorry about what I said. I didn't intend for you to hear it."

"That, I got," she scoffed.

"That's not what I meant," he growled.

They passed the security checkpoint and entered the parking lot. There were several more vehicles in the makeshift area now than there had been when they'd arrived.

"It doesn't matter. You can't control how you feel. I get that. But neither can I. Seeing you again, being with you again, it's brought up a lot of emotions I thought I'd dealt with a long time ago. But that's not your problem. If you don't feel the same way, then you don't."

Xavier laid a hand on her arm, gently stopping

her from moving forward. "I didn't say I didn't feel something for you."

"But not enough." She turned her face away from him so he couldn't see the tears that were threatening to fall although her voice was thick with them.

"I—"

The rest of his words were caught in the sound of an explosion that rocked the light blue sedan parked several spaces away.

Not far enough away to keep the blast from lifting her and Xavier from their feet and flinging them backward, across the parking lot.

Bria landed on the asphalt, pain reverberating throughout her entire body. Darkness swelled behind her eyes and she knew she was only seconds away from losing consciousness.

She turned her head, looking for Xavier, her fear for him palpable despite the pain she was in.

What she saw sent terror shooting through her alongside the pain.

Eliot.

He was beside her, lifting her into his arms.

"You're mine. Everything is going to be okay now."

Those were the last words she heard before the darkness claimed her.

Chapter Twenty-Three

"I need to get out of here. Now," Xavier said, struggling into a sitting position in the hospital bed.

He reached for his IV line but the nurse grabbed his hand before he could rip it out of his arm. "Mr. Nichols, you can't leave yet. You were unconscious for several minutes. The doctor has ordered a CT scan."

"I don't care what the doctor ordered. I'm leaving." He'd awoken in the back of an ambulance on the way to the hospital. If he could have, he'd have forced them to turn around and take him back to the movie set. He didn't have time for a hospital visit. He needed to find Bria.

"Xavier, listen to the lady." A voice boomed from the door.

Ryan strode into the room, followed closely by Shawn. The brothers wore matching expressions of concern on their faces.

"Sykes has Bria. Do you have a line on where he's taken her?" Xavier shot the question at Ryan.

"Not yet. But the police have put out a BOLO on

Eliot and his vehicle, and West has employed all of our resources. We will find them."

"The panic button," he said, desperation lacing each word.

Shawn shook his head. "She hasn't hit the button."

Xavier's heart leaped with fear. He had no doubt that West and the police were doing everything they could, but would it be enough?

The brothers shared a glance.

"What? What aren't you saying?" Xavier demanded.

"The cops also went to Sykes's apartment. The doorman said Sykes hasn't been there in a couple days and the building's management wouldn't let them into the place."

"Okay, so they need to get a warrant."

Ryan and Shawn glanced at each other again.

"Spit it out," Xavier growled through his teeth.

"There's only your word that Sykes took Bria and you were half-unconscious," Ryan said. "The police say they don't have enough to formally open an investigation into Sykes for kidnapping, and without it, they can't get a warrant to search his apartment."

He squelched the urge to bellow. Instead, he pointed to the IV and trained his gaze on the nurse. "Take it out now or I will pull it out."

The nurse studied him, ostensibly gauging just how serious he was. He reached for the line again.

"Okay, okay." She went to work taking the line out of his arm. "But if you are going to leave, you'll have to sign a paper saying you left against medical advice."

"I'll sign whatever you want, but you better bring it now. I've got work to do."

"Dude, you aren't going to be any help to anyone if you pass out," Shawn said. "Do what the doctors say and let us handle finding Sykes."

Xavier glared at the two men. "Would you, if it was Addy out there somewhere with a deranged man?" He looked at Ryan. "Or Nadia?"

His friends stayed silent.

"Exactly."

The nurse finished removing the IV. "Stay here. I'll be right back with the AMA form."

He was itching to get out of the hospital and start searching for Bria, but he nodded. Two minutes. That was all he was giving her before he took off. Long enough to put on his shoes, if he could find them.

He rose as the nurse left the room and headed for the closet. Luckily, he'd come to before they'd taken his clothes off him so he didn't have to worry about walking out of the hospital in a gown.

"What do we know so far?" He opened the closet door and found his shoes, watch, wallet and cell phone on the shelf inside in a large clear plastic bag.

He reached up, stifling a groan and fighting back dizziness.

Shawn gently nudged him out of the way and grabbed the bag. "The camera facing the parking lot caught the explosion, but we can't see you or Bria." Shawn carried the bag with his things back to the bed while Xavier followed at a slightly slower pace.

"Did anyone on set see anything? Which direction Sykes took off in, maybe? The make and model of the car? Anything?"

Ryan shook his head. "At the moment, it looks like you and Bria were the only ones in or around the parking area. The cops are questioning everyone on set at the time of the explosion."

Xavier sat much more slowly than he'd have liked and put on his shoes. "The cops aren't going to tell us anything even if they happen to get something from a witness."

"I know that." Ryan frowned. "Which is why I've also got people asking questions. We have to be discreet though, given we don't have any power or jurisdiction. But everyone on set knows that you were protecting Bria and so far people have been forthcoming."

"They just don't know anything," Xavier snapped, the frustration and fear bubbling in his chest.

"I sent Gideon to keep an eye on Sykes's place in case he shows up."

"Fine." Xavier finally finished lacing his boots and stood. "He can help me search Sykes's apartment when I get there."

"Let's just slow down a minute," Ryan said, stepping in front of Xavier.

"Let's not slow down," Xavier barked. "We don't know what that maniac is doing to her right now." He paused to swallow back the emotion that had swelled in his chest and throat. "I'm not waiting another minute before doing everything I can to find her. Now help me or get the hell out of my way."

Ryan blew out a deep breath before stepping aside. He and Shawn fell into step beside Xavier as they made their way down the hospital corridor, only stopping briefly at the nurses' station so that Xavier could sign himself out of the hospital against doctors' orders.

Shawn drove and they made good time getting from the hospital to Sykes's Chelsea apartment. Shawn illegally parked the SUV a block from the building and they walked back.

Gideon met them in front of the building's revolving glass doors. "The doorman agreed to let you go up to Sykes's apartment. You only have five minutes."

Shawn's eyebrows rose. "How did you manage that?"

A ghost of a smile crossed Gideon's lips. "The old-fashioned way. A bribe."

Gideon resumed his post outside the apartment, keeping an eye out in case Sykes showed up while the rest of them marched into the lobby and past the doorman who barely spared them a glance. They were silent on the elevator up to the eleventh floor.

Shawn picked the lock on the door and they were

inside Sykes's apartment within a minute of stepping out of the elevator.

"Careful," Ryan warned. "If the cops ever do get a warrant, we don't want them to know we were here."

The apartment wasn't large and the decor was minimal. The four of them split up with Shawn taking the living/dining/kitchen combination, Ryan taking the second bedroom, and Xavier heading for the main suite.

A king-size bed with a leather headboard sat against one wall, facing a sleek, black wall-mounted television. The bedside tables were empty and the closet and single dresser in the room held nothing other than clothing.

Xavier crossed the room into the adjoining bathroom. Another door on the other side of the room opened into the hallway. He found cleaners and a sponge under the sink but nothing that would lead them to where Sykes might be holding Bria.

"Xavier, Shawn," Ryan called. "In here."

Xavier entered the room behind Shawn and pulled up short. Ryan had the closet doors open. The walls inside were covered in photos of Bria. Some of them were of her in Los Angeles, while others had been taken more recently in New York. There were even a few of him and Bria together.

The pictures made his blood boil, but he tried to focus on what they might tell them about Sykes and where he could be.

"He's obsessed with her," Xavier whispered.

He stepped forward, examining the photos more closely. A knot formed in his stomach. Several had been taken through the windows of Bria's townhouse, likely with a long-range lens but still too close for his comfort.

"Nothing here tells us where Sykes has taken Bria." Xavier slammed his palm against the open closet door.

"Maybe there is. Look at this." Shawn held a notebook open, flipping through the pages. "I found it under the bed."

Ryan and Xavier each took a side and looked over Shawn's shoulder.

The notebook was full of Sykes's fantasies about the life he and Bria would live together.

"Here." Shawn turned the page and pointed. A photograph of a farmhouse had been taped onto one page above more ramblings about Sykes and Bria going somewhere where it would be just the two of them.

"Doesn't look like there's an address visible."

Xavier reached over Shawn's shoulder and pulled the photo out of the book, hoping to find an address or some writing on the back that would tell them where to find the house. There was nothing.

It took all his strength not to rip the photo into tiny pieces.

"If Sykes owns this place, it's not under his own name," Shawn said.

"Look under the name Morgan Ryder. He may have inherited it, so we should also look under his parents' names and any siblings' or any other family members'."

"I'll call into the office as soon as we're back in the car," Ryan said. "We should get out of here. We've already spent more than the five minutes Gideon paid for." He laid a hand on Xavier's shoulder. "We will find her."

Chapter Twenty-Four

Bria woke on an unfamiliar sofa, in an unfamiliar room. She had no idea how long she'd been unconscious, but she could see through the large window in front of the sofa that she was lying on that it was dark outside. The moon was bright though, so she could see that there was nothing beyond the window but a large lawn that ended where a copse of trees began.

Her head throbbed. She lifted her hands to her head and found that they'd been tied.

Xavier.

He'd been beside her when the car exploded. Where was he now? And was he okay?

He had to be. There was so much she hadn't said. So much time they'd wasted.

She pushed herself into a sitting position. Someone groaned. It took a moment before she realized that someone was her. Her entire body ached, almost enough to outweigh the fear coursing through her. Almost.

Eliot stepped into her sight line. "You're awake.

Good." The smile she'd once found charming looked grotesque now. "I made us a romantic dinner to celebrate the first night of our new life together."

Fear clouded her already foggy brain. Eliot was her stalker. He was delusional. Dangerous.

She had to break through his delusions. Get him to let her go.

"Eliot, I think I need a doctor. I need you to take me to the hospital."

Eliot went to his knees in front of the sofa. "You bumped your head. I got you two aspirin. I'll take care of you." He reached out and pushed a lock of hair off her forehead.

She fought against the desire to shrink away from his touch. Swallowing her revulsion, she said, "I think I need a doctor. Please, Eliot."

He pushed to his feet as if he hadn't heard her at all. "After you've taken your pills, I'll help you to the dining room. Everything is ready."

There was no way she was going to swallow any pills he was offering her. Her head was pounding, but right now what she needed more than anything was for it to clear. "I don't think I need aspirin. My head is feeling better."

Eliot grinned. "That's great. Let's eat, then."

He reached for her arm and helped her get to her feet. She wobbled but found her footing quickly. Eliot didn't let go of her arm. They moved into the formal dining room. Eliot had set the table with two elaborate place settings complete with salad and bread plates and crystal. Her eyes glanced over the silverware. He'd set a fork by her place setting, but only his had a knife. Of course, it would be a lot easier to use them to defend herself if her hands weren't tied.

She hoped it wouldn't come to that. Eliot was clearly not in his right mind, but maybe she could talk him back into his senses. Make him see that this was not the way to win her love.

He pulled out a chair for her at the table and she sat.

The change in position drew her attention to something in her pocket.

Her panic button.

If she could get her hand into her pocket and hit the button without Eliot seeing, Xavier would know exactly where she was.

She held her still tied hands out in front of her. "I can't eat with my hands tied."

Eliot had already placed the food, in covered dishes, at the center of the table.

"Yes, you can." Eliot reached for the open bottle of red wine on the table between them and poured them each a glass. "I'll help you. It will be romantic. I can feed you."

Her stomach turned. So he wasn't going to untie her. Fine. She could still hit the button. Maybe without even reaching into her pockets. The fabric of her slacks wasn't that heavy.

She shifted her hands back into her lap in what she hoped was a pose that looked casual to Eliot. He didn't seem to be watching her closely at all, lost in what he imagined was some sort of romantic dinner. And where did he think this romantic dinner would lead?

The thought sent a shudder through her. She moved her hands toward her left pocket.

Eliot stood. He whipped the covers off the platters on the table with a flourish, revealing a roast and vegetables. He sliced the roast, then doled out food onto each of their plates before sitting down again.

"Now, isn't this lovely? I can't tell you how long I've waited for us to be together like this. No agents, no fans, no costars. Just the two of us, the way it should have been since *Murder in Cabin Nine*." Eliot reached across the table and used his knife to cut her meat.

She recoiled, not wanting him near her with a knife in his hand. Or at all.

Eliot frowned.

She plastered a smile on her face and tried to look as if she'd moved just to give him more room to slice her food. It seemed to work. In more ways than one.

Eliot returned her smile, but she was more concerned with the fact that the shift in her body allowed her easier access to the panic button. She pressed the button through the material of her slacks, feeling the small fob pressing into her leg.

Please work. Please work.

"I know you had a part in *Murder in Cabin Nine*."

"You were so nice to me. I've never forgotten that, although I know you didn't remember who I was."

"I'm sorry I didn't remember you. Is that why you've done all this? Because I didn't remember you?"

The look he gave her reflected genuine shock. "Of course not! I mean, I've loved you since we met on set, but I totally understood you had to focus on your career. I don't hold your ambition against you."

The way he spoke, as if they'd had some type of relationship that didn't solely exist in his mind, sent a shiver through her. But she wanted to keep him talking. It might be the only way to bring him back to reality.

"I think we should spend some time together, just the two of us, laying a strong foundation for our relationship going forward, but after a few years, I wouldn't have any problem with you going back to work. I mean, it would be a shame to let everything I've done to further your career go to waste."

Eliot giggled as if he was in on a secret that she wasn't.

A sinking feeling in her gut said he wasn't just talking about the public relations work he'd done for her. "Are you talking about your PR work?"

He giggled again. "That's just the little stuff." He leaned across the table, all wide grin and wild eyes. "I killed Derek Longwell."

Bria sucked in a sharp breath, but Eliot didn't seem to notice.

"I saw what he did to you. Well, I saw him on top of you in the woods and you hit him with a rock. Good girl." His smile was grotesque. "You ran away, but Derek was stunned. When he saw me approaching he barked at me to help him. I helped him all right. I picked up the rock you'd hit him with and hit him again. It only took one blow."

Bile rose in Bria's throat despite her empty stomach.

"And Bernie? Did you kill him too?" She knew the answer, but something compelled her to hear it directly from Eliot.

He nodded, spearing a bit of potato and meat with his fork and popping it into his mouth. "He was easy." Eliot spoke around the food in his mouth. "I'd been keeping tabs on your place. I saw that bodyguard of yours get into it with Bernie. Bernie had no right to follow you like that," Eliot said with a frown and no hint of irony. "Taking pictures of you everywhere you went. Invading your privacy."

"Why did you leave Bernie's body in front of my house?"

Eliot's head dipped and he looked at her out of the side of his eye, shyly. "I wanted you to know what I was willing to do for you. How much I loved you. I didn't tell you about Derek and that was a mistake. I wasn't going to make that mistake again."

He'd let his delusions get the best of him, but this was not the moment to tell him that.

"So everything…the emails, the flowers. You killed Bernie. You did it all?"

"For you," he said. "I followed you to New York to keep an eye on you while you were filming. I wanted to be close to you. I always want to be close to you."

How had she missed it? Eliot had lost all connection with reality.

"Eliot, you know I care for you and respect you as a friend."

He kept cutting as if he hadn't heard her.

"This isn't the way to get me to fall in love with you. You need to let me go."

"Why? So you can run into the arms of that bodyguard of yours? Do you really think I don't know that you're sleeping with him?"

She sucked in a deep breath. She hadn't thought twice about having Eliot over to her apartment in Los Angeles or the townhouse in New York. Had he planted some kind of listening or video devices? No, no, he couldn't have. And even if he had, she and Xavier had been together at his house not hers. Still, the thought of Eliot somehow watching them, even if he hadn't had a view inside their homes, was sickening.

A deep scowl twisted his lips. "I see I hit the nail on the head." He stuttered out a deep breath. "It's okay. I can forgive you one indiscretion. As long as it never happens again, of course."

"That's why you sent me that photograph and the threats against Xavier. You wanted to frighten him away from me."

He scoffed. "I should have known better. A meathead like him. All brawn and no brains. I should have just killed him like I killed Bernie."

Eliot sawed her meat faster.

The words coming out of his mouth were terrifying but not nearly as much as the knife in his hand. "Eliot," she said in a voice she hoped was soothing. "We can work this out. Just untie me."

The knife slid off the plate, and Eliot's hand hit her wineglass sending it toppling over. Red wine spread across the white lace tablecloth.

Eliot surged to his feet, throwing the fork and knife down on the table. "Look what you made me do! I wanted our first dinner as a couple to be perfect." His eyes flashed with anger.

Terror swelled in Bria's chest. She cut her gaze up at him.

He reached down and yanked her to her feet, pulling her to his chest. "Now you'll have to pay for that."

Chapter Twenty-Five

Xavier's heart hadn't stopped beating as if it would pop out of his chest at any moment since he regained consciousness and realized Bria was gone. It had already been nearly four hours, and with each passing moment, he found it harder to breathe. Sykes could have taken her anywhere in four hours.

Focus.

He, Shaw and Ryan returned to West Investigations' headquarters while Gideon remained at Sykes's building, keeping lookout. Now they sat in the conference room, awash in the information that West's researchers had been able to find on Eliot Sykes, aka Morgan Ryder. In his early twenties, Sykes had embarked on a middling acting career that included only one credit for a deodorant commercial. They'd been able to turn up a couple of Morgan Ryder's headshots. The man in the photograph was definitely a younger Eliot Sykes. Tate Harwood had also been able to dig up a thin file on Sykes from his work on *Murder in Cabin Nine*, which had included Sykes's application for the production assistant's job. He'd listed his older brother, Joseph, as his emergency contact, and Ryan was working on finding contact information for him now, but he was apparently doing a stint with Doctors Without Borders so it was slow going.

The police weren't telling them anything officially, but Brandon was using his police contacts to funnel information to them unofficially. Unfortunately, the cops hadn't made any more progress on finding Bria than he had. Where was she?

Xavier pushed the file he was reading away and let his head fall into his hands.

"Hey, why don't you take a break?" Shawn dropped a hand on his shoulder and squeezed.

"I can't." Xavier reached for the background report on Sykes again. "There has to be something in here that gives us a clue to where he's taken Bria."

Excited voices mingled with hurried footsteps in the hall. Ryan and Tess burst into the room.

"Bria activated her panic button," Ryan said.

Xavier pushed to his feet and dashed around to the other side of the table where Tess had sat the laptop she'd carried into the room.

"She's too far away to get an exact location but we can tell the general area. She's, or at least the panic button's signal, is in Putnam County about an hour and ten minutes away," Tess said.

"I've already got Gideon on his way and we'll let the cops know when we're en route," Ryan said, falling in step beside Xavier as he headed from the room. "The signal should get more precise as we get closer to the button's location."

"Good," Xavier said, forgoing the elevators and pushing through the door to the stairwell.

Ryan grabbed his arm, forcing him to stop. "Are you sure you're up for this? I can't have you running on pure emotion. I need to know your head is on straight."

He understood where Ryan was coming from. He'd be no good to Bria and a potential danger to Ryan and whoever else was at his back if he couldn't rein in his emotions and think rationally.

He took a deep breath and let it out. "I can do this."

Ryan nodded, but Xavier read hesitancy in his eyes.

Xavier was able to cut the hour-and-ten-minute drive down to something closer to forty minutes. They kept Tess on the speaker, giving them updates on the panic button's location.

"Damn," Tess's anxious voice carried through the SUV's speakers.

"What is it, Tess?" Ryan said.

"The GPS in the panic button just went offline."

Xavier's heart thundered. "What does that mean?"

"We lost the signal."

Ryan swore.

Xavier was too terrified to react. If they couldn't follow the panic button's signal, they had no idea where to look for Bria.

"Have we found any connection between Sykes and a house, a business, a shed, anything out here in Putnam County?" Ryan barked.

"Nothing yet. We're still looking though," Tess responded.

Xavier wracked his brain. There had to be a way to locate Bria. He couldn't get this close and fail her. "I've got the photo of the farmhouse on my phone," he said, an idea blossoming in his head.

He navigated the SUV into a hard right turn, bouncing into the parking lot of a combination convenience store and gas station.

Ryan slanted a glance across the car at him. "What are you doing?"

"We need to know where that farmhouse is. That's the best lead we have to where Sykes might be holding Bria and since the panic button's GPS leads us to this area, it stands to reason it's located somewhere near here."

Xavier swung into a parking space and slammed the car into park. "When you're lost you ask for directions. We show the photo around and ask if anyone can direct us to it."

He hopped out of the car with Ryan on his heels.

The man behind the counter inside the convenience store looked up as they entered. "Hello, can I help you find something?"

"I'm hoping you can." Ryan took the lead. He pulled the photo of the house up on his phone. "We're trying to get to this house, but our GPS has died and we don't have the exact address. Do you recognize it?"

The man's eyes narrowed with suspicion. "I'm not sure."

Xavier reigned in his frustration. "Sir, a woman has been kidnapped. She's being held in this house." He tapped the phone's screen. "If you know where this house is, please help us find her."

The man studied them for a long moment. "Are you cops?"

Xavier and Ryan shared a glance.

"No," Ryan answered. "We're private investigators and friends of the woman who has been kidnapped."

"PIs." The man's expression morphed from suspicion to eagerness. "I always wondered what it was like to be a PI. Like that *Magnum PI*, you remember the old show?"

"Sir, please," Xavier pressed. "The house. Do you know where it is?"

The man sighed. "It looks like the old Dobrinsky place although no Dobrinsky has owned it for more than thirty years. People around here still call it that though."

"Do you know who owns it now?" Ryan pressed.

"Um…some doctor and his family bought it way back when."

Xavier shot a look at Ryan. Sykes's father and brother were doctors.

"No one has lived in the house for years now though. Not since the old doctor died. I guess his wife, if she's still alive, or his kids own it now."

"How do we get to the house from here?" Xavier asked, impatiently.

The man frowned but gave them the address for the house and sketched a map out on a napkin.

Ryan threw a hurried thank-you over his shoulder as they ran back to the car.

Xavier gunned the SUV in the direction the man had told them to go, while Ryan called Gideon and Tess to give them the house's location.

Since Xavier wasn't about to allow the fact that they had no legal authority to go after Sykes stop them, he, Ryan and Tess decided on the drive up that Tess would call the local police once they'd safely rescued Bria.

Xavier spied the semi-obscured driveway that the convenience store clerk said led to the farmhouse. He could see how they could have had trouble with the GPS tracker in Bria's panic button. The house was almost completely obscured by trees. There was no way they'd have seen the structure simply driving by. From the looks of it, the property encompassed several acres. Which also meant that there could be other buildings on the property where Sykes was holding Bria. Buildings it would take time to find and clear. Time Bria might not have.

Xavier stopped the car and cut the engine as soon

as the house came into view. He and Ryan stepped out of the SUV just as Gideon pulled to a stop behind them.

They met in the space between the two vehicles.

"Gideon, you go around the back," Ryan said, pulling his gun from its holster. "Xavier and I will enter through the front."

They crept toward the farmhouse. The exterior confirmed the convenience store clerk's statements about the home having been sitting vacant for an extended period. The lawn was overgrown and the siding needed to be replaced in several places. The stairs leading to the porch were crumbling and several shutters were missing from the front windows.

Gideon cut across the lawn and headed for the back of the house.

Xavier and Ryan waited several moments, giving Gideon the opportunity to get into place before they moved up the crumbling stairs to take position on either side of the front door.

"Ready?" Ryan whispered.

Xavier said a quick prayer that they'd find Bria inside and safe, then nodded.

"On three," Ryan said. "One, two, three!"

Chapter Twenty-Six

"You need to understand that you are mine!" Eliot's face twisted with rage. "I love you."

"You killed two people. You blew up a car and kidnapped me. That's not love."

Eliot's eyes darkened. He let out a scream that felt as if it shook the foundation of the house.

Bria's heart thundered in her chest. There was no reasoning with Eliot. He was lost in the delusion he'd created for himself.

Her hands were still bound, but she lunged for the table and grabbed the knife. In one quick motion, she turned back to Eliot and slashed it across his face.

Blood spilled from the wound and Eliot howled, hitting her across the cheek and sending her tumbling into the back of her chair. The knife fell from her hand and slid under the table, out of reach. Luckily, she managed to stay on her feet.

"You bitch!" Eliot pressed the palm of his hand to the wound on his face and glared at her. "I'll kill you."

He took a step toward her, but she lowered her

head and drove her body into his chest, sending him reeling backward.

Bria kept moving forward, past him and out of the dining room.

The layout of the house was a mystery to her, but she'd seen a set of stairs from the living room sofa when she'd regained consciousness and she headed that way now.

The hallway was pitch-black, which was a double-edged sword. On the one hand, it made it harder for Eliot to see, but it also made it harder for her to see. Presumably Eliot knew the layout of the house so the advantage went to him. The hallway was long and curved. She tried the doors lining it, finding the first two locked.

She ran for the third door, as the sound of Eliot's footsteps trailed down the corridor. The door opened without a sound and she darted into the room, turning the flimsy lock, despite knowing it wouldn't stop Eliot if he really wanted in.

"Bria. Oh, Briiiiiiaaaaa." Eliot called out her name in a singsong voice. She could hear what sounded like the handle on one of the other bedroom doors being jiggled and then footsteps moving again.

She worked her wrists in hopes of loosening the ropes enough to slip them free, as her eyes darted over the room searching for something to use as a weapon. There was nothing in the room except a bed, stripped down to the bare mattress, and a dresser. She considered for a moment, searching in the dresser drawers, but rejected the idea as the footsteps in the hall drew louder and closer. It didn't seem like Eliot was forcing the locked bedroom doors open. Not yet, at least. And as long as he wasn't, she had time to come up with a plan.

"Come out, come out, wherever you are," Eliot sang. "Really, Bria, I'm tired of this game. Why don't you come on out here and we can talk about this like adults. I can be reasonable."

The handle on the door to the room she was hiding in moved up and down. There was nothing but a thin piece of wood separating her from Eliot and she was terrified he could hear her thundering heart.

After what seemed like an eternity, she heard his footsteps continue down the hall, away from the door. She let out the breath she'd been holding. She couldn't hide in this room forever. Eventually, Eliot would start forcing the locks and there wasn't even a closet in the room that she could hide inside of.

She was finally able to loosen the knot on the rope Eliot had tied her hands with enough to slip one of her hands, and then the other, free. Ugly red marks marred her skin, but at least now she'd be able to fight back.

She had to move. Back toward the living room and presumably a door. She didn't know where they were exactly, but Eliot had to have driven her here, so there must be a road somewhere nearby. She just had to get to it and hitch a ride with a passerby to a nearby town or police station. And all while avoiding Eliot. It wouldn't be easy but the alternative…

She shuddered.

More footsteps and the squeak of the floorboards sounded faintly from down the hall. And then another sound, rusted door hinges being forced open. Apparently, Eliot had found an unlocked room. There wasn't likely to be a better time.

Bria eased the door open and peeked into the hall. It was empty but a door at the far end stood open. It was now or never.

She slipped from the bedroom and ran as quickly and quietly as she could back toward the front of the house. But not quietly enough. She threw a glance over her shoulder just in time to see Eliot step into the hallway.

Their eyes met as she turned the corner and raced out of the hall.

Eliot bounded after her.

Bria fled down the stairs and past the dining room and through the living room, past the sofa that she'd woken up on. Just beyond the living room was another hallway that split in two different directions. She had no idea which way led to the door and no time to figure it out.

She lurched to the right.

"Bria!" Eliot thundered behind her.

Her lungs burned, but hope swelled in her chest

when the large front door came into view. She grabbed the handle and pulled, but it didn't budge. She flicked the lock and still nothing happened.

Eliot must have done something to keep it from opening.

She turned, looking for another exit.

Eliot stood at the fork in the hallway.

His gaze sent ice through her veins. There was no doubt in her mind he was going to kill her.

Unfortunately, there was only one direction to go in, and it required heading back toward the stairs. Well, she wasn't going to go without a fight.

Bria gave a primal scream and raced at him. A look of surprise colored Eliot's face as she threw herself into him and they both hit the floor hard.

She'd trained six days a week, weights, cardio and some martial arts, while she was filming the Princess Kaleva movies. She reached for that training now, throwing punch after punch to Eliot's face and neck. She heard a crunch as one of her blows made contact. A satisfying gush of blood flowed from his nose.

She scrambled to her feet.

But Eliot recovered fast. He pushed to his feet, driving his shoulder into her stomach as he rose.

The attack stole the breath from her lungs, sending her wobbling on her feet.

Eliot's arm whipped out and around in a circular motion, connecting with Bria's jaw. Tears swam in her eyes and she fell to her knees.

Don't lose consciousness. She fought against the desire to go to sleep. Every instinct in her body said that if she did, she'd likely never wake up. She shook the drowsiness off in time to see Eliot's foot kick out.

Surprising herself she caught his leg before it made contact with her ribs.

Shock flashed across his face when she yanked with all the strength she had. Shock turned to surprise as he realized he was losing his balance.

She scrambled to her feet as he hit the floor on his back and ran for the dining room. There had to be a kitchen in the house. Hopefully, it led to a back door, and if not, she'd at least be able to grab a weapon to defend herself.

She made it to the living room before Eliot tackled her from behind. She landed on the hardwood floors hard enough to rattle her teeth.

He flung her onto her back.

She reached for the wound on his face, scratching at it, his eyes, wherever she could reach. He yelled in pain, then grabbed her by the hair, slamming her head into the floor.

Bria's ears rang and her vision swam. She tried to focus, to make her body move, but the signals weren't getting from her terrified brain to her limbs. She couldn't just lie there. She had to keep trying. She needed to stay alive until Xavier found her.

It took every bit of strength she had, but she managed to flip onto her stomach and begin crawling away from Eliot. The room spun, but she could make out the long hallway she'd been headed for when he'd tackled her.

"I thought you were the one." Eliot's voice came from behind her. She glanced over her shoulder and saw that he was standing in the middle of the room, watching her, tears falling from his eyes. The sight was equal parts pitiful and petrifying.

She moved faster and the front door of the house came into view.

Eliot's footfalls sounded behind her.

He yanked her to her feet just as the door crashed open.

Xavier stood in the doorway, his gun held outstretched.

Eliot's arm came around Bria's throat, cutting off most of her air supply.

"Let her go," Xavier demanded.

"No! She's mine. We belong together." Eliot took several steps back, dragging her along with him.

Xavier stepped farther into the house, followed by Ryan West. Both men had their guns pointed at her and Eliot. But she knew they wouldn't shoot. She was in the way.

She heard a door burst open somewhere behind her.

"You've got nowhere to go, Eliot. We've got you surrounded. Let her go and we can talk about all of this. If you hurt her, you're a dead man."

Eliot's arm tightened around her neck and he dragged her back several more steps.

Xavier and his men hadn't heard Eliot earlier. They didn't know that there was no chance that he'd give up. He'd see them both killed first.

Bria could feel herself getting light-headed. She didn't have long before she passed out, and who knew what Eliot would do then. She needed to do something to get herself out of the line of fire.

She lowered her head and bit down on Eliot's forearm.

He yowled and loosened his grip enough that she could slip under it. She launched herself away from Eliot.

Xavier and Ryan thundered forward, barking at Eliot to get onto his knees, while Gideon rounded on Eliot from the kitchen. It must have been him she'd heard bursting into the house from the back door.

Eliot reached behind him and a shard of light glinted off the knife as he whipped it forward toward Xavier.

The gunshot thundered through the room.

Eliot froze, the knife still outstretched. He looked down at his stomach where blood had already begun blooming over his shirt. He stumbled, then collapsed.

Ryan rushed forward, grabbing Eliot's hands and placing them in cuffs while the third man kept his gun trained on Eliot.

Xavier hurried to Bria's side and pulled her into his arms. "Baby, are you okay?"

She looked into his eyes and told the truth. "No." Her hands trembled, adrenaline still surging through her body. "Is he dead?" She tried to peer over Xavier's shoulder to get a look at Eliot, but he shifted, making it impossible for her to see past him.

She could hear Ryan on the phone with 9-1-1, asking for an ambulance immediately. Eliot must still be alive. She wasn't sure if she was relieved or not.

She wrapped her arms around Xavier, pulling him close and burying her face in his chest.

"It's over. You're safe now."

And for the first time in months, she actually felt like that might be the truth.

Chapter Twenty-Seven

Bria watched through the tinted windows as Xavier made his way over to the SUV from the front of the police cruiser where he'd been speaking to the Putnam County police detectives. They had not been happy to discover that Xavier and his men had taken it upon themselves to rescue her instead of alerting their department. The detectives still weren't happy, but her statement describing her kidnapping and Eliot's loud and unhinged ravings that she was his, had done a lot to neutralize the tempers of the local cops. It had also helped that West Investigations had implied that they'd let the Putnam County chief of police take credit for having saved Hollywood's darling from the stalker who'd kidnapped her.

Xavier opened the back door of the SUV and slid in beside Bria. She had the heat cranked up and a blanket wrapped around her shoulders, but she didn't begin to feel warm until he wrapped his arms around her.

They held each other for several minutes before pulling away.

"Is everything okay? Are you and your guys in trouble?" she asked.

Xavier shook his head. "I don't think so. At least, nothing major anyway. The chief is too busy dreaming about all the press he's going to get."

She let out a deep breath. "That's good, I guess."

"I don't like that he's trading on you being kidnapped to advance his career."

"I'm used to it. It's not just Hollywood that's cutthroat. If that's all it takes to keep you, Shawn and Gideon out of jail, I'm happy to let the cops have their fifteen minutes at my expense."

"Are you really okay?" Concern shone in Xavier's eyes.

He ran a finger over the bruise that was forming on her cheek. She had several other bumps and bruises from her fight with Eliot. They would take a few weeks to heal completely, but no permanent damage had been done, which was what she told the EMTs who had tried to take her to get checked out at the local hospital.

She didn't want to leave Xavier, and the police hadn't been through questioning him so she'd declined the offer.

She leaned her forehead against his. "I was terrified in that house with Eliot. But one thing I knew for sure was that you were looking for me and that you would move heaven and earth to find me. And you did."

"I will always be there for you when you need me. Always." He kissed her softly.

She was still struggling to process that Eliot, a man she'd considered a friend and trusted confidant, was her stalker. Xavier was right. She hadn't known Eliot at all. His delusions had run deep. The police had already discovered that Eliot had followed her to New York a few days after she'd crossed the country to start filming *Loss of Days*. He'd been the one delivering the flowers, and feeling threatened by Xavier's presence and the obvious feelings she had for him, he'd escalated his stalking.

"There's something I need to tell you." She'd promised herself that when she got out of that house and away from Eliot, she'd tell Xavier how she felt about him and she wasn't going to waste another moment before keeping that promise to herself.

"I let you go fifteen years ago without telling you how much you mean to me. I loved you then and I love you now. And I'm hoping it is not too late for us. I don't know exactly how we'd make it work, but I know I want to make it work with you and I'll do whatever it takes. Move to New York and commute back and forth to Los Angeles when I have to. Or I'll focus my career on projects that film on the East Coast. Whatever it takes. I just know that as hard as I've worked to become Brianna Baker, movie star, that's how hard I'm willing to work to build a relationship with you that lasts," she said pointedly, remembering what he'd told Ryan about their relationship not being meant to last.

"Bria, about what you overheard me say—"

She held up a hand. "I don't want to look back. Let's start from here. Committed to making us work. What do you say?"

She waited anxiously for what felt like hours until a wide grin began spreading across Xavier's face.

"I love you too."

She grinned. "You do?"

"I do." He grinned back. "And you don't have to change a thing."

Her heart beat fast. She was having trouble processing what he was saying beyond the joy she felt at hearing he loved her as much as she loved him. "Why? What do you mean I don't have to change a thing?"

"Ryan and Shawn have been planning to open a West Coast office for a while now and they offered me the job of heading it up some time ago."

"You mean you'd be willing to move to Los Angeles?" She could barely believe what she was hearing. She hadn't even considered that he'd move to be with her.

His smile grew wider. "I'd be more than willing. I don't care where I live as long as you're there too."

Love swelled in Bria's chest. She threw her arms around Xavier and kissed him with all the passion and yearning that had laid dormant in her heart for him over the last fifteen years and all the hope she had for the years to come.

Chapter Twenty-Eight

"I could get used to this life." Xavier stretched his arms over his head and burrowed further into the oversize deck chair next to her.

The Pacific Ocean stretched out in front of them as far as the eye could see. The breeze off the ocean cooled the sun's warm rays. She understood where Xavier was coming from, but a few days was all they could manage, budget wise and time wise.

Bria laughed. "I suggest you don't. Renting a yacht is okay for a couple days for our honeymoon, but we both have to go back to work eventually."

He reached across the short space separating their chairs and took her hand, turning it over and kissing her palm. Love tugged at his heart every time he saw his ring on her finger. It had been such a long road for them getting here. But here they were. Together, forever.

"I guess I'll just have to be content with a long weekend with my wife and the wide open sea."

"It's not so bad." She smiled at him and his heart fluttered.

"It's not bad at all."

And it wasn't, especially after everything they'd gone through in the last eight months. Eliot had insisted on going to trial on the stalking and murder charges. The case was a slam dunk for the prosecution. The cops had found the knife that had killed Bernie Steele in Eliot's apartment and they'd been able to find traces of Bernie's blood under the handle, even though the knife had been cleaned. He and Bria had been called to the stand as witnesses. Testifying had been especially difficult on Bria, who'd had to relive her kidnapping and being held captive by a man she'd thought of as her friend. They'd both been relieved when the jury had come back with guilty verdicts for Bria's kidnapping, Bernie's murder and a host of other charges. It wasn't clear that he'd ever be charged for Derek Longwell's murder, unfortunately. Eliot had insisted that Bria was lying about his having confessed to that murder, and given the years long lag and the shoddy police work that had been done back then, it was unlikely the prosecutors could get a conviction. Still, Eliot would be in jail for a very long time for the crimes he'd been convicted of, which was exactly where he belonged.

Xavier had wasted no time in asking Bria to marry him after the trial was officially over. He'd taken her out for a romantic dinner the very next day and proposed. And she'd accepted.

He'd have married her that night, but Bria had wanted a wedding, nothing big and definitely something private, but she'd wanted all their friends and family to know how much they loved each other. Their schedules had kept them too busy to plan a wedding. He'd moved across the country to California and had opened West Investigations' West Coast office. He was happy to say the new office was taking off, but it had been a lot of work in a short time.

And Bria had been traveling a lot promoting *Loss of Days*. The audiences and critics loved the movie and her performance in particular. She'd already been nominated for several awards and there were even whispers that she'd be nominated for an Oscar next year. They'd been ships passing in the night to some extent, but they'd made the most of the time they'd been able to spend together over the last several months.

Then, two days earlier, she'd surprised him by renting the yacht and proposing they have the boat's captain, who was also a justice of the peace, marry them at sea.

They'd exchanged vows the night before, under a setting sun, the first mate and the yacht chef acting as their witnesses.

It was perfect. Just like his wife.

"What are you thinking right now?" Bria asked.

He leaned over and kissed his bride. "How much I love you and how lucky we are to have found our way back to each other."

"I couldn't agree with you more."

* * * * *

INTRIGUE

Seek thrills. Solve crimes. Justice served.

Available Next Month

A Place To Hide Debra Webb
Swiftwater Enemies Danica Winters

....

K-9 Detection Nichole Severn
The Perfect Witness Katie Mettner

....

Wetlands Investigation Carla Cassidy
Murder In The Blue Ridge Mountains R. Barri Flowers

Larger Print

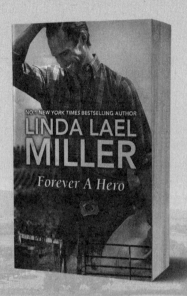

MILLS & BOON

Want to know more about your favourite series or discover a new one?

Experience the variety of romance that Mills & Boon has to offer at our website:

millsandboon.com.au

Shop all of our categories and discover the one that's right for you.

MODERN

DESIRE

MEDICAL

INTRIGUE

ROMANTIC SUSPENSE

WESTERN

HISTORICAL

FOREVER
EBOOK ONLY

HEART
EBOOK ONLY

Subscribe and fall in love with a Mills & Boon series today!

You'll be among the first to read stories delivered to your door monthly and enjoy great savings.